A Whisper *of* Secrecy

Darcy Burke

USA TODAY BESTSELLING AUTHOR

OLIVERHEBERBOOKS

For my dear friend, Jen
I will never be able to fully express what you mean to me or how glad I am to have you in my life. Here's to all the memories yet to come.

CHAPTER 1

London, May 1868

Hadrian Becket, Earl of Ravenhurst, watched the play of emotions across his investigative partner's beautiful, familiar features. Matilda—who went by Tilda—Wren's green eyes flickered with surprise, then sorrow, and finally with how she most often viewed the world: avid curiosity. Detective Inspector Samuel Teague of the Metropolitan Police's Detective Branch, their friend and occasional associate, had handed Tilda a scrap of parchment on which was written Tilda's father's name.

Tilda sucked in a breath, and Hadrian's pulse quickened. She glanced toward Teague. "It's more than his name. There's the date he died too."

Not just died—the date he was *murdered*. Sergeant Thomas Wren had been killed when he'd stumbled upon a theft in progress over a decade ago.

And last night, a former inspector from the Met, Padgett, had been found dead with the paper Tilda now held in his pocket.

Hadrian could well imagine the questions ricocheting in her mind, chief among them—what did Padgett have to do with her father's death?

"Yes, it's peculiar," Teague said with a slight frown.

Peculiar was not the word Hadrian would use to describe the paper that had been found in Padgett's pocket. It was shocking. And suspicious.

Tilda gestured with the parchment. "Do you know if this is written in Padgett's hand?"

Teague nodded. "I did compare the handwriting to one of his reports, and it appears to be."

They stood in Tilda's grandmother's small parlor at the front of her terrace house in Marylebone. Hadrian wondered if they should sit but didn't want to interrupt. Not when Tilda's focus was so fiercely fixed on Teague.

"Did you examine the scene of Padgett's death?" she asked.

"I did not, but I can tell you he was found at his lodgings," Teague replied. "He lived in a pair of rooms in Villiers Street."

Tilda glanced at the parchment. "Have you any idea why he had this?"

Teague shook his head. "Nor does Inspector Lowther yet."

Tilda's blonde brows shot up. "Lowther's been assigned the case? Not someone from the Detective Branch?"

Tilda was familiar with a great many of the Metropolitan Police due to her father's career there. Lowther, in particular, was a friend and sometimes investigative associate. Hadrian had met him during the first case he'd worked on with Tilda several months ago. Lowther had also been the constable who'd found Tilda's father over a decade ago after he'd been murdered.

"Lowther is being considered for a promotion to Detective Branch," Teague said. His expression seemed to hold more than a bit of skepticism.

"You aren't in favor of that promotion?" Hadrian was disinclined to support it. Lowther was not above accepting bribes to share information about investigations. Tilda had explained that Lowther needed extra money to provide for his family, which included an ill child, and that constable wages were not sufficient. However, Lowther was no longer a constable, and Hadrian found the acceptance of bribes by members of the police, for any reason, distasteful.

Teague shrugged. "I've been asked to work with Lowther on this case in order to make an assessment of his readiness for the job. From what I know of him, I'm not sure he's up to snuff."

Tilda exhaled and seemed to relax slightly. "I'm glad to know you will be involved."

Teague gave her a wry look. "That doesn't mean I can be as forthcoming with information as I have in the past when we've worked together on matters. In those cases, you'd been hired to investigate something parallel to my own investigation. I can't imagine you'll have anything to do with determining the cause of Padgett's death."

"Not as of yet," Tilda said with a feeble smile. "However, you can count on seeing me at the inquest. It's tomorrow?"

"Yes. I'll let you know when and where," Teague said.

Tilda's gaze fell to the parchment once more. Her thumb moved slowly, almost lovingly, over the ink, as if she were hoping to touch her father and not just his name.

Hadrian held out his hand. "May I?"

She locked eyes with him, then blinked. "Of course." There was an eager quality to her response as she put the paper into his palm.

The reason for that was simple to identify. She hoped that Hadrian would touch the parchment and see someone's memory. After being stabbed one night as he'd left Westminster several months ago and hitting his head on the pavement when he fell, Hadrian had been burdened with the ability to see others' memories when he touched an object or another person's bare flesh. The power did not work with people he knew well, such as his mother, his retainers, and Tilda, nor had it ever worked when he touched a corpse. However, it had, on rare occasion, been triggered when he'd handled an item that had been touched by a deceased person.

Hadrian had been shocked and horrified by the ability, and he had no way of controlling it. But recently he'd met two gentlemen who possessed the same ability. Now, Hadrian knew it passed within families and that he could learn to guide the power, if not completely control it.

However, Hadrian had been struck in the head just a few days earlier at the end of their most recent case and since then, he hadn't seen a single memory. He'd told Tilda about it before Teague's arrival, but she was apparently still hopeful that Hadrian would see something when he touched the paper. Hadrian hoped so too. In fact, he'd never wanted to see a memory more than he did right now.

He stared down at the paper, as much to concentrate on seeing something as to avoid Teague seeing his eyes glaze over, which Tilda had recently reported observing when Hadrian handled an object and saw a memory. He couldn't close his eyes, for that made the memory disappear.

Nothing was happening.

Hadrian was now worried there was something wrong with his strange ability. He'd only just begun to stop thinking of it as a curse, due in part to learning that he wasn't alone in having it. He'd met two men—a father and son—who possessed the same ability to experience memories. Captain Vale, the father, had been instrumental in informing Hadrian about it and offering counsel. His son, Thaddeus, had used his power for personal gain and founded a spiritualism society in which he tricked people into thinking he was contacting their deceased loved ones.

Captain Vale had been horrified to hear of his son's abuse of his power but delighted to see how Hadrian used his with Tilda. It had been extremely useful in guiding their investigations, and with Vale's advice, Hadrian had finally begun to find success in controlling it. Now, when he needed it most—to help Tilda with something so personal and vital—it had abandoned him.

Hadrian silently swore. Then he handed the paper back to Teague.

Tilda was still watching Hadrian. He gave her the slightest shake of his head to communicate that he hadn't seen anything. He hated the disappointment that shadowed her eyes.

Teague tucked the parchment into his pocket. "Congratulations on your successful investigation with Inspector Maxwell in the City. You've solved yet another pair of murders, and I'm not at all surprised. I'm confident they're pleased they hired you." He smiled at Tilda.

"It was most gratifying to work with Inspector Maxwell," Tilda said.

The inspector sent a sly look toward Hadrian. "And you nosed your way into the investigation, I heard."

"His involvement was both helpful and welcome," Tilda replied with the barest touch of heat. Hadrian quashed a smile.

"Are you working on an investigation now?" Teague asked, seemingly unbothered by Tilda's response. And he was likely only needling Hadrian, for they had an excellent working relationship.

The truth was that Hadrian *had* inserted himself into the matter. He'd shown up unannounced with his own disguise as Tilda's "brother." Thankfully, Inspector Maxwell had allowed Hadrian to remain and contribute to the investigation, albeit somewhat reluctantly.

Tilda nodded in reply to Teague's query. "I've a case to track down stolen items."

"Well, should you require any assistance from me, you need only ask," Teague offered.

"I make the same offer to you regarding Padgett's death," Tilda said.

"To the best of my ability." Teague gave her an apologetic half-smile. "Whilst Scotland Yard allows some female involvement, they would not hire you to assist as the City of London did. Indeed, my colleagues were surprised you were brought on."

"Hopefully, they saw the benefit, considering how the case turned out," Tilda said coolly.

"Not to mention Tilda's contributions to the apprehension of the Levitation Killers," Hadrian noted. That had been the case they'd worked on before they'd gone to work in the City investigating corruption in a friendly society and then a pair of murders associated with the society.

"Some have noticed," Teague said. "Though that doesn't mean they're ready to employ Miss Wren." He gave Tilda an apologetic look.

"Will you tell us why you believe Padgett was murdered?" Tilda asked. "We'll learn the details at the inquest tomorrow."

"You will indeed." Teague lifted a shoulder. "I don't see a reason not to tell you. Padgett was choked to death. The imprint of the murderer's hands is bruised onto his neck."

Hadrian's pulse picked up speed. Whilst he might not be able to see Padgett's memory by touching his corpse, he ought to see that of the murderer, perhaps as he was choking Padgett to death. Not that Hadrian wished to see such a thing, but it could lead them to the killer.

"Have you any idea why he was killed?" Hadrian asked.

"Not yet. There was no evidence of a forced intrusion, but there seemed to be a struggle. A chair was overturned, and ale was spilled." Teague scrutinized Tilda a moment. "You're going to ask me if you can see his lodgings."

"I might." She arched a brow at him. "Would that be possible?"

"Not tomorrow. I'll let you know." Teague inclined his head at Tilda and Hadrian. "See you at the inquest." He turned and left the parlor.

Tilda waited until Vaughn closed the front door before speaking. She turned to Hadrian with an anxious expression. "You saw nothing when you held the parchment?"

"Unfortunately, no." He hated confirming that.

She exhaled with disappointment. "I suspected you wouldn't since it was in Padgett's possession, and he is dead. I hope it was for that reason and not because there is some…problem with your ability." Tilda turned and went to the table situated near the front window that looked out to the street. Mrs. Acorn, the housekeeper, had set up the tea tray which they had not yet touched due to, first, Tilda's mother's arrival and then Teague's.

Tilda poured the tea as Hadrian joined her. She briefly met his gaze. "Perhaps you don't miss the ability to see others' memories? You have often called it a curse."

"I have done so less and less as it has come to help us. I hope it will be of use to you now."

"To me or my investigation regarding stolen items?" Tilda blinked at him as she sat.

"Don't tell me you don't want to discover the connection between Padgett and your father's death. There must be a reason Padgett had that information written down and stashed in his pocket."

She gave him a wry look. "You know me too well. Alas, I am not sure what's to be done right now. I really must focus on this case with Mrs. Goodwin."

"But we'll go to the inquest tomorrow?" Hadrian knew she was planning on it and wanted to make sure she was aware she could rely on him to be with her.

"You wish to accompany me?" She sipped her tea.

"Of course. That shouldn't surprise you. I'll pick you up, as usual."

She smiled again—warmly this time. "I'm sure Leach will be happy to have things back to normal."

Hadrian chuckled as he thought of his coachman's delight to be needed once more. "He did miss ferrying us about whilst we were working in the City and unable to use my coach." They'd been in disguise and would not have been able to afford such a luxury in the roles they played.

They sipped their tea and nibbled on Mrs. Acorn's delectable almond cake for a few minutes. Hadrian could see that Tilda was pensive.

"This has been a tumultuous afternoon," he said softly. "First your mother arrives unannounced and then your father's name appears in a dead former inspector's pocket."

"A former inspector we know was corrupt," Tilda added. She sounded surprisingly even, given what Hadrian had just pointed out. "Yes, it has been an…interesting day so far. Honestly, I can't decide which of those things you mentioned is more troublesome." She cracked a sardonic smile.

"I imagine they provoke different reactions," Hadrian said. "I can see your curiosity about Padgett and the note. With your mother, you seem guarded and, well, perhaps annoyed."

Tilda grimaced faintly, causing fine lines to crease her heart-shaped face. "My mother and I do not have the closest relationship, which you may recall me telling you. I did tell you that, didn't I?"

Hadrian nodded. "I know you don't see her often and when she does come to town, it seems her focus may be on other things. Doesn't she usually come with her husband?"

"Yes, and they don't stay here. They lodge with his daughter and her husband." Tilda pursed her bow-shaped lips. "I confess I'm not looking forward to sharing a roof with my mother. I haven't done so in eight years. I was more than happy to come live with Grandmama whilst my mother moved to Birmingham with her new husband. Truly, things could not have worked out better."

She barely took a breath before continuing. "Are you worried about not being able to see anyone's memories for several days now?"

Hadrian noted that she changed the subject away from her mother. That was fine—he would not press her but would remain her ally and offer support as needed. And he supposed they had been talking about his ability before.

He wasn't sure he wanted to discuss it. His frustration at not being able to help Tilda today with Padgett's note was great. He was beginning to think he ought to travel to Swindon to consult with Captain Vale about this problem. In fact, he would plan to do just that if his power did not return tomorrow. "I don't know that I'm *worried,* but I dearly wish I'd been able to see something with the piece of paper."

Tilda lifted a shoulder. "That may not have anything to do with whatever is preventing you from having a vision. You don't always experience one."

Whilst that was true, Hadrian hadn't ever gone this long without seeing a memory. Not since he'd gained the power in January.

"How is your head?" Tilda asked. "Perhaps your ability to see memories will return when it is fully healed. Draper only struck you four days ago."

"It's still a bit tender to the touch, but it doesn't ache." Hadrian had thought the same thing—that the blow had disrupted things. He hoped it was temporary. "I'm sure you're right," he said with a confidence he didn't quite feel.

There was another commotion in the entrance hall, and Hadrian heard Tilda's grandmother's voice. She appeared in the parlor a moment later wearing a broad smile.

"I'm so pleased you're still here, Lord Ravenhurst. But Vaughn tells me there's another guest." Mrs. Wren glanced about the room.

Tilda pressed her lips together before addressing her grandmother. "My mother arrived. She's gone upstairs to rest."

Mrs. Wren, a petite woman in her seventies with white hair

and bright blue eyes, stared at Tilda. "Did you know she was coming?"

"Of course not," Tilda replied. "I would have told you. I would have prepared the entire household."

"Why is she staying here?" Mrs. Wren went to the chair near the hearth and sat, her expression weary as her shoulders drooped slightly.

"Presumably because she came alone—Sir Bardolph is not with her," Tilda said. "I'm sorry, Grandmama," she added in a kind whisper.

"But why has she even come by herself?" Mrs. Wren clucked her tongue. "She's never bothered before."

"She heard about my investigative work and has come to persuade me to stop. And to marry, probably. She's already decided that Ravenhurst and I must be courting." Tilda rolled her eyes.

"I can't say I'd be upset about that," Mrs. Wren said with a delighted smile.

Tilda cast her a stony glance. "Do not start on that, Grandmama."

Hadrian tamped down his curiosity. Was this a frequent discussion? Particularly since they'd returned from the City? When he'd last seen Tilda, he'd confessed his strong feelings for her, and she'd acknowledged their "closeness," which had been threatened when he'd been struck in the head the other day. He'd hoped to hear more about whatever epiphany she'd had—if she'd had one—today. And now, hearing that a courtship had been discussed between her and her grandmother, he couldn't ignore a jolt of giddiness. He would very much like to court Tilda—if she would allow it.

However, now was definitely not the time to address such matters. Tilda had far too much to deal with at present.

Mrs. Wren waved her hand. "We will make the most of your mother's visit. What can we do to occupy her time?"

"I don't know, but I need to work on my case with Mrs. Goodwin. And I need to attend an inquest tomorrow afternoon with Lord Ravenhurst."

"Another inquest?" Mrs. Wren asked with concern, her brow furrowing. "Please don't tell me this missing items case is now a murder? Why does this always happen? I thought for sure when you went to the City to investigate a friendly society, there would be no chance of a murder. Then there were two *and* you ended up investigating them."

That did seem to happen with their cases, which both Tilda and Hadrian had observed. They started with an investigation, and it ended up involving a murder. Or two. Or three.

"This inquest has nothing to do with my case," Tilda told her reassuringly. "It's the death of a former inspector who investigated Lord Ravenhurst's stabbing. He wanted to go, and I am accompanying him."

Hadrian noticed how Tilda misrepresented things but said nothing. He understood why she wouldn't want to tell Mrs. Wren about the note in Padgett's pocket regarding her son.

Mrs. Wren eyed them with clear interest. "How familiar the two of you have become. Is it any wonder your mother assumes you may be courting?"

Hadrian saw the flash of irritation in Tilda's eyes, but before she could respond, her mother, Lady Pierce, returned. She looked to her former mother-in-law.

"Good afternoon, Barbara," Lady Pierce said without a hint of warmth.

"Welcome to my home, Edith," Mrs. Wren replied with a smile.

The tension between the two women was obvious, and Hadrian wondered if it had always been that way or if something had caused them to dislike one another. Perhaps it wasn't even dislike, but neither seemed eager to see the other.

Hadrian decided it was time to take his leave, despite how

curious he was to stay and learn more about the relationships between the three women. "I'm afraid I must be going." He rose, and Tilda stood with him.

Lady Pierce gave him a wide smile. "Don't rush off on my account. I decided to come back downstairs in order to become acquainted with you."

"We can do that another time," Hadrian assured her. "Indeed, I will speak to my mother about inviting you for tea at her house."

"Would you?" Lady Pierce's eyes warmed with enthusiasm. "I would be most obliged."

Hadrian smiled. "Excellent. We'll look forward to seeing you all then." He made a point of looking to Mrs. Wren to communicate that she would be included.

Tilda's grandmother gave him a small but appreciative smile and the faintest nod.

"I'll walk you out," Tilda said.

They moved into the entrance hall together where Vaughn handed Hadrian his hat and gloves. "Have a good afternoon, my lord."

Hadrian inclined his head at the very tall but hunched butler. Though in his seventies, he was quite spry. He'd come to Tilda's household after his employer—Tilda's grandfather's cousin—had been murdered. That had been their first case together.

"Thank you, Vaughn. I'll see you tomorrow when I fetch Miss Wren." Hadrian looked to Tilda. "If I can be of service in any way, please send word," he said softly.

Tilda nodded as their eyes met. "Thank you."

Donning his hat and pulling his gloves on, Hadrian departed through the door held open by Vaughn.

Leach stood at the coach and opened the door as Hadrian approached. "Did you have a pleasant visit, my lord?"

"I did, but it was…odd. You may have noticed the woman who arrived after us. That is Miss Wren's mother. She lives in Birmingham and arrived unannounced. They are not close."

"Indeed?" Leach's brow creased. "I am sorry for Miss Wren. I don't like to think of her being inconvenienced or troubled."

"I don't either," Hadrian said. "I will offer my support as I can."

"I couldn't help noticing Inspector Teague's arrival," Leach said. "Will you and Miss Wren be investigating another murder?"

Hadrian gave the coachman a wry look. "Not officially, though that has never stopped us before."

CHAPTER 2

Tilda stifled a yawn as Clara finished pinning her hair. "Pardon me."

"Did you not sleep well, miss?" Clara asked, her brown eyes warm with concern as they met Tilda's in the mirror at her dressing table.

"I did not. But I shall persevere." She gave Clara a reassuring smile, and the maid departed the chamber.

In truth, Tilda had fought to fall asleep and hadn't been successful until probably close to dawn. She had not been able to stop thinking of the note in Padgett's coat and the mystery of why he'd had it and why he'd been murdered. Mostly, however, she'd been consumed with thoughts of her father. The grief had eased over the years, but the ache of loss was always with her. It felt sharper today than it had in some time.

She looked toward the small desk situated beneath the window—to one of the few things that had belonged to her father and were still in her possession. Standing, she went to pick up the wooden letter opener. The handle was carved with the head of a fox. It was a good reminder of her father, who was sly and cunning—like a fox. Holding the object made her feel closer to him, her hand touching where his had once been.

How she wished Hadrian could touch this letter opener and see one of her father's memories. But he typically didn't see the memories of the dead. Though he had on at least two occasions, so perhaps he could try? But she couldn't imagine a letter opener would tell her anything about Padgett or why he had a scrap of paper bearing her father's name.

Though perhaps it would just be nice to have some sort of connection with her father again. She thought of the case she and Hadrian had investigated involving the mediums who'd claimed to speak to the dead. They'd been frauds and had tried to lure Tilda with a possible message from her father, but she hadn't bought into it. She also hadn't wanted it. Her father was gone, and communication from beyond—even if it was possible— wouldn't bring him back to the here and now.

Still, the idea of Hadrian seeing one of her father's memories stuck with her. Perhaps she *would* ask him to try. Though not now, as it seemed his power wasn't functioning properly at the moment. Hopefully, when his head fully healed, he'd be able to see memories again.

Tilda slid her thumb over the carved fox. She was incredibly eager to attend the inquest in a short while. There had to be a reason Padgett was carrying her father's name and the date he'd died, not that she expected to learn it at the inquest. She only hoped there would be something to explain the link or to offer some sort of clue.

Particularly since the inspector assigned to the case—Edwin Lowther—had been the man to find her father after he'd been killed interrupting a theft at an apothecary shop. In the years since her father's death, Lowther had been kind and helpful to her. When she'd started conducting investigations, he'd provided aid when he could. Sometimes, she paid him a small "gratuity" because his family needed it, just as she knew he would be in trouble if anyone at the Met learned he'd helped her.

She intended to speak with him following the inquest.

A soft rap on the door drew Tilda to turn from the desk. She hoped it wasn't her mother. "Come in."

Mrs. Acorn entered the bedchamber. "A letter was just delivered for you." She handed the envelope to Tilda and looked upon the letter opener in Tilda's hand. "That was your father's, wasn't it?"

Tilda nodded.

"Have you been thinking of him more with your mother here?" Mrs. Acorn asked gently.

"I suppose so." It wasn't due to her mother's arrival, though Tilda did not plan to tell anyone in the household about the paper in Padgett's pocket.

Tilda wondered what her mother would say. Did she miss her first husband or think of him at all? Tilda doubted it. They'd never had a close marriage that Tilda could remember. Her mother hadn't liked being married to a bobby. She'd hoped her husband would become a magistrate like his father. But Tilda's father hadn't wanted that. He'd told her his passion was working directly with people to keep them safe and solving crimes. The latter was why he was eager to join the Detective Branch.

"Lady Pierce wants to know if you're coming down for tea," Mrs. Acorn said.

"It's a bit early for that," Tilda noted. "Did you tell her I was going out?"

"I did not." Mrs. Acorn smiled benignly. "Would you like me to?"

"No, I'll be down in a moment. Thank you, Mrs. Acorn."

The housekeeper left, and Tilda used her father's letter opener to unseal the envelope. She removed and read the short missive from Mrs. Goodwin, her new client, which confirmed their meeting for tomorrow afternoon.

Setting the letter on her desk, Tilda gave the letter opener a silly, sentimental squeeze before putting it down. She fetched her hat and gloves from her dressing table, then went downstairs.

Vaughn was just closing the door as Tilda approached the entrance hall. He turned and his eyes reflected surprise upon seeing her. "Miss Wren."

"Who was that?" Tilda asked.

"Mr. Orchard," Vaughn replied. He appeared discomfited—his neck was red as his gaze darted toward the parlor.

Mr. Orchard lived across the street and had been attempting to court Tilda for the past couple of years. Every few months, he called and asked her to promenade or to take tea. Tilda was kind in her refusals, but he persisted. So, she'd been rather firm at their last encounter. Since that had been about four months ago, Tilda believed she'd finally been successful in deterring him.

Apparently not.

"Matilda, are you there?" Tilda's mother's voice carried from the parlor into the entrance hall.

Tilda bristled. No one called her Matilda, except for her mother.

Vaughn gave her a warm smile. He said nothing, but Tilda understood his wordless support, nonetheless. She handed him her hat and gloves, then squared her shoulders and went into the parlor to face her mother.

Grandmama sat in her usual chair near the hearth, her expression bland, whilst Tilda's mother perched on the settee with her fashionable gown draped perfectly over her legs and along the front of the settee. Last night at dinner, she'd expressed her relief that Tilda was finally wearing garments in the current fashion. Tilda hadn't bothered to point out that if her mother cared so deeply about her wardrobe, she could have provided Tilda with an allowance for such things. The truth was that Tilda didn't want her mother's husband's money. But she acknowledged—privately—that it would have been nice if her mother had offered.

Directing her attention to her mother, Tilda frowned slightly. "Did Mr. Orchard call?"

"He did," her mother replied crisply. "I sent him on his way. I informed him you have much loftier prospects than him."

Tilda drew in a breath. "You didn't really say that."

Her mother lifted her chin in a haughty manner. "I did."

Glancing toward her grandmother, Tilda received proof as she gave a slight nod.

"Mother, you may not meddle in my life," Tilda said.

"Barbara said you aren't interested in Orchard." Her mother darted a look at Tilda's grandmother. "How am I meddling if I only did what you would have done?"

Tilda kept her voice even. "I would not have been rude about it. Nor would I have lied. I do not have 'loftier prospects.' I have no prospects. *By choice.*"

"That's preposterous. You can't *choose* to remain unwed. Sooner or later, you will need a husband, and you've an astonishing opportunity to snare an earl!" Her mother's eyes gleamed with excitement.

"I do not wish to wed," Tilda said as she clenched her jaw. "I am not you. If you insist on pestering me about such nonsense, I will ask that you leave. In fact, you should go home. There's no reason for you to be here at all."

"Well, now who is being rude?" Her mother sniffed. "You are ruining your life flouncing about playing inspector." Her nose wrinkled. "It's unseemly, and you'll never catch a husband behaving in such a manner."

Playing inspector? Tilda's job was more than a passion for her. The income from it, which continued to grow, supported this household. Indeed, if not for her employment, they would not have been able to afford to take in Vaughn or Clara, nor would they live as comfortably as they did with the added expense of

Grandmama's medication. And it wasn't comfortable at all—Tilda worked hard to ensure there was enough money to keep the household running. Why else had she foregone updating her wardrobe until her income supported doing so?

Tilda kept a rein on her temper—barely. "Has it not occurred to you that the money I earn as an investigator supports this household? I suppose not, since I doubt you've given much thought as to how we subsist. Furthermore, there is no *flouncing* involved with investigating crime. I don't expect you to understand my desire to work in this field, not when you never supported Papa."

Her mother inhaled sharply as her eyes rounded. "You dare speak to me like that?"

"That is enough," Grandmama said quietly but firmly. "I won't have you arguing in my parlor. I would ask you to apologize to one another."

Tilda blinked at her grandmother—why should she apologize to her mother? Grandmama gave her a stern but kind look.

"Apologies, Mother," Tilda murmured.

"I see no reason I should apologize," her mother announced. She looked at her former mother-in-law. "You can't think Tilda's *work* is acceptable. Do you really want to see her unwed and alone? You aren't going to live forever."

Tilda's neck and shoulders tightened. She had to fight to keep from demanding her mother leave immediately. It was cruel of her to play on Grandmama's sentiments like that. But then her mother wasn't sentimental in the slightest. Tilda wasn't even sure if she was capable of love.

A horrid thought struck Tilda. Was she like her mother? She didn't think she was particularly sentimental either. And she was far more interested in furthering her career than in finding a mate or establishing a home. The notion of falling in love didn't hold appeal. That made Tilda feel cold and sounded too close to her mother.

"I do hope Tilda will wed." Grandmama sent Tilda an apologetic glance and a small but incredibly heartfelt smile. "She has so much love to give. And that is what it will take for her to agree to marriage—a deep and abiding love. I hope that will happen, but it may not, and Tilda mustn't settle."

Tilda's heart constricted. That was how Grandmama saw her? Perhaps Tilda *wasn't* exactly like her mother. Her father, after all, had been very loving. Perhaps she just needed to allow that side of herself to be more present.

"She won't have to settle," Tilda's mother said with great confidence. "She has an earl on the hook."

"There is no hook!" Tilda grunted with exasperation. Hadrian would be here any moment, and she didn't want him coming inside where he'd be subject to her mother's blatant matchmaking.

"You are wrong, my dear. We are to have tea with Lord Ravenhurst and his mother. We will take our best advantage."

Movement outside the front window drew Tilda's eye. Hadrian's coach had pulled up, and he was already stepping out. *Blast.*

"You must excuse me," Tilda said hurriedly. "I need to go to the inquest."

"An inquest?" her mother asked with horror. "You can't mean to go to one of those."

"I've been to several," Tilda said wryly. "It is part of my work. Really, you must excuse me, for Lord Ravenhurst is here. He is accompanying me."

Tilda's mother's eyes lit, and she clapped her hands together. "Oh! That makes all the difference. Of course you must go."

Vaughn welcomed Hadrian into the entrance hall. Tilda sent her mother a dark look. "We must be on our way. Please don't detain his lordship."

Hastening into the entrance hall, Tilda glanced at Hadrian. "I just need my hat and gloves."

The butler already had her accessories. Tilda gave him a brief, grateful smile and donned the hat. She then took the gloves and started toward the door.

But they were not to escape so easily.

"Good afternoon, Lord Ravenhurst!" Tilda's mother had come into the entrance hall.

Hadrian executed a smart bow. "Good afternoon, Lady Pierce."

"I'm so looking forward to tea with your mother. Do you know when that will be?" She smiled expectantly.

Tilda sent a glare toward her mother. It was as if she hadn't listened to a word Tilda had said.

"I'm awaiting confirmation from my mother, but probably Wednesday," Hadrian replied.

"We must go." Tilda started toward the door, and Vaughn scrambled to open it.

"Lady Pierce," Hadrian said with a nod.

"Have a pleasant inquest," Tilda's mother said.

Tilda couldn't resist rolling her eyes as she marched from the house toward Hadrian's coach. He caught up to her just before they arrived at the coach door, which Leach held open.

"Good afternoon, Miss Wren," the coachman said affably.

"Good afternoon, Leach." Tilda smiled, and the tension in her features mostly evaporated.

Mostly.

"I understand you have a new case," Leach said. "I look forward to doing my part." He'd been instrumental during their past cases—not just driving them about but fetching the police when necessary. He was an important part of the team.

"I'm glad to hear it," Tilda replied before stepping into the coach. She sat on the forward-facing seat, and Hadrian did the same. They'd gone back and forth over their acquaintance with both sharing the seat and not. They hadn't shared it at first, then they had, then they'd kissed, then they'd returned to not sharing the seat. Now, it seemed, they were back to sharing.

Would another kiss follow?

Tilda thrust that thought away. She'd had enough talk of love and marriage today. Not that kissing Hadrian had anything to do with love *or* marriage.

They were shortly on their way, and Hadrian turned his head toward Tilda. "I sense your frustration with your mother."

"She has come to meddle in my life. She insists I must give up my career and marry. It's preposterous." Tilda exhaled. "I wish she would go home."

"That must be incredibly difficult. I'm sorry."

Tilda pressed her spine against the squab and briefly closed her eyes as she marshaled her emotions and pushed her mother from her mind. "Let us focus on other matters. You told Leach about my investigation into Mrs. Goodwin's stolen items?"

"I mentioned that we may be needed," Hadrian replied. "Is that all right?"

"Certainly. Though I don't wish to take up too much of your time so soon after we finished our investigation in the City. I'm sure you have matters in the Lords that require your attention."

"Somewhat, yes, but I always want to help you with investigations." He grinned. "I find I enjoy solving crimes more than I ever imagined. I've you to thank for that."

Tilda sent him a small smile. "I never meant to corrupt you, but I'm grateful for your assistance. I've a meeting with Mrs. Goodwin tomorrow afternoon if you'd care to accompany me."

He took a moment to respond. "I'm afraid I have other plans tomorrow. But Leach can certainly transport you, if you like."

His hesitation sparked her curiosity. Was there something he wasn't saying? No, of course not. Sometimes, she had to remind herself to leave off her investigative sensibilities. "Thank you, but that isn't necessary. I didn't invite you so that I'd have transportation."

"I didn't think you did. Since I will not require Leach tomorrow afternoon, I only wanted to be courteous." He waggled his brows. "And Leach truly does love to help with our investigations."

"Well, then I will accept the offer. I wouldn't want to disappoint him."

"I'll let him know," Hadrian said. "Just tell him what time to fetch you. I'm sorry I'm not able to accompany you."

Tilda gave him a reassuring smile. "It's quite all right. I know you have responsibilities, and our investigations often take too much of your time."

"Never," he said rather vehemently. "Every moment we work together is of great importance to me."

She believed that to be true, and when his duties were great, he did occasionally divert himself from their investigation, as he would be doing tomorrow. "How is your head today?"

"Still faintly tender, but I'm hopeful I will see something of the killer's memory when I touch Padgett's body."

"Because we know the murderer touched Padgett with his bare hands," Tilda said almost breathlessly. "I hadn't considered that. I do hope you'll have the chance to get close enough." Tilda wanted nothing more than to learn something of use today.

He met her gaze with determination. "I'll make sure I do. How likely is it that we'll be trying to solve Padgett's murder?"

"Probably not as likely as you may think, given our history," she said sardonically. "I realize our cases tend to involve a murder. However, my current case with Mrs. Goodwin has nothing to do with Padgett. I'm not sure even I can find an excuse to investigate his death."

"I know people in the Home Office, Tilda. I'll make sure this investigation is conducted with skill and integrity."

"That is kind of you, but I would rather you not cause a stir. Inspector Lowther will do his best, I'm sure. I plan to speak with him today."

He arched a dark brow at her. "And will you offer your services?"

"I will certainly make myself available to him." Tilda doubted he would consult with her, but she would hope he would at least share information. If not, Teague would, as he'd already demonstrated by coming to see her in the first place. She was most grateful to him, for without his thoughtfulness, she would have no idea about a potential connection between Padgett and her father.

A small voice in the back of her head asked if that might have been preferable. Tilda wouldn't rest until she discovered the truth.

CHAPTER 3

They arrived at the Green Dragon in the Strand where the inquest was to take place. As Hadrian escorted Tilda into the pub, he thought of their conversation in the coach. He would be gravely disappointed if he was not able to see anything when he touched Padgett. Ideally, he would touch the man's neck where he'd been choked. Hadrian believed that would give him his best chance at seeing the memory of whomever had killed him.

But there were two distinct obstacles in his way. The first was getting close enough to the body and being able to touch Padgett's neck; the coroner and police would be nearby, along with everyone else in the room, including the jury, spectators, and the press. The second, of course, was whether his ability would even function properly. He still hadn't seen a memory since he'd been struck in the head.

He'd been careful not to touch anything or anyone that might give him a memory since learning of Padgett's murder. He didn't know why he was avoiding doing so, except that after meeting with Captain Vale, he now knew that managing his power was possible. Conserving his energy to encourage the return of his ability made sense—and he truly couldn't think of what else to do.

If today was a failure, he planned to visit Captain Vale in Swindon tomorrow, which was why he'd told Tilda he couldn't accompany her to meet with her client, Mrs. Goodwin. He'd hated to refuse her invitation, but regaining his lost ability was at the forefront of his mind.

He hadn't told Tilda why he couldn't go with her and wondered why he was hiding his plans. He supposed he didn't want her to see how worried he was. And he wanted her to focus on her case, which she'd set aside to assist Inspector Maxwell, not on his troubles.

The interior of the pub looked much like the other inquests they'd attended. A table in the center held the body of the deceased which was covered with a cloth. The jury of twelve men stood on the far side of the room and kept to themselves. The coroner, Julius Graythorpe, whom Hadrian recognized, stood at the head of the table along with several uniformed constables. It seemed there were other non-uniformed members of the police, including Detective Inspector Teague. Hadrian also noticed Inspector Lowther, whom he'd met during his first investigation with Tilda.

Tilda surveyed the spectators who'd come and were either seated in the rows of chairs or lingered about. "Ezra Clement is here." She referred to the reporter for *The Daily News*, with whom they worked on occasion. In their last two cases, they'd traded information with Clement.

Hadrian hadn't liked him at first because he'd tried to pester Hadrian's mother about her interest in the spiritualism society Hadrian and Tilda were investigating. But Clement had redeemed himself by being helpful and true to his word.

Clement approached them. He wore his signature plaid trousers. Today's colors were brick red and brown.

The reporter regarded them with his shrewd brown eyes

before fixing on Tilda. "What brings you here, Miss Wren?" He glanced toward Hadrian. "Ravenhurst. Are you working on a case to do with Padgett?"

Tilda lifted her shoulder. "Merely curious."

Hadrian wasn't surprised that she didn't offer any information, such as Padgett's connection to Hadrian's stabbing.

"I imagine you've come because of your association with Padgett," Tilda said smoothly. She referred to Clement having paid Padgett for information regarding the spiritualism case. Padgett had shared details from the police with Clement—and that had been *after* Padgett had left the Met.

It occurred to Hadrian that Padgett had a contact inside the Metropolitan Police Department. Who was that person, and did they know anything about Padgett's murder? He glanced at Tilda, certain she'd already posed those questions in her mind along with many others.

"The murder of a former police inspector is of interest," Clement replied evenly. "Regardless of whether I know them or not."

"Do you know anything that would help find Padgett's killer?" Tilda asked. "Such as who Padgett was obtaining information from inside the police after he retired?"

Hadrian was glad she'd asked the question—and not at all surprised.

The reporter pursed his lips. "I don't, unfortunately, though I'm not sure that would have anything to do with this. Is there something you know that connects Padgett's murder with whomever was giving him information?"

"No, but since we know Padgett was corrupt, it makes sense to investigate his unethical and potentially illegal activities."

"It does indeed," Clement said. "I don't know that he had a single source of information. Padgett has always been a bit like a fly—able to avoid detection until he became annoying. I'll poke around and see if I can learn anything."

Tilda smiled like a cat, and Hadrian knew she'd wanted Clement to offer to do just that. "That would be incredibly helpful."

Clement inclined his head then studied Tilda intently. "Helpful to whom? You're sure you're not working on anything to do with this?"

"I am not," Tilda replied.

"I thought you might be, given your comment about my being helpful. Also, because Padgett was the inspector who investigated his lordship's stabbing several months ago. From what I understand, Padgett closed the case, then you solved it." He moved his gaze to Hadrian. "Would you care to comment on the former inspector's murder?"

Hadrian's jaw tightened. "No."

Clement's eyes narrowed once more. "Are we not friends? You don't need to keep secrets from me."

"We have no secrets to keep regarding this case," Tilda said. "For we are not working on it. I only meant it would be helpful to the police."

"I see." Clement sounded slightly uncertain as if he didn't believe they weren't working on the case.

Hadrian wondered why she wasn't telling Clement that they were. How else was she going to obtain information from him? Especially since it sounded as though he may be able to learn something useful.

"If that changes, you know where to find me." Clement touched the brim of his hat before turning and making his way to the back wall, where he would likely stand and take notes, as he typically did during inquests they'd attended.

"I suppose he knew that Padgett investigated my stabbing because Padgett told him?" Hadrian asked quietly.

"Probably." She sent a slight frown toward Clement's back. "I wonder how long Clement was working with Padgett."

"I'm surprised you didn't ask," Hadrian said. "Why didn't you tell him about the paper Padgett was carrying?"

Tilda's mouth straightened, but her brow continued to furrow. "I don't want Clement probing into my father—at least not until I learn more about what's going on."

Hadrian sent her a dark look. "It's entirely possible he already knows about the paper and the mention of your father."

"*If* Clement is now in direct contact with Padgett's source in the Met, I would believe that. However, it doesn't sound like he is, and I had the distinct impression he was seeking more information." Tilda exhaled. "I will likely need to confide in him because chances are he knows *something* that could help the investigation." She gestured toward the chairs. "Let's sit."

They claimed seats in the front row, and a few minutes later, the coroner called the inquest to order. Graythorpe was of somewhat short stature, but his sharp blue eyes and deep voice commanded attention and respect. He explained the purpose of the inquest, which was to examine the questionable death of former Inspector John Padgett.

First, the coroner interviewed Inspector Lowther about how Padgett had been found. Lowther described Padgett's lodgings and said the police had been summoned by a neighbor who'd found the body.

"How did you find Mr. Padgett?" Graythorpe asked.

Lowther must have been a fearsome constable for he was tall and burly. Though in his forties, he still sported a thick head of ink-dark hair. Bushy brows capped his deep-set brown eyes. "He was on the floor of his lodgings next to an overturned chair. He was clearly deceased as his eyes were open, and his lips were blue. His neck was bruised, and his face was swollen. Looked to me like he'd been strangled by someone with his bare hands."

"Did you find any clues at the scene that would lead you to the killer?"

"No, but the rooms had been ransacked," Lowther replied.

"We can't say if anything was missing. None of the neighbors we interviewed observed anything unusual."

There was no mention of the paper that had been found in Padgett's pocket. Hadrian glanced at Tilda, but she was riveted on the testimony.

Graythorpe's brow creased. "I've determined Mr. Padgett was killed sometime between midnight and three. No one saw anyone enter or leave the lodging house?"

"That's right," Lowther said with a nod. "Everyone I spoke with said they were asleep before midnight. I was careful to ask for the time they retired."

It seemed to Hadrian that Lowther wanted to make sure he was demonstrating his ability to become a detective inspector.

"Thank you, Inspector." Graythorpe then interviewed the two constables who'd arrived ahead of Lowther at the lodging house. Following that, he spoke with the landlord.

Turning to face the jury, Graythorpe instructed them on their duty to determine whether Padgett's death was a murder. It didn't take them long to reach their decision. They ruled Padgett had been choked to death. Graythorpe thanked them for their service. Overall, it was a very boring inquest—and a short one.

Hadrian pivoted toward Tilda as they stood. "I need to get close to that body before they cover him up again." He was surprised they hadn't done so already.

"Let's hurry," Tilda said quietly. She made her way toward Lowther, who stood near the head of the table.

Hadrian followed behind, removing his gloves as he went and stashing them in his pocket.

Lowther smiled warmly at her. "Miss Wren, I'm a little surprised to see you here."

"Only a little?" she asked with a small smile, angling herself so that Lowther would not be facing the table.

Realizing she was creating an opportunity for him to investigate Padgett's body, Hadrian quickly moved as close as he could. Surreptitiously, he reached for Padgett's neck.

The bruising was horrid and spanned the front and sides of his neck. Hadrian could make out the thumb and finger marks of the killer's hands. He noted an odd stripe of bruising on the little finger of what would have been the left hand. It was a bit darker than the surrounding bruise.

Someone nearby coughed, and that prompted Hadrian to finish his task. He pressed his fingers against Padgett's cold flesh and thought of the man's demise. He imagined the hands wrapping around the poor man's neck.

Nothing came to him. No vision. No sentiment. Along with the memories he saw, he often sensed what the person was feeling at the time.

Frustration curled through him. Hadrian had long bemoaned his inexplicable and sometimes frightening new power, but he'd grown used to it. In fact, he depended on it to aid Tilda in her investigations. Without it, was he any use to her?

It couldn't just be…gone.

The irony that he'd hated this ability at first and was now upset because it wasn't functioning properly was not lost on Hadrian. He had to determine what had happened and how he could get it working again. He refused to accept that he'd lost it.

Hadrian's plans to visit Swindon were now imperative. He desperately wanted to speak with Captain Vale about the disappearance of his power. Turning away from the body, he joined Tilda and Lowther.

"You do know about the note then," Lowther said quietly. "Teague said he planned to tell you, but I wasn't sure if he had."

"Why wasn't it mentioned in the inquest?" Tilda asked.

Lowther glanced about and lowered his voice even more. "We don't want the press to know about that yet."

"I see," Tilda murmured. "So you're investigating the connection then? Do you have any idea what it could mean? You were there that night. When my father was killed, I mean."

"Yes." Lowther's expression turned somber. "I can't think of any connection between Padgett and Wren, other than they both worked for A Division. They weren't friends. Your father was gregarious and well-liked. Padgett was always rather stoic. He was a solitary fellow for the most part."

Hadrian watched Tilda's expression soften as Lowther discussed her father. The description was very nice. Hadrian could hear in Lowther's tone that Thomas Wren had been admired. "Was Padgett *not* well-liked?"

Lowther shrugged. "I don't think he was *dis*liked." He grimaced faintly. "Actually, some of the constables didn't care for him in the last few years. He did grow somewhat cantankerous as he aged. That was why he retired."

"Was it?" Tilda asked, though she knew it wasn't. Padgett should have been prosecuted for accepting bribes from the man who'd had Hadrian stabbed. Instead, he'd quietly retired and taken up work as a private investigator.

"That's my understanding," Lowther said. "I should go. It's always good to see you, Miss Wren."

"Please give Peggy and the children my best," Tilda said with a bright smile. It was almost *too* bright, as if she was masking something.

Looking closer, Hadrian noted the faint lines forming the number eleven between her brows. He sensed her agitation. This had to be difficult for her.

"Shall we go?" he asked softly.

She turned toward him. They stood very close to one another. Tipping her head back, she searched his face. "Did you see anything?"

He shook his head. "I'm sorry."

Her eyes dimmed with disappointment, and Hadrian's anger

over his missing power burned anew. How could he not see what he needed to in order to help Tilda? It was bloody unfair.

"I did notice something," he said. "It may be nothing. I'll tell you in the coach."

He escorted her outside and they walked to where Leach stood. He immediately opened the door, and Tilda climbed inside wordlessly.

Hadrian followed her in and sat beside her. "There was a strange mark on Padgett's neck."

"I saw the bruising," Tilda said. "I glanced over at the table before I distracted Lowther. You observed something beyond the discoloration?"

"There was a darker stripe on the contusion—where the left little finger of the killer's hand pressed into Padgett's flesh. I think he might have been wearing a ring."

Tilda sucked in a breath. "That's brilliant, Hadrian." Her eyes shone with admiration. "Excellent detective work."

He couldn't help feeling a surge of pride at her praise. "Thank you. I have a brilliant teacher."

Her brow creased. "But why wasn't that mentioned at the inquest? I can't imagine a coroner of Graythorpe's caliber would miss such a thing."

"Perhaps they're aiming to keep that from the press as well," Hadrian said.

She seemed to ponder that a moment. "That would be my guess. I find this secrecy questionable. I may ask Teague, however, he might not be able to tell us anything."

"Because he doesn't know, or because he isn't in on the secret?"

"That is a question I'd like to know the answer to. Along with many others." She gave him a wry look. "And before you say it, yes, I am going to try to investigate this murder—as I can. I really must give attention to my paying client after having to delay the work whilst we were in the City."

"I was hoping you would say that—about investigating the murder. You deserve to know why Padgett had your father's name and the date he died in his pocket." He gave her an earnest look. "I will do everything in my power—*everything*—to help you."

She arched a brow at him. "Does that mean you intend to bring the full influence of your earldom to bear?"

"Whatever it takes."

Tilda laughed softly. "I never imagined to befriend an earl, let alone have one working alongside me."

Hadrian hoped it would always be thus. Which was why he needed to regain his power to help her.

"You do realize that we may be investigating a ring once more," she said.

A ring had been at the center of their first investigation. Touching it had first alerted Hadrian to his ability to see memories, though he'd no idea at the time what was happening to him. He'd stripped the ring from his assailant's hand. When he'd picked it up a few days later, he'd seen his first vision. Unraveling that mystery had been challenging. He couldn't have done it without Tilda's help.

"So it seems," Hadrian said. "And I'm confident we'll be successful again."

She gave him a hesitant look. "Would you mind if we made a detour before you take me home?"

"Not at all." For the first time, he saw a cautious, almost timid shadow in her gaze, and he would have agreed to anything she asked. "Where to?"

She glanced toward the window. "An apothecary shop just off Knightsbridge."

He thought a moment before asking, "Can I ask why?"

"It's where my father was killed."

Hadrian felt as though he'd been socked in the chest. He

hadn't expected that answer. "Why do you want to go there today?"

She didn't immediately respond. He watched as the furrows in her brow deepened. Then they relaxed. "Padgett's death and that paper in his pocket have brought my father to the forefront of my mind," she said carefully. "I've never visited the shop. In fact, I've purposely stayed quite clear of it. I think it's time I went, if only to see it."

"Are you hoping to learn something?" Hadrian wasn't sure what. The crime had occurred over a decade earlier.

"I'm always hoping to learn something," she said with the hint of a smile that soothed Hadrian's concern for her. "But I don't know that I expect to."

Hadrian knocked on the roof of the coach, which would prompt Leach to pull to the side of the road. Once they were stopped, Hadrian opened the door and informed the coachman of their change of destination.

They were quiet a few minutes. Hadrian wanted to ask about her father but also didn't want to cause her any upset. In the end, he decided their friendship was close enough for him to probe, at least a little. "Is it good that you're thinking of your father more?"

"Yes, and also no." She smoothed her hand over her lap. "I always wanted to know more about what happened. For instance, why was my father there? A Division ends at Knightsbridge, and the shop was in B Division."

"And he was a sergeant at A Division," Hadrian said.

She nodded.

"Lowther showed up there too. Why?"

"At the time, he was a constable with B Division," Tilda replied. "Lowther being at the shop makes sense. The supposition is that my father was patrolling the park side of Knightsbridge and saw something that drew him to cross the street. But we've no way to confirm that, of course."

"I didn't realize there were questions around your father's death."

"I can't say I did either, until that paper was found in Padgett's pocket. The explanation for his presence at the shop so close to A Division made sense to me."

"It does to me too." Though Hadrian could understand how her opinion might change. "Now you aren't so sure?"

She lifted a shoulder. "As I said, we have no way of knowing what prompted my father to go to the apothecary shop. Now a former inspector who seemed to have knowledge of something surrounding my father's death is dead."

"You think, perhaps, you may move closer to the truth?"

A brief smile lifted her mouth. "That is my hope. Although, I don't want to have unrealistic expectations. I would like to visit this shop as an investigator looking into an old crime, not as a daughter searching for answers she may never find."

Hadrian thought that was brilliant of her, but he couldn't help feeling for the daughter who wanted those answers. "Should I try to touch something in the shop?" He so badly wanted to help her.

"I'm not sure it would be helpful." She sent him a slightly nervous glance. "It also doesn't seem as though your power has returned. Your head likely needs more time to heal."

"Probably." He buried his frustration. Tomorrow, he would hopefully find answers to this conundrum when he visited the Vales. He *needed* to be able to see memories to help Tilda.

"Furthermore, it may not even be an apothecary shop anymore," Tilda said. "That was over a decade ago."

They'd find out soon enough.

They arrived at the address, and it was still an apothecary shop. He noted the relief in Tilda's features as she looked out the window before they departed the coach.

Tilda paused before walking inside, her gaze moving over the sign hanging over the door. It read: R. Williams, Apothecary. "I'm glad it's still here," she murmured.

Hadrian was too. He opened the door for her and a bell tinkled as the door moved inward.

The shop was small and lined with shelves containing bottles, tins, and pots of various sizes. There was a section of "Beauty Aids" as well as one for "Female Maladies."

"Have you any idea what you're going to ask?" Hadrian whispered.

"Not entirely," Tilda replied as she made her way to the counter.

A bespectacled man in his sixties stood off to the side poring over a book that was open on the counter. He looked up at them and smiled. After glancing at the book for another brief moment, he removed his glasses and carried them in his hand as he moved toward them. "Good afternoon."

"Good afternoon," Tilda said. "Are you Mr. Williams?"

"I am," he replied with a nod.

"And were you the same apothecary who was here in December of 1857?" Tilda asked.

"I've been here since 1845," he said proudly. "What is special about December 1857?"

"My name is Matilda Wren. My father, Sergeant Thomas Wren, was killed here."

Williams was a fair fellow, with white hair and blue eyes, but he became even paler. "Oh, dear. Yes, of course. I'd forgotten the precise month after so much time. That was a terrible tragedy."

"I'm an investigator now," Tilda said. "I wondered if you would satisfy my curiosity about what happened here." She gave him a gentle smile.

His gaze cradled her with concern. "I will share what I can, my dear. I do remember the event quite clearly. Nothing like that had ever happened before—or since, thankfully."

"Thank you." She regarded him expectantly.

"I live upstairs," he said. "But I didn't see what happened. A sound woke me around one in the morning, though I can't say exactly what it was. My wife—God rest her soul—was also awakened, but she didn't think I should go downstairs. I had to soothe her for a few minutes before I could make my way to the shop. When I arrived, I saw the source of the sound—the front window was broken. Then I found your dear father. He was just there." Williams gestured toward an area near the door—next to the shelf for Beauty Aids.

"Was he still alive?" Tilda asked. Hadrian heard the hope in her voice, and his chest tightened.

"I'm afraid not," he said kindly. His brow furrowed. "You know how he was killed? I don't want to say anything upsetting."

"Yes, his throat was cut," she said stiffly.

"I'll tell you what was strange." Williams frowned briefly. "There should have been a great deal of blood on the floor with such a wound. But there wasn't. Indeed, there was hardly any blood at all. I mentioned that to the police, and they said the killer had likely cleaned it up."

"That hardly makes sense," Hadrian blurted.

"I agree," the apothecary said. "Nor was there time to do so between when I was awakened and when I came downstairs."

Tilda turned her head toward Hadrian. "Then perhaps he wasn't killed here." She looked back to the apothecary. "That makes the most sense, doesn't it?"

Williams nodded. "I suggested it at the time, and the police said they would investigate every possibility. That was the last I heard of it."

"Was there no mention of the lack of blood at the inquest?" Tilda asked.

"Not that I recall," Williams replied after a brief moment of consideration.

Tilda looked at him with appreciation. "Do you remember who was here from the police?"

"I do recall the man who arrived first—Constable Lowther. He was most upset. After ascertaining that I and my wife were all right, he left to fetch additional help. Two more constables and an inspector arrived a short while later."

"Do you recall any of them?" Tilda asked hopefully.

"The inspector's name was Padgett, and the constables were Jurgens and Fellows, I believe."

Hadrian masked his surprise. Had Tilda known that Padgett was here? Wouldn't she have mentioned that before?

"You're certain of those names?" Tilda's eyes had turned steely. Hadrian didn't think she'd known about Padgett.

"I am, though I'm sure you could consult the report." Williams blinked. "I assume that's still available somewhere."

"I'm sure it is," Tilda said. "Which one of them suggested the killer had cleaned up the blood?"

"Inspector Padgett." Williams responded without the barest hesitation.

"Is there anything else you remember about that night?" Tilda asked.

Williams thought for a moment. "I don't think so. It was very somber. The police were saddened by your father's death. They were most committed to finding his killer."

"But they never did," Tilda said softly.

"I wasn't certain," William said. "I'm sorry to hear that's the case. But you're looking into it now?"

She shook her head slightly. "Not really. I was only curious."

"My apologies. You said you were an investigator, and I made a poor assumption." He inclined his head. "You did also say you were satisfying your curiosity."

Tilda cocked her head. "What did the thief steal from you that night?"

"Not much, but I suspect that was because he was interrupted by your father. He nicked some laudanum and opium tinctures— just a few bottles of each."

"Thank you for your time, Mr. Williams." Tilda gave him a warm smile.

"My pleasure, Miss Wren. I extend my deepest sympathy for your enduring loss. I'm sure your father would be proud of you now."

"That's kind of you to say." Tilda nodded gently, then turned.

Hadrian looked toward the apothecary in silent gratitude, then moved to open the door for Tilda. They didn't speak until they were back in the coach on the way to her grandmother's house.

"Seems that was an excellent idea," Hadrian said once they were moving. He looked sideways at Tilda. Her expression was surprisingly serene after what they'd just learned.

"I am going to ask Teague if he'll obtain the police report for me, as well as the inquest report. I want to see what they wrote about the crime scene, though it sounds as though it won't match what Williams just told us." She turned toward Hadrian. "Why would Lowther lie? He's always recalled the events as if he'd found my father not long after his throat had been cut. He has said on more than one occasion, 'If only I'd been a few moments sooner!'"

"You think he lied?"

Tilda's jaw tightened briefly. "He had to have. Or Williams is lying, but that doesn't seem likely after listening to him. He pointed out the lack of blood, and that Padgett had an explanation for it." She shook her head. "I can't believe I've never asked these questions before."

"Don't follow those thoughts, Tilda. There's no benefit." Hadrian realized he sounded a bit stern, but he didn't want her to chastise herself. Not only was there no point—she wasn't to blame. "What's important is that you're learning it now, when you're equipped to investigate the matter. Will you speak with Lowther?"

"I think I must. But first I want to see the reports. I've no doubt he lied, however. I mean to find out why."

"What about Padgett?" Hadrian asked.

Her eyes turned frosty. "Between the paper in his pocket and his presence at my father's murder scene, there's an undeniable connection between them. Are you prepared to help me find out what that is?"

"Absolutely." Nothing would keep Hadrian from her side.

CHAPTER 4

As Tilda prepared for her meeting with Mrs. Goodwin, she thought of the night her father had died, as she'd done almost incessantly since visiting the apothecary shop yesterday. There had to be a reasonable explanation for the lack of blood at the apothecary shop. Part of her wanted to simply go to Lowther and demand to know the truth, but if he'd lied once, he'd almost certainly lie again.

That didn't mean she wasn't going to investigate the matter. She had to. Hopefully, Teague, whom she trusted, would be of assistance.

Now, she needed to focus on her paying client, Felicity Goodwin, the widow who'd hired her to find items stolen from her house a few weeks ago. Tilda picked up her reticule from her desk just as there was a knock on the door. "Yes?"

The door opened without a reply. Tilda managed not to frown as her mother entered.

She surveyed Tilda, her focus settling briefly on the reticule in Tilda's hand. "You look as if you're going out. How fortuitous. I thought we could go shopping."

"I *am* going out," Tilda replied shortly as she glanced toward the door. "I have an appointment."

"I could come along with you," her mother said, seemingly oblivious to Tilda's haste. "And we can shop afterward. You need a new gown for tea with his lordship and the dowager countess."

"I don't, actually." The idea of shopping with her mother was about as attractive as spending the afternoon doing needlework, which wasn't remotely interesting to Tilda. "In any case, I'm not sure how long my appointment will take."

Her mother's brows pitched over her eyes, and she twisted her lips into a peeved expression. "What appointment is this?"

"If you must know, I'm meeting with a client." Tilda moved to grab her hat and gloves from her dressing table.

Her mother exhaled. "Oh, that silly *job* of yours. Is that why you were so distracted at dinner last night and again at breakfast this morning? Or dare I hope you were thinking of the earl?"

"Why would I be thinking of Ravenhurst?" Tilda asked.

Her mother lifted her shoulders as her eyes rounded briefly. "Oh, I don't know, because he's an attractive, wealthy earl who seems to like you very much?"

Tilda ignored her sarcasm. "I have no time for romance, nor am I interested in it."

Her mother put a hand on her hip. "Why not? Girls always dream about the man they will marry someday, the household they will run, the children they will have."

"Did you do that?" Tilda asked, then held up her hand. "Never mind. I don't care. I have none of those dreams. I'm surprised you would think I did, given the upbringing I had."

Her mother's cheeks hollowed as she drew in a breath. She glanced away from Tilda, then pressed her lips together. "Whether you want that or not, you must think of your future. Marriage will give you security, if nothing else. You needn't have a grand romance."

Tilda wondered if her mother had loved either of her husbands, but she wasn't going to ask. The answer didn't matter. "I'll secure my own future. We have very different opinions on marriage. I see no point in marrying at all *unless* it's for love."

"That's ridiculous," her mother said. "Love isn't as important as money or position."

Tilda had no trouble believing her mother meant that. She certainly hadn't loved her father. Which begged the question… "Why did you marry Father? Because it certainly wasn't for any of those reasons." She regretted the hasty comment as soon as it passed her lips.

Her mother actually looked slightly uncomfortable, much to Tilda's surprise. "His family had enough money for us to be comfortable, and…I thought he would rise to be a magistrate like his father, or perhaps even a member of Parliament."

Of course, Tilda's father hadn't done either of those things. Instead, he'd been murdered. She briefly thought of telling her mother what she'd learned yesterday, that the story they'd always heard of Thomas Wren's death might be false, but she wasn't sure her mother would care. Furthermore, Tilda didn't want to discuss it until she learned the truth.

"Are you happy now, Mother?" Tilda asked quietly. "As the wife of a baronet?"

"I am," her mother replied without hesitation. "I daresay, you would be even happier as a countess."

Tilda rolled her eyes. "That is not even possible—either becoming a countess or being happy as one."

"I disagree," her mother said vehemently. "You could easily become a countess. You and Lord Ravenhurst are friends, and that's unheard of. Indeed, you're a breath away from courtship. You're already moving in the same social circle, *and* you know his mother. Besides, I see the way he looks at you. He cares for you."

Tilda gritted her teeth. "That's because we are friends. We have been in several…tense situations." She'd been about to say dangerous but decided her mother didn't need to know that since she was already against Tilda's work.

"You can't continue *working* together in that fashion," her mother insisted. "I can't believe there aren't rumors about you and the earl already."

"Nobody notices us or cares what we do," Tilda said.

"I doubt that's true. You've been in the newspaper," her mother said. "You will draw attention now."

"We don't swan about Society solving crimes. No one that you would deem important sees us doing anything. We do *not*, as you said, move in the same social circle." Tilda didn't hide her exasperation. "You really must leave off discussing my work and Ravenhurst. I've been clear that you mustn't meddle in my life. If you can't refrain from doing so, I must ask that you leave. Excuse me, as I need to leave for my appointment." Tilda moved forward.

Her mother stood blocking the door a moment, eyes narrowed as she surveyed Tilda. "I still think you need a new gown before having tea with Lord Ravenhurst and his mother. Will you please consider it?"

"I can't afford another gown at the moment," Tilda said plainly. "Now, please step aside so I won't be late."

Her mother opened the door and moved into the corridor. Tilda followed her, closing the door behind her and then starting toward the stairs.

"I'll pay for it, Matilda," her mother called after her.

Tilda looked back at her mother over her shoulder but didn't reply. She wanted to provide financial support now? Was that part of her campaign to persuade Tilda to end her investigative career? Irritated, Tilda hastened down the stairs and bid farewell to her grandmother before departing the house.

Leach was waiting for her at the end of the street with Ravenhurst's coach. He jumped down to open the door for her as she approached. "Good afternoon, Miss Wren."

"Good afternoon, Leach. Thank you for meeting me here."

Tilda hadn't wanted him to fetch her at the house because her mother would have made much of the fact that Tilda was taking Hadrian's coach to her appointment. She would have pointed to the overture as further proof that they were practically betrothed.

"I'm glad to be of service, Miss Wren," Leach said as he helped her into the coach. He closed the door, and they were shortly on their way to Mrs. Goodwin's house in Maddox Street.

Tilda was glad she'd listened to her grandmother and Hadrian, who'd both encouraged her to purchase new gowns so that she looked more successful as an investigator. She would have felt self-conscious calling on Mrs. Goodwin in Mayfair in one of her outmoded gowns.

Her mother's offer to buy a dress continued to grate on Tilda. She'd never wanted to spend money on Tilda before. Indeed, she hadn't even offered an allowance when Tilda had decided to move in with her grandmother after her mother had married Sir Bardolph. The fact that her mother only wanted to buy her something now, either because she wanted Tilda to stop working as an investigator or, even likelier, she thought Tilda could snare an earl's hand in marriage, rankled her. Even if she wanted to pursue a courtship with Hadrian, she wouldn't accept her mother's assistance or support.

The coach came to a stop, and a moment later, Leach opened the door. He helped Tilda to the pavement. "I'll wait here, Miss Wren."

"Thank you, Leach." She smiled at the coachman before looking up at the elegant stone façade. The house was not as big as Hadrian's or his mother's, but it would surely be one of the nicest Tilda had ever entered.

She knocked on the door, which was promptly opened by a gray-haired butler. Tilda estimated his age to be at least sixty. His blue eyes regarded Tilda astutely but also with kindness.

"Good afternoon," she said. "I've an appointment with Mrs. Goodwin."

"Miss Wren?" he asked.

"Yes," Tilda replied with a smile.

"Come in." He held the door for her as she entered and closed it firmly whilst she paused in the marble-floored entrance hall. "This way, please." He led her into a staircase hall with an ornate wrought-iron railing and proceeded upstairs to the drawing room at the front of the house. He stood to the side of the door as Tilda moved past him. "Miss Wren is here."

Mrs. Goodwin, garbed in a beautiful yellow gown, was seated in a chair by the windows facing the street. She rose. "Welcome, Miss Wren, I'm so pleased you could come."

The butler departed, and Tilda made her way to the seating area. Mrs. Goodwin was in her middle-fifties with auburn hair streaked with white at the temples. There was also a white streak that started on the left side of her forehead. Her eyes were a pretty Wedgwood blue and sparkled with an amiable warmth as she regarded Tilda.

"I apologize that it has taken me so long to meet with you," Tilda said.

"I understand that you had a pressing matter." Mrs. Goodwin gestured for Tilda to sit in a chair angled near hers and retook her seat. "I'm sure you're a very busy investigator," Mrs. Goodwin said.

Tilda suppressed a laugh as she situated herself on the attractive rose-colored chair. "Perhaps not as busy as you might think. There aren't a great many people who would hire a woman."

"That would be their loss, I'm sure," Mrs. Goodwin said. "Whereas I was thrilled to read about you in the newspaper. I would much rather hire a woman to help me find my stolen items, particularly since the men with the Metropolitan Police have not been that helpful." She shook her head. "I'm being unkind. They did find where three of the items had been sold."

"Let us start at the beginning." Tilda withdrew her notepad from her reticule, along with a pencil. "Your inquiry letter said the theft occurred on the thirtieth of April," Tilda confirmed.

Mrs. Goodwin nodded. "That's right."

"And how did you discover the items were missing?"

"That morning, my housekeeper noticed the pieces were gone when she passed through the dining room," Mrs. Goodwin replied. "All the items that were stolen were displayed on a cabinet."

"Tell me about the items," Tilda said. "The more detail you can provide, the better."

Mrs. Goodwin took her time describing each piece, which were all silver—a pair of candlesticks, a teapot with a matching sugar bowl, a tureen, and a salver. "The salver and the tureen were particularly dear to me. The tureen because it was costly and made by the French silversmith, Balzac, in the mid-eighteenth century. The lid featured a pair of fighting stags. Their antlers were so detailed and beautiful." She smiled gently. "But the salver is my favorite because my son purchased it for me last year as a birthday gift. It was designed by Hester Bateman and has one of her armorial etchings."

Tilda recognized that name. Bateman had been a successful silversmith in London during the last century. "Can you describe the coat of arms?"

"Certainly. The top portion is divided into two halves with a stag on the left and a sword on the right. A chevron separates that from the bottom where three martlets are in flight. Those are mythical birds with no legs that are constantly in the air from birth to death. I believe they signify everlasting effort and perseverance."

After making notes about the items, Tilda looked up at Mrs. Goodwin. "Nothing else was missing besides those items?"

"No. I wonder if the thief just grabbed what was easily available."

"Did anyone hear the thief?" Tilda asked.

"The butler, Sperling, heard something, but he thought it was in the library. He did quickly check there and, finding nothing, returned to bed."

"What time was that?"

"About half one, he said." Mrs. Goodwin inclined her head toward Tilda. "You're welcome to speak with him, as the police did."

"I may do that," Tilda said. "Have you any idea how the thief entered your home?"

"It seems they came in the front door," Mrs. Goodwin replied with disdain. "They did something to the lock. I had to have it replaced."

Tilda continued to write in her notebook as Mrs. Goodwin spoke. "What did the police do?"

"Inspector Nicholson published a list of the items in the newspapers."

"That's what I would have done," Tilda said.

Mrs. Goodwin smiled. "I'm glad to hear he did something right. Someone made a report to the police station that they'd seen my candlesticks, the teapot, and the sugar bowl at a jeweler on Greville Street."

Tilda was surprised that someone had gone to the trouble to report that to the police. "Was the inspector able to recover those items?"

"Unfortunately, no. The jeweler, Mr. Timms, claimed the person was mistaken, that he'd never had those items. The inspector searched the shop and was unable to find them. He believes the jeweler may have already sold them or even melted them down." Mrs. Goodwin frowned sadly.

It sounded to Tilda as though Inspector Nicholson could have done more. "I will speak with the jeweler," Tilda said. "What of the other items—the salver and the tureen? Did Inspector Nicholson have any information about what happened to those?"

"No, but I wonder if they were sold to a collector due to their value."

That would mean the thief knew what they'd stolen. Or perhaps the jeweler had acted as a fence and sold the items. If he'd displayed the other pieces in the shop as the person had reported, that seemed possible. Whatever the truth, Tilda would discover it. "I don't imagine Inspector Nicholson offered any assurance that he would find the thieves?"

"Not at all," Mrs. Goodwin said with a light chuckle. "He quite plainly told me I shouldn't hope anyone would be caught, that the best they could do would be to find items and return them to me. But he said even that was highly unlikely. You see why I hired you."

Tilda smiled. "Yes." She would also speak with Inspector Nicholson. She needed to determine what he'd done so that she didn't duplicate any of his efforts, though she had the sneaking suspicion she would be far more thorough. Hopefully, he would be open to sharing information with her. Some police were not.

"Were any of your neighbors robbed?" Tilda wondered if the thief had known of Mrs. Goodwin's easily accessible silver display, or had the theft been random?

Mrs. Goodwin shook her head. "I spoke with all of them. I was—and continue to be—distressed that someone was able to break into my house. Everyone on the street was also horrified and upset. All I can think is the thief must have chosen my house because I'm a widow living here with a rather small staff."

"Who else resides here besides your butler and your housekeeper?"

"A cook, a maid, and a footman. I also have a coachman and a groom, but they're at the mews."

"Of course," Tilda said. "No one else heard or saw anything that night?"

"That's correct," Mrs. Goodwin said. "You may speak to all of them, if you'd like. I told them you may do so."

"If it's convenient, I would like to speak with them now," Tilda said. "I'm going to do everything I can to find your stolen silver."

Tilda would ask Hadrian to help her, particularly in speaking with the jeweler. Hadrian's ability could be very useful in exposing the truth of what Mr. Timms had done—assuming Hadrian's power had returned. She hoped that when she saw him next, his head would be fully healed, and he would once again be able to see others' memories. Would he be happy to regain it, or was he relieved to no longer be troubled by what he'd once referred to as a curse?

Mrs. Goodwin stood. "Come, I'll take you downstairs to speak with the staff. And before I forget, I must give you the deposit for your fee."

"Thank you."

Tilda waited as Mrs. Goodwin went to her desk. She returned with a bank note for the first third of the fee Tilda had communicated. The thrill of earning money through her work was intoxicating.

Recalling the conversation with her mother earlier, Tilda felt a pang of sadness that she would never understand what it meant to Tilda that she could take care of herself and not rely on a husband. How she wished that was a sentiment she could share with her mother. However, they hadn't much in common.

In fact, Tilda wondered if blood and her father were the only things they shared. And one of those was gone.

"After you," Tilda said, tucking the bank note into her reticule.

Mrs. Goodwin moved toward the door, and Tilda followed. As interested as she was in Mrs. Goodwin's stolen items, she was eager to turn her attention to her father's murder.

Unfortunately, it seemed far likelier that she would find her client's silver than solve a decade-old case.

∾

"Welcome, Lord Ravenhurst." Captain Vale greeted Hadrian in the large library of his home just outside Swindon. In his early fifties, Vale had light blond hair and hooded brown eyes. "I trust your trip was pleasant."

"It was indeed, thank you," Hadrian replied. He'd already given his hat and gloves to the housekeeper. Last time he'd visited—with Tilda—they'd wondered if there was a butler in the household. Today, he learned there was not. "I greatly appreciate you sending your coach to fetch me at the train station."

Hadrian had sent a telegram yesterday asking if he could come for a visit today. Captain Vale had responded immediately, indicating Hadrian was more than welcome and that he'd send his coach to fetch him at the train station.

"I'm so pleased you wanted to come," Captain Vale replied. "I said I would always be available if you ever needed my help or counsel, and I meant it."

"I trust you've recovered since I saw you last?" Hadrian asked with genuine concern. The captain had been stabbed by one of the Levitation Killers, whom Hadrian and Tilda had revealed.

"Quite, thank you." Vale briefly touched his midsection where he'd suffered the wound. "Still not riding yet, but soon. How have you been?"

"Well, thank you."

The captain's eyes narrowed faintly. "I sense a hesitation in your tone. Let us sit." He gestured to a seating area with a pair of matching mahogany chairs upholstered in dark green velvet. "From your tone, I gather there is something troubling you. Your telegram indicated you wished to speak with me about a discreet but urgent matter, and since you are seeking me out, I have to wonder if the issue is to do with our shared ability."

"It is." Hadrian didn't settle back against the chair, for he was quite tense. He sincerely hoped Captain Vale would be able to help him. "I haven't been able to see any memories for nearly a week now."

The captain's brows shot up. "Has that ever happened before?"

Hadrian shook his head. "I was hit in the head last Sunday, and I haven't seen a memory since. I wonder if the blow has caused some sort of interruption. At least, I hope it's an interruption and not a permanent loss. Miss Wren and I are conducting another investigation. It's imperative I regain the ability to see memories."

"I see." Vale's brow furrowed.

"Have you ever had this problem?" Hadrian asked.

"No, nor am I aware of it occurring, which isn't to say it hasn't." He gave Hadrian a reassuring look.

That was not the answer Hadrian had been hoping for. He feared he'd come all this way for nothing. "Since you've never heard of this, I don't suppose you have any suggestions about how to regain my ability." Hadrian tried not to sound disappointed but was certain he failed.

The captain's gaze was apologetic. "I'm afraid I don't have any suggestions." He cocked his head as he drew a breath. "I will offer a bit of advice. I recommend you seek calm and reflection. Allow your mind to be at peace as much as possible. Perhaps it needs a rest."

Hadrian exhaled. "That is close to what Tilda thinks. She theorized the power may return when my head is fully healed, perhaps in another few days."

"That seems reasonable," Vale said with a hopeful smile. "I'm glad to hear you and Miss Wren are still working together. I like her very much. I did wonder if your relationship is more than just business associates."

"We are good friends," Hadrian said carefully. "And we enjoy working together." He wasn't going to share the depth of his feelings about Tilda—not with Captain Vale. Not with anyone.

"Do you see her memories?" Vale asked.

"No. Never."

"Not even when you first met?"

Hadrian shook his head. "I didn't have occasion to touch her bare flesh, and I don't think I touched anything of hers until after we'd become associated with one another."

"Interesting," Vale murmured. "That could speak to why the two of you formed a close bond. It's as if your mind knew before you did." He smiled gently.

If Hadrian hadn't been in possession of a strange and inexplicable ability to experience others' memories, he would have rolled his eyes at such claptrap. However, Vale, with his experience and knowledge, knew of what he spoke.

Vale leaned back in his chair and rested his elbow on the arm. "It is curious, though, isn't it? You're an earl and she's… Well, you aren't from the same class, are you?"

Hadrian stiffened. "No, we are not, and I'm not sure I appreciate you making something of that." He was all too aware that he and Tilda were not of the same social status—because Tilda often reminded him.

"I meant no offense," Captain Vale said with an earnest expression. "It's just unusual. I certainly find no fault with it. I hope no one else does either. Still, with your responsibilities, your activities with her must draw notice."

In fact, whilst Hadrian had been working in the City with Tilda for about a week, his absence from the House of Lords had been noted. He hadn't explained where he'd been, just that he had other matters that required his attention.

Captain Vale wasn't wrong in thinking that Hadrian's partnering with a woman, particularly one not from his class, to investigate crimes would likely be frowned upon. But Hadrian didn't care. He could hear his mother's argument in his head. *"That's because no one knows, dear, but if they found out, you would change your mind."* That was perhaps true, as he didn't care to be the subject of gossip. Much to his chagrin, he'd been through that several years earlier when his betrothed had broken things off to marry someone else.

Captain Vale blushed faintly and looked down at the floor for a moment. "Please accept my apologies. I did not mean to speak out of turn. I like you and Miss Wren, and I hope you'll be able to work together for a long time to come. You indicated she's aware of your loss of power. Is anyone else?"

"She's the only person besides you and your son who know about it."

Vale blinked at him in surprise. "You haven't told your mother yet? I thought you'd planned to do so."

In fact, Vale had given him excellent advice on how he might reveal his secret to her, but Hadrian hadn't been able to do it. He wanted to wait until he felt more comfortable with the ability. When he could better control it. Now that it was gone, he was glad he hadn't said anything. What if it never returned?

"Not yet," Hadrian replied. "I want to, but the timing has not been right. I did visit my grandmother after meeting you and learned I was not alone in this odd situation. I discovered that my great uncle, who I thought had died young, was, in fact, committed to an asylum. She said he had hallucinations."

"They lied about his death?" Vale asked grimly. At Hadrian's nod, he went on. "It certainly sounds as if he shared the same trait we do. I'm sorry that was his fate. Do you know if he still lives?"

"My grandmother indicated he did not, but perhaps I should question that." Hadrian couldn't imagine what the man might have endured over the past thirty or more years. "I wish he'd met someone like you. You've helped me immensely."

Vale smiled. "I'm glad to hear it. I'm sorry I'm not able to help you with this problem, however. Would you mind if we spoke to Thaddeus about it? I know he's not your favorite person."

That was certainly true. Thaddeus Vale, under the guise of Lysander Mallory, had been responsible for fleecing a great many people, including Hadrian's mother, by convincing them he could speak to their dead loved ones. Hadrian didn't know how much money his mother had paid to Mallory's London Spiritualism Society or if she'd received any recompense.

"Has he been able to pay anyone back?" Hadrian asked. The younger Vale had promised to do so, though Hadrian wasn't sure how he could. It seemed he hadn't retained enough of the money he'd swindled.

"Everyone," Captain Vale replied.

Hadrian was surprised to hear that and could think of only one way he may have accomplished it—Captain Vale had a decent-sized fortune. "Did you help him?"

"Of course. You would do the same for your son if he'd owned up to his mistakes and was making a true effort to improve himself."

"Is he?" If true, Hadrian was glad to hear that.

"He is," the captain confirmed. His features softened. "He's writing again, which pleases me greatly, as you know."

Last time Hadrian had visited with Tilda, they'd learned Thaddeus Vale was a gifted writer. In fact, it was his writings, which they'd briefly perused, that had revealed his villainy.

"If you think Thaddeus can aid my predicament, I'm eager to speak with him," Hadrian said. He was desperate to regain his ability to experience memories and would try anything.

"I'll send for him." Vale stood and left the room.

Hadrian looked around the library, his attention drawn to the seating area where he and Tilda had sat during their last visit. That was when he'd learned he shared the same ability with the captain. Their hands had grazed one another over the teapot, and since they were both gifted with the power to see memories, they were able to identify one another by the jolt of energy that shot through them when they touched. Hadrian hadn't realized it at the time, but the captain had explained.

Vale returned and said his son would join them shortly. He pulled a third chair into their area.

A few minutes later, Thaddeus Vale, who Hadrian still thought of as Lysander Mallory, entered the library. He'd cropped his blond hair, and he wasn't as quick to smile as he'd been when Hadrian had known him as the head of the spiritualism society.

Thaddeus regarded Hadrian with uncertainty. He did not appear to be the same confident, charming man whom Hadrian had met in London.

Hadrian decided he should put the man at ease. "Good afternoon, Mr. Vale. Your father says you've taken up writing again."

Thaddeus seemed to relax as he dropped into the empty chair. His eyes were hooded like his father's and nearly the same brown. "It has been a balm as I've worked to accept my mistakes and forge a better path forward."

"I'm pleased to hear it." Hadrian glanced at Captain Vale, who nodded.

"Thaddeus, his lordship has come to me with a perplexing problem. He sustained a mild head injury nearly a week ago and has not experienced anyone else's memories since. That has never happened to me, and I don't think you've encountered that either, have you?"

The younger Vale shook his head. "I've not ever experienced any interruption, but neither have I injured my head after the initial occasion that triggered the ability."

Hadrian recalled that Thaddeus had fallen from his horse, which had prompted him to start seeing others' memories. "I suppose I must be patient and wait for my head to fully heal. Hopefully, then the ability will return."

Thaddeus's brows creased. "I would encourage you to calm your mind as much as possible. When I was first struck with this power, I was overwhelmed by it. It wasn't until I learned to rein my thoughts and feelings that I was able to lessen the impact.

And now that I am spending a great deal of time thinking and writing, I find I have even more control over what I see and when. Every morning, I meditate for a time before I leave my chamber. That has helped me immensely. You may wish to try that and see if it will encourage your ability to return." He cocked his head. "If you still possess it." He reached for Hadrian. "May I?"

Realizing Thaddeus meant to see if they both still felt a jolt when they touched, Hadrian held out his bare hand—he'd removed his hat and gloves when he'd arrived and given them to the housekeeper. Thaddeus put his palm over Hadrian's hand and met his gaze.

Hadrian did not feel the same frisson of energy as when he'd touched the man—and his father—in the past. Worry unfurled in Hadrian's chest and made his pulse leap. "I don't feel anything." His voice was low and perhaps a bit ragged as he worked to tamp down his anxiety. He couldn't lose this. Not now.

"I do," Thaddeus said, his dark eyes narrowing slightly. "It's faint, but it's there. I don't think you've lost it. Not yet anyway." He pulled his hand away and sat back in his chair.

"Not *yet*? You think I should expect to lose it permanently?" Hadrian's voice had climbed. He hated that he sounded so affected.

"I couldn't possibly say. But I do recommend you do what I suggest. Show your mind that you want to continue as you have, that you are ready to hone your skill." Thaddeus smiled. "I'm trying to call it that instead of a power or an ability. It really is a skill we've been gifted with that will either flourish or fade depending on how we use it."

Hadrian wondered if the derision he'd initially felt for the *skill* had somehow affected his ability to use it. Except, he'd begun to learn how to manage it in the last several weeks, after speaking with Captain Vale and learning about the power.

"I might make another suggestion," the captain said kindly. He regarded Hadrian with sympathy. "Perhaps you should confide in your mother. Discussing your ability—your newfound skill—might encourage it to grow stronger again. I do think having support helps us manage the skill."

"I certainly felt that way," Thaddeus said with a fervent nod. "Once I began to confide the depth of my ability and how badly it affected me to my father, I finally started to make progress with managing it. That was in addition to meditating and finding quiet in my mind."

Hadrian chuckled because he had to let something out. "All right, you've convinced me to try." He took a deep breath but didn't feel any better.

"Is Miss Wren aware of your predicament?" Thaddeus asked.

"Yes. I'm keen to regain the ability to see memories so that I may assist her with an important investigation."

"It's good that she knows," Thaddeus said. "As my father said, talking to someone close to you could help matters. I assume you don't see her memories?"

"No."

"Then she is close enough for you to not confuse things for you, meaning you needn't worry about seeing her memories and having that clutter your mind. That is why it can be helpful to lean on those we love." Thaddeus sent his father a warm smile.

Love? Hadrian acknowledged that he had romantic feelings for Tilda, but love? He wasn't ready to consider that. Not when she didn't even share his romantic sentiments. But ignoring how he felt didn't mean the emotion didn't exist. His pulse quickened again.

He couldn't think about that. All his energy needed to be focused on regaining his ability—rather, his skill.

"Thank you both for your time today," Hadrian said, rising from the chair.

The other men also stood.

"If we can be of further help, please send word," Captain Vale said. "I'd be happy to help in any way possible."

Hadrian smiled. "I appreciate that." He looked to Thaddeus. "I'm glad to see you're working toward redemption. Tilda will be glad to hear it too."

A few minutes later, Hadrian took his leave in Captain Vale's coach. He would spend his time on the train trying to meditate. And he would do the same before bed tonight and again in the morning. He'd also contemplate how to hone his skill and write, though he'd no idea what yet.

He'd do anything to see memories again. For Tilda.

CHAPTER 5

Tilda closed the door to her bedchamber and started toward the stairs. After spending yesterday at home with her mother and grandmother, she was eager to leave the house and call on the jeweler, Mr. Timms, in Greville Street.

Following her meeting with Mrs. Goodwin on Saturday, she'd sent a note to Hadrian asking if he was available to accompany her on the errand today. He'd replied that he would be delighted and would fetch her at noon. Tilda had then written again to ask him not to come to the house. She asked him to park the coach at the end of the street as Leach had done the other day. The last thing Tilda wanted was for them to be bothered by her mother's meddling.

There would be enough of that on Wednesday when they would attend tea at Hadrian's mother's. He'd confirmed the event in his missive to Tilda. She'd waited to tell her mother until Sunday when it would be impossible to go shopping. That hadn't stopped her mother from trying to recruit Tilda's grandmother in persuading Tilda to change her mind about a new ensemble for the tea.

To her grandmother's credit, she'd resisted. Though Tilda

could see she'd wanted to encourage the idea. Grandmama preferred seeing Tilda dressed in current fashions. The truth was Tilda did too, but she wasn't going to accept anything from her mother. Tilda hoped she would return to Birmingham on Thursday once the tea had happened.

As Tilda made her way into the entrance hall, she was surprised to find her grandmother waiting for her. "Is everything all right, Grandmama?" she asked.

"Yes. I know you're going out, and I wondered if your errand is to do with your new investigation? I understand you don't want to say much in front of your mother, but I'd like to know where you're going." She smiled at Tilda.

Tilda nodded. "It's to do with my investigation."

"Isn't Lord Ravenhurst helping you, as usual?" Grandmama asked.

Tilda glanced about to make sure her mother wasn't nearby. "He is, and he is accompanying me on this errand. I asked him to pick me up at the end of the street."

Grandmama pursed her lips and shook her head. "I'm sorry it's come to that, but I understand why you wouldn't want him to come here." She pouted briefly. "It only means I'm not able to see him either, which is unfortunate."

"You will see him Wednesday when we all go for tea at his mother's," Tilda reassured her.

"I'm to be included?" Grandmama blinked in surprise.

"Of course," Tilda said. "If his mother's going to meet my mother, I certainly want her to meet you too, so that she can have a better impression of our family."

Grandmama pressed her lips together, but her blue eyes revealed her amusement. "Don't be unkind, Tilda."

"I am speaking the truth. As you well know," Tilda added archly.

Tilda bussed her cheek and turned. Vaughn opened the door and bade Tilda a pleasant afternoon.

Hurrying down the street, Tilda saw both Leach and Hadrian standing outside the coach waiting for her.

Hadrian smiled as she approached, and Tilda's breath caught for the barest moment. He looked particularly handsome in a black coat with light beige trousers and a crisp cream-colored waistcoat. "Good afternoon."

"Good afternoon," she replied, glad that her voice was even and that the suddenly rapid beat of her heart was not discernible. At least, she hoped it wasn't.

Why was she so inordinately happy to see him? There were often several days—or even weeks—that went by when they did not see each other between investigations. However, their last investigation had only concluded a week ago, and here they were, enmeshed in another. So, why did it feel as though they'd been apart longer than the two days since she'd seen him last? The longer they worked together, the more she missed his absence.

Perhaps her mother's presence was making her crave Hadrian's company more than normal. Unlike her mother, Hadrian understood Tilda, and he made her feel completely at ease with herself and the life she'd chosen.

"I'm eager to conduct our first inquiry regarding these stolen items," Hadrian said. "I've given Leach the address of the jeweler."

"Excellent." Tilda thanked Leach before climbing into the coach.

Hadrian followed and sat beside her on the forward-facing seat. Sometimes it was easier if they sat opposite one another as they conversed, but Tilda was glad he'd sat next to her. She wasn't entirely sure why, nor did she want to ponder that. Just as she preferred not to think overly much about why she was so pleased to see him.

"Are we to pick you up at the end of the street for the duration of your mother's visit?" Hadrian asked.

"Probably," Tilda replied. "It's easier than having to listen to her badger me about my work and the fact that we are investigative partners."

"She takes issue with that?"

"I believe she finds it odd or even inappropriate that someone like you would work with me in this manner. It's bad enough that I do it, you see." Tilda rolled her eyes. "I do appreciate you not coming to the house. My mother would insist on speaking with you, and we would be inconveniently delayed."

"I'm sorry things are difficult for you," Hadrian said softly. "How long will she be here?"

"I wish I knew." Tilda turned her mind to the investigation and informed him of all she'd learned from Mrs. Goodwin the other day.

Hadrian listened intently until she finished. "I see why this visit to the jeweler is the first inquiry you want to make."

"Yes." She hesitated slightly before continuing, hoping that her next statement wouldn't cause any upset. "I'm hopeful your ability has returned, and you'll be able to see Mr. Timms's memories. I want to know if he's lying about having had Mrs. Goodwin's teapot, sugar bowl, and candlesticks."

Hadrian's features didn't show a reaction. "You think he lied to the police?"

"It seems likely," Tilda said. "Why would someone go to the police and fabricate a story about seeing Mrs. Goodwin's items at Mr. Timms's?"

"I suppose there's no gain in doing so."

"Precisely." Tilda paused again. She wanted to know about his ability. Did he not wish to discuss it? "Has your power returned?" she asked gently.

"Not that I've noticed," Hadrian said with a touch of heat. "But I haven't been out or with people unknown to me, either today or yesterday."

That wasn't encouraging. "Is your head feeling better at least? I hope so."

"Yes," Hadrian said, his tone clipped. "I do expect I'll have success today." His expression was determined, and Tilda hoped he was right. If he wasn't, they'd manage without his ability. She'd been investigating long before she'd met him, and she imagined she'd still be doing so long after their association ended.

Did she expect that to happen? Honestly, she couldn't imagine it. Nor did she particularly want to. Which was a troubling thought since she'd always seen herself as an independent woman of business. But it wasn't as if she *needed* Hadrian. She simply liked having his assistance. He'd proven most helpful, and his ability was only a small part of that.

"I'd also like to determine if Mr. Timms might have the salver and the tureen." Tilda looked at Hadrian shrewdly. "I would like you, as the Earl of Ravenhurst, to pose as a silver collector."

Hadrian grinned. "I do like it when we assume roles for our investigations. Who will you be?"

"A friend of particular interest." Tilda had thought about the role she ought to play and determined it would be best if Hadrian was trying to secure silver to impress her. Such a scheme would hopefully persuade the jeweler to help them.

"A *particular* friend?" Hadrian asked, his brows raised. "As in, we are in a courtship?"

"Something like that," Tilda replied. "We are aligned by our passion for silver. You have an interest in Balzac, the French silversmith, and I like to collect pieces by Hester Bateman."

"Because the salver and the tureen were designed by them," Hadrian said.

"Precisely. You shall indicate that you'll pay any price, regardless of provenance."

"I can do that." Hadrian's dark blue eyes gleamed with anticipation. "This will be fun."

The coach arrived at the jeweler's shop in Greville Street a short while later. Leach opened the door, and Hadrian stepped out. He helped Tilda to the pavement and tucked her arm through his. "Ready, my dear?"

Leach's brows shot up, and Hadrian chuckled. "We're playing roles," he said softly to the coachman.

Sniggering, Leach nodded as he closed the door. "I'll wait here until you're finished."

Hadrian escorted Tilda into the jeweler's shop. The interior was dim after the brightness of the late May afternoon. Tilda's eyes adjusted as she looked about the small shop. There was a rectangular, glass-topped display cabinet behind which were a table and a desk. A gentleman in his early fifties sat behind the latter. He looked up as the door closed behind them.

"Good afternoon," he said in a gravelly voice. He stood, and Tilda could see he was a squat fellow with wispy white brows and gray hair slicked back from his wide forehead. "I'm Timms. How may I help you?"

His mouth lifting into a benign smile, Hadrian guided Tilda to the display cabinet. "I am Ravenhurst, and this is my very dear friend. We've come in search of silver. We're collectors." He sent Tilda a heated look that rattled her. "It's one of many things we have in common."

Tilda had not expected the thrilling jolt that shot through her as Hadrian committed rather convincingly to his role. She batted her lashes at him before turning her attention to Mr. Timms. "I do hope you can help us find something to add to our collections."

Timms had leaned forward over the cabinet as soon as Hadrian had said his name. His sable eyes glowed with something discomfiting. Avarice, perhaps. "Is there something specific you're looking for?"

"I have several items from Balzac and am always looking to expand my collection," Hadrian replied smoothly. He looked over at Tilda. "She snatches up any Hester Bateman piece she can find."

Tilda clutched Hadrian's arm more tightly. "His lordship is keen to provide me with a piece of Hester Bateman silver today." She looked up at Hadrian. "What was it you said? Whatever the cost?" She laughed and fluttered the fingers of her free hand near his chest.

Hadrian chuckled. "That *is* what I said." He settled his gaze on Mr. Timms. "And I don't care where it came from," he added in a dark whisper.

Timms's eyes glimmered once more with greed and excitement. It didn't seem to bother him that Hadrian had all but said he would buy stolen goods. In fact, the jeweler seemed even more keen to help them.

"I don't suppose you have any salvers or candlesticks?" Tilda didn't want to just say salver, lest Timms realized what they were about. They didn't want to be too obvious in looking for Mrs. Goodwin's exact items.

"I may, in fact," Timms replied. "If not, I know where to find something. Not today, unfortunately, but could you return in a couple of days?"

Tilda pouted. "I was dearly hoping for something today. But perhaps if I have to wait for my Hester Bateman, you can at least satisfy Ravenhurst. He would love something from Balzac. Please tell us you have at least one item. Perhaps a salt cellar or a tureen?" She smiled prettily at the jeweler.

Timms grimaced. "I know for certain that I don't have any Balzac pieces. I could probably find one of those too. Again, it would be in a few days." He clasped his hands together and gave them an earnestly apologetic look. "I am terribly sorry I can't meet your needs today."

Exhaling, Tilda turned her body towards Hadrian. "I suppose we can try other shops."

"Yes, but I'd heard that this one would have what we wanted. Perhaps we should just be patient." Hadrian sent an expectant look at Timms.

"I can definitely help you," Timms assured them quickly and eagerly. "I'll obtain as many pieces created by both silversmiths as I can." He'd gone from one piece to multiple items. Would he promise them the moon if they asked for it? "Can you return on Thursday?"

Tilda pursed her lips. "Do you *promise* you'll have something? From both Hester Bateman *and* Balzac?"

Timms placed his hand over his heart. "I give you my solemn vow. You will have to choose between multiple items. Or perhaps you'll want to buy them all." He tittered, and Tilda had to force a laugh to join him. She found the man odious.

"Could you perchance show us some silver you do have?" Tilda asked. "Something may catch our eye." She smiled up at Hadrian.

"Yes, do bring out your best pieces," Hadrian said.

"Right away." Timms pulled a ring of keys from his pocket and practically tripped over himself in his haste to move through a doorway at the back of the shop.

"I wanted you to be able to touch something he has handled," Tilda whispered.

Hadrian nodded. "I thought that was your intent."

A few moments later, Timms returned with a large velvet-lined tray bearing several silver pieces and set it atop the cabinet. Tilda quickly surveyed the items and determined that none were any of Mrs. Goodwin's missing silver, not that she'd expected them to be.

Timms made a show of presenting each piece of silver and describing it, including the maker and when it had been produced. One was a pretty hand mirror with roses along the handle and an intricate vine of roses around the edge of the glass. "This belonged to my wife," Timms said with a sad smile. "She died three years ago, and I only recently decided I should sell this so someone else may love it as she did."

"I'm sorry to hear your wife is no longer with you," Tilda said kindly.

"This is beautiful." Hadrian removed his glove and picked up the mirror. "I like to feel the silver against my bare flesh. I can see why your wife loved it," he added, turning the object in his hand.

Tilda watched Hadrian closely to see if he was experiencing Timms's memory. When he touched an object and saw a vision, his gaze flattened, almost as if he were in a trance. He never closed his eyes, for then the memory would disappear.

His jaw tightened, and he allowed his eyelids to drop for the barest moment. Tilda knew he hadn't seen anything. His power must not have returned.

"I'll take the mirror." Hadrian handed it to the jeweler. "Would you wrap it please?"

"Of course, my lord." Timms looked quite pleased. He took the mirror to the table behind the counter and wrapped it with paper before moving to a shelf stacked with boxes.

"Why are you buying that?" Tilda asked. Was he merely trying to convince the jeweler of their ruse?

He glanced at Tilda. "When my power returns, I'll have this and will hopefully see Timms's memories."

That was brilliant. Indeed, Tilda was almost annoyed she hadn't thought of it. "I'm so very glad you're here," she said softly.

He looked at her with warmth and appreciation. Tilda smiled at him as another flash of heat dashed through her.

Timms returned with the boxed mirror, and Hadrian paid the man. "Thank you, my lord," the jeweler said excitedly.

"We'll see you on Thursday," Hadrian said, taking the box from Timms. "Do send word to Ravenhurst House if we are able to come sooner. That would be most appreciated." He gave the jeweler a bland smile, then looked to Tilda. "Ready, my dear?"

"Of course," she murmured. They departed the shop.

"*Blast,*" Hadrian breathed as they made their way to the coach.

Tilda assumed he was frustrated about not being able to see

Timms's memories. "Don't fret," she said quietly. "Would you mind if we visited C Division to speak with Inspector Nicholson?" she added in a regular volume.

"Not at all." Hadrian directed Leach to drive them to C Division headquarters.

Hadrian tossed the box with the mirror onto the opposite seat, then settled himself next to Tilda. He let out a ragged breath.

She could still sense his frustration. "Your power will return."

"I hope so."

"Do you?" She turned towards him. "I wondered if you might be relieved to no longer be cursed."

"Once upon a time, I would have been. However, not now." He scowled. "Not bloody now."

"We'll solve this case with or without your ability to see memories," Tilda said.

"Are you speaking of Mrs. Goodwin's missing silver or your father's murder?" Hadrian asked. His anguished gaze met hers.

Tilda was surprised by the depth of his emotion. "I meant the silver, but I suppose I would also include…the other."

"I hate that I can't help you."

"You are helping." Tilda touched his arm. "I've told you before that your value to our investigations is not just your ability to experience memories. You have become an excellent investigator, and I would not want to work on either of these matters without you."

Their eyes held for a long moment. Tilda had the strange sensation that the world was falling away, that only the two of them existed.

She blinked, and the spell was broken. Turning her head, she took a deep breath to calm her racing heart. Last week, when Hadrian had been struck in the head by a killer, she'd acknowledged to herself that her feelings for him went far deeper than she cared to admit. Still, she wasn't sure what that meant. Nor was she ready or willing to acknowledge it to anyone else.

"Thank you for saying that," Hadrian said quietly. He squared his shoulders against the squab. "I will regain my ability. I simply must."

Tilda couldn't help thinking he was trying to convince himself as well as her.

~

*H*adrian thought about what Captain Vale and Thaddeus had said to him the other day. He'd meditated the past two nights, and his power still hadn't returned. Perhaps he wasn't doing it right.

And why hadn't he told Tilda about going to Swindon? Or about what he was trying to do to bring his ability back?

He supposed he didn't want to share the depth of his concern. It was better that he tried to demonstrate optimism and confidence. He'd already displayed his frustration after visiting Timms and regretted doing so. He needed to direct his energy towards regaining his ability and not feel defeated when it didn't happen. It *would*. It had to. He would try again at the police station; he removed his gloves to be prepared.

They arrived at the station at 21 Great Marlborough Street a few minutes later, and Hadrian escorted Tilda inside. She approached the constable on duty at the desk and asked to speak with Inspector Nicholson.

"I'm not sure if he's here," the constable, a very young man with light brown hair and wide brown eyes, said. "Just a moment."

"Is he old enough to be a police constable?" Hadrian asked quietly.

"Apparently," Tilda replied. "He did look quite young."

A few minutes later, the constable returned with a man in his middle thirties. He had dark sable hair and small brown eyes.

"Inspector Nicholson?" Tilda asked.

"He's not here, I'm afraid. I'm Inspector Jurgens." The man smiled, his thin lips stretching. "How can I help?"

Jurgens. That was one of the names the apothecary had given them. Could it be the same man? Hadrian glanced at Tilda and saw her pulse ticking in her throat.

"I'm Mrs. Harwood," she said, using the fake name she'd employed during their last investigation when she'd posed as the wife of a City of London police inspector. Why wasn't she using her name? "This is Mr. Nigel Beck." Again, she used the alias Hadrian had taken during their last case. "We're making inquiries into a rather old case. May we have a few minutes of your time?"

An old case? What was Tilda doing? Was she going to ask Jurgens about her father's murder?

"Certainly." Inspector Jurgens gestured toward a door to an office just off the entrance hall. "We can meet in here."

The small chamber held an oak desk and several chairs. Jurgens gestured toward the chairs. "Would you care to sit?"

"No, thank you," Tilda said with a faint, rather strained smile. She looked at Hadrian and glanced toward the door.

Hadrian understood—he moved to close it. His pulse leapt as he contemplated whether this inspector could be the same man who'd reported to the apothecary shop over a decade ago.

Tilda fixed him with an expectant stare. "Are you the same Jurgens who arrived at the scene of the murder of Sergeant Thomas Wren at an apothecary shop near Knightsbridge in December 1857?"

The inspector's reaction was impossible to ignore. His eyes rounded, his nostrils flared, and his flesh lost a shade of color. There was no hiding the fact that he was, indeed, the same man.

"I can see that you are," Tilda said brusquely.

"That was a long time ago, when I was a new constable. I don't remember much." Color returned to his cheeks—perhaps a bit too much of it, so that he now appeared flushed.

Tilda's lips pulled into a humorless smile. "But you clearly remember that you were there. I would simply like confirmation of something we've recently learned. Sergeant Wren wasn't, in fact, killed at that shop. There wasn't enough blood. Since his throat was cut, he would have bled all over the floor and that did not happen. He was killed elsewhere and moved to the shop."

Hadrian watched the inspector closely. His reaction was more subtle this time, but there was still a slight twitch of his nose, and he paled again.

"Why are you asking about this old case?" Jurgens asked. "That was solved at the time. Wren was killed by the thief he interrupted."

"Except he couldn't have been because of the lack of blood." Tilda pursed her lips at him. "And please don't say the thief cleaned it up. That simply isn't possible, and for you to expect anyone to believe that is insulting."

Jurgens's cheeks turned bright pink. "There's no call to be rude."

"I'm not the one expecting you to believe a lie," Tilda said with an ice Hadrian had never heard from her before. "Why was Wren's body moved, and why did the police lie about the circumstances?"

"Why are you asking these questions?" Jurgens sounded shaky, almost nervous. "I don't know anything. As I said, I was a new constable at the time. I was mostly watching and learning. I don't know why anyone would have moved the sergeant's body. That doesn't make any sense."

Hadrian wasn't sure he believed the man. He removed his watch from his pocket and "accidentally" dropped it near the inspector's feet. "Pardon me."

Jurgens bent to retrieve it just as Hadrian did. The contact would be brief, and Hadrian would need to focus all his thoughts on seeing something, *anything*.

Reaching for the watch, Hadrian brushed his hand against the inspector's. Nothing happened. But perhaps the contact was simply too quick. He allowed the inspector to retrieve the watch and deliver it into Hadrian's palm.

"Thank you." Hadrian closed his hand around the watch and again tried to see something. Still, there was nothing. But at least now he had the man's touch on the watch. As with the mirror he'd purchased from Timms, Hadrian could hope that he'd have a chance to see Jurgens's memories when his power returned.

"How long have you worked here in C Division?" Tilda asked.

"Six years," Jurgens replied. His eyes narrowed. "I thought you asked for Nicholson when you arrived. He had nothing to do with the case you're asking about."

Tilda arched a brow. "How do you know? You just said you'd been a new constable at the time and were learning the job."

Jurgens scowled faintly. "I know that Nicholson has never worked at B Division as I did then."

"I see," Tilda murmured. "Did you know that Padgett died recently? Or are you going to pretend you don't remember him?"

Hadrian held his breath a moment, worried that she'd gone too far. Her anger was palpable. At least to him.

Jurgens glowered at Tilda. "I am not pretending anything, and I do not care for your insinuations, Mrs. Harwood. Of course I remember Padgett, and I had heard he was killed in his lodgings. He transferred to A Division the year after Wren's murder, and we did not remain in contact. I was sorry to hear he died." He took a step toward Tilda, and Hadrian instinctively moved closer to her.

"What is your interest in this *closed* case?" Jurgens asked.

Tilda kept her gaze level with his. "Sergeant Wren has living family members who may wish to see this case reopened, given the revelation of this new information regarding the lack of blood at the scene."

Hadrian gave Tilda great credit for her ability to provide an alias as well as a valid reason for her interrogation of the inspector. But what would Jurgens do if—or when—he discovered "Mrs. Harwood" was, in fact, Wren's living family?

Jurgens swallowed. "Until his family demonstrates interest, there is nothing to be done."

Tilda blinked. "Is that all it will take?"

"I couldn't say. It would be up to the superintendent of B Division where the murder occurred, I should think."

"I have one last question," Tilda said. "You said you did not maintain contact with Padgett. What about Lowther and Fellows, who were also there that night? And before you prevaricate, I'll tell you who I really am. My name is Matilda Wren. I am Sergeant Wren's daughter."

Jurgens's jaw dropped. "Why did you lie?"

"I didn't know if you'd speak to me," Tilda said evenly. "Now, please answer my question."

"I know Lowther." Jurgens's tone was hesitant, as if he didn't particularly want to admit that. "I believe Fellows works in the Home Office. I have not stayed in contact with him either."

"Thank you. I'm sure you understand that it's important to me to learn the truth of what happened to my father. He was killed somewhere else and moved to the apothecary shop. I mean to find out why and who was behind the falsification of what truly occurred."

"You're rather good at making inquiries, if you don't mind my saying," Jurgens noted. "I suppose your father left an impression on you."

"Miss Wren is a private investigator," Hadrian said coolly. "She's solved many murders, and she'll solve this one too." He looked at Tilda. "You should give the inspector your card—in case he recalls something he'd like to share." Hadrian turned an icy stare on the man and fished his own card from his pocket. He presented it to Jurgens. "Or you can contact me."

The inspector took Hadrian's card. His eyes widened as he read the script, then he snapped his attention to Hadrian. Apprehension lined Jurgens's features, which Hadrian found quite satisfying.

Hadrian adopted his most authoritative tone. "Inquiries will be made, Inspector Jurgens. I recommend you make yourself useful. Those who seek to sidestep the law will not fare well."

Jurgens inclined his head. "My lord."

Tilda handed two cards to the inspector, her lips tightly pursed. "I really did wish to speak with Inspector Nicholson. About another matter—a theft he is investigating. I've been hired to find the items that were stolen. Will you give him one of my cards and tell him I'll call another day?"

Nodding, the inspector looked at her card. "A private investigator, eh? I'm sure your father would be proud."

"I expect he would be," Tilda said flatly. "But I can't be sure because he's dead. Someone ended his life and has lied about the circumstances for over a decade. What would make him proud is my bringing the truth to light and ensuring that justice is served." She met Jurgens's gaze. "I aim to do just that. Good day, Inspector."

Tilda turned on her heel and left the chamber. Hadrian followed her. They did not speak until they were outside the station.

"Are you all right?" Hadrian asked softly.

"Yes." Tilda took a pair of deep breaths and shook out her arms. "I'm disappointed we weren't able to speak with Nicholson. Hopefully, we can do so tomorrow."

That disappointed her? "You've nothing to say about happening upon one of the men who was present the night your father was murdered?"

"It's certainly a coincidence—and a very helpful one at that. I'd intended to search for the other police who were there besides Lowther and Fellows. I'm sorry Padgett is dead. But it's clear to me that Jurgens is hiding something. Which means Lowther likely is too."

They'd reached the coach. Hadrian instructed Leach to return them to Tilda's grandmother's.

Tilda climbed inside. Hadrian had barely sat down beside her before she turned toward him. "I'm angriest about Lowther. He's been kind to me all these years. I've dined at his house, met his family. He's helped me with investigations."

"For a fee," Hadrian pointed out, since she sometimes offered him small bribes, as she did with other police contacts.

"Not always, but often. He has an ill child. I'm happy to help him. Or I was until I discovered he's been lying to me all this time." She sounded both furious and sad.

"What do we do next?" Hadrian asked. "About your father's case, not Mrs. Goodwin's."

"I think Jurgens gave us the direction we must take. I will speak to the superintendent of B Division and demand he reopen the case. And if he won't, I'll investigate it myself."

"You're going to do that anyway, aren't you?"

Her eyes gleamed with determination. "Yes, we are."

Hadrian noticed she said "we." It wasn't surprising, but it *was* wholly gratifying. Despite what she'd said about his helpfulness, he worried that without his power, he wouldn't be of use.

Even without it, he'd do anything to work alongside her on this of all cases. Nothing was more important than giving Tilda the justice she deserved.

CHAPTER 6

Tilda stood from the chair in the library situated at the back of the house. The room had once been her grandfather's study. Now, it was where she and her grandmother liked to read the newspaper in the morning and where they completed correspondence. Tilda's mother had gone shopping, so things were blissfully quiet and relaxed.

Now it was time for Tilda to meet Hadrian. If she'd known her mother wouldn't be there, she would have had him come to the house so her grandmother could see him.

"Are you off to make more inquiries with Lord Ravenhurst?" Grandmama asked.

"Yes. We've a call to make." Tilda hoped they would be able to speak with the superintendent in Chelsea at B Division. If he wasn't there, she'd make an appointment to see him another time. But she dearly hoped he would be there.

Tilda heard Vaughn open the front door, followed by her mother's distinctive voice. "Careful with that," she said loudly. She'd taken Clara with her to assist with carrying packages.

"Sounds like your mother has returned," Grandmama said. She rose and accompanied Tilda to the entrance hall.

If only Tilda had left a few minutes earlier, she could have avoided her mother altogether. Alas, she could hopefully just slip by her. Tilda stopped short at seeing Clara juggling several boxes. Then she hurried to take a few of them from her.

"I've found the perfect ensemble for you to wear to tea," Tilda's mother announced. "Come into the parlor and I'll show you."

Tilda didn't have time for such nonsense. "I have an appointment, Mother. I'll have to look at it later."

"It will only take a moment." She whisked off her gloves and swanned into the parlor, apparently assuming Tilda would follow.

"May as well go," Tilda's grandmother murmured.

"Fine." Tilda exhaled before moving into the parlor. She placed the boxes on the settee and motioned for Clara to do the same with the packages she still carried.

Tilda's mother removed the largest box from the pile and set it atop the others. "I believe this will require minimal adjustment, but Clara can take care of any alteration that may be required." She opened the box and shot Tilda a slight frown. "It would be best if you could try this on before you leave so that Clara can get started."

"I cannot," Tilda said, trying not to grit her teeth. "As I said, I've an appointment, and I'm already going to be tardy."

"I'm sure it's to do with your *investigation*," her mother said with distaste. "They'll just have to be patient. Ensuring you are well-outfitted for the dowager countess is far more important."

If Tilda had time, she would argue that point. Not that it would matter. Her mother would not be convinced otherwise.

Her mother lifted the top part of the ensemble from the box. The garment was long-sleeved, rose-colored, and affixed with three bows along the front. The neck was high and decorated with a small ruffle. The style was fussier than Tilda would choose, and the color was too…pink. However, she supposed it looked quite fashionable.

"Isn't it lovely?" her mother asked rapturously. "So feminine." She laid the garment over another box, then removed the skirt. It had a short train—Tilda despised trains as unwieldy—and another bow over the bustle along with several ruffles.

"It's beautiful," Tilda's grandmother said. She looked at Tilda with a warm smile. "You will look wonderful."

"I purchased a new bustle because this ensemble requires something larger than what you're currently wearing." Tilda's mother eyed her gown with mild derision, which Tilda found offensive since she'd only purchased it recently. "I also obtained new shoes. They have a darling heel. Oh, and there's a matching hat, gloves, and a reticule. I couldn't resist. You will be utterly splendid!"

Tilda could only imagine the expense. On the one hand, she was frustrated by her mother's meddling and the fact that she'd never bothered to spend money on—or time with—Tilda at all in the last several years. And yet, she was finally doing so and seemed rather pleased to make the effort.

Except it was entirely because she was hoping to match Tilda with Hadrian. Not because she loved Tilda and wanted to do something that would make Tilda happy. Tilda didn't even know what that would be.

Yes, she did. She wanted her mother to accept Tilda's chosen profession and even support it.

Which was silly. It wasn't as if Tilda needed to have her mother in her life. They had never been particularly close, not like Tilda had been with her father, and they had grown even further apart since her mother had remarried.

"Don't you like it?" Tilda's mother asked, her gaze wary.

Tilda chose her response carefully. "It's very pretty. I'll try it on with Clara when I return later this afternoon." She smiled at the maid, who nodded in acknowledgment.

"Now, I must be off." Tilda sent a stern look toward her mother. "Truly." She turned and said goodbye to her grandmother, then went to the entrance hall to fetch her hat and gloves, which she'd placed there earlier.

Vaughn opened the door for her, and Tilda departed after thanking him. She made her way quickly to where Hadrian was waiting with his coach at the end of the street. He stood outside with Leach, who reached for the door as she approached.

"My apologies for being late," Tilda said. "My mother delayed me. She purchased garments for me to wear to tea tomorrow." She sent Hadrian a faint grimace.

"You don't like them?" he asked.

"They are not what I would have chosen." Tilda inclined her head toward Leach and thanked him before climbing into the coach.

Hadrian sat down beside her. "What's wrong with the ensemble?"

"It's…not my taste. There are bows and ruffles. And it's pink."

"I think you'll look quite nice in pink." He smiled at her. "In truth, I can't think of anything that would detract from your beauty."

Heat shot into Tilda's cheeks, and she turned her head whilst taking a breath to slow her suddenly speeding pulse. "You may change your mind when you see me at tea tomorrow."

Hadrian chuckled. "I look forward to it."

Tilda wished to direct their conversation to their investigations. "I do hope Superintendent Yates is present when we arrive." They were on their way to Rochester Row, where the superintendent's office was located.

"And if he's not?" Hadrian asked with an elevated brow.

"I'll be greatly disappointed." Tilda took a deep breath. "I'll ask for an appointment to see him as soon as possible."

"I know how important this investigation is to you. We will find answers. I promise." His gaze was dark and steady.

Tilda believed him, but how could he keep that promise? Particularly when his power wasn't working? She didn't dare ask if it had returned. Indeed, she didn't really want to discuss it unless he raised the topic.

"Will you allow me to ensure we see the superintendent?" Hadrian asked. "Provided he's there."

"You plan to use your title?"

His lips curled into an almost wicked smile that made Tilda's heart race once more. "Of course."

They arrived in Rochester Row and departed the coach. Leach would wait for them, but he'd move forward so the coach wasn't directly in front of the station.

Inside, they could see into the charge room, where an inspector was speaking with someone, and a woman was searching another woman who'd almost certainly been arrested. Tilda and Hadrian made their way to the desk, and Tilda asked to speak with Superintendent Yates.

"Do you have an appointment?" the constable on duty asked.

"No," Hadrian replied. "Please inform him the Earl of Ravenhurst requires an interview."

The young constable's eyes rounded. "Right away, my lord." He took himself off, racing through a doorway down a corridor. It sounded as though he were running up a set of stairs.

"He must be here," Hadrian said with a nod.

The back of Tilda's neck was hot, and she felt generally flushed and…anxious. She never felt this way during an investigation. But then she'd never investigated anything so personal before.

She supposed she ought to consider helping Hadrian to find his assailant when they'd first worked together, but that had been different. She hadn't known him as well then as she did now. He was also still here, whereas her father was not and hadn't been for some time.

An image of her father rose in Tilda's mind. He would have

liked Hadrian. At least she thought he would. She acknowledged that it was difficult to think she really knew her father when she'd been so young. To know him now, as an adult, would be quite different. And wonderful. When she thought of how they'd been robbed of all this time, she became angry and sad. Emotion welled up inside her, and she worked to push it down, to bury it in the recesses of her soul, where it had lurked mostly dormant for over a decade.

"Are you all right?" Hadrian asked softly.

Tilda blinked and focused on him once more. "I'm fine. Why do you ask?"

"You're a bit flushed," he said. "It's warm today."

Tilda would seize that excuse. She did not want to reveal what she'd been thinking about.

The constable returned. "Superintendent Yates will see you. Please come with me." He led them back the way he'd gone and returned.

They trailed him into a corridor, then turned to the left to climb the stairs to the first floor. The constable guided them to a large office in the front corner of the building. He gestured for them to go inside but remained in the corridor.

Superintendent Yates, a broad-shouldered man in his early fifties with thick side whiskers and dark hair flecked with gray, looked up from his desk. "Ravenhurst?" he asked.

"Good afternoon," Hadrian replied. "This is my associate, Miss Wren. We've come to speak with you about an old case regarding the murder of Sergeant Thomas Wren."

Yates's dark brown eyes snapped to Tilda as his bushy brows briefly rose. "Wren? Sergeant Wren was a relation?"

"My father," Tilda replied.

"I recall that incident." Yates set down his pen and straightened in his chair. "That was a decade or so ago, wasn't it? I don't know how I can help you."

"It seems the investigation may not have been as through as it ought to have been." Tilda's throat felt tight as she worked to keep her anger at bay. "We spoke with the owner of the apothecary shop where my father was allegedly killed."

"'Allegedly?'" Yates asked dubiously.

"That was the conclusion at the time. However, the apothecary informed us that there was not enough blood at his shop for my father to have been murdered there. He was killed elsewhere, and his body was moved."

Yates frowned. Then he took a deep breath and clasped his hands on his desk. He gave Tilda a patronizing smile that made her want to chuck her reticule at his head. "You've decided this based on the word of an apothecary ten years on? Why didn't he report that at the time of the murder?"

"He did, but he was told the killer cleaned the mess. He found that highly unlikely, as do I," Tilda said with a measure of heat, despite her best efforts to remain calm. "Mr. Williams said there would not have been time for the killer to wash the blood away before he arrived downstairs. He was alerted to the presence of the criminal by the sound of breaking glass."

"Perhaps the glass was broken after the murderer cleaned up," Yates said with a shrug. He looked to Hadrian. "What is your role in this…inquiry, my lord?"

"As I said, Miss Wren is my associate. She is a private investigator, and I assist her."

The superintendent blinked in surprise. "Do you? How odd. And why are you investigating this old murder?"

"As Miss Wren has already stated, it appears the original investigation was not thorough," Hadrian said crisply. "Thomas Wren was an esteemed sergeant, and he was about to become a detective inspector. I should think the Metropolitan Police would like to ensure the case was handled correctly."

"Wren interrupted a theft in progress, and he was killed. It's awful and I'm very sorry for your loss, Miss Wren." He met Tilda's gaze. "However, there is nothing to be done about it now."

"Why not?" Tilda asked. "You could reopen the case. Two of the constables who were present are still with the Metropolitan Police. They could shed light on what really happened."

"Why would their stories change now?" Yates shook his head. "I appreciate you wanting some sort of satisfaction since his killer wasn't found, but I'm afraid that will be elusive, my dear, if not impossible."

Tilda clenched her hands into fists briefly at his use of an endearment. She took another deep breath lest she capitulate to her violent urge and launch her reticule at him.

Hadrian fixed a dark, lordly stare on the superintendent. "I would very much like for you to reopen the case."

Yates unclasped his hands and flattened them atop his desk. "Some things are better left alone, my lord. Too much time has passed, and I would advise you not to trust the memory of an aging man who likely partakes of the items he sells."

What was that supposed to mean? Was the superintendent implying that Mr. Williams was drug-addled?

Tilda pursed her lips. "I found Mr. Williams quite credible."

"As did I," Hadrian added coolly. "I ask that you reconsider reopening the case, Superintendent. I should hate to have to speak with the Home Secretary about this matter."

"Hardy won't want to commit resources to such folly." Yates's tone was stern. He tipped his head down a moment and when he looked back up at Tilda and Hadrian, his features had softened. "I do understand your plight, Miss Wren, and I'm sorry your father died in such a horrible manner. He was a fine member of the Met." Though the superintendent seemed to speak genuinely, Tilda couldn't help feeling frustrated.

"Will you at least allow us to review the investigation files?" Tilda asked.

"Certainly. Though, it may take the clerk some time to find them."

"We'll wait," Hadrian said with a humorless smile.

Yates stood. He was quite tall, a bit taller than Hadrian even. "I'll send the clerk to fetch the files. You can wait downstairs. There is a bench outside the charge room."

"Thank you." Hadrian turned to Tilda.

She swept from the room and stalked to the stairs. Hadrian followed. They returned to the entry area and watched as the superintendent spoke with the constable. Without looking toward Tilda and Hadrian, Yates pivoted and walked back through the doorway toward the stairs. The constable went the same way.

There was indeed a bench outside the charge room, but it was occupied by a nervous-looking woman wearing glasses and clutching her reticule in her lap. Tilda moved to stand on the other side of the entrance area, and Hadrian joined her, taking a position to her left.

"Yates was incredibly disagreeable." Tilda looked over at Hadrian. "Will you really speak with the Home Secretary?"

Hadrian nodded. "First thing tomorrow. Something isn't right. May I tell him about the paper that was found in Padgett's pocket?"

Tilda hesitated. "I don't want to cause trouble for Teague."

"I won't mention Teague, and I won't mention the paper at all unless I feel it's necessary."

"Thank you. What do you suppose the superintendent meant when he mentioned Mr. Williams's products?"

Hadrian scoffed. "I found that rude. That comment along with what he said about leaving things alone seemed suspicious to me."

Relief washed through Tilda. "Thank goodness it wasn't just me." She gave him a grateful smile. "I am grateful for your support in this."

"I'm more than happy to give it. We will discover the truth, Tilda."

A constable dragged in a very drunk man. His odor was quite

pungent, and he could barely walk. He fell at Tilda's feet and grabbed at her skirt.

"Get up!" The constable hauled the drunkard up and cast an apologetic look at Tilda before pulling the man into the charge room.

Tilda and Hadrian waited for quite some time. At last, the woman on the bench was called into the charge room.

"Shall we sit?" Hadrian asked.

"I don't know how much longer we should wait."

"We can wait all day." Hadrian gave her an encouraging smile, and Tilda couldn't help but relax.

She really needed to moderate her emotions. This was not the way to conduct an investigation. She had to distance herself from the fact that her father was the victim. Except that he was the entire reason she was doing this.

It occurred to Tilda that she was, apparently, capable of feeling a great deal of emotion. Perhaps she was not like her mother at all then. That gave her some comfort.

Finally, the constable returned. Tilda immediately approached him without waiting for him to come to them. Hadrian accompanied her.

Right away, Tilda realized the constable wasn't carrying anything. "Where is the report?"

The constable glanced at Hadrian as crimson flushed his cheeks. "I'm afraid it isn't there. It may have been misfiled."

"You were gone for some time," Hadrian said. "May we assume you conducted a thorough search?"

"I did try, my lord," the constable responded. "I can look again later, if you like."

"I would like that very much." Hadrian gave the young man a direct, expectant stare. "Perhaps when you are not assigned to the desk, you can take more time to search."

"Thank you, my lord. I will do my best. Where shall I send word if I find it?"

"*When* you find it, please bring it to Ravenhurst House. I would appreciate that very much."

"Certainly, my lord," the constable replied eagerly.

Hadrian looked to Tilda. "Shall we go?"

"I suppose." She didn't bother hiding her disappointment. Turning, she strode to the doorway.

Hadrian made it there in time to open the door for her, and they walked outside. Tilda blew out a breath. "Do you really think he'll find the file?"

"You don't?"

"No. I think it's missing on purpose. Just as I think the superintendent didn't want to reopen this investigation because there is something to hide." There was no other good explanation for what had happened. The paper in Padgett's pocket was too curious to ignore. Why had he been carrying it?

They reached the coach, and Leach commented on how long they'd been gone. He also observed, somewhat regretfully, that they looked as if they hadn't been successful.

Tilda paused before climbing into the coach and looked at Leach. "Actually, it was rather enlightening."

Hadrian blinked at her. "Was it?"

"We learned the police would rather this case remain closed, and they don't care that it doesn't make sense for my father to have been killed at the apothecary shop. And, perhaps most importantly, we discovered the files are missing." She focused on Hadrian. "I'm reminded of when we tried to see the file about your investigation—when you were stabbed several months ago."

"It wasn't missing though," Hadrian said. "We weren't allowed to see it."

Tilda narrowed her eyes. "I'm not sure those are different things."

Hadrian's brow furrowed. "You think the constable lied and the files were there?"

"I think I don't trust anyone at the police, save Inspector Teague," Tilda replied. "Indeed, I'd like to speak with him soon."

"To share information or to determine if he's actually trustworthy?" Hadrian asked.

"Both." Tilda climbed into the coach, and Hadrian sat beside her. "I hope Teague will help me. I'm not sure we can discover the truth without someone in the police providing assistance. Unless you're able to convince the Home Secretary to reopen the investigation. But even then, I'm not sure I'd trust whomever they assigned."

"It certainly can't be Lowther or Jurgens."

Tilda scowled. "I'm so angry with Lowther. How could he deceive me like this?"

Hadrian gazed at her with sympathy. "I don't know." His features hardened briefly. "But we *will* find out."

Tilda was surprisingly comforted by Hadrian's assurances, and his willingness to use his position to help her. She didn't particularly like that it was necessary, but she wasn't going to decline his offer to speak with the Home Secretary. Though Hadrian had described her as his associate, they were so much more to each other than that. He was her dear friend and confidante.

Tilda didn't know how she would navigate this investigation without him. And she was very glad she wouldn't have to.

CHAPTER 7

For days now, Hadrian had been taking time to meditate and focus on regaining his ability to see others' memories. He started every day trying to see something by touching the mirror he'd bought from Timms. And every morning, he was disappointed when he saw and felt nothing at all.

Perhaps the failure of his power was driving him to do whatever necessary to aid Tilda in her investigation into her father's murder, such as calling on the Home Secretary this morning. She'd been so distraught yesterday. Hadrian had never seen her so upset. She possessed one of the coolest temperaments he'd ever encountered, particularly when it came to investigations.

Hadrian regarded himself in the full-length mirror in his dressing chamber. He was garbed for business and would change part of his ensemble before the tea that afternoon at his mother's house with Tilda and her mother.

"Forgive me, my lord, but I must ask something." Hadrian's valet, Sharp, pressed his thin lips together as Hadrian turned to face him. "What is the purpose of that rather feminine hand mirror that's appeared next to your bed?"

Hadrian kept the mirror on the table beside his bed so that he could easily grasp it in the morning. "It's a gift for someone. I'm waiting for the right time to present it." The lie came forth with ease. Hadrian credited his investigative work with Tilda for preparing him to come up with a fabrication without notice.

Though Hadrian should have devised an excuse for having it. Just as he should have expected Sharp to ask. The valet had been with him a decade, and he knew Hadrian exceptionally well. He did not, however, know about Hadrian's missing ability.

Sharp's light brown brows arched with curiosity. "Who is it for?"

"I'd rather not say."

"I will assume it's Miss Wren," Sharp said as he moved to tidy the dressing chamber, not that it was in disarray. The valet kept a very neat space.

"I don't know why." Hadrian wasn't sure why he wasn't confirming Sharp's suspicion. Indeed, he realized his "lie" wasn't far from the truth, for he did intend to give it to Tilda at some point.

Sharp surveyed him with a slightly narrowed gaze. "I can't decide if you have a secret affair going on or if you're keeping her at arm's length because of the difference in your positions."

"Neither," Hadrian said. "We are investigative partners and friends."

"You forget that I know you. I'm well aware of when you are fixated on a female, though it doesn't happen often." Sharp cocked his head. "And I don't believe it's ever happened to this extent."

Hadrian put a hand on his hip. "What does that mean?"

Sharp shrugged. "I can see she's very important to you, that the days you spend with her are when you are in your best spirits."

Blast. That sounded rather obvious. "I suppose I should expect you to notice such things. Has anyone else?"

"Not that I know of. Why are you waiting to give her the mirror?"

Hadrian supposed they were dispensing with the pretense of Hadrian not identifying the recipient of the gift. "I'd rather not say. And it's nothing to do with our relationship," he added. It was to do with Tilda and when she might be ready to pursue the feelings they both seemed to have for one another. Though Hadrian suspected his were stronger at the present time, or that, at least, he was more willing to acknowledge them. "It's complicated."

"I see." Sharp's brow creased. "Do you think your mother will not approve of someone of Miss Wren's station?"

"My mother's approval, whilst nice, is not required."

"Then Society's approval," Sharp said. "I'm sure that matters."

"Not as much as you think." It probably should factor into things, but Hadrian didn't care what anyone thought about him wanting to marry Tilda.

Did he want to marry her?

He did. He could think of no better partner—not just in their work but in all things. He'd never met a woman he admired or liked as much as Tilda. And Sharp was right, the time they spent together made for the very best days.

"I must be on my way to my meeting with Hardy." Hadrian picked up his hat and gloves and departed the dressing chamber.

Leach was waiting with the coach outside. They left for Whitehall, and Hadrian turned his focus to the upcoming interview.

He'd sent a note yesterday afternoon requesting the meeting and had received confirmation in the evening. Even so, Hadrian had gone to one of his clubs after dinner in case he happened upon Hardy there. A great deal of government business happened at clubs, not that this was government business. However, Hadrian had not encountered the Home Secretary.

They arrived at Whitehall, and Hadrian made his way into the Home Office. He was immediately shown to Hardy's suite.

The Home Secretary was in his middle-fifties with rather long, fuzzy side whiskers. He was very well spoken and regarded as an important figure in the Conservative Party. Whilst Hadrian did not agree with all of Hardy's views, he found the man to be of good temper and keen intelligence. He particularly liked that Hardy had supported last year's Reform Act, which increased the electorate.

"Morning, Raven," Hardy said. "You wanted to speak with me about a police matter?"

"Yes. May we sit a moment?" Hadrian looked toward the seating area.

Hardy nodded, and they each took a chair.

Hadrian went straight to the purpose of his visit. "Yesterday, I asked Superintendent Yates at B Division to reopen a murder case. Sergeant Thomas Wren was killed during a robbery that he interrupted at an apothecary shop in December 1857. New information has been revealed that indicates the investigation was not conducted properly. However, Yates refused to reopen the matter."

Frowning, Hardy fixed his attention on Hadrian. "What information has been brought to light?"

"I spoke with the apothecary, Mr. Williams, the other day, and something about the murder never sat right with him. He said there wasn't enough blood for Sergeant Wren to have been killed in his shop. When he raised that point, the inspector told him the killer must have cleaned up the blood. However, Williams doesn't believe that would have been possible in the amount of time before Williams came downstairs and discovered Wren's body."

"Was the killer found?" Hardy asked.

Hadrian shook his head. "The case was closed. There is something amiss about this investigation, and this business with the lack of blood is just one puzzling piece."

Hardy's blue eyes lit with curiosity. "What else do you know?"

"One of the constables who was present that night, a man called Padgett, was recently murdered." Hadrian thought it important to mention the clue found on Padgett. "He had a piece of paper in his pocket with Thomas Wren's name and the date he was killed."

"That is odd." Hardy stroked one of his side whiskers in contemplation. "Suspicious, even." He lowered his hand to the arm of the chair and returned his focus to Hadrian. "How did you come to gather all this information?"

Hadrian had somewhat expected this question or one like it. He didn't want to lie and saw no reason to. "I occasionally assist a private investigator with her cases. Her name is Matilda Wren. Thomas Wren was her father. She is investigating his death, and I am helping."

Hardy blinked at him, his disbelief evident. "You work with a private investigator? And she's a woman?"

"She's brilliant," Hadrian said proudly. "She was instrumental in apprehending the Levitation Killers and, most recently, she worked with the City of London Police on cases of corruption and murder."

"Ah yes, I do recall that a woman investigator was involved in the case involving the murders of those mediums." Hardy clasped his hands, whilst his elbows rested on the arms of the chair. "May I presume you've come to ask me to direct Superintendent Yates to reopen the investigation into Wren's murder?"

"I have."

Hardy shook his head, and Hadrian's stomach clenched. "I'd rather not do that. This is a matter for the Detective Branch. I'll ask them to handle it. If there is new information and we've a chance to solve the murder of a police sergeant, we must try."

Hadrian exhaled with relief—and gratitude. "Thank you."

"I can see this is of personal importance to you, which is another reason I'm inclined to help," Hardy said. "Will Miss Wren allow the Detective Branch to investigate this matter? She oughtn't be involved in something so close to her."

There was no way Tilda would stand aside. But she was very good at pretending she wasn't investigating something when she absolutely was. The key would be in who was assigned to the case. Hadrian hoped it would be Teague.

"Miss Wren only wants to see justice done," Hadrian said evenly. "So long as she's kept abreast of the investigation, I'm confident she'll be happy to support the Detective Branch in whatever way she can. Even if that means doing nothing," he added.

Apparently, he was willing to lie.

Because he would move heaven and earth to help Tilda and give her the peace she deserved.

Hardy stood, indicating the meeting would conclude. "I'll send a note once I know who will be conducting the investigation. I'm sure the detective inspector will want to speak with you and Miss Wren about what you know."

"Thank you again." Hadrian shook the man's hand. He couldn't help the surge of anticipation that he might see one of the man's memories. Unfortunately, Hadrian was once again disappointed. He tamped down his frustration.

Hadrian took his leave and made his way through the Home Office. He encountered a man called Ernsby, a clerk he'd known for several years.

"Morning, Lord Ravenhurst," Ernsby said. "It's been a while since I've seen you. I think the last time was Sir Henry Meacham's funeral."

Sir Henry had been Tilda's grandfather's cousin. His murder was the first case they'd worked on together, though it hadn't started with his murder. Indeed, his death hadn't even been ruled a murder at first.

"That's right," Hadrian said. Sir Henry had been an under-secretary with the Home Office before retiring, so several people from the office had attended his funeral. "Keeping busy here?"

"Always," Ernsby replied with a chuckle. "I'm glad Fellows is back. He was gone for nearly a fortnight taking care of his mother in Leeds. Poor woman passed away."

Fellows? Hadrian recognized the name, though he didn't know the man as well as he knew Ernsby. How had he not recalled the name after hearing it from the apothecary the other day? Could this Fellows be Constable Fellows who'd been at the apothecary shop the night Thomas Wren was killed? "How long has Fellows been with the Home Office?"

"Let me see… Almost ten years, I think?" Ernsby replied. "He was with the Metropolitan Police before that, but he preferred clerical work and came to work here after someone retired."

Hadrian's pulse sped. It had to be the same Fellows. "I believe there was a Constable Fellows with B Division around 1857 or so. That must be him."

Ernsby smiled. "Indeed it is."

"Is he here?" Hadrian glanced around. He didn't think he'd recognize the man but thought he had a widow's peak and angular features.

"Not at the moment." Ernsby's wide brow furrowed, and his gray brows drew together. "Do you need to speak with him?"

Hadrian waved his hand. "No. I was merely curious. Always like to convey my thanks to you fine gentlemen in the Home Office. Your hard work is appreciated."

Ernsby inclined his head. "Thank you, my lord."

"Have a good day," Hadrian said before departing. He was anxious to tell Tilda what he'd learned and would find a moment to do so that afternoon.

In the absence of his ability to see others' memories, Hadrian was glad he could help in other ways. Particularly since Hadrian had begun to fear that his ability was gone forever.

adrian had insisted on sending his coach to Tilda's grandmother's house to convey them to his mother's for tea. Tilda's mother had been ecstatic. She'd also taken it to mean that Hadrian had taken a special, *personal* interest in Tilda. Beleaguered by her mother's tireless efforts to make more of her relationship with Hadrian, Tilda had only said that he was a gentleman and was always thoughtful of everyone, not just her. He was being kind in sending his coach for *all three of them.*

That had not dampened her mother's enthusiasm for a possible match. Whilst Tilda was excited to hear how Hadrian's meeting with the Home Secretary had gone, she was just as eager for the tea to be over.

They arrived at the dowager countess's elegant terrace on Hill Street near Berkeley Square. Leach smiled as he helped Tilda from the coach. "May I say you look especially lovely today, Miss Wren," he said softly.

Tilda didn't think her mother or grandmother, who'd exited the coach first, had heard his comment. She was glad because her mother would surely gloat about Tilda's ensemble. "Thank you, Leach."

Even Tilda had to acknowledge that the rose-colored outfit wasn't terrible. It just wasn't what she would have chosen. If there were fewer bows and ruffles, she would have liked it fine. She was at least satisfied that the hat wasn't overly decorated. It was small and sleek with an attractive black and white speckled feather.

Tilda followed her mother and grandmother to the door, which the butler, Peverell, opened as they approached the threshold. He welcomed them to the dowager countess's home and bestowed a particular smile on Tilda. "It's lovely to see you again, Miss Wren."

"I trust you are well, Peverell," Tilda said as she moved into the entrance hall. A marble statue of Hestia, the Greek goddess of the hearth, greeted them from an alcove on the right. It was beautiful, but to Tilda, it was the epitome of extravagance and wealth. She couldn't imagine having something like that in her home rather than observing it in a museum.

"Very," the butler replied. "I hope the same for you."

Tilda gave him a warm smile. "Thank you. Allow me to present my grandmother, Mrs. Wren, and my mother, Lady Pierce." She probably ought to have introduced her mother first due to her rank, but Tilda thought age was more important. In Tilda's opinion, her grandmother had lived long enough to earn the highest amount of deference and respect.

"The dowager countess and his lordship are in the drawing room, if you'll come with me." Peverell led them into the staircase hall and up to the drawing room. Tilda's mother took the lead directly behind the butler.

At the top of the stairs was a portrait of Hadrian, his younger brother Gabriel, and their father. Hadrian had been fifteen when it was painted and Gabriel just ten. Gabriel had died in India several years ago, and their father was also gone. The dowager countess had placed the painting there so she would pass it multiple times a day. Tilda had learned all this from Hadrian, of course. They'd really come to know each other quite well. In fact, she thought he knew her better than almost anyone just now, given all the time they spent together. That acknowledgment gave her a very pleasant feeling.

Tilda entered the drawing room, which she'd visited on several occasions. Her focus went immediately to Hadrian who stood near his mother's chair, his attention on the doorway—and now on her. He wore an exceedingly bright orange waistcoat. It wasn't hideous, but it was odd for him. Indeed, she would have expected to see something like that on Ezra Clement, along with his ostentatious plaid trousers. Lifting her gaze to his once more, Tilda saw Hadrian smile.

"Welcome," Lady Ravenhurst said, rising from her chair.

Tilda inclined her head to the dowager. "This is my grandmother, Mrs. Wren, and my mother, Lady Pierce." Again, she decided not to bother with what propriety might have demanded.

This time, her mother gently pursed her lips at Tilda before smiling widely toward Hadrian's mother. "I'm delighted to make your acquaintance, Lady Ravenhurst. Thank you for inviting us today."

"I'm glad you could come." The dowager looked to Tilda's grandmother. "I'm pleased to meet you, Mrs. Wren. Your granddaughter speaks so warmly of you."

Tilda imagined her mother didn't appreciate the dowager saying that and not indicating the same about her, but then Tilda didn't speak warmly of her mother. She rarely spoke of her at all.

"The tea is arranged over near the windows," the dowager said, moving past Hadrian toward the round table that was set with five chairs today.

"What a delightful arrangement," Tilda's mother said.

The table was adorned with all the accoutrements of an elegant tea, including pretty pink floral-patterned teacups. Two tiered stands featured small sandwiches, cakes, and, Tilda's favorite, scones. There was clotted cream along with jam and lemon curd, plus the teapot. A beautiful arrangement of pink peonies stood in the center.

The dowager looked to Tilda. "Would you mind pouring, Miss Wren?"

"Not at all." Tilda noted her mother was smiling approvingly. She likely thought this was some sort of sign the dowager liked her, which she did. However, that didn't mean she wanted Tilda to marry her son.

"I understand you're working on a new case involving stolen items," the dowager said to Tilda as she poured the tea.

Tilda nodded. "Some silver pieces went missing, unfortunately. But I believe we have a lead on recovering them."

Hadrian's mother smiled. "How wonderful. I'm sure your client will be pleased. I did ask Hadrian who it was, but he said he couldn't reveal their identity for privacy's sake, which I understand."

After finishing with the tea, Tilda sat and plucked a scone from one of the tiered trays. She sliced it open and went about covering it with lemon curd and clotted cream.

"Surely they would never know if you told us," Tilda's mother said with a light laugh. She looked at Tilda expectantly as if she were waiting for Tilda to reveal Mrs. Goodwin's identity.

"It would be highly inappropriate," Tilda said coolly. "And unprofessional."

"Tilda is a trustworthy and reliable investigator," Tilda's grandmother said with pride.

"She is indeed," the dowager agreed. "She was most helpful to me when I hired her to make inquiries."

Tilda's mother shifted her focus to the dowager. "What was that about?"

"Let us not speak of business," Hadrian interjected smoothly. Tilda was sure he didn't want the conversation to drift into a discussion of the corrupt spiritualism society they'd investigated. His mother had been swindled, albeit it mildly.

Hadrian looked to Tilda's mother. "Do you enjoy living in Birmingham?"

"I miss certain things about London, but I like it very much," Tilda's mother replied. "We've a grand home, and I've enjoyed decorating it." She looked at Lady Ravenhurst. "Your home is beautiful."

"Thank you." The dowager sipped her tea and replaced the cup in the saucer. "I confess I found it odd that your daughter did not move to Birmingham with you, nor did she have a Season here in London. Were you not interested in that?"

Tilda froze before taking another bite of scone. Her mother's features stiffened, and her eyes briefly turned to frost. "Unfortunately, Matilda did not wish to come to Birmingham with us. She preferred to stay in London with her grandmother."

"I can't say I blame her," the dowager said, sending a smile toward Tilda. "There is no city like London." She looked back to Tilda's mother. "Surely you could have stayed here to give her a Season."

There was simply no good way to respond to that. Even if her stepfather had offered to fund a Season, Tilda would have declined. The dowager would almost certainly find Sir Bardolph's disinterest in Tilda's standing or future, as well as Tilda's disinterest in finding a husband, disappointing.

"I don't think anyone regrets Lady Pierce's move to Birmingham or Tilda's choice to remain with me," Tilda's grandmother said diplomatically. "I certainly don't." She smiled at Tilda, her blue eyes gleaming with love.

"I don't either," Tilda added softly.

Tilda's mother glanced at her, and Tilda knew she was going to respond. Tilda braced herself.

"Unfortunately, Matilda has resisted having a Season and the Marriage Mart entirely. She has preferred to care for her grandmother. Whilst that is incredibly thoughtful, she can continue to do so after she is wed. In caring for my mother-in-law, Matilda has become quite skilled at managing a household. There's a housekeeper, a butler, and a maid. Matilda keeps all of it running smoothly." She smiled at Tilda with something akin to pride, but Tilda didn't think that was it.

Instead of feeling flattered by her mother's words, Tilda saw them for what they were—a shameless attempt to show Lady Ravenhurst that Tilda could manage a household. As if overseeing their small complement of retainers would qualify her for the demands of being a countess. There was no comparison, and Hadrian's mother would recognize that.

"Miss Wren seems quite accomplished at all she sets her mind to," the dowager said as she dolloped clotted cream on her scones. "I did wonder at her choice of occupation and even the fact that she *had* an occupation, but I can see how much she enjoys her work. And how clever she is. I'm sure that makes you proud." She fixed her gaze on Tilda's mother as she bit into her scone.

The dowager countess's words infused Tilda with warmth. With that came the reminder that she wished her own mother would say such things.

"Quite." Tilda's mother's tone was brittle. But what else could she have said? "I do wish she would take time to find a husband. Though it seems she and Ravenhurst get on very well."

Tilda closed her eyes for the barest moment. Had her mother really said that? Of course she had.

"They are worthy professional partners," the dowager said. "I don't imagine they'd have much in common socially."

No, they did not, though Tilda could imagine her mother disagreed. Which was ludicrous. Tilda and Hadrian did not move in the same circles, contrary to what her mother believed. Tilda didn't even *belong* to a social circle.

Tilda's mother's features had tightened once more, and her smile was both faint and lacking good humor. "This is a social engagement, is it not?"

Unable to tolerate another moment of this exchange, Tilda removed the napkin from her lap and looked to Hadrian. "Might we step aside for a moment to discuss our case?"

"Certainly." Hadrian rose with alacrity and moved to help Tilda from her chair.

She placed her napkin on her seat and gave everyone a mild smile before walking to the farthest corner of the thankfully large drawing room.

"Do you really want to discuss the case, or did you just want to escape?" Hadrian whispered as they neared the opposite side of the room.

"Both." She turned to face him when they'd reached the corner.

Hadrian swept her with an admiring perusal. "You do look lovely today. Your ensemble is more rose than pink, I'd say. It's a flattering color on you."

"I can't quite say the same about your orange waistcoat," she said wryly. "I've never seen that garment before, and I'm honestly surprised you'd borrow fashion sense from Ezra Clement."

Laughing, Hadrian's blue eyes twinkled as he regarded her. "I hadn't considered that, but now that you compare it to him, I can see it would match a pair of his garish trousers."

"Why would you wear that?" Tilda asked.

He shrugged. "If you were going to wear something you didn't particularly care for, I thought I would do the same."

Tilda stared at him as warmth spread through her. "Oh." She simply couldn't manage to say anything else. There were too many words and thoughts crowding her brain to push any of them out. She was flattered and delighted. She was also nearly smitten with his thoughtfulness.

Smitten.

She'd known at the end of their last investigation, after Hadrian had been injured, that her feelings for him had deepened. But just as she'd recognized that, she'd also needed time to understand how things had changed for her. Now it seemed she knew. He was more than a friend and a business associate.

This was ill-timed, however. She could not indulge whatever feelings she had for Hadrian in the midst of their current investigation. Truthfully, she wasn't sure she *ought* to recognize them. How would that turn out? As his mother had just pointed out, they had nothing in common socially. Nor did they share any commonality with regard to their economic status. They were worthy professional partners, as the dowager countess had aptly stated, and that was all.

Except the more Tilda reminded herself of that fact, the more a tiny voice at the back of her head said it didn't have to be that way. That voice reminded her that they'd kissed and shared a number of warm, even heated, moments. And they'd acknowledged that they cared for one another.

Still, having and acknowledging those feelings did not mean anything would—or even could—come of them. They were a mismatch in nearly every way.

Nearly. Tilda did not care for how that word had stolen into her thoughts.

She cleared her mind and turned her thoughts to their case. How could she have been distracted when she was eager to hear about his meeting this morning? "Please tell me about your interview with the Home Secretary."

His eyes continued to gleam, but the merriment from earlier was now replaced with an excitement she'd seen before, usually when he had something important to share from a vision he'd seen. Had he regained his ability?

"I'm pleased to report that Hardy is going to assign a detective inspector from the Detective Branch to reopen your father's case."

Tilda sucked in a breath. This was more than she'd hoped for. "Did he say who?"

Hadrian shook his head. "I'm sure you're hoping it will be Teague, as am I. But there is more."

"Don't keep me in suspense." Tilda could see his enthusiasm and wondered what more there could possibly be after such wonderful news.

"I'd completely forgotten there is a clerk in the Home Office called Fellows."

Tilda stared at him. "Is it the same Fellows?" she breathed.

"It is." Hadrian's expression was triumphant. "He moved to the Home Office about ten years ago."

"Is it odd that a constable would become a clerk?" Tilda wondered aloud.

"Perhaps."

"I'd like to ask Teague about that." Tilda dearly hoped he would be appointed to this case. And if he wasn't, she'd hope he could keep abreast of it and let them know what was happening. "Let's call on him tomorrow after we visit Mr. Timms."

"I was going to suggest the same," Hadrian said with a smile. He glanced toward the tea table and sobered. "I suppose we should return. I'm sorry things are…awkward."

"Only because my mother is making them that way." Tilda blew out a breath, then met his gaze. "I'm sorry. I do appreciate you humoring my mother. I hope she will leave soon, especially once she realizes her efforts to persuade me to stop investigating aren't effective in the least."

Hadrian looked at her with sympathy. "I can't imagine that's been pleasant for you to endure this past week."

Tilda lifted a shoulder. "I can handle her. But I will be grateful for peace in the household once more."

They returned to the table, and the conversation seemed as stilted as when they'd left. Tilda's grandmother looked at her with something between apology and discomfort.

After enduring another half hour or so of Tilda's mother's attempts to align her with Hadrian as more than just professional partners, Tilda's grandmother thanked the dowager for her hospitality.

"Perhaps we'll see you at a social event," Tilda's mother said as they stood. "I've accepted an invitation to a ball at Lord and Lady Trumbull's next week."

Tilda snapped her attention to her mother. She had? This was the first Tilda was hearing of it and, judging from her grandmother's expression, it was the same for her.

"I am not able to attend," the dowager said. "But it's lovely that you've been invited." Something about her tone didn't quite ring true. Tilda wasn't sure Hadrian's mother thought the invitation was, in fact, *lovely*.

They said goodbye and were shortly on their way back to Marylebone Lane in Hadrian's coach. Apparently, Hadrian had walked to his mother's and would return in the same manner.

When they were underway, Tilda's grandmother pursed her lips at her former daughter-in-law. "It would have been preferable for you to inform us of these social plans somewhere other than in the company of others."

"It slipped my mind." Tilda's mother waved her hand. "In any case, the invitation didn't include you." Her tone wasn't rude exactly, but excluding Tilda's grandmother sparked Tilda's ire when she was already fairly annoyed.

"I'm not going," Tilda said firmly. "You didn't even ask if I was available. You can't presume to make appointments for me without my consent."

"This is an excellent opportunity for you to move in the same circle as Ravenhurst. You can show his mother that she's wrong, that the two of you *are* socially matched."

"Except we are not." Tilda brushed her hand over her brow. "I don't want to argue with you about this, Mother. I thought you'd be returning to Birmingham after this tea, not planning more events that don't interest me."

Her mother's eyes widened briefly. "You didn't enjoy yourself today? You seemed to, particularly when you and Ravenhurst went to the corner for your *private* conversation. You also clearly favored your scone." She arched a brow at Tilda, as if daring her to respond to the contrary.

"It was a very good scone," Tilda murmured. "This tea was for your benefit, Mother, not mine. I'm already well acquainted with Ravenhurst and his mother."

"I could see that. I don't think it would take much to convince them that you and he will make an excellent match."

Tilda stared at her mother. "You can't think the dowager countess was in favor of that. I believe she made it clear she's not." She glanced toward her grandmother, hopeful that she'd have some support.

"She wasn't encouraging," her grandmother added quietly. She sent Tilda an apologetic look, but Tilda didn't need her sympathy.

"I have no expectations," Tilda declared, perhaps a trifle too loudly for the interior of the coach. "I am content to work with Ravenhurst. Anything other than that would be…awkward."

Like the kiss they'd shared. Only it had been quite wonderful before the awkwardness had set in.

Her mother regarded her dubiously. "Will you still feel that way when he's moved on to someone else and is wed?"

The idea of that sent a sharp dread straight through Tilda. Her pulse picked up speed, and her body tensed. She couldn't imagine him being married. Nor could she foresee them continuing to work together if he was. He would be busy with his wife, and they would probably have a family. There would be no room for their investigations. Or for Tilda.

A disquieting feeling settled into Tilda's bones. She couldn't shake the sensation that something had changed for her, and she was powerless to force things back to the way they were. She liked her life, her independence, her investigative work.

She did not care to contemplate surrendering any of that. Not even for whatever she was feeling for Hadrian.

CHAPTER 8

ilda was waiting at the end of Marylebone Lane when
Leach slowed the coach to a stop. He hopped down
from the box as Hadrian opened the door and stepped out.

"I hope you haven't been waiting long," Hadrian said,
appearing mildly concerned.

"No, but in hindsight I should have come much earlier. The
weather is pleasant, and my mother isn't here." She gave him a
wry smile, then looked to the coachman. "Good afternoon,
Leach."

The coachman inclined his head. "Good afternoon, Miss
Wren."

Tilda shifted her gaze to Hadrian. "Do you mind if we go to
the police station in Great Marlborough Street first? I'd like to
try to speak with Inspector Nicholson again, since he wasn't
there the other day."

"Of course." Hadrian nodded toward Leach, who moved to
hold the door whilst Tilda climbed into the coach.

Tilda hesitated. She'd spent far too much time since the tea
yesterday thinking of her evolving feelings for Hadrian, and now

she was questioning where she ought to sit. If she took the forward-facing seat, he'd sit beside her as he'd done of late, and Tilda wasn't sure she wanted to be that close to him. She needed to focus on the investigation. But if she sat rear-facing, he would ask why, and she didn't want to have an awkward conversation.

Ultimately, she decided she would deal with her own awkwardness. She could sit beside him and keep her mind wholly on the investigation. It was imperative.

Settled on the forward-facing seat, Tilda tensed as she waited for Hadrian to sit beside her. Instead, he sat opposite her. She instantly relaxed.

She also suffered a wave of disappointment. Blast, this was irritating!

"We've a busy day and likely much to discuss," Hadrian said. "As we've realized in the past, sometimes it's easier if we're facing one another when we are deep in conversation." He flashed a smile.

"Yes, there is a great deal to accomplish, especially now that I've added this extra call at Great Marlborough Street."

"It's important we do that." Hadrian studied her a moment. "How long will we continue to fetch you from the end of the street instead of your house?"

Tilda exhaled. "I was hoping it would be tomorrow, but now that my mother has accepted an invitation to this infernal ball next week, I can only hope it will be the day after that."

Hadrian arched a brow at her. "You think your mother is going to abandon her campaign—whatever it is—so easily?"

"I can hope," Tilda grumbled.

"If it helps, I've also accepted Lord and Lady Trumbull's invitation."

Whilst Tilda was always glad for his company, in this case, it was the opposite of helpful. Now her mother would spend the evening trying to push them together. Tilda would have to go out of her way to stay clear of Hadrian when she wanted to do the opposite, particularly at a social event where she wouldn't know anyone and would feel completely out of place.

Perhaps she'd plead a terrible headache.

"I'm sorry you've been dragged into my mother's machinations," Tilda said. "I'm hoping to avoid going, especially since my mother didn't see fit to include my grandmother."

"I confess I found that a trifle…impolite."

"That is a nice way of saying rude." Tilda chuckled. "I want to say my mother means well, but I'm not sure she knows how to do that. I hope your mother wasn't put off by her behavior." Tilda didn't think that was possible, not when her mother had been entirely off-putting at the tea yesterday.

"She didn't say anything negative," Hadrian replied, though Tilda wasn't sure she believed him.

"Well, I do apologize for my mother's shameless attempts at matching us. Please convey that to your mother, if you don't mind."

"I will, but it isn't necessary." His brow creased with sympathetic concern. "Has your mother always tried to persuade you to wed?"

"Not always, no. Which is why this is particularly frustrating. I made it clear to her several years ago that I had no interest in marrying. Since she only comes to London once a year, it wasn't an issue. Indeed, I believe she was relieved to not have to do anything to shepherd me toward marriage. Her purpose in coming here now was to convince me to stop investigating. Marriage only became of interest to her when she met you and saw that we are associates. She ridiculously thinks we are poised for a romantic relationship."

Tilda wished she hadn't said the last, for she could feel heat rising in her face. Was her skin flushing? Could Hadrian see? It was unfortunate that he was across the coach and not beside her, for she wasn't able to turn her head away from him.

"I don't want to tell Inspector Nicholson that we're meeting with Timms today," Tilda said, eager to change the topic. "I only want to determine what he's done to locate Mrs. Goodwin's missing pieces."

Hadrian nodded. Thankfully, he didn't appear to have noticed Tilda's reaction to their conversation. "That makes sense."

They arrived at the police station and made their way inside. Right away, Tilda glimpsed Jurgens in the charge room speaking to someone. A sliver of unease raced up her spine.

She met Hadrian's gaze. "I can't shake the feeling there's something very wrong with what happened to my father. All the police who were present that night lied. One of them has now been murdered and was carrying my father's name in his pocket. And another now works for the Home Office. It's all suspicious."

Hadrian's brows drew together. "I agree."

They went to the desk and asked the constable on duty if they could speak with Inspector Nicholson.

"I believe he's here," the constable said. "What are your names?"

"Lord Ravenhurst and Miss Wren," Hadrian replied.

The constable's eyes widened as he regarded Hadrian. "Just a moment." He hurried through a doorway and returned quite quickly. "This way." He led them again to the small office adjacent to the entry area.

Inspector Nicholson was in his late thirties with blond hair and moss-green eyes. He stood as they entered, revealing that he was shorter than most police, like Inspector Teague. The Metropolitan Police had a height requirement, and both of them seemed to just meet that.

"Good afternoon, Inspector," Tilda said in her most professional tone. "I'm Miss Wren and I'm investigating Mrs. Goodwin's missing silver."

Surprise and disbelief flashed over Nicholson's round face. "You're doing what now?"

"She's investigating the theft of Mrs. Goodwin's silver," Hadrian said loudly, as if the inspector suffered from hearing loss.

"I'm investigating that," Nicholson said with a slight scowl. "Did she hire you?"

"Yes," Tilda replied. "I've come to ask what inquiries you've made so I don't duplicate your fine efforts." Though it galled her to compliment the man when he was being disagreeable, Tilda knew she would obtain better results if she was pleasant or even deferential.

Nicholson straightened his shoulders. "That's wise of you."

"I understand you listed the items in the newspaper, and someone reported seeing them?" Tilda asked.

"That's right. They were seen at a jeweler's shop, but when I called on the owner, he said he didn't have those items."

"Did you believe him?" Tilda asked. "What I mean is, did you find him trustworthy?"

"I had no reason to think he wasn't." Nicholson lifted a shoulder. "It's very difficult to recover stolen items. And it's just as hard to apprehend the culprit, unfortunately. It's too bad Mrs. Goodwin is wasting her money on an investigator. I hope you aren't preying on the woman's sadness over her lost silver."

Hadrian glowered at the inspector. "I hope you aren't trying to insult Miss Wren."

Tilda touched Hadrian's arm briefly. "It's all right, Lord Ravenhurst." She used his name to remind the inspector of Hadrian's rank. "I'm sure Inspector Nicholson is just being protective of Mrs. Goodwin." She smiled at the inspector despite wanting to kick him in the shin.

"Precisely," Nicholson said, though he cast a nervous glance at Hadrian. "How are you involved with this investigation, my lord? Are you a friend of Mrs. Goodwin's?"

"I work with Miss Wren. I would appreciate if you would

share all the information you've collected regarding these stolen items. We mean to find Mrs. Goodwin's missing silver, regardless of how *difficult* you say it will be."

"The jeweler is Timms in Greville Street, if you'd care to call on him." Nicholson pursed his lips. "I already searched his shop, and I didn't find any of Mrs. Goodwin's items."

"Have you any leads on the missing salver or tureen?" Tilda asked.

"As I said, it's very difficult to find stolen items, and it has been several weeks now. I do not expect to locate them." Nicholson exhaled. "It's a shame, but I did advise Mrs. Goodwin to accept that her items would not be returned."

"Did you check with other divisions about missing silver?" Tilda asked, though she suspected she already knew the answer.

"I did not," Nicholson said flatly. "This is a simple theft, Miss Wren, not a conspiracy or anything that would indicate coordination with other divisions."

"Of course," Tilda murmured. "Thank you for your time, Inspector."

"We'll let you know if you can be of further help," Hadrian said with a fleeting, humorless smile.

Tilda turned and left the office. She led Hadrian from the station.

"That was a supreme waste of time," Hadrian scoffed as they walked to the coach.

"Not entirely," Tilda said. "We have confirmation that Nicholson's investigation was not at all thorough."

"Will you be checking with other divisions about silver thefts?" Hadrian asked. "I hadn't even thought of that. This is why you're the investigator, and I'm your humble assistant."

They arrived at the coach, and Hadrian directed Leach to take them to Mr. Timms's shop in Greville Street. Inside, Hadrian again sat in the rear-facing seat opposite Tilda.

"I will speak to Teague about it," Tilda said. "Unfortunately, Nicholson is correct in that most stolen items are not recovered. However, after our initial visit with Timms, I'm confident he's hiding something. I am optimistic we may find at least some of Mrs. Goodwin's silver."

Hadrian inclined his head. "I am too. I hope we'll have good luck with Timms today."

Tilda hoped so too. Then she could turn her mind to investigating her father's murder. She was both glad for the distraction of Mrs. Goodwin's case and agitated that she couldn't put her full focus on untangling a decade-old web of deceit.

~

They arrived at Mr. Timms's shop, and Hadrian helped Tilda from the coach. "Ready to resume our roles?"

She gave him a saucy look that stirred sensations in Hadrian that were not at all appropriate for this time and place. "Most certainly." Tilda linked her arm through his, and they strolled across the street and into the shop.

Mr. Timms looked up as they entered and immediately leapt from his chair behind the desk. He hurried to the glass display cabinet and smiled broadly at them. "Welcome, welcome. I'm so pleased you've returned. As promised, I have several pieces of silver for you. Let me fetch them."

The jeweler removed a ring of keys from his pocket as he turned from the case and went through a doorway. He returned a moment later with two salvers and placed them on the glass cabinet. "Here are the first items. These are Hester Bateman salvers, of course. I'll be back with the Balzac pieces." He disappeared once more.

Tilda frowned. "Neither of these salvers are Mrs. Goodwin's." She gestured to the one on the right. "This has an armorial etching, but it's not the one she described."

Timms emerged once more, this time with a large tureen which he set on the glass cabinet beside the salvers. "This is a Balzac. It's quite special. I've two more Balzac pieces," he said excitedly before ducking through the doorway once more.

Tilda sucked in a breath and glanced at Hadrian. "That's Mrs. Goodwin's tureen."

Hadrian's pulse ticked up. "You're sure?"

"Positive. It has the fighting stags on the lid." Tilda turned slightly toward him. "I found it interesting that both the Balzac and the Bateman pieces stolen from Mrs. Goodwin feature stags."

"But not the other items?" Hadrian asked.

Tilda shook her head as Timms returned with a bowl and a salt and pepper shaker set. She picked up the tureen. "This is heavier than I anticipated," she said with a laugh. "Wherever did you find such a piece?"

Timms glanced toward Hadrian. "I believe his lordship said provenance did not matter." His tone was sly.

Gasping softly, Tilda handed the tureen to Hadrian and leaned slightly toward Timms. "Does that mean it was stolen?" she asked in a breathless whisper.

"It means I am not aware of who owned it before, just who I obtained it from."

Tilda affected a faint pout for a brief moment and once more pivoted toward Hadrian. "Is it bad that I was hoping for something with a checkered past? Those pieces have secrets. They speak to me," she added dramatically.

Hadrian silently applauded Tilda's acting—and her method. This was an excellent way to try to coax the truth from Timms. Hadrian set the tureen down on the cabinet and fixed an expectant stare on the jeweler. "You heard my dear friend. This tureen will be more valuable to her if it has a story to tell." He winked at Timms

Timms chuckled. "I can certainly fabricate something if that would help. I'm afraid I don't know anything extraordinary about this piece, except that it is a Balzac from around 1760. I do imagine it's changed hands many times, likely smuggled here by a family fleeing the Terror in France." He waggled his brows as if he were discussing something charming and not a horribly violent period of time. But then, they were encouraging him to be salacious.

Hadrian smiled. "I don't think my friend wants fabrications. Surely you know something. From whom did you purchase this? Or did you *not* purchase it?" Hadrian arched his brow.

"I didn't steal it," Timms replied coolly. "Nor will I disclose the person who asked me to sell it for them. I must keep confidences, or I will lose important clients."

"You're selling it for someone?" Tilda asked. She flashed a smile at Timms that made Hadrian's blood thrum. "Would you tell us if we paid more?"

The jeweler seemed to hesitate. But he ended up shaking his head. "There is nothing I can tell you, unfortunately."

Hadrian found his reply puzzling. Timms seemed an avaricious fellow. Hadrian withdrew several banknotes from his pocket and fanned them on the cabinet. "You're certain?"

Tilda edged closer to Hadrian and touched his arm. He turned his head toward her, and she gave him a heated stare rife with anticipation. He knew it was for their performance, but how he wished she would look at him like that because she couldn't help herself.

Timms stared at the money for a long moment before lifting his eyes to Hadrian. "You understand that I can't betray the trust of my clients. They must never know that I told you anything."

"It's not as if you're going to give us their direction," Hadrian said with a short burst of laughter. He sobered and placed another banknote with the others. "Are you?"

The jeweler's features darkened and grew guarded. "Why would you want to know that?"

"We don't," Tilda said quickly, and Hadrian realized he'd

pressed a little too hard. "His lordship was in jest. We are going to buy the tureen. I just want my story. Please?"

Sweeping the banknotes up from the cabinet, Timms nodded. "The man who brought the tureen occasionally brings other items he asks me to sell."

"Is he a thief?" Tilda asked with a rapturous exhalation.

"I don't believe so," Timms replied. "At least he doesn't look like how I imagine a thief would appear."

"In what way?" Tilda pressed.

"He looks more like a man of business. He wears a dark gray suit of clothing and round spectacles. And he speaks in a cultured tone. Like you," he said with a flattering smile.

"I see," Tilda murmured. "Well, that is fascinating. I wonder how he obtained this magnificent tureen."

"He could still be a thief," Hadrian said. "One ought to never judge a person by their appearance. Or their speaking manner."

"That is true." Tilda gestured at the jeweler. "Just look at Mr. Timms. He is a fine jeweler with a respectable business and yet he's likely a receiver. Or…what's that other word?" She blinked at Hadrian.

"A fence?" Hadrian supplied.

Timms put up a hand—the one that wasn't gripping Hadrian's money. "Wait just one moment. I never said this tureen was stolen."

"No, you did not, but it is just the same," Tilda said with an edge of smugness that made Hadrian want to smile.

"You can't know that," Timms sputtered.

Tilda gave him an icy stare. "Indeed, we can. The owner hired me to find it. I do thank you for your assistance."

Timms paled. "I didn't know it was stolen. As I said, the man who asked me to sell it is respectable!"

"And yet, this tureen belongs to my client and will be returned to her." Tilda flicked a glance at Hadrian. "I do think you should return Lord Ravenhurst's money as well, unless you'd prefer we involve the police."

Now ashen, Timms thrust the banknotes back at Hadrian. "What am I to tell *my* client?"

"That he gave you a stolen tureen to sell," Hadrian said as he tucked the money back into his coat pocket. "Or we could tell him for you. What is his name, and where can we find him?" Hadrian presumed this was the information Tilda wanted. He glanced at her, and she looked upon him with approval—and perhaps admiration.

Timms clasped his hands together as his eyes darted to the left and then the right. He appeared quite agitated. "I don't know where you can find him. His name is Dorris."

"What of the other items he brought you at the same time as this tureen?" Tilda asked.

"There wasn't anything else." Timms put his hand to his chest. "I swear."

"We know there was," Tilda said sternly. "In fact, the police came here to ask you about the pieces—a pair of candlesticks, a teapot with a matching sugar bowl—and you lied to them. Someone reported seeing those items for sale here. Now that we know you have the tureen, it's not difficult to believe the person who saw the other items wasn't mistaken. Shall I have Inspector Nicholson return to question you again? Or perhaps he'll just come to arrest you as a receiver of stolen items."

"I didn't know they were stolen!" Timms waved his hands as his face flushed. "Yes, I had those items, but I sold them."

Tilda pursed her lips at Timms. "Let's hope you keep good records so that we may regain those pieces and return them to my client."

"And why didn't you show us you had the tureen the other day?" Hadrian asked. "You clearly had it then."

Timms's gaze dipped, and his voice lowered. "I thought I had a buyer for it, but I did not."

"What of the salver that was stolen from my client?" Tilda asked. "Did you already sell that as well?"

"There wasn't a salver," Timms declared. He blinked at Tilda.

Hadrian fixed a dark glower on the jeweler. "Why should we believe you amidst all the lies?"

"I swear on my wife's grave there was no salver." Timms swallowed, and his features creased with defeat. "I suspected the items might be stolen, but I didn't know for sure."

"Have you sold items for Mr. Dorris before?" Tilda asked.

The jeweler hung his head. "Yes."

"When and what were they?" Tilda pulled her notebook from her reticule and began to make notes.

"I would have to review my records, but it's been some time since he was last here, over a year. Before that, he came perhaps a handful of times, starting about twelve years ago."

Hadrian was shocked to hear it had been so long. "You truly don't know where we might find Mr. Dorris?"

Timms shook his head.

"Describe what he looks like," Hadrian commanded.

"He wears gold-rimmed spectacles. His hair is dark brown with a bit of gray at the temples, and his side whiskers come down to about here." Timms indicated a spot in front of his ear.

"Is he tall, short? Broad-shouldered? Spindly?" Tilda asked.

"I'd say tall," Timms replied. "Not as broad in the shoulders as his lordship." He glanced at Hadrian.

Tilda gestured toward the back doorway. "Fetch your records then, so I may see what other items Dorris gave to you to sell and the dates on which he did so. Ravenhurst will go with you."

Hadrian moved behind the glass cabinet and accompanied the man through the doorway to his back office. There, Timms pulled some books from a shelf. He glanced nervously at Hadrian, then returned to the front where Tilda waited. Hadrian glanced around the office, but nothing of import stood out to him. How he wished he had his power! The things he could learn from touching Timms or the tureen… Not being able to see Timms's memories was bloody infuriating.

It took some time for Timms to go through his books and find the dates when Dorris had brought him stolen items. He read out the date and a description of each item as well as what he sold it for and how much he paid Dorris. He, of course, kept a fee for himself.

Tilda wrote everything down with meticulous care. Hadrian watched over her shoulder, impressed at how quickly and neatly she made notes.

When they'd finished, Tilda closed her notebook and tucked it back into her reticule. "Explain what happens after you sell one of these items for Mr. Dorris." She looked at him expectantly.

"I send him a note and—"

"You *do* know where he lives," Hadrian snapped.

"No, I give the note to the publican of the Yellow Dog in Leather Lane. Dorris calls the next day, always in the evening after I close, and I pay him."

Tilda slid a look at Hadrian who nodded faintly. They would visit the Yellow Dog next before going to Scotland Yard.

Straightening her shoulders, Tilda regarded Timms with authority. "This is what will happen next. You will dispatch a note to the publican of the Yellow Dog. You will not inform Mr. Dorris that you know the tureen was stolen. Obviously, you will not tell him about us."

Timms regarded them warily. "What do you plan to do?"

"We will be here when Dorris arrives tomorrow after you close. If you warn him in advance, and he doesn't come, we'll have Inspector Nicholson here in a trice." Tilda inclined her head at Timms. "We'll wait whilst you write the note."

The jeweler went to his desk and wrote out a note. "I'll take it over after you leave. I promise."

"If you do not follow our instructions, Inspector Nicholson *will* pay you a visit." Tilda narrowed her eyes at Timms. "And

Lord Ravenhurst will ensure you are prosecuted for your crimes. I'm sure Mr. Dorris is not the only person who provides you with items you claim aren't stolen."

"I will do everything you've said." Timms came back to the glass cabinet. "Thank you for giving me the chance to make things right."

Hadrian didn't think that was the man's motivation at all. He wanted to preserve himself. What Hadrian wondered was whether Tilda would ensure he was prosecuted anyway. He suspected she would, and Hadrian wholeheartedly supported that.

"Do not make a mess of things," Tilda warned. She looked to Hadrian. "Will you carry the tureen?"

Hadrian nodded. "Of course."

Timms turned and moved toward a shelf beside the doorway to the back of the shop. "I have a box." He took one from the shelf and brought it back to the cabinet.

Hadrian placed the tureen into the box. He didn't thank the man. "Deliver the note immediately, Mr. Timms. I don't wish to be disappointed." He used his haughtiest tone.

"No, my lord," Timms croaked.

Tilda turned from the cabinet and started toward the door. Hadrian moved to open it for her. After she stepped outside, he cast a final glare toward Timms before closing the door and joining Tilda on the pavement.

"That went well," he said.

"It was rather invigorating, wasn't it?" She smiled at him, and once again, his body reacted in ways it should not. He was in real danger, he realized. His heart was completely in peril. What was he going to do?

Tilda started across the street. Hadrian pulled himself from his brooding thoughts and hastened to catch up to her.

He saw a movement from the corner of his eye. A horse-drawn cart was moving much too fast for a city street. And it was heading right for Tilda.

Fear tore through Hadrian, icing his veins and seizing his lungs. His heart stopped as the world froze. He lunged for Tilda, desperate to push her out of the way, heedless of his own safety. He knew, with a crystal clarity, that he would gladly give his life for hers.

CHAPTER 9

*H*adrian dropped the box with the tureen before wrapping his arms around Tilda and carrying her as he raced toward the other side of the street. The small cart with its speeding horse flew past, but Hadrian's attention was entirely on Tilda and keeping her safe.

She blinked up at him as he held her in his arms. His heart was galloping faster than the horse had been.

"I didn't see the cart," Tilda said, sounding breathless. The pulse in her throat appeared to be moving as quickly as Hadrian's. "Thank goodness you did." Her eyes were a deep, earthy green, and Hadrian feared he could lose himself quite easily.

The emotion of the moment, coupled with what he'd been feeling all day, surged through him. Yes, his heart was imperiled—if love was a danger. For he was most definitely in love.

And he had to keep that to himself.

Leach approached them. "That was a near thing!"

Tilda stepped back, and Hadrian dropped his arms to his sides. They couldn't stand there embracing all day. Even if he wanted to.

Hadrian met Tilda's gaze. "Are you all right?"

"A little shaken, but I'm fine."

"I'm sorry to have startled you. I didn't really think. I just needed to move you from the path of the cart."

"I'm so glad." Tilda let out a nervous laugh. "What happened to the tureen?"

Hadrian turned his head and saw the box in the street. The tureen had fallen out. He also observed several bystanders watching them. One of them, a man who looked to be in his fifties, ambled toward them.

"I saw what 'appened," the observer said in an East London accent. "That cart was up the street. Started moving when ye came out of the shop. The driver whipped that 'orse into a gallop right fast."

Then it hadn't been accident. Hadrian's blood iced as fury rose within him. If he could find that driver, he would show the man true fear. "Did you happen to see the driver well enough to provide a description? I'm Lord Ravenhurst," he added, thinking that his rank may be of use in this situation.

"Only that 'e wore a wide-brimmed 'at and it was pulled low over 'is 'ead." The man gave Hadrian an apologetic frown. "I wish I'd seen more, my lord."

"It's all right. I appreciate you sharing what you know." Hadrian withdrew a coin from his pocket and pressed it into the man's hand. "If you think of anything else, please call at Ravenhurst House on Curzon Street."

The man nodded. "I'm Elias Parker. Ye can find me in Cheapside. I own a butcher shop with me son."

"Thank you, Mr. Parker," Tilda said.

As Parker departed, Hadrian looked to Leach. "What did you see?"

"The cart came out of nowhere. I wasn't facing that direction, unfortunately." The coachman looked angry. "I'm terribly sorry, my lord."

"You needn't be," Hadrian assured him. He turned and loudly

asked the other bystanders if anyone else saw what happened or could identify the driver. Two observers corroborated Parker's story but weren't able to describe the driver beyond the hat. One of them added that the horse was brown, which Leach confirmed. That much he'd seen.

Hadrian thanked the bystanders and paid them as well, asking them to call on him if they learned of anything else as he'd done with Parker. Finally, he went to the box and tureen, picking up the latter first.

He was immediately swept away to a different time and place. It was dark—nighttime—and he was in a dining room. He could tell because a small lantern sat on the edge of the table and cast a faint light. Hadrian smelled tallow and felt both urgency and apprehension.

There was another person in addition to whose memory Hadrian was seeing. It was a man dressed in simple clothing made of rough fabric—it wasn't difficult to conclude that he was lower class or at least dressed that way. He was short and stocky, with a wide mouth and a pockmarked face. His hair had receded from his forehead, and Hadrian would estimate he was in his middle-thirties. Most importantly, he clutched a salver in his hand. Hadrian couldn't see the top of it, where the armorial etching would be, but the beading on the edge was visible. That alone revealed it as a Hester Bateman design, and he was sure it was Mrs. Goodwin's. Careful to look down at the hands of the person whose memory he was experiencing, Hadrian noted that he held the tureen. He wore knit gloves with holes in the forefinger and thumb of the undeniably masculine right hand.

"Hadrian, you need to move out of the street."

Tilda's voice broke through the vision, and Hadrian blinked, which banished it completely. Sharp pain splintered through his head, and he grimaced. He hadn't missed that aspect of his ability.

Clutching the tureen and picking up the box, Hadrian turned and joined Tilda on the pavement. Her green eyes were dark, and her features creased as she looked at him with urgency. She clearly wanted to ask him something but could not in front of Leach.

"Do you still want to go to Scotland Yard?" Leach asked.

"Yes," Tilda replied quickly. She turned to Hadrian. "Or should we go to the Yellow Dog first?"

Hadrian put the tureen back into the box. "I'm wondering if we should speak with the publican today and try to find Dorris right away or just wait to interview Dorris until tomorrow evening when he shows up at the jeweler's shop."

She looked at him shrewdly. "I've been contemplating the same. I think we should try to find him through the publican. If we can't, we'll catch him tomorrow evening. We must prepare Leach to fetch Inspector Nicholson if Dorris doesn't come. We'll use a signal through the window to tell him to go."

"Excellent plan," Hadrian said, glancing at Leach.

The coachman nodded. "I'm glad to help."

Hadrian frowned slightly. "Even if we've convinced Timms not to warn Dorris, do you think the publican at the Yellow Dog may deter him from coming?"

Tilda's eyes narrowed. "We'll make it worth his while not to do so."

"You need me to bribe him?" Hadrian asked.

"You can if you prefer, but I do have money for such purposes. You're just usually faster than I am," she added with a smile. "I'll include the expense with Mrs. Goodwin's invoice."

"Then let us go to the Yellow Dog." Hadrian gave Leach the direction and escorted Tilda to the coach.

Hadrian sat down beside her this time. He knew they would discuss their encounter with Timms, but he wanted to be close to her. Not just because he'd recognized the strength and truth of his feelings, but because he'd been afraid he would lose her. He simply didn't want to be too far from her, even across the coach.

Before they started moving, Tilda turned toward him. "You

saw something when you picked up the tureen, didn't you? Has your power returned?"

Hadrian had been so overcome with the realization of his love for Tilda and the fright of the racing cart that he'd failed to truly feel the return of his ability. He was both relieved and elated. And his head still ached.

"Yes. The moment I touched the tureen, I had a vision."

She stared at him, her expression incredulous. "What happened to provoke it to return?"

"I don't know, and I won't question it. I do hope it's here to stay, however. Despite the pain." He grimaced again as he rubbed his temple.

Tilda opened her reticule and withdrew a small bottle. She pulled off her glove and opened the bottle, then pressed the mouth against her forefinger. She tipped the bottle then transferred it to her other hand. "It's lavender," she said as she spread the oil across his forehead with her fingertips. She repeated her actions as Hadrian lowered his hand and surrendered to her ministrations.

He was shocked that she was tending to him in such a personal way, but also delighted, particularly because of her thoughtfulness. "You're carrying lavender oil for me?"

She met his gaze. "It seemed prudent. I'm only sorry I didn't think of it sooner."

"You've kept it in your reticule, even though my power has been absent?"

"Of course. I wanted to be prepared for when it returned."

When, not if. She'd believed he would regain his ability, even when he'd begun to lose hope. His love for her surged within him. How was he going to keep this wondrous feeling inside?

He simply would. Because he must.

She finished with the lavender oil and returned the bottle to her reticule. Then she drew on her glove. "Better?"

It was actually. The pain was still there, but it had soothed. "Quite."

"Please tell me what you saw," Tilda said eagerly. "I can't wait another moment."

Hadrian chuckled. "I don't want to keep you in suspense."

Except he had to, for the coach had stopped and Leach opened the door.

Tilda put her hand on Hadrian's sleeve. "I don't think we should go in until after Timms delivers his note. I don't want to be speaking with the publican when Timms arrives."

Hadrian nodded. "That makes sense. We'll watch for him." He turned his head toward the coachman. "Leach, we'll let ourselves out when we want to go in."

"Very good, my lord." The coachman closed the door.

Tilda's eyes glittered with excited impatience. "Now, tell me everything."

Hadrian related what he'd seen in exacting detail, including the smell and the sensations he'd felt. When he finished, Tilda cocked her head. "You were seeing Mrs. Goodwin's dining room. She had the silver on display. There were two thieves?"

"At least, but I don't think there were others." Hadrian was fairly confident on that point. "I was in the memory long enough that I would have known if someone else was with them. It was just the pair."

"And the man whose memory you experienced had the tureen, whilst the other man had the salver? It's too bad you couldn't see the armorial etching."

"I've no doubt it's the one we're looking for," Hadrian said. "What do you suppose the connection is between the thieves and Dorris?"

Tilda's brow creased. "The thieves could be working for Dorris. I am very much looking forward to speaking with him."

Hadrian eyed the tureen in the box, which he'd placed on the opposite seat. "Are we keeping that for now or returning it to

Mrs. Goodwin? I confess I'd like to keep it. I want to really focus on these thieves and Dorris, and also try to see something else."

"Do you think you can do that?"

In the past, Hadrian had seen different visions from touching the same thing. He'd also experienced the same memory from different points of view. He'd begun to be able to direct what he saw, at least somewhat. He owed that to Captain Vale, who'd introduced the idea and said it was possible. Hadrian needed to write to Vale and tell him he'd regained his ability.

"I do," Hadrian said in answer to Tilda's query. "What about the other items that Dorris brought to Timms? I was surprised their relationship went back twelve years."

"There doesn't seem to be a specific connection between the items," Tilda said. "They were all silver or jewelry, but it's not as if they're all Balzac or all Bateman. Or all stags," she added wryly. "What I would like to know is why Mrs. Goodwin's salver wasn't given to Timms to sell with the other items."

"I found that peculiar too. Hopefully we can find out why from Dorris." Hadrian glanced out the window. "I haven't seen Timms, have you?"

"No, but perhaps he went in through a back door." Tilda arched a brow. "I might do that if I were conducting his shady business. Let's go in."

Hadrian opened the door, and Leach moved to hold it. After stepping from the coach, Hadrian helped Tilda down. They turned toward the pub, where a sign with a yellow dog hung over the door. Hadrian escorted Tilda inside.

The common room was small with low ceilings and a lingering scent of ale. A few patrons sat at tables, and a barkeep with somewhat unkempt blond hair stood behind the bar, speaking with a patron who clasped a tankard.

Hadrian inclined his head toward the barkeep. "Perhaps that is the publican."

"Let's find out. You should do the talking. He'd likely rather hear from a man." Tilda made a slight face.

"Sadly true," Hadrian replied softly. He gently brushed his hand along the small of her back as they approached the bar. He'd done that many times since he'd known her, but now it felt different. Probably because *he* felt different. He was now a man in love.

The barkeep moved along the bar from the man with the ale toward Hadrian and Tilda. He was around Hadrian's age and of middling height with thick, dark curls and a wide mustache. "Afternoon."

"Good afternoon," Hadrian said. "We're looking for the publican. Are you him?"

"No. That's Akers. He's not here."

Hadrian looked over at Tilda, who frowned faintly. He returned his attention to the barkeep. "Do you expect him back soon?"

The barkeep shrugged. "Mayhap. Mayhap not."

"Thank you." Hadrian turned away from the bar, and Tilda did the same.

She took a few steps and exhaled. "I suppose we must rely on catching Dorris tomorrow evening."

"That seems our best plan."

"Then let us go to Scotland Yard," Tilda said.

Hadrian nodded, and they departed the pub. He helped her into the coach, and even the touch of her gloved hand in his was a keen reminder of his newly acknowledged emotion toward her.

⁓

As they drove to Scotland Yard, Tilda's mind was awhirl with the events of the afternoon. They'd made great progress with Mrs. Goodwin's case. Now it was time to turn her thoughts to her father's murder. Though she also planned to tell

Teague about Mrs. Goodwin's case and solicit his opinion about Dorris and his long history of having stolen items fenced.

The thing bothering Tilda most at the moment was the coach that had nearly struck her and Hadrian. It did not sound as if it was an accident. Since it had occurred outside the jeweler's shop, was it to do with Mrs. Goodwin's case?

Tilda couldn't shake the notion that it wasn't, that the act was instead linked to her father's murder and Tilda's interest in it. Something had been hidden at the time of Thomas Wren's death, and Tilda was now seeking to uncover it. That could very well have provoked someone to ensure the truth, whatever it was, remained buried.

They arrived at Scotland Yard and, fortunately, Teague was there. They went upstairs to his office, and he greeted them warmly.

"It's coincidental that you would stop by this afternoon," Teague said to Tilda. "I was planning to call on you on my way home later. I've been assigned to reopen the investigation into your father's murder."

An immense wave of relief washed over Tilda. "I'm so glad. I was hoping it would be you."

Teague's auburn brows rose. "You knew the case was to be reopened?"

Tilda nodded and looked toward Hadrian. "Ravenhurst called on the Home Secretary yesterday."

The inspector's brows arched even higher as he regarded Hadrian. "Did you? It appears an earl is able to affect police investigations." He gestured to the seating area. "Shall we sit?"

When they were all situated in chairs, Hadrian replied to Teague. "There was more than adequate reason to reopen the matter. It never would have been closed if the true facts had been documented. Not that we've seen the file. The clerk was unable to locate it in B Division."

"That's because it would be kept in the Detective Branch—the death of a police sergeant is an important crime. Except it isn't there," Teague said with a frown. "When the case was assigned to me earlier today, I sent a constable to find the file. However, he returned empty-handed. I plan to speak with the constables and inspector who were on the case. Of course, one of them—Padgett—is dead, so I can't talk to him."

"We spoke with Jurgens the other day," Tilda said. "We encountered him at C Division as we were investigating another case. I'll tell you about the case later, as I'd like your opinion on something. Jurgens did not care for us inquiring about my father's case, particularly when we brought up what we learned after visiting Mr. Williams, the apothecary."

Teague's forehead creased. "That's the shop where Wren was killed?"

"*Allegedly*," Tilda said. "Williams told us there was not enough blood for my father to have been murdered there. When he pointed that out to the police, they told him the killer cleaned up." She rolled her eyes, and Teague let out a snort.

"No thief would take the time to clean up the murder of a police officer who interrupted his robbery." Teague scoffed. "They would run away as soon as possible, for they are now a murderer."

Tilda appreciated the inspector's sense. "Precisely. Furthermore, Mr. Williams indicated that he heard glass breaking and went downstairs to the shop. There would not have been time for the criminal to clean up. There would also have been evidence of his work—he would have had to use supplies from the apothecary's shop. It's simply unbelievable."

"I agree." Teague's features darkened. "Which means the police lied and are hiding something. You think your father was killed elsewhere?"

"He had to have been. The question is where. And why was he moved?"

"I shall endeavor to discover both those things. I'll speak with

Jurgens, as well as Lowther and Fellows." Teague gave his head a slight shake. "Hearing this information about Wren's death, I don't like that Lowther is assigned to Padgett's murder."

"I don't like it either," Tilda said. "Nor the fact that he has lied to me for years, all whilst pretending to care for me." The pain of his betrayal was still fresh.

"Fellows works for the Home Office now," Hadrian shared. "We found his elevation from constable to clerk following Tilda's father's death suspicious. That seems a strange path of advancement."

"It is unusual," Teague agreed with a wrinkled brow. "However, the timing of it may be nothing more than a coincidence. I prefer to let the evidence lead me and not lead the evidence to a conclusion I desire."

"As do I," Tilda said. "Is it too much to hope that you'll keep me abreast of your investigation?" she asked hopefully. She had a good relationship with Teague, and they'd worked together on several investigations. He'd always shared what he could, but she also knew this would be a highly sensitive matter, and he may have been tasked with abject confidentiality.

"I will to the best of my ability, though we must be careful. Your involvement will not be appreciated by some, and not just because you're a woman."

"Because she's Wren's daughter," Hadrian said flatly. "I should also like to be kept informed. That shouldn't be frowned upon since I'm the reason the investigation was reopened."

Teague met Hadrian's gaze. "That's true. I will use that as my reasoning for being in contact with you. You can always convey information to Miss Wren."

"I appreciate that," Tilda said softly. "Truly."

"I know how important this must be to you." Teague's expression was solemn. "I would do exactly what you are if my father had been murdered and facts were hidden, particularly since one of the men who may have buried the truth has been murdered."

"Why was he carrying my father's name in his pocket after all this time?"

"I am investigating that too—carefully, given Lowther's involvement," Teague replied. "I plan to search Padgett's lodging again."

Tilda sat slightly forward in her chair. "I would go with you, if you'd allow it."

"I'll consider it. I wouldn't want anyone to see you. The last thing I want is to be removed from the case."

"That is also the last thing I want," Tilda said. "I can disguise myself as a man. No one will know it's me."

Teague chuckled. "Of course. You've done that before."

During a past investigation, Tilda and Hadrian had gone to a gentleman's club to conduct an inquiry, and her disguise had been most convincing. Tilda smiled. "William Taylor from Somerset can make a reappearance."

"Speaking of Padgett, I noticed something about him at the inquest," Hadrian said. "The marks on his neck were clearly made by two hands choking him. I noticed an odd mark made by the left hand. It looked as though the killer was wearing a ring."

Teague nodded. "Very good. I recognized the same thing when I viewed the body. The coroner also made note of it, though he didn't say so during the inquest."

"We're looking for a man wearing a ring on his left hand," Tilda said. "I also plan to speak with Ezra Clement."

Exhaling, Teague's brows drew together. "I don't want him writing about this case."

Tilda shook her head. "I don't either, at least not now. He's a potential informant or witness. He has a connection with Padgett—Clement paid him for information on occasion, and it hasn't been terribly long since he last did so."

Teague fixed her with a direct stare. "I can't say I mind you making your own inquiries. I expected you to. However, and I don't wish to offend you, do you promise not to take matters into your own hands?"

"I would never." Tilda straightened her spine as she regarded Teague. "I seek justice, not vengeance."

"I thought so," Teague said. "But I would have been remiss if I didn't confirm that. May I expect you to share what you learn?"

"Certainly. You will be the one to ensure justice is served."

"We should mention something else that happened today," Hadrian said, his eyes darkening as he glanced at Tilda. "We were nearly run down by a speeding cart in the course of an investigation we're conducting. This happened on Greville Street."

Teague blinked at them. "You're sure it was intentional?"

"Witnesses said the cart started forward after we exited the shop we were visiting, then sped toward us," Tilda replied.

"Really, it raced toward Tilda," Hadrian clarified. "She started across the street before I did. I rushed to push her out of the way."

"Good heavens, that's horrible," Teague said. He shifted his focus to Tilda. "Do you think it was to do with your investigation?"

"I don't know. The case isn't terribly serious—I am merely searching for stolen items. I did want to tell you about it because it appears the man trafficking the items has been at this for at least a dozen years."

"That's a long time. Tell me about it."

Tilda related the details, from being hired by Mrs. Goodwin, to the items that were stolen, to tracking them to Timms's shop and obtaining a list of pieces brought by Dorris, and, finally, their intent to trap Dorris tomorrow evening.

"It sounds as though you may want to have an inspector or constable on hand when you catch Dorris."

"We spoke with the inspector assigned to the case, but he wasn't very helpful," Tilda said with disdain. "Nicholson at Great Marlborough Street."

Teague snorted. "He's fairly worthless, unfortunately. If you like, I can try to assign a constable from the Detective Branch to accompany you."

"I don't think I want to bring anyone from the Met into the meeting." Tilda wanted to obtain as much information from Dorris as possible without scaring him off. "I'm not sure Dorris is the man behind the thefts. I mean, he is, though there may be others involved." Dorris was not the man who'd committed the actual theft of Mrs. Goodwin's items, at least the most recent theft—that much they knew from the vision Hadrian had seen from the tureen. "I'd rather not involve the police until I know more. But I do thank you for the offer. I'd like to review whatever information the Met might have about the items stolen and fenced by Dorris."

"You said you have a list?" Teague asked. At Tilda's nod, he stroked his forehead a moment. "You'd have to review the occurrence books, but then you'd have to know which divisions' books you'd need." Teague grimaced. "You may want to query the criminal clerk in the Home Office and see if he can help in some way."

Tilda turned her head toward Hadrian. "Is that Fellows?"

"I'm not sure, but it actually might be."

"Perhaps you should call on him and ask about this matter," Tilda said. "I already stirred things up when we spoke with Jurgens."

Hadrian shrugged. "I was there too."

Teague looked at Tilda. "I think you should talk to Fellows with Ravenhurst. Request an appointment and provide a written list of the items you're seeking to track down in reports. I'll be curious how he responds to you. That could tell us something. If you don't mind doing this."

"Not at all," Tilda replied. Indeed, she would be glad for the chance to speak with Fellows, and this gave her the perfect opportunity. However, she thought it would be best if Hadrian made the request. "Do you mind setting the appointment?"

"Not at all," he replied with a quick smile.

"Depending on what you find, the Detective Branch may want to investigate," Teague said. "This sounds like a longtime operation." He fixed on Tilda. "Back to the incident in Greville Street today, if it wasn't to do with your investigation into the stolen items, what do you think was the purpose?"

"It could be linked to my father and my interest in his death," Tilda suggested. "We know the police are involved in covering up whatever really happened the night he was killed. We've spoken to several members of the Met about the murder and how the facts of the case don't make sense. As for the stolen items, we just learned of Dorris and confirmed Timms's fencing of stolen items today. It doesn't seem likely to me that anyone associated with their operation would seek to run us—or me—down. Not today, anyway."

"That seems logical." Teague frowned. "Though I do not like the idea that anyone from the Met may be behind trying to injure you."

"Or just frighten me," Tilda said. "I'm sure someone doesn't care for the questions I'm asking or the fact that the investigation has been reopened. You learned of that this morning?"

Teague nodded.

"And I spoke with the Home Secretary yesterday," Hadrian said. "It's entirely possible that someone within the Home Office or the Metropolitan Police was aware of the case being reopened yesterday afternoon. That would be plenty of time to set someone up to follow Tilda and frighten her." Hadrian looked at her with grave concern. "I don't like this one bit."

"Neither do I," Teague said darkly. "You've made an excellent connection—and point, Ravenhurst. I will do my best to move quickly on this investigation. Aside from wanting to ensure Miss Wren's safety and learning the truth, it seems there is a rot within the police or even the Home Office, and I will stamp it out," he vowed.

Tilda appreciated his commitment and enthusiasm. "Thank you." She rose, and the gentlemen joined her, then she and Hadrian departed.

They didn't speak again until they were settled in the coach on their way to Tilda's grandmother's house. "I'd like to talk with Clement tomorrow," Tilda said. "We should be able to find him at his coffee house around lunchtime. I also want to pay a visit to Lowther, but I'd rather call on him at home in the evening, after we conclude our business with Timms. I've been to the Lowthers' on several occasions. His wife is lovely and has always been very kind to me. I'd like to strike at Lowther where he's most vulnerable—in his home."

"Whilst that is calculating, I wholly agree. This man has lied to you, and it's time he revealed the truth. You're more likely to obtain that from him away from his work."

"I'm glad you think so." Tilda smiled at him. "Shall we visit the Home Office the day after tomorrow?"

Hadrian nodded. "That gives me time to have my secretary arrange an appointment with Fellows."

"Excellent. I appreciate you doing that. Please don't mention my name. I'd rather Fellows didn't know in advance that I will be there."

"An ambush." Hadrian chuckled. "I endorse that."

Tilda laughed with him. "I'm glad." She sobered and met his gaze. "I truly appreciate your support. You have always been a stalwart assistant—and friend. I feel I'm relying on you more as the latter in this case, and I am grateful."

His eyes warmed with affection, and he smiled in that way that made Tilda's stomach quiver as if butterflies were trapped inside. She was becoming increasingly aware that her feelings for him might actually surpass friendship. But now wasn't the time for such thoughts. She needed to keep her focus on finding her father's true killer.

CHAPTER 10

It was too late to call on Tilda, but Hadrian didn't care. He had to see her.

After dining and conducting business at his club, Hadrian had gone home, eager to attempt to see a memory from the mirror he'd purchased from Timms. He'd been nervous that his ability might vanish again, but it hadn't. And now he had to tell Tilda what he'd seen.

Leach stopped in front of Tilda's grandmother's house, and Hadrian didn't wait for him to open the door of the coach. Leaping down to the pavement, Hadrian waved at Leach. "I'm not sure how long I'll be."

As he approached the door, he hoped he wouldn't be causing trouble for Tilda. He knew her mother would make much of his visit.

Hadrian barely knocked before Vaughn opened the door.

"Good evening, my lord," the butler said with a measure of surprise. "We weren't expecting you."

"No." Hadrian met the man's gaze, thinking that if Vaughn wasn't stooped, he would have been one of the few people

Hadrian looked up at. "I've important information to share with Miss Wren regarding our investigation. It couldn't wait until tomorrow."

Vaughn's mouth pulled into a brief smile. "That sounds exciting. I'll fetch Miss Wren, if you'd care to wait in the parlor."

"I will, thank you." Hadrian removed his hat and gloves and set them on the table in the entrance hall. He paused a moment, struck by how comfortable he felt in this house. That made him smile.

He went into the parlor and stood near the hearth. His attention was drawn to the photograph of Tilda's father in his police uniform. Hadrian hated to think of how he'd died. It wasn't fair.

Tilda entered a few minutes later. She wore a simple gown made of brown cotton—something she wouldn't wear out. It was rather outdated, as all her wardrobe had been when they'd met. He understood why she wouldn't bother to purchase new clothing that no one would see, not on the household's limited budget.

"Hadrian, I'm surprised to see you. Vaughn said you had exciting news?"

"Yes." Hadrian grinned. He was relieved his power had returned and that it had shown him something useful. He was also happy to see her, even though they'd only parted a few hours ago. "May we sit?"

Tilda moved to the settee and sat, angling herself toward the vacant side, which seemed a clear invitation to him that he should join her there. Hadrian also pivoted his body so they were facing one another.

He immediately launched into his tale of what had happened. "After my dinner at the club, I went home and sought to see a memory with the mirror I purchased from Timms."

"I take it you were successful?" Her eyes glowed with curiosity and zeal.

"Yes, but it took time. I sat down with the mirror, and before touching it, I focused my mind on Timms and on Dorris. I tried to summon an image of what Dorris looked like based on Timms's description. I also thought of what we know of Dorris, that he's been bringing silver and jewelry to Timms for over a decade.

"At first, I only saw Timms's shop and various patrons. Based on the fashions, I would say the memory was of an event that occurred several years ago."

Tilda's eyes rounded. "How many visions did you see?"

"Several over the course of a few hours." He grimaced. "Before you ask, I took breaks in between, and yes, I did suffer a terrible headache, but it was worth the pain. I finally saw Dorris. It had to be him, as he matched Timms's description, and he had the mirror. He set it down on a piece of fabric. I believe it was draped over the glass cabinet."

"If he had the mirror…" Tilda sucked in a breath.

"I could see his memories." Hadrian nearly laughed with his giddiness.

"And did you?" Tilda breathed. "I'm afraid to ask what this cost you in terms of agony."

It had been rather awful, but Hadrian had drunk two glasses of whisky and bathed his face in lavender water. He'd also smoothed lavender oil into his temples and forehead, as Tilda had done.

"Again, it was worth it, because I focused on Dorris and the mirror." He stopped abruptly and held up his hand. "In my eagerness, I'm skipping ahead. First, I must tell you that there were other items on the cloth when he set the mirror down. And I am sure they matched some of those that Timms described today—these were the first things Dorris brought to Timms twelve years ago and that Timms had recorded in his ledger."

"The silver stag candlesticks, the pearl and garnet earrings, and the snuffbox with the armorial crest?"

"You remembered all that?" Hadrian asked. He withdrew a

small notebook from his pocket. "I wrote all that down after the vision. I recalled the stag candlesticks as being from the first batch of items from Dorris. Your memory is astonishing."

Tilda chuckled. "Well, I have also reviewed my notes extensively. In fact, I was doing so when you arrived." She sobered, her eyes narrowing. "You saw the mirror twelve years ago. Timms must have given it to his wife instead of selling it."

"That was my thought as well."

Eyes alight with excitement, Tilda leaned toward him. "What did you see?"

"I saw Dorris meeting with a pair of men. I recognized one of them as the thief in my vision from the tureen." Hadrian had made the connection immediately, and he'd almost been jolted from the vision. "But he appeared younger. His face was thinner, and his hair had not yet receded."

"So Dorris is directly connected to the thieves!" Tilda clasped her hands together and grinned at Hadrian. "How happy I am that your visions have returned."

"No happier than I am," Hadrian said with a laugh. "We'll have much to discuss with Mr. Dorris tomorrow evening."

"We will indeed. This is splendid, Hadrian. I'm so glad you came to tell me, despite the hour."

Hadrian glanced at the clock. It was nearly ten. A truly terrible time to call like this. "I hope my presence won't be troubling for you."

"Because of my mother?" Tilda shook her head. "She retired early, thankfully. And my grandmother had just gone up before you arrived, else she would probably have come with me to greet you."

"That would have been...inconvenient." Hadrian couldn't think of a better word.

"Quite. Though I would have told her that we needed to discuss the investigation, and it would bore her. Still, her presence would mean I would have had to wait to hear your brilliant news."

"I'm not even finished yet," Hadrian said, enjoying the slight widening of her eyes in response.

"Please continue," she urged with a wave of her hand. "Did you see what happened between Dorris and the thieves? Or perhaps where they were located? Could you tell the time of the memory based on their clothing?"

Hadrian chuckled. "One of the thieves handed Dorris a bag, and the other—the one I recognized—had a painting."

"A painting?" Tilda asked in surprise. "So they don't just steal silver and jewelry. Did you see the painting?"

"A little. It was angled, but I could see it was a portrait of a woman. I think her clothing was from the 1780s or so." Hadrian moved on to her next question. "I don't know where they were, but it was dark. There was a lantern on a table. There was also a fireplace behind the thieves. I believe they were in a residence."

"You picked up so many details." Tilda's brow furrowed. "I hope you used some lavender for your pain."

"I did, in fact. Thank you for asking. I did have to rest a bit before coming here, which was most difficult."

She nodded. "I'm sure. I can see how eager you were to share everything—I would have been the same."

"To address your last question, I am not exactly sure of the time of the vision, but since I was seeing Dorris's memory from the mirror, we know it happened at least twelve years ago. I don't think I would see any of his memories from the time he was no longer in possession of the mirror, unless he's somehow touched it again since giving it to Timms."

"That's an excellent point," Tilda said. "And it helps us narrow the time of this memory. What about their clothing? Did it look as though it was from the mid 1850s?"

"I couldn't say. The thieves were dressed in dark, nondescript garments."

"No matter. You certainly obtained a great deal of other details. Well done, Hadrian." She leaned forward again. "I shouldn't assume you are done. Is there more?"

He heard the hope in her voice. "In fact, there is. I also handled my watch in an effort to see one of Jurgens's memories. Whilst I did glimpse something, it wasn't of use. I only saw one of his memories at Great Marlborough Street. I recognized the charge room."

Tilda shook her head. "I can't believe you suffered through all those visions. Your head must have felt as though it was splitting in two."

"It was painful, but I'd do it again. I *will* do it again in case there is more to see. The lavender helped immensely. As did a tumbler—or two—of whisky." He winked at her.

"That is comforting," she murmured with a smile. "I can see you're managing all right, and I'm so pleased. You must be relieved to know that your ability is apparently here to stay."

"I certainly hope so."

"What do you think prompted its return?" she asked.

Hadrian had been contemplating that, and he wasn't sure. He gave Tilda a sheepish look. "I must confess something to you. The day you invited me to accompany you to meet with Mrs. Goodwin, I was unable because I went to see Captain Vale. I wanted to consult with him about my ability vanishing."

Tilda stared at him. "You kept that from me?"

She sounded hurt. He hated that. Regret ate at him. "I was worried the power was gone forever. I didn't want to discuss it. I'm sorry. It's not that I don't trust you."

"I knew it troubled you greatly when the ability disappeared." Her blonde brows pitched into a V. "I thought I was supportive."

"You were," Hadrian assured her. "You *are*. I was foolish. I worried you wouldn't need me anymore."

"I told you that I would." Now she sounded exasperated. "You must take me at my word."

"I will. I should have told you about visiting Captain Vale and what he told me. He encouraged me to meditate and quiet my mind as much as possible to invite the ability to return. I even spoke with Thaddeus Vale, who said much the same thing."

Tilda gave him a sardonic look. "You must have been truly desperate to speak with Lysander Mallory."

Hadrian grinned. "Horribly desperate." He schooled his features and met her gaze with a direct, heartfelt stare. "I am just so glad to have this power back. I hated that I wasn't able to help you, especially now. Of all the cases to not have the ability to assist you." He exhaled. "We're going to find out what happened to your father. I'm going to touch all the men who were there that night and see what really happened."

Tilda's eyes sparkled, and he realized there was moisture—not full tears, but she batted her lashes before they could form. "Thank you," she whispered.

"What about you?" Hadrian had pondered whether he ought to try to see her memories, not that he'd ever experienced them before.

Her features creased in puzzlement. "What do you mean?"

"I could try to see your memories from when your father was alive. Perhaps you knew something that could help the investigation, something that you've long forgotten."

"I don't know what that could be."

"Of course you wouldn't, not if you've forgotten." He flashed her a quick smile. "I know you've said you don't know if you'd want me to see one of your memories. I won't try unless you agree."

"What makes you think you'll see one now when you never have before?" she asked dubiously. "It's not as if you haven't had the chance. We've...touched."

"I know." How he wanted to touch her now. He longed to stroke her cheek, to hold her against him as he'd done not even a fortnight ago at the end of their last case, to kiss her again and feel the softness of her lips against his. "I don't know if it will be possible, but I'm willing to try. Even if I don't learn anything helpful, perhaps I'll see something that will make you smile when I share it." Hadrian realized part of his desire in seeking a memory of Thomas Wren was so that he could "meet" him in the only way that would ever be possible.

"All right." She flattened her palms against her lap and straightened her shoulders. "What should I do?"

"Nothing. I'll just take your hand, if you don't mind." Hadrian's pulse leapt at the prospect of just holding her hand.

Tilda lifted her right hand from her lap and held it toward him.

Hadrian took a deep breath and focused his thoughts on Tilda and her father. He glanced at the photograph of Thomas Wren on the mantel and imagined the bond between father and daughter.

Lifting his hand, he clasped Tilda's. Her flesh was soft and warm. He felt a jolt of energy, but it was nothing to do with his ability. It was entirely due to his feelings for her and how her touch was a balm he hadn't realized he craved. The dull ache that had lingered in his head eased, much as it had done earlier that day when she'd smoothed lavender oil into his forehead.

"Anything?" she whispered.

"Not yet." Hadrian tried harder to see her father.

Tilda clasped his other hand, surprising him and sending a shiver of delight up his arm and into his chest, where it settled and grew, warming him with a delicious heat. She pressed his palm to her cheek and closed her eyes. "Perhaps it will help you if I tell you that I see him in my mind—his kind brown eyes, his quick smile. The cleft in his chin that I inherited from him."

Hadrian wished he could help her, that he could see Thomas Wren. But his mind was already full. Every thought was trained on Tilda and his love for her. There was simply no room for him to see her memories.

It wasn't fair. And yet he would not trade the way he felt about her. Not for anything.

Tilda opened her eyes. "This isn't working, is it?"

"I'm afraid not." He gave her a wry smile. And gave in to the overwhelming desire to stroke his thumb along her cheekbone. "I'm sorry."

"It's all right." She smiled at him in return and let out a soft sigh. "I knew it was unlikely to happen."

"My goodness, what have I stumbled upon?"

Hadrian turned his head to see Lady Pierce standing on the threshold of the parlor. She wore a dark red dressing gown and a cap that covered her pale hair.

Hadrian watched as Tilda's eyes grew round as the full moon. He dropped his hands to his lap, and she scooted away from him, which made him realize how close they'd moved toward one another.

"Nothing, Mother. Lord Ravenhurst was just leaving."

"That didn't look like nothing," Lady Pierce declared. She arched a brow at Hadrian. "Do I need to insist you marry my daughter?"

Tilda stood and huffed, her cheeks flushing. "You will do no such thing. I had something in my eye, and Ravenhurst was trying to see what it was."

Hadrian continued to be impressed by her ability to fabricate a believable lie without notice. It was an excellent skill during their investigations. Lady Pierce appeared less impressed. She arched a dubious brow at her daughter.

Lady Pierce didn't say anything, however. She shifted her gaze to Hadrian and smiled. "How delightful to see you here, Lord Ravenhurst. But what an odd hour to be calling. I might presume you and my daughter share a particular...intimacy. Why else would you be here so late?" She blinked expectantly.

"We're working on an investigation, Mother," Tilda replied crossly. "Our *intimacy* is borne of our close professional relationship." She looked over at Hadrian and, with her eyes, urged him to agree.

"I truly was helping Miss Wren with something in her eye," Hadrian said. "I am here this late because I made an important discovery in our investigation and needed to share it." He gave Tilda's mother his most charming smile. "I would never mean to intrude, but it was simply vital that I call."

Hadrian wished they could have a little more time together, but he knew that wouldn't be possible with her mother present. He turned to Tilda. "I'll see you tomorrow."

"Yes. For our meeting with Mr. Clement," Tilda said. "And our other inquiries."

"Just so." He had an overwhelming urge to kiss Tilda's cheek but could not, of course. Would he have done so if Lady Pierce hadn't interrupted them? Alas, he would never know.

"Thank you for coming," Tilda said.

Hadrian inclined his head, then pivoted to face Tilda's mother. "Good evening, Lady Pierce." He moved into the entrance hall, where he fetched his hat and gloves.

Vaughn opened the door for him. "Good night, my lord."

"Good night, Vaughn."

Hadrian made his way to the coach, where Leach was waiting.

"Did all go well?" Leach asked.

"Yes. It was good that I came." He climbed into the coach, and they started back toward Ravenhurst House.

Hadrian imagined Lady Pierce was badgering Tilda about his visit. He was sorry they'd been caught by her—not because of any impropriety but because he knew Tilda's mother would likely press her hope that there might be more between Tilda and Hadrian than their professional attachment.

And the truth was that there *was* more, just not as much as Hadrian wanted. It was odd to think he and Tilda's mother were aligned. He would like nothing more than to make Tilda his wife. He knew that with absolute certainty.

Just as he knew Tilda would never agree.

~

As soon as the door closed behind Hadrian, Tilda attempted to escape her mother's critical stare. "I believe I'll retire."

"You can't think I'll let you evade this situation so easily," her mother said in a tone Tilda hadn't heard since she'd been a child. "Sit."

Tilda opened her mouth to decline, but her mother held up a hand.

"Don't bother." She gave Tilda a prim look as she moved to sit in one of the chairs. "I do believe that you and Lord Ravenhurst are adhering to a professional relationship." One of her pale brows arched. "However, I also sense something simmering beneath the surface. Is it that he sees you as beneath him?" Her expression creased with concern and…sympathy?

"Not at all." Tilda begrudgingly perched on the settee she'd recently vacated. "We have not discussed any other sort of attachment." That wasn't exactly true. After their kiss, a couple of months ago now, she'd told him that she wasn't interested in marrying. And whilst she did feel *something* toward him, her sentiments about marriage hadn't changed.

"Perhaps you should. I believe you're well suited, and if I'm not mistaken, Ravenhurst appears to be quite fond of you."

"Do not confuse our friendship, which is strong, particularly for a man and woman of differing backgrounds, for romantic inclination, Mother." Tilda gentled her tone. "You will be greatly disappointed."

"I don't think I will," her mother said with confidence. "You should at least consider it. Marriage to an earl would offer you many benefits, and Ravenhurst clearly supports your eccentricities. You're unlikely to find another man who will."

Tilda didn't know whether to laugh or rage. She chose to change the subject. "You may be interested to know that the Metropolitan Police have reopened the investigation into Papa's murder."

Her mother's eyes rounded briefly, and she stared at Tilda in surprise. "Why?"

"I uncovered new information. Rather, old information that was ignored." Tilda didn't want to delve into the specifics. She doubted her mother wanted to hear about how much blood was or wasn't present where Thomas Wren was allegedly killed.

"You've been investigating your father's death?" She gaped at Tilda. "You said you were searching for stolen items."

"They are separate cases. A retired inspector was recently murdered, and he was carrying Papa's name written on a piece of parchment. It's rather curious, so I made a few inquiries." Tilda wasn't sure why she'd shared that detail. Perhaps she thought her mother would want to know what had really happened to her first husband. Or perhaps Tilda simply hoped she would care.

"That is curious," her mother murmured. She blinked and spoke louder. "I was going to tell you that whilst I've been here, I finally went through a few crates of things that your grandmother had stored in the attic. I found a diary of your father's from when he died."

Tilda jolted. She braced one hand on the front edge of the settee as she leaned slightly forward. "When did you find it? I need to see it."

"Just today." Her mother stood and went toward the entrance hall. "Vaughn, will you go up to my room and fetch the book sitting on my desk? It's bound in brown leather."

"Yes, my lady."

Tilda heard Vaughn's halting gait as he walked to the stairs.

Her mother returned and sat in the chair once more.

"What else did you find?" Tilda asked, wondering why she'd never known about these crates.

"Only some things from our house—mostly clothing from when you were young and a few items that belonged to your father, including his police hat. I suppose you want that too?"

"Yes," Tilda whispered. She couldn't believe that a diary—words written by her father—had been in this house for years and she hadn't known it. "Did Papa always keep a diary?"

"For many years, but they were always to do with his work," her mother replied. "I didn't think I'd kept any of them. I offered them to the police after your father died."

Tilda could try to recover them but wasn't even sure where to start. "I wish you'd kept them for me."

"How was I to know such things would be of interest to you?" She pursed her lips briefly. "They wouldn't be if you were a typical young lady."

"Well, I am not. And I'm sorry that disappoints you." Actually, she wasn't sorry at all. Tilda wouldn't apologize for who she was. "Papa would be proud of me."

"Yes, he would." Her mother's agreement surprised Tilda.

Vaughn returned a moment later with the book.

"Give it to Matilda," her mother said.

Tilda accepted the diary from Vaughn and thanked him. She immediately stood. "I'll retire now." She'd no desire to read her father's diary in front of her mother.

"Will you have time to shop tomorrow for your gown for next week's ball?" her mother asked as Tilda made her way toward the entrance hall.

Pausing, Tilda pivoted and noted that her mother had also risen. "No. I have a gown that is appropriate." She had the ensemble that Hadrian had procured for her when they'd gone to Northumberland House during their first investigation. Surely that would be satisfactory for a ball.

"May I see it?" her mother asked with a patient smile.

"Of course. Just ask Clara tomorrow. Good night, Mother."

Tilda turned and moved into the entrance hall. After bidding Vaughn good night, she made her way upstairs to her chamber.

She closed the door securely and allowed the emotions she'd held at bay. Touching the book, she imagined her father's hands on the leather, where hers were now. It was almost as though she were touching him. This wasn't the memory Hadrian had tried to see for her, but it was just as significant.

Tears stung her eyes as she made her way to her bed. She sat on the edge and took a deep breath.

Blinking, Tilda opened the diary. Her father's handwriting leapt at her from the parchment. Despite her best efforts to rein her emotions, a tear fell onto the paper.

She tipped her head back and mentally chastised herself. "Now is not the time for sadness. There could be something helpful here," she whispered.

Inhaling deeply once more, Tilda dashed her hand over her eyes and fixed her attention on the diary. The first page was dated the ninth of September 1857. It was the day her father had received word that he was being considered for the Detective Branch.

Tilda lost herself in his words, most of which were about his work. Now and again, there was a mention of Tilda. He marveled at her curiosity and her voracious appetite for reading. He was always looking for ways to find books to bring home to her. Tilda smiled. Love for her father expanded in her chest.

In late October, he began to mention a case he was working on involving a series of thefts in Mayfair. Though he hadn't yet been officially promoted to the Detective Branch, he was assisting a detective inspector—a man called Knowles—with the case.

During one of the thefts, a footman had been injured when he'd tried to stop the thieves. Her father wrote that the footman reported seeing two men. The entry concluded rather abruptly.

Tilda couldn't help thinking it was a coincidence that there were two thieves, just as Hadrian had seen in his vision. For a moment, she thought of the pain Hadrian must have endured as he'd worked to see as much as possible with the mirror, as well as with his watch that he'd dropped at Great Marlborough Street.

She was so relieved his power had returned but didn't feel entirely good about it. The visions were taxing, and their investigation had been going well. Still, the memories he experienced so often pointed them in a useful direction, and when it came to solving her father's murder, she would take any help she could.

Hadrian had been so thoughtful to try to see one of her memories with her father, even knowing it would hurt him and that it was likely impossible. And why was it? He could see others' memories.

She knew why. It was because they were close. He wasn't able to see his mother's memories or those of the people in his household, with whom he interacted every day. But he didn't see Tilda every day, nor was she his relative. She wondered if he could see his sisters' memories. She didn't think he'd seen any of them since gaining the ability.

What's more, Hadrian had never been able to experience Tilda's memories, not even when they'd been newly acquainted. Granted, they hadn't touched until they'd known each other better, but they'd handled the same things and he'd never seen a glimpse. Again, she wondered why.

Her mother's words came back to her—*Ravenhurst appears to be quite fond of you.* Did his emotions toward someone affect his ability to see their memories? Did he, perchance, care more for her than she realized?

Tilda blinked and refocused her attention on the diary. She needed to concentrate on her father's case, not her mother's silly conjecture.

He didn't mention the theft case again until late November. Tilda's blood ran cold when she read the entry for the twenty-eighth.

We recovered one of the items stolen from Lord Edgemere today. The brooch, a bouquet of five flowers featuring different colored gems, purchased from a jeweler in Greville Street was seen on the Duchess of Glenmuir. It's remarkable to have found this since it was stolen over a year ago. Her Grace was very disappointed to have to relinquish the beautiful piece.

The description of the brooch matched one of the pieces Timms was given by Dorris the first time he'd visited his shop twelve years ago. That would have been 1856, the year before this diary entry. And the timing of the loss of the brooch matched when it had appeared at Timms's shop.

Tilda's hands shook. Was her case with Mrs. Goodwin connected to the one her father had been investigating? She quickly read through the remaining entries, but there were only a few more before she read the last one dated the tenth of December. That was just three days before he'd died.

She stared, unseeing, at the door to her chamber. The connections between her case and her father's were too similar to ignore: a series of thefts, a pair of thieves, Dorris fencing the stolen items at Timms's shop.

Had her father and Detective Inspector Knowles solved that case? She had to find out.

And did that case have anything to do with Thomas Wren's murder? There was no evidence of that, but Tilda thought it was important to make inquiries since he'd been working on the investigation at the time of his death. She hoped Knowles would be able to help her. And Dorris, of course.

Jumping from the bed, Tilda paced. She stopped and reread the entry from the twenty-eighth of November. Then she paced some more. She could hardly wait to tell Hadrian what she'd discovered. In fact, if it wasn't so late and he hadn't already strained propriety by coming here, she might have gone to his house.

If she thought he could gain any more information by touching the diary, she would likely go straightaway—propriety be damned. However, it was exceedingly rare that he saw a vision from a deceased person, and she highly doubted he'd experience anything from the diary.

She could ask him tomorrow, she supposed. How was she ever going to sleep?

CHAPTER 11

*A*fter meeting with his secretary and taking care of correspondence, Hadrian departed to fetch Tilda for their meeting with Ezra Clement. Not that they had an appointment with the reporter. Hopefully, they'd find him at his favorite coffee house on Fleet Street.

As Leach drove to Marylebone Lane, Hadrian thought of last night. He wondered how the evening may have progressed if they'd not been interrupted by Tilda's mother. A kiss had not seemed impossible—at least then. When Hadrian thought of it now, he doubted Tilda would have allowed it. And if she had, Hadrian worried that she would have only done so because of her emotional vulnerability. This case regarding her father's death was affecting her greatly.

Hadrian hoped Lady Pierce hadn't troubled Tilda after he'd gone. The woman clearly wanted him and Tilda to make a match, and she had likely been encouraged by what she'd interrupted.

Which was what exactly? It certainly hadn't been anything to do with Tilda's eye.

Hadrian didn't want to think too much about it. It was best if he focused on their investigations.

Upon arriving at Tilda's grandmother's, Hadrian didn't reach the door to the house before Vaughn opened it and Tilda walked outside. She met him with a dark urgency in her gaze that piqued Hadrian's curiosity.

As soon as they were in the coach, seated side by side on the forward-facing seat, and Leach closed the door, Tilda turned toward Hadrian. "My mother found my father's diary in a crate in my grandmother's attic. It's a record of his days, primarily his work, in the months leading up to his death."

Hadrian couldn't keep his jaw from dropping. Tilda's demeanor indicated the diary contained something important— something she was desperate to reveal. "You didn't know he kept such a diary?"

Tilda shook her head. "Apparently there were others, but my mother gave them to the Metropolitan Police." She frowned as her eyes heated with irritation. "I'm just glad she didn't give them this one. Hadrian, it has the most astonishing information. My father was working with the Detective Branch when he died. He and Detective Inspector Knowles were investigating a series of thefts with two thieves, and they recovered an item." Her eyes gleamed with anticipation. "It was a brooch of a bouquet of flowers made of different colored gems."

Hadrian sucked in a breath. "Timms described a brooch like that when he reviewed the items in his ledger with us." He remembered it clearly because the piece sounded so distinct— and beautiful.

"Yes, it was one of the first items Dorris brought to him twelve years ago," Tilda said excitedly. "It had been stolen from Lord Edgemere in 1856. Someone recognized the brooch on the Duchess of Glenmuir. It was purchased from a jeweler on *Greville Street*."

"This is—" Hadrian shook his head. "I don't know what it is. A coincidence?"

"Certainly. I have to think the thefts my father was investigating were linked to the theft of Mrs. Goodwin's silver. Dorris was involved with both."

"Perhaps he's a known fence that thieves use?" Hadrian suggested. He'd no idea how such things worked, of course.

"I suppose that's possible. We'll soon obtain the answers from Dorris himself," she said with a steely determination.

"I hope we can," Hadrian said. "How will we persuade him to reveal the truth?"

Tilda's brow furrowed. "I've been thinking about that. I hope Timms has followed our instructions and not alerted Dorris to who we are."

"I have to think Dorris won't show up if that is the case."

"I think so too," Tilda replied with a nod. "I thought we could pretend to want Dorris to procure some items for us."

"That's a good idea." Hadrian was not surprised that she'd come up with something. "Do you have items in mind?"

Tilda's gaze turned shrewd. "I thought we'd ask for salvers crafted by Hester Bateman."

Hadrian grinned. "The item that's still missing. What if Dorris never had it?"

"That's possible, but why would he have the other items stolen from Mrs. Goodwin and not the salver?" Tilda arched a brow. "I have a theory. What if Dorris keeps the items he likes?"

"Interesting. I could offer him a great sum to entice him to part with the salver."

She smiled at him, and his heart tripped. "That would be brilliant."

"Then we have a plan," Hadrian said.

Tilda settled back against the squab. "I do hope we can find the occurrence books with the entries for the other items Dorris fenced over the years."

Hadrian slapped his palm against his thigh. "I nearly forgot to tell you. When my secretary set the meeting with the criminal clerk, he confirmed the clerk *is* Fellows." He eyed Tilda to see her reaction.

"That's unfortunate. We'll have to hope he doesn't continue to hide information as he did when my father died." Her tone was rife with disdain.

"I've been thinking about that since I confirmed he's the criminal clerk. So many police were involved in burying the truth—Fellows, Jurgens, Lowther, and Padgett."

"That we know of," Tilda said darkly. "These men covering up the truth about the death of another member of the Met is unimaginable. I can't fathom why they would have done that. Unless there is some sort of conspiracy."

Hadrian frowned. "What would that be?"

"That is what we need to determine. If we can solve this case with Dorris and the stolen items, perhaps we'll move closer to discovering what happened. There is a clear connection between Dorris and my father, though it's possible it has nothing to do with his murder. We need to track down Detective Inspector Knowles. I'm not familiar with him—I don't believe he's still with the Detective Branch. Perhaps he retired. I hope Teague can help us find him."

"I'm sure he will," Hadrian said. "And now no one can frown at your involvement since your case with Mrs. Goodwin is now tied to your father's investigation. Will you tell Teague about your father's diary and the case he was investigating?"

Tilda nodded. "I think I must. I trust him to use the information to help us uncover the truth. I'm just so glad to have the diary." She smiled gently. "It was wonderful to read my father's words."

Hadrian loved seeing her excitement and her happiness. He imagined her reading the diary and was immensely glad for the joy it clearly gave her. The urge to hold and comfort her was great. But he needed to keep his emotions in check. It was becoming more difficult, especially with the personal nature of this case.

They arrived at the coffee house in Fleet Street, and Hadrian escorted Tilda inside. Right away, she looked toward the table where they'd seen Clement before. He was seated there again today, his head bent over a newspaper.

Tilda strode to the table, and Hadrian moved quickly to keep up. Clement looked up as they approached. The reporter's brown hair was thinning near his hairline, but he had long side whiskers.

"Ravenhurst, Miss Wren." The reporter sat straight. "What a pleasant surprise."

"May we sit?" Tilda asked, her hand already on the chair.

"Of course," Clement replied with a nod.

Hadrian held the chair whilst Tilda sat, then took the one beside her.

Clement set his newspaper aside and clasped his hands on the end of the table. "Have you come to ask if I've discovered from whom Padgett was collecting information?"

"Not specifically that." Tilda arched a brow at him. "But do you know who?"

"I heard a rumor—from multiple people—that he may have had informants in other divisions or even the Home Office," Clement replied. "Not terribly helpful, I know, but it's something."

"Yes, thank you," Tilda said. "I am actually more interested in hearing about your relationship with him."

Clement's expression turned wary. "You know all about that."

"*All?*" Tilda sent him a skeptical look. "I doubt that. How and when did you begin working together?"

"We met a few years ago at a pub near Scotland Yard—the Standing Bear. I go sometimes to try and overhear information about cases." He sent a sheepish glance toward Hadrian, likely thinking Hadrian would find fault with that. And he was right.

"That's rather shameless," Hadrian said. At first, he hadn't liked Clement and his manner. The man could be ruthless about finding a story. He'd even gone to Hadrian's mother's house to question her about something, but Hadrian had put a stop to Clement's attempt to gather gossip fodder.

Clement shrugged. "One does what is required in my line of work. It's the same with Miss Wren." He inclined his head toward Tilda.

"Miss Wren doesn't compromise her principles," Hadrian pointed out.

"Neither do I." Clement's features hardened. "There are lines I won't cross."

Hadrian snorted. "Bribing an inspector isn't one of them."

Tilda turned her head and gave Hadrian an impatient frown. "I've had to bribe the police for information. As Mr. Clement said —one does what's required."

Hadrian knew that, of course. And he felt appropriately admonished. Clement had helped them on numerous occasions. Hadrian supposed he was concerned the reporter may not help them now, and Tilda absolutely needed his assistance.

She shifted her attention to Clement. "You met Padgett at the Standing Bear?"

"Yes. He often sat alone. I joined him one evening, which he didn't particularly care for." Clement smiled briefly. "Padgett was a surly fellow."

"I recall that from the one time I met him," Hadrian said. "I found him rather disagreeable."

"Did you offer to purchase information from him?" Tilda asked Clement.

"I don't typically do that. I'm willing to pay, but I prefer the request comes from the other party. I asked if he had anything to share that might interest the readers of the *Daily News*. He glowered at me for a long while, then asked what it was worth to me. I told him it depended on whether he had anything worthwhile.

Then he tossed out a number, and I paid it." Clement sipped his coffee.

Tilda kept her gaze pinned to Clement. "What sort of information did he give you and how often?"

Clement leaned forward. "Why are you asking me all this? What aren't you telling me?"

"I'll get to that," Tilda clipped out.

"He would tell me about interesting investigations. Occasionally, he just gave me the information, but more often, he offered me a clue that led me in the right direction to find a story. That way he had plausible deniability if anyone asked whether he told me anything."

Tilda straightened her spine and lifted her chin slightly. "I wasn't entirely truthful with you at Padgett's inquest."

Clement blew out a breath. "Neither was I."

"I'll go first," Tilda said. "Provided you plan to reveal your secret second." Clement nodded, and Tilda continued. "Padgett had a piece of paper in his pocket when he died. My father's name and the date he was murdered were on it."

"*Bloody hell.*" Clement paled, and Hadrian's pulse sped.

Tilda put her hands on the table and clutched the edge. "What?"

Clement's jaw tightened. "Padgett had asked to meet with me the day after he was murdered—the day he was discovered. That paper was for me."

~

Tilda gaped at Clement. "You're certain?"

"It had to be," Clement said without hesitation. "That is precisely the sort of clue he would give me, and we were due to meet." He clenched his jaw. "I should have told you about the meeting."

"You would have if I'd told you about the note," Tilda said.

"However, I didn't think it wise to share that information just yet. Honestly, I am not sure who I can trust right now."

"But you're trusting me," Clement said. His eyes gleamed with appreciation. "Thank you. I trust you as well. I won't make the same mistake in the future. We lost valuable time by not sharing what we knew."

"Agreed." Tilda looked over at Hadrian. He appeared as surprised as she felt.

"So Padgett was going to give you that note," Hadrian said. "Would he just slip you the parchment and wish you luck?"

A vague smile lifted Clement's lips. "Something like that. We would meet at the Standing Bear, and he'd tuck his clue beneath my glass. He'd grunt and I'd pay him. Then he'd leave."

"That's it?" Tilda asked. "What if you had questions? What would you have done with my father's name and the date he was killed?"

"I would not have known what the date meant," Clement replied. "And I wouldn't have known your father's name. Indeed, I don't know his Christian name."

"Thomas," Tilda supplied.

Clement inclined his head in response. "I would have recognized the surname, of course, and wondered if there was a relation to you. I imagine I would have called on you to ask about him and the date."

"And I would have explained to you the circumstances of his death." Tilda did so then, concluding with, "My father allegedly interrupted the theft."

Clement's brows arched. "You don't know what happened?"

"I thought I did." Again, Tilda glanced at Hadrian. He was watching her with concern. She could see how much he cared, and it truly made her feel better. She went on to share what they'd learned at the apothecary shop, particularly that there hadn't been enough blood for her father to have been killed there. "When the apothecary pointed that out to the police, they said the killer had cleaned it up."

"What utter horsesh—" Clement pressed his lips together. "Pardon me. That's nonsense. No thief who cut a police sergeant's throat is going to take the time to clean anything."

"Exactly our thoughts," Hadrian said, glancing at Tilda.

"Why do you think Padgett wanted me to investigate Thomas Wren's murder?" Frowning, Clement picked up his coffee but then set it down almost immediately. "It seems that was what he wanted me to do."

Tilda made the connection for Clement. "Padgett was the inspector at the apothecary shop that night. There were also three constables present—Lowther, Jurgens, and Fellows. Lowther and Jurgens are inspectors now, and Fellows is currently the criminal clerk at the Home Office."

Clement gasped, and Tilda went on to explain the rest of what they'd learned so far, including the missing police report and the fact that her father had been investigating a series of thefts with the Detective Branch. Tilda didn't mention her father's diary. She didn't want anyone to know the specific evidence she had. She wouldn't put it past one of the men who'd covered up the truth to try and steal it from her.

"This is a conspiracy to hide the truth of your father's death." Clement's tone was heavy. "What are you going to do?"

"We'll continue making inquiries," Tilda replied. "Padgett had to have known what happened that night. But instead of telling you, he gave you that paper to investigate the matter. You said he often did that, but I can't help thinking he didn't want to be caught revealing the truth."

"That does make sense." Clement drummed his fingers on the table. "What is your next move?"

Tilda chose her words carefully. "We have found a connection between the case my father was investigating and the one that I'm currently working on."

Clement's brows shot up. "How did you manage that?"

"I'd rather not say just yet, but I have proof the two investigations are connected."

"When you're ready to disclose that information, I hope you'll let me know." Clement sounded disappointed but didn't appear angry.

"I will. I'm sure you plan to investigate my father's death now too," Tilda said. "I would ask that you share whatever you can. Please. It would mean a great deal to me." She hoped he understood why this case might be different than the usual way they traded information—piece for piece.

"Of course." Clement's brow pleated into sympathetic lines. "I imagine this has been upsetting for you, to have something you've long held as truth turn out to be a lie."

"I am committed to discovering the real truth," Tilda said with determination. "My father deserves that."

Clement nodded in agreement. "He certainly does. I would do the same for my father, though he is just a schoolmaster in Canterbury."

"A noble profession," Hadrian said.

Tilda looked toward Clement. "Our first inquiry into the connection between my case and my father's is to find the police reports for other items that were stolen and fenced by the same man. We've a meeting with the criminal clerk in the Home Office tomorrow."

"Fellows?" Clement asked with a smirk. "That should be interesting. I look forward to hearing about it."

"We will be speaking with the fence this evening," Hadrian said.

"And with Lowther," Tilda said. "He and his wife have been very kind to me in the years since my father's death, and to learn that Lowther was part of whatever conspiracy that buried the truth is particularly upsetting. I am going to demand he tell me what really happened the night my father died."

"Do you think he'll be honest with you at last?" Clement sounded doubtful.

"I hope so." But Tilda wasn't sure what to expect.

Hadrian looked to Tilda. "Do you want to tell him about our interview with Jurgens?"

"Oh yes." Tilda shifted her attention back to Clement. "Jurgens is an inspector at Great Marlborough Street now. We encountered him when we went to the station to speak with the inspector who was investigating the theft of my client's silver. We questioned him about my father's death, but he didn't reveal anything helpful. He seemed agitated when I brought up the case. He tried to say my father's murder had been solved, but we set him straight."

Clement shifted in his chair. "This is all very suspicious. What can I do? I'm not sure it's wise for me to go poking about into your father's death. That will draw even more attention."

"The investigation into his death has been reopened," Tilda said. "Detective Inspector Teague is overseeing it. But I don't know how you would know that, and I don't wish to cause trouble for Teague."

"I understand." Clement cocked his head. "Perhaps I can help with the investigation into the thefts. I can search newspaper archives."

Tilda smiled. "That would be helpful, thank you. The thefts go back at least twelve years. That's the first time the fence is known to have stolen items. I can provide you with a list of items that were fenced—and when—with a jeweler called Timms in Greville Street." She pulled her notebook from her reticule and found where she'd written the details. "Can you write this down now?"

"I can," he said as he took the notebook. "This will help my search." Clement's dark brows drew together. "I do hope you'll let me know more when you can. Beyond the story of a conspiracy that I would dearly love to write, I want you to find justice for your father."

"That's kind of you to say," Hadrian noted softly.

"Yes, it is," Tilda agreed. "I will definitely tell you what I can as soon as possible. We'll keep in contact." She glanced at Hadrian, who nodded.

"One other thing," Hadrian said. "The stolen items may not be limited to jewelry or silver. There may be paintings or other art."

"Do you think there's another fence beyond Timms?" Clement asked. "The jeweler wouldn't have been able to sell a painting."

"No, he would not," Tilda agreed. She sent an admiring look at Hadrian, glad he'd remembered to mention the painting he'd glimpsed in his vision.

Tilda and Hadrian left after Clement finished copying her notes about the stolen items. Outside, Hadrian looked over at her. "Is there anything else for us to do this afternoon before we go to Timms's shop, or shall I take you home for now?"

"I wish there was something for us to do," Tilda said with grave disappointment. "My mother will almost certainly want to drag me shopping. She insists I need a new gown for the Trumbull ball, though I've tried to assure her that the dress I wore to Northumberland House is more than adequate." Tilda made a face and waved her hand dismissively. "Never mind that. I am very glad we sought Clement out today."

"I am too. Now we know why Padgett had your father's name in his pocket."

They arrived at the coach, and Leach opened the door. Tilda climbed inside, and Hadrian sat beside her after instructing Leach to drive to Marylebone Lane.

"I wonder why Padgett wanted to share this with Clement now, after all this time." Tilda pivoted toward Hadrian. "Something had to have prompted him."

"And yet he didn't just come out and tell Clement. He simply invited him to investigate." Hadrian made a sound in his throat. "I can't say my impression of Padgett has improved."

Tilda tried to think of what could have motivated Padgett to push Clement to look into the past. "Padgett was also murdered. Perhaps someone learned that he was going to share information and killed him."

Hadrian's eyes glinted. "It is notable that he planned to meet Clement and was murdered. Do you think there could be a splinter in the conspiracy?"

"First, I'd like to prove there *is* a conspiracy." Tilda was most eager to speak with Lowther. He could potentially reveal all.

"We will," Hadrian said with confidence.

"I am most anxious for this evening's plans," Tilda said.

"As am I." He met her gaze with a steely resolve. "We will have answers, Tilda. Before this day is through."

CHAPTER 12

$\mathscr{H}$adrian picked Tilda up at her grandmother's house instead of down the street that evening. Once again, she came from the house before Hadrian even reached the door. That was probably for the best, so they weren't delayed by Hadrian needing to make small talk with the members of her household.

When they were on their way to Greville Street, Hadrian asked about Tilda's afternoon. "Did you end up shopping with your mother?"

Tilda exhaled as she set her reticule beside her. "Yes. Apparently, a ballgown is a very specific garment, and the dress I wore to Northumberland House is not, officially, a ballgown." She rolled her eyes, then smiled at him. "I'm glad you will be at the Trumbulls', too. At least I won't feel completely out of place."

Hadrian returned her smile. "You will fit in very well. In fact, you may find it entertaining. I can't believe I don't know this, but do you dance?"

"No. I learned a little, but I've not had occasion to practice." Her expression turned sardonic. "You can see why I am not enthusiastic about attending a ball. My mother assures me I dance well enough. I'm just hoping no one asks." She blew out a breath. "It's just such a waste of time when I do not have time to waste."

"Perhaps you should look at it as an opportunity to relax and enjoy an evening without thinking of the investigations."

Tilda's gaze snapped to him in surprise, then her brows drew together. "Do you really think I'll be able to set aside the investigation into my father's death?"

Hadrian grimaced. "No, I don't. My apologies. Perhaps we will solve it by then."

"That's in four days." Tilda scoffed. "It seems unlikely."

"It's possible," Hadrian said. "In my experience, our investigations often gain momentum and come to a conclusion rather quickly."

"You may be right." Tilda smoothed her hand over her forehead. "I suppose I just feel overwhelmed right now. You were right earlier; we will find answers. It was a dreadful afternoon waiting for this evening to arrive."

Hadrian looked at her with sympathy. "I hope the time spent shopping with your mother wasn't too taxing. Did she pester you about our association?" He asked the question in part so he could determine if Tilda's opinion about their relationship may have changed. He supposed he was eager for any chance that she might reciprocate his feelings, even a little.

"Thankfully, my mother didn't bring it up," Tilda said with satisfaction. Then she cast a sly glance toward him. "But that's likely because I made her promise not to if she wanted me to agree to accompany her."

Hadrian couldn't help but laugh. "She must have really wanted you to go shopping."

"Apparently." Tilda turned toward him slightly. "Are you ready for our scheme at Timms's shop?"

Hadrian nodded. "I am."

"I'd like you to take the lead," she said. "Once again, your title will almost certainly be helpful and influential."

"I'm happy to do that," Hadrian said.

When they arrived in Greville Street, Leach stopped the coach before they arrived at Timms's shop.

Hadrian peered out the window. "I wonder why he stopped here."

Leach opened the door, and Hadrian marked his grim expression. "There's a police wagon in front of the jeweler's," the coachman said.

Hadrian stepped down and turned to help Tilda. Her brow was creased with concern. "I don't like the sound of that."

"Nor do I," Hadrian replied. He glanced down the street toward the jeweler and saw the police wagon, as well as a constable standing outside. "Let's see what's happened."

Tilda took his arm, and they hurried toward the shop. The constable turned toward them as they approached, his eyes wary.

"Good evening," Hadrian greeted the constable. "I'm Ravenhurst." He didn't introduce Tilda because he wasn't sure what name she wanted to use. He should have asked.

"I'm Miss Wren," she said. "We have an appointment with Mr. Timms this evening about a case we're investigating. Has something happened?"

"I'm afraid so," the constable said darkly. "You won't be able to meet with Mr. Timms."

Hadrian's stomach clenched. He looked over at Tilda. Her features had gone stiff. "Is there an inspector inside?" she asked.

The constable nodded. "Inspector Emery."

"You're from G Division?" Tilda asked.

"Yes."

Tilda nodded. "We'll just have a few words with him then."

The constable pressed his lips together, then glanced behind him toward the closed door to the jeweler's shop. "I'm not sure I should allow you inside."

"It's fine," Tilda assured him. "I'm a private detective."

"We may have helpful information for the inspector," Hadrian added. He gave the constable an authoritative nod, then escorted Tilda into the shop before the constable could stop them.

The inspector stood with another pair of constables behind the glass cabinet where Hadrian and Tilda had stood earlier that day. The glass was shattered, and it looked to Hadrian as if several pieces of jewelry that had been there earlier were now missing.

"I think Timms is dead," Tilda whispered.

They couldn't see Timms's body, but Hadrian agreed with her assessment. "Let's find out what happened," he replied softly.

They walked farther into the shop, and the inspector and constables looked over at them.

"Who are you? What are you doing in here?" the inspector asked crossly. He looked to be a few years older than Hadrian. He had dark, curly blond hair and hooded brown eyes. He also sported a neat mustache.

"I'm Ravenhurst," Hadrian replied. "And this is Miss Wren. We had an appointment with Mr. Timms this evening to discuss a case we're working on."

The inspector's brow furrowed as his eyes narrowed. "What case is that?"

"I was hired to find some stolen silver pieces," Tilda said. "It seems Mr. Timms may have sold some of them."

"Is that right?" The inspector glanced at the floor. "Well, he's not going to sell anything else."

"May we come closer?" Hadrian asked.

The inspector exhaled. "May as well."

Hadrian and Tilda stepped around the glass cabinet. Timms lay on the floor on his back. His throat was cut. Immediately, Hadrian thought of Tilda's father, who'd been killed in the same manner. Except in this case, there was plenty of blood.

Tilda fixed on Timms's body for a long moment before she

lifted her focus to the inspector. "How were you alerted to the murder?"

"A patron came into the shop and found him like this. He alerted a constable who was on patrol."

"Then it happened when the shop was still open." Tilda met Hadrian's gaze briefly. "We were to meet Timms right after he closed."

"I would estimate this happened within the past hour," the inspector said. "The coroner should be here soon."

"Did you find the murder weapon?" Tilda asked.

Inspector Emery shook his head. "Not yet. We need to conduct a more thorough search—only arrived a short while ago. So far, we haven't seen it."

Hadrian surreptitiously removed his gloves and placed his bare hand on the wooden side of the glass cabinet in the hope that he would see the killer's memory. He wouldn't see Timms's since the man was dead.

The light in the shop changed, and Hadrian saw Timms showing necklaces. They were displayed on a cloth atop the glass cabinet. This was not the memory of a killer. It was that of someone eager to purchase something—Hadrian could feel the person's interest in the necklaces. Hadrian lifted his hand from the cabinet, and the vision faded.

He moved toward the desk where Timms had sat when they'd first come to the shop. Touching the edge, Hadrian focused his energy on seeing a memory from today and from someone who wished to harm the jeweler.

Nothing happened.

Concentrating, Hadrian redoubled his efforts. At last, he saw a flicker of something. He glimpsed Timms—his features were a mask of fear. Then the vision was gone. Pain exploded in Hadrian's head. He closed his eyes briefly and focused on what one of the constables was saying.

"It does look as though some things were stolen from the case."

"Definitely," Tilda said. "There are pieces missing from when we were here earlier."

"I don't suppose you recall what those were?" Inspector Emery asked.

Tilda moved carefully to survey the interior of the cabinet, which was littered with glass, as was the floor. "I don't recall them exactly, but I know there were brooches here." She moved her hand over an area. "I'd estimate five or six are gone. And I think some rings from this part." She gestured to another space. "I can't be sure how many."

The inspector wrote in a notebook and nodded. "Thank you. That's very helpful."

Tilda glanced around, then settled on Hadrian. "I wonder where the silver we looked at earlier is?"

"What silver?" Inspector Emery asked.

"Mr. Timms showed us several pieces—we were looking for my client's stolen items," Tilda replied.

"There are several locked cabinets in the back," one of the constables said. "Perhaps they're in there, but I haven't found a key."

"He keeps a ring of keys in his coat pocket," Hadrian said.

The constable looked toward Timms, then back at Hadrian, before going to kneel next to the body. He removed the keys and inclined his head at Hadrian. "Thank you."

"Do you mind if we look in the cabinets with you?" Tilda asked. She glanced at the inspector.

"Go ahead. You'll let us know if you don't find the silver you saw earlier?"

"Of course." Tilda followed the constable into the back room, and Hadrian followed.

The constable worked to open the four locked cabinets. Three contained silver pieces and one had jewelry. Hadrian saw the silver pieces that Timms had shown them that afternoon in the third cabinet. He gestured toward them and looked at the constable. "They're here."

"They're quite valuable," Tilda said. "As is some of the jewelry, I imagine. I'm surprised the thief didn't try to open these cabinets."

"Could be they didn't have time," the constable said. "Inspector Emery thinks it was a robbery."

Tilda walked back out to the inspector, and Hadrian trailed her. "Does it make sense to you that a thief would kill the jeweler?" she asked. "Why not knock him unconscious or tie him up? Thieves steal. They don't murder."

The inspector shrugged. "I think some do. It was clearly a robbery. You said yourself that some of the jewelry is missing. Perhaps Timms tried to fight."

"That sort of wound is not indicative of a fight," Tilda noted. "More likely, Timms would have been stabbed with a knife." She bent down and studied Timms's neck. "The knife was drawn from left to right. If the killer was in front of him in a fighting position, he would be left-handed. But if he stood behind him, he would be right-handed."

The inspector nodded. "That makes sense. You're a detective, you say?"

"Yes," Tilda replied, rising.

"A very good one," Emery said with a note of admiration.

Hadrian couldn't tell what Tilda thought of that, but he was glad for her. She deserved accolades more often than she received them.

"I don't think this was a robbery," Tilda concluded. "I suspect the goal was to kill Mr. Timms, perhaps because he was going to speak with us. We'll get out of your way now, Inspector. Thank you for allowing us to come inside and survey the scene."

"I will make sure the coroner invites you to the inquest," Inspector Emery said.

Tilda withdrew one of her cards from her reticule and handed it to the inspector.

"Thank you, Inspector," Hadrian said, and he escorted Tilda from the shop.

As they walked toward the coach, she glanced back at the shop over her shoulder. "I know you were trying to see something, and did you?"

Hadrian touched his head. "Very briefly, I saw Timms. He was deathly afraid, but that was all I glimpsed."

When they arrived at the coach, Tilda put a hand on her hip and frowned. "This is incredibly frustrating. I suppose we must pressure the publican at the Yellow Dog in order to find Dorris."

"We can go there now, if you like," Hadrian offered. He could see how upset Tilda was, and he wondered how much of her agitation came from the manner in which Timms had been killed.

"As much as I would like to go now, I prefer to call on Lowther."

"I understand," Hadrian said.

Tilda climbed into the coach, and Hadrian told Leach they would continue to their next destination as planned. Hadrian followed Tilda inside and sat down beside her. Her jaw was set in a hard line, and her hands were clasped tightly together.

"Are you all right?" Hadrian gently touched her arm. "Was that difficult to see—the way Timms was killed, I mean?"

Tilda turned her head and met his gaze briefly. "It was unsettling, yes."

"I'm sorry," Hadrian whispered.

Tilda shifted away slightly, and Hadrian withdrew his hand. "I just need to focus on this investigation."

Hadrian understood, but her disinterest in his efforts to comfort her stung. It shouldn't. None of this was about him. This was the most personal investigation she'd undertaken, and Hadrian would support her every step of the way.

CHAPTER 13

The sun was low in the sky when they arrived at the home of Inspector Lowther and his family in Adelaide Street near Charing Cross Station. Tilda hoped they would arrive after the Lowthers had completed dinner, but if they hadn't, she would not be deterred.

Tilda was already anxious about speaking with Inspector Lowther, but the death of Timms and failing to encounter Dorris meant she was even more agitated. She took a deep breath as they approached the door to the Lowthers' home, which they shared with his brother-in-law.

"I don't plan to say much," Hadrian said.

She looked over at him to see he was watching her with a kindness that softened her nerves. "I just appreciate you being here. And you must feel free to speak whenever you wish. I certainly don't mind."

Hadrian nodded. "Ready?" At her responding nod, he knocked on the door.

A few minutes later, Mrs. Lowther answered. A cap covered her blonde curls. Her blue eyes rounded briefly. "Tilda! Did

Edwin forget to tell me you were coming for dinner?" Her eyes narrowed.

Tilda smiled. "No. We did not come for dinner. Have you not already eaten?"

Peggy Lowther shot a look toward Hadrian. "We were just finishing, actually. Is something amiss?"

There was no good way to answer that question, so Tilda didn't. "I came to speak with Edwin. This is Lord Ravenhurst." She gestured to Hadrian.

"Come in." Peggy opened the door wide and motioned them into the small entrance hall. "Do you mind waiting in the parlor for a moment?" She gestured to the right.

"Not at all."

Again, Peggy looked at Hadrian. She appeared slightly nervous. "Edwin told me you were working with an earl. I thought he was being fanciful."

"We do indeed work together," Tilda said. She sent a smile toward Hadrian. "Lord Ravenhurst has proven himself to be an excellent investigator."

Peggy cocked her head as her brow pleated. "How…odd. I would think his lordship would be far too busy for such undertakings."

"I find working with Miss Wren to be fulfilling in ways I never imagined," Hadrian said.

"How nice." Peggy clasped her hands together. "I'll fetch Edwin. Please make yourselves comfortable."

She left, and Hadrian turned toward Tilda. "Is she from the north?"

"Yes, York. Her accent gave her away."

"Indeed. You know this family very well." He frowned, but there was sympathy in his eyes. "I know that makes Lowther's betrayal even worse."

Tilda's throat felt tight. She swallowed and took another deep breath. Her pulse was moving quickly.

"Shall we sit?" Hadrian suggested as he moved toward a worn settee. There was a small hole in the blue damask on the front edge of the cushion.

"We may as well." Tilda sat, and Hadrian joined her.

"Tilda!" The Lowther children, led by the youngest, Michael, raced into the parlor. He was followed by his sister Edwina, and the oldest, Nancy.

Michael was six but still jumped onto Tilda's lap as if he were a toddler. Edwina was nine and squeezed herself onto the settee between Tilda and Hadrian, who obliged by scooting over. Nancy, at thirteen, behaved in a more sedate fashion, but she smiled widely at Tilda as she came to stand before her.

"We haven't seen you in ever so long," Michael whined.

Tilda put her arms around Michael as he perched on her lap. "It hasn't been terribly long, has it?"

"It was Epiphany," Edwina said. "Ages ago."

"I suppose so." Tilda grimaced apologetically. "I've been busy with my work. Forgive me."

"All right." Michael looked at her expectantly. "Did you bring Mrs. Acorn's spice biscuits?"

Tilda felt bad that she hadn't, but she'd been too focused on the case. "I did not, but in my defense, my mother is visiting us from Birmingham, and the household is a bit busy. I promise I'll bring some soon—and I mean that. It won't be so long next time."

Michael sent a curious look toward Hadrian. "Who's he?"

"This is my friend, Lord Ravenhurst."

Nancy's eyes widened. She looked a little pale, and Tilda hoped she hadn't been too ill of late. She suffered from asthma. "Lord?"

"He's an earl," Tilda whispered as if it were a secret. "But a very nice one."

Hadrian chuckled. "You make it sound as if earls are not nice by nature."

Tilda only shrugged in response, which made Hadrian laugh again.

Edwin Lowther appeared in the doorway. "Children, you mustn't pester Tilda or his lordship."

Tilda tensed. She looked over at Lowther, who was smiling. Though he cut a formidable figure, he possessed the kindness of a father who adored his children. That made his betrayal even worse.

"Tilda's going to bring us Mrs. Acorn's spice biscuits soon," Michael said as he slid off Tilda's lap.

"That is very kind of her and of Mrs. Acorn. Go and help your mother tidy up." He looked at all three children, but only the girls made their way from the parlor—after hugging Tilda. A knot formed in her throat as she embraced Edwina and then Nancy. She hated that their father was likely involved in something nefarious.

Michael loitered. He narrowed his eyes at Hadrian. "What does an earl do? Do you have horses? I would like to ride a horse."

"I do have horses," Hadrian said. "Perhaps we can arrange for you to at least meet them?" He glanced at Inspector Lowther, whose eyes rounded slightly.

"That is very generous of you to offer, my lord," Lowther said.

Michael looked up at his father. "Can I, Papa?"

"If his lordship invites you, yes. But go help your mother now."

Casting a grin toward Hadrian, Michael turned and skipped from the parlor.

"You don't really have to show him your horses," Lowther said as he came into the parlor and sat in a chair near the hearth.

"I don't say things I don't mean," Hadrian said evenly, but Tilda caught the steel in his gaze and the tightness of his jaw. She wanted to hug him.

"We've come to speak with you about a matter we're investigating." Tilda was glad she sounded normal and that the tension inside her was not leaking out—not yet at least.

Lowther leaned slightly forward with interest. "How can I help?"

"By being completely honest and answering my questions," Tilda replied. "I'm investigating my father's death. I have learned some new facts that are most concerning, and since you were present the night he died, I'm sure you can help me determine what truly happened."

Tilda watched Lowther's response carefully. He stared at Tilda, his features controlled, but she observed his speeding pulse in his neck and the way he suddenly clutched his legs just above the knees. She wondered if he was aware he'd done that.

"I don't know how I can help."

"As I said, I only need you to honestly answer my questions." She gave him a patient smile. "I think I deserve that," she added softly. "Mr. Williams, the apothecary who owns the shop where my father was found dead, says he could not have been killed there due to the lack of blood. As you know, my father's throat was cut, and there should have been considerable blood on the floor. Mr. Williams says there was nothing, and when he mentioned it to the police, he was told the killer must have cleaned it up. Is that true?"

Lowther opened his mouth, but closed it again as his cheeks flushed dark pink. His chest rose and fell quite rapidly. "I don't recall that."

"Don't lie," Hadrian snapped, surprising Tilda. "You found Sergeant Wren, didn't you? I can't believe you wouldn't remember what you saw. What kind of detective inspector do you hope to be?" He was harsh, but Tilda thought it was necessary if Lowther was going to prevaricate.

"Was there blood or not?" Tilda pressed.

"There was not." Lowther sounded as though someone were standing on his throat.

Tilda fixed her stare on him. "You can't think the killer took the time to clean up the mess. Surely there would have been evidence of that."

Lowther brushed his hand over his brow, which was glistening with perspiration. "I don't remember. I found your father, then I went to fetch another constable."

"Who was that?" Tilda asked.

"Jurgens. He went to the station and brought Inspector Padgett and Constable Fellows. I swear, my memories of that night are murky. It was…upsetting."

"If you think it was more upsetting for you than it has been for Tilda—for years—you are incredibly selfish and inconsiderate," Hadrian said with a dark glower. "Why have you all lied about what happened?"

For a moment, Lowther looked as if he were going to protest, but his features creased, and his shoulders drooped. "I only did what I was told," he whispered brokenly. "I said it looked as though he'd been moved from wherever he was killed, but Padgett told me I was wrong."

Lowther looked over at Tilda, his eyes wet with tears. "I was a new constable. I did what I was told."

Tilda felt sympathy for Lowther, but her anger and hurt were greater. "Great effort has been made to hide the truth of my father's death. The investigative report is now missing."

"I don't know anything about that." Lowther wiped his damp forehead again. "Truly."

"You know that my father's name and the date he died were written on a piece of paper found in Padgett's pocket," Tilda said. "Why did he have it?"

Lowther shook his head. "I don't know."

"You also know Padgett was present at the apothecary shop that night my father was killed—you just said so." Tilda looked at Lowther with disappointment. "You must at least suspect Padgett's murder had something do with my father's death."

When Lowther didn't immediately respond, Hadrian made a sound in his throat. "Or have you been told to cover up any connection?"

"I—I shouldn't discuss the investigation," Lowther said shakily.

"I believe you have been told to suppress any information that would link Padgett's murder to my father's," Tilda said. "Which is why I will be investigating both. I am saddened you would behave in this manner after all the kindness you've shown me. I wonder what Mrs. Lowther would say."

Lowther glanced over his shoulder, then looked at Tilda with a nearly panicked expression. "Please don't tell her. Will you give me some time to try to fix this? I don't know how, but—"

"I won't tell her now, but I will continue with my own investigation. Perhaps you could muster enough grace to help me find someone. My father was investigating a series of thefts when he died. He was working with Detective Inspector Knowles, but he is no longer with the Detective Branch. I assume he retired. Do you know how I may contact him?"

"He died some years ago."

"How many?" Tilda demanded.

"1861, I believe—a heart attack."

"It's remarkable that you recall those details and not anything to do with Sergeant Wren," Hadrian noted with great sarcasm.

"Is there anything else you will tell me right now?" Tilda did not bother to hide her frustration.

Lowther briefly met her gaze. "No." He sounded as though he'd swallowed a rock and coughed.

"I will bring the weight of my rank to these investigations, Inspector Lowther," Hadrian said with an authoritative growl. His lip curled. "You will not be able to hide from justice."

Tilda stood. "I'm very disappointed, Inspector," she said quietly. "How could you have treated me the way you have this past decade, knowing that you are hiding the truth about my father's death? It's unforgivable."

Lowther looked up at her, his eyes sad and his jaw quivering. "I didn't have anything to do with his death. You must believe that."

"I don't think I can believe anything you say. You know where to find me when you are ready to reveal the truth. In the meantime, we will work on uncovering it ourselves." Tilda strode from the parlor and left the house with Hadrian on her heels.

They walked in silence to the coach in the near darkness, as the sun had set whilst they were inside. "Back to Marylebone Lane?" Leach asked solemnly. He was quite good at reading a situation and could likely see that Tilda was upset.

"Yes, thank you." Tilda climbed into the coach as he held the door.

She sat on the forward-facing seat and hoped Hadrian would sit beside her. She'd been keeping the majority of her emotions about her father at bay, but they were so close to the surface right now. She feared they were going to bubble over like a boiling pot left atop the stove. Perhaps with Hadrian at her side, she could borrow some of his strength to take the pot from the heat.

"I'm sorry," he said in a low, gravel-filled tone.

Tilda could hear his frustration. He was completely with her, and she was so grateful. "Thank you for everything you said to Lowther. You were magnificent."

Hadrian turned his head toward her and arched a brow. "I was angry."

"Magnificently angry," she said with a smile that didn't linger. The emotions rose in her throat. She recalled the embrace they'd shared a fortnight ago, after he'd been struck in the head. She'd needed to touch him, to hold him then, to alleviate the fear that she might lose him.

Now, she felt something similar. Only, she didn't need him to banish the fear. She wanted him to ease her despair and soothe her anger. And, perhaps, she hoped he would give her something else to cling to.

Tilda scooted closer to him until their thighs were touching, or, at least, their clothing was. She laid her head against his shoulder. "Is this all right?"

"More than." He put his arm around her and held her.

As her sadness and ire began to settle, a new emotion fought to break through. She turned toward Hadrian and looked up at his familiar profile, the masculine angle of his jaw, the fringe of black lashes on his dark blue eyes, the slight bump in his nose that made his features imperfectly perfect.

He turned his head toward her, and his eyes met hers. Her heartbeat careened into a wild rhythm. She should move away, but she wanted comfort. And she wanted it from Hadrian. There was no one else in the world she would turn to in this moment. He understood her, and he'd demonstrated his unerring support.

She leaned up and pressed her lips to his, closing her eyes and praying she wasn't making a mistake. But how could she when this seemed the most appropriate, the most *natural* thing to do?

Hadrian cupped her head and neck with his free hand as he returned the kiss. He pivoted toward her, and Tilda understood what she was feeling now—desire. And perhaps even…joy.

But a joy she'd never experienced before.

The kiss went on and on, as Hadrian wordlessly led her. It deepened until she felt wonderfully breathless.

Vaguely, she pondered whether they were nearing her grandmother's house. She ought to pull away, but this was so very lovely.

Hadrian's thumb stroked her jaw, and he lifted his head. "We're nearly there."

Tilda blinked. The reality of what had happened, of what she'd invited, rushed over her like a cold bucket of water on a winter morning. "I'm sorry," she whispered. She moved her hands, which had been clasping his neck, to her lap.

"You don't need to apologize, but perhaps I should. I hope you don't think I was taking advantage."

She briefly looked at him. "Not at all," she replied vehemently. "That was entirely my fault. I wanted…comfort."

"I hope I was able to provide it."

Yes, along with many other things. That was certainly true. He'd comforted her but also stirred something within her she hadn't known existed.

It frightened her.

She just didn't know what to do with all she was feeling—not the desire or the joy and certainly not the fear. However, things were changing, both with Hadrian and within herself. Tilda wasn't sure she was the same woman who'd stepped into the coach a short while ago.

But she didn't have time for such complications! Not now. Not when she was in the midst of the most important case of her life.

"Er, thank you," she said awkwardly. The coach began to slow, and she was relieved to be leaving in a moment.

Hadrian clasped her hand. "I hope you won't regret that. I will not."

She risked another glance at him. It was hard to look at him and not want to kiss him again. "You said that last time," she pointed out with a wry smile.

"Well, I suspect I will never regret kissing you. I care deeply for you, Tilda. Surely you know that."

"I do." She released his hand as the coach stopped. "But can we not discuss this? For now, anyway."

"Yes." The door opened, and Hadrian looked at her intently. "For now."

He climbed out and helped her down, then walked her to the door. "I'll pick you up tomorrow for our meeting with Fellows."

"Thank you. I'll see you then." She gave him a bright smile, grateful for his patience and understanding. She quickly ducked into the house and found she had to fight to catch her breath.

What foolishness had she indulged in? How was she going to face Hadrian tomorrow?

The same as she always did, she told herself calmly. They would continue with the investigation.

But there would come a time when she wouldn't be able to ignore what had happened, or what was *happening* between them. Hadrian had all but said so.

She was beginning to think that perhaps she didn't want to. That meant facing the fear that was holding her back.

First, she had to determine whatever that was.

CHAPTER 14

*A*s Hadrian arrived to fetch Tilda for their appointment with Fellows at the Home Office, he had to set aside his consuming thoughts about the kisses they'd shared last night in the coach. Though he longed to talk to her about what happened, he would not. He would honor her request that they not discuss it.

He recognized that she'd been upset and vulnerable. However, he didn't think he'd taken advantage, not when she'd initiated the intimacy.

Departing the coach, Hadrian made it all the way to the door and even knocked before Tilda appeared. Vaughn answered, and the entrance hall contained not only Tilda but her mother and grandmother as well. Apparently, he would need to exchange pleasantries today, not that he minded.

From the small pleats between Tilda's brows, he could see that she didn't care for the delay. That was not surprising, as Tilda was about business and efficiency above all else. Besides, she wouldn't want to spend time with her mother in Hadrian's presence so she could continue her matchmaking campaign.

Not that Hadrian minded that either, truth be told.

Lady Pierce smiled brilliantly. "How pleasant to see you again, Lord Ravenhurst. Tilda says you have more business today. My goodness, I had no idea your investigations demanded the two of you spend so much time together." She looked at him and then Tilda somewhat expectantly.

Her message seemed clear to Hadrian. They spent a great deal of time together, and they got on well. The natural progression would be that they make a match. Except Tilda wasn't interested in such progression, not that her mother paid any attention to what Tilda wanted.

"Will you be back for dinner?" Tilda's grandmother asked, thankfully changing the subject.

Relief flashed in Tilda's warm green eyes. "I should be. We must be off."

"So quickly?" her mother asked with a faint pout.

"I'm afraid so," Hadrian said apologetically. "We have an appointment, and we mustn't be late."

"I see," her mother said. "Well, I hope you're looking forward to the ball next week. We are."

Hadrian glanced toward Tilda's grandmother. "Remind me, Mrs. Wren, are you also attending?"

"I am not." She slid a mildly irritated glance toward her daughter-in-law.

"That is unfortunate," Hadrian said. "I'd hoped to see you there. I'm sure the invitation would include you if you wanted to go," he added benignly. He settled his gaze on Tilda's mother. "You can arrange that, can't you, Lady Pierce?"

Tilda's mother blinked. "Certainly. I didn't know she wanted to come." She sent what seemed to be a forced smile toward her mother-in-law. "I'm so glad she'll join us."

"Excellent," Tilda said as she turned toward the door. "See you later." She departed the house.

Hadrian touched his hat as he made eye contact with Tilda's grandmother. She gave him a grateful smile whilst arching a sardonic brow at her daughter-in-law. Hadrian had to swallow a chuckle as he turned toward the butler.

Vaughn inclined his head. "My lord."

Pivoting, Hadrian stepped outside and hastened to catch up with Tilda.

At the coach, she pivoted toward him. "Thank you for that."

He lifted his shoulder in a faint shrug. "You'll have a much better time if your grandmother attends, won't you?"

"Undoubtedly," she replied.

Leach opened the door for her, and she climbed into the coach. Hadrian briefly considered sitting across from her so that last night's activities would not be close to mind, but he decided they needed to focus on their investigation, not Hadrian's profound reaction to what had happened. He knew he loved her, but for the first time, he had a spark of hope that she may feel something for him in return.

"I have to apologize about last night." Hadrian said.

Tilda snapped her gaze to his. "What do you mean? I thought we weren't—"

Hadrian realized how badly he'd misspoken and held up his hand. "What I mean is I should have tried to touch Lowther or something in his house so that I could perhaps see what he was hiding from us. However, I was too caught up in the moment and neglected to do my part. I'm rather annoyed with myself."

Tilda exhaled, and he could see the relief in her features. She had thought he was going to discuss the kissing. Of course she had. He'd stupidly worded his apology.

"It's all right," she said. "Honestly, I didn't even think of it." She pursed her lips with faint disdain. "That's how upset I've been. This is such a betrayal by someone whom I have long trusted. But I need to set my feelings aside. Lowther is utterly entwined in this situation, and his role is not benign."

"Do you think there's a chance he may be criminally prosecuted?" Hadrian asked.

"I don't know," Tilda replied. "Since he's employed by the Metropolitan Police, I'm not sure what will happen."

"That's true." Hadrian thought of how he'd reported Padgett's behavior after their first case. Hadrian was all but certain the inspector had bribed witnesses and nearly ensured an innocent man was prosecuted for murder. However, nothing had happened to him. He'd simply retired from the police and continued to traffic in information with Clement and who knew who else.

Tilda looked over at Hadrian. "You must use your rank and influence as you see fit today. It may be important in ensuring that Fellows responds."

Hadrian nodded. "I'll do that. And I won't make the mistake I made with Lowther last night." He removed his gloves and tucked them into his coat pocket.

They arrived at the Home Office a short while later and made their way to Fellows's small office on the first floor. The room had a window and a hearth. Two chairs stood on the opposite side of Fellows's desk from where he sat.

Fellows rose as they entered. He was in his mid-forties and of average height. He had a lighter build but a slight paunch. His face was angular, with a long nose and a sharp chin and small hazel eyes. His dark hair was streaked with several gray strands and formed a widow's peak at his forehead. He inclined his head toward Hadrian. "Lord Ravenhurst." He shifted his attention to Tilda, expectantly.

Hadrian had not mentioned that he would have company when he'd requested this meeting. "Thank you for meeting with us today. Allow me to introduce my investigative partner, Miss Matilda Wren."

Fellows arched a brow. "Are you related to Sergeant Thomas Wren?"

"He was my father," Tilda replied. "I believe you knew him."

"No," Fellows said. "I only met him in death, I'm afraid." He gave her an apologetic look. "Please sit." He gestured to the chairs in front of his desk and moved to close the door before sitting back down.

Tilda set her reticule on her lap and addressed Fellows. "In fact, that is why we've come today. We wanted to speak with you about the night my father died."

Fellows clasped his hands on top of the desk and nodded. His brow creased with concern. "May I ask what has sparked your interest after all this time?"

Hadrian wondered if Tilda would mention the note in Padgett's coat pocket.

"I suppose I've always been curious." Tilda lifted a shoulder. "I appreciate you indulging my inquisitiveness. Would you mind telling me what happened that night?"

"Not at all." Fellows looked at her with sympathy. "I imagine it was difficult to lose your father, and I'm sorry for that. I was a constable with B Division. I was summoned to the apothecary shop by Constable Jurgens, I believe. I saw the front window had been broken. Mr. Williams was inside. He was rather distressed. Your father, of course, was already dead, and it was evident he'd been exsanguinated by a cut to the neck. If it's any solace to you, I imagine he died quickly and without pain."

Tilda's lips pressed together and tightened. It wasn't really a smile but an acknowledgment of what Fellows said.

"I did notice the lack of blood, however," Fellows continued. "The apothecary also mentioned that, and Inspector Padgett, who arrived before me, insisted the killer had cleaned up. He said he'd found evidence of that—an empty bucket with a bit of dirty water at the bottom that may have contained blood. That's all in the occurrence book as well as a separate report, which I'm sure you've read."

"No, I have not," Tilda said. "I tried to obtain the records from B Division, but they didn't have anything."

Fellows's dark brows pulled together. "That's strange. Did they look carefully?"

"Apparently," Hadrian replied. "The constable is to let us know if he finds something. You're the criminal clerk. Can you think of anywhere else the records might be?"

"I suppose they could be in storage here at the Home Office. I'll ask an assistant clerk to look."

"We would appreciate that," Hadrian said.

Tilda cocked her head. "Do you find Padgett's murder strange?"

Fellows seemed to ponder her question a moment. "Since I used to work for the Metropolitan Police, I find all murder questionable. But I have to say, I'm not terribly surprised that is how Padgett met his end. I don't know how well you knew him, or what you may have heard, but he was involved in shady dealings. I think he knew and associated with some rather unsavory people."

"Then you weren't surprised to hear he'd been choked to death?" Tilda asked.

"Not terribly, no," Fellows replied. "I am sorry for him, however."

"You knew him well?" Tilda asked.

"Not really," Fellows said. "Our paths crossed a few times, but most of what I know of him is from others."

"Rumors then?" Tilda clarified.

Fellows chuckled. "I suppose so." Sobering, Fellows frowned. "I know the investigation into your father's death has been reopened. I can't say I'm sorry to hear it. I haven't yet spoken to Detective Inspector Teague, but I imagine he may wish to speak with me, as you have today. I'll be as helpful as I can."

"What was your deduction about the lack of blood?" Tilda asked. "Did you believe the killer had cleaned it up?"

"I didn't have any reason to doubt Padgett at the time."

"But perhaps you do now?" Hadrian asked. "Because of his reputation since then?"

Fellows's brow creased with concern. "It's probably a question Detective Inspector Teague should ask and pursue. At the time, I had no cause to distrust Padgett. There was the bucket, and there seemed to have been time for the killer to clean. Mr. Williams, the apothecary, said he'd consoled his wife before coming downstairs."

"Do you think the killer must have taken the cloths or whatever he used to wipe up the blood with him since they weren't found at the shop?" Tilda asked.

"That was our conclusion," Fellows said.

Tilda clutched her reticule tightly—Hadrian could see her tension. "Did you ever think my father might have been killed elsewhere and moved to the shop?"

Hadrian studied Fellows closely for any hint of reaction, but there was nothing. The man was either telling the truth or incredibly good at lying.

"I confess it occurred to me once or twice over the years that he may have been moved," Fellows replied. "But as I said, I had no reason not to believe what Padgett said."

"May I ask why you moved on from the Met?" Tilda asked. "Forgive my saying so, but I can't imagine a great many constables would seek to be a clerk."

Fellows gave them a sheepish smile. "I'm afraid I preferred the clerical aspects of the job. I enjoyed working the desk at the station and assisting in the charge room. I eagerly accepted a clerical position here at the Home Office, and I've been most content."

Tilda abruptly stood, and in doing so, knocked a file off the corner of the desk. It landed near Hadrian, and he knew exactly what she'd intended.

He bent to retrieve it and clasped his bare hand around it. He focused all his thoughts on the night that Tilda's father was killed. He imagined Mr. Williams' apothecary shop and delved deep to reach into the past.

The shop filled his vision, and he was standing over the body of Thomas Wren. His neck was cut open, and blood stained his flesh and clothing. His eyes were mercifully closed. Seeing Tilda's dead father shook Hadrian.

He clung to the vision. In it, he felt pleased and relieved. He looked up from the body and saw Lowther and Jurgens straightening. Lowther looked pale and apprehensive, whilst Jurgens arched his back and stretched his arms. Padgett was there too. He had his hands on his hips, and he nodded, appearing satisfied. The vision began to fade, and Hadrian reluctantly allowed it. He couldn't be absent too long.

As Fellows's office came into view once more, Hadrian blinked. He straightened, then stood and set the file back on the desk.

Fellows, who'd stood whilst Hadrian retrieved the file, inclined his head toward Hadrian. "Thank you."

"We appreciate you taking the time to speak with us today," Hadrian said.

"Do let me know if I can be of further help," Fellows replied.

Hadrian nodded, then went to open the door for Tilda. She said goodbye to Fellows, and they departed.

As soon as they were outside, she looked over at Hadrian as they made their way to the coach. "You had a vision, didn't you? I was hoping you would."

Hadrian wasn't sure he wanted to tell her every detail. He preferred to leave out the part about her father but prepared himself for the likelihood that she would ask.

"I did," Hadrian said. "I was in the apothecary shop the night your father was killed."

CHAPTER 15

$\mathcal{T}$ilda's heart pounded. She both wanted to hear everything Hadrian had seen and to ask him to only tell her what she needed to know.

"What did you see?" she whispered, her body tense as she angled herself toward him on the seat. He also pivoted so they were facing each other as best as they could.

"It was definitely Fellows's memory, because I saw the three constables, Padgett, Lowther, and Jurgens," Hadrian said. "I sensed Fellows was nervous but also pleased."

"About what, I wonder? I don't suppose you've acquired the ability to hear what they were saying."

A regretful smile lifted his lips. "Unfortunately, no, but I think I could surmise their moods from looking at them. Padgett seemed confident and satisfied—he had his hands on his hips. Jurgens was arching his back and stretching his arms. It was almost as if he were—"

"If he had just moved something heavy?" Tilda asked, her pulse continuing its frantic beat.

Hadrian nodded. "Exactly what I thought. Lowther appeared apprehensive. I thought he looked pale."

"I suppose that should make me feel better—perhaps he didn't care for whatever they were doing." Tilda's lip curled. "It doesn't."

Hadrian met her gaze with understanding. "I don't blame you."

"How do you know it was the night my father died?" Tilda hesitated before whispering, "Did you see him?"

"I did."

Tilda took a deep breath and exhaled as her pulse spiked even more. An unsettling energy rushed through her. "You saw that he was dead?"

"Yes."

"I can't decide if I want to know more than that. I've thought about his death so many times over the years. I want to say it's become easier to think of him killed in that way, but I know now, with everything being brought up again, that it really hasn't." The familiar ache of loss tightened her chest. "Were his eyes open?" she asked softly.

Hadrian shook his head. "They were closed."

Tilda let out a long breath. "It's silly, but that gives me a bit of comfort."

"Nothing you could feel about this is silly," Hadrian said vehemently. "It's all real and it's true, and you should have no shame."

"Thank you." Tilda warmed at his words. She tried to think about the investigation and not just her emotions. "Was there blood?"

"Not on the floor," Hadrian replied. "The wound was bloody, but it looked dry to me. The floor was completely clean. I can't imagine a killer would have tidied it so well." His brow darkened. "Nor do I believe any of the men from the Met who were present that night could have thought that either."

"If they did, they were terrible at their work," Tilda noted wryly.

"Well, Fellows did say he prefers clerical work," Hadrian said. "I confess the interview with him surprised me. I expected

Fellows to be shifty. Instead, he sounded almost credible. I wondered if he was perhaps unaware of what had truly gone on."

"Given the vision you had, I don't think that's possible. I think we must presume he's an excellent liar."

Hadrian nodded. "Do you have any suggestions for how we might persuade him to reveal the truth?"

A frown twisted Tilda's lips briefly. "Not at the moment, but I will think on it. A memory that would help us pressure him would be helpful, and it doesn't necessarily need to be *his* memory." Tilda gave him a hopeful look.

Hadrian considered trying to see Lowther's or Jurgens's memories. "I wonder if we'd have better luck spending our energy on Lowther. Between the apprehension I sensed in Lowther during Fellows's memory and your close relationship with him, don't you think we can persuade him to tell the truth?"

Tilda agreed that was their best path, but she thought they would probably have to truly break him, and perhaps even involve his wife. Which Tilda would do if it became necessary. Nothing was more important than discovering what really happened and finding justice for her father.

"I think we have to try," Tilda said. "Let's go to his house again after we're finished at the Yellow Dog."

"Good enough." Hadrian straightened on the seat, and Tilda eyed his profile. It was difficult to sit here and not think of what had happened last night. She'd lain awake for quite some time, unable to sleep, as she recalled his kisses and how wonderful he'd made her feel.

She could not afford to think about that, both because she wasn't ready to acknowledge whatever she was feeling and mostly because she needed to focus on the investigations. Pivoting, she faced forward, straightening her spine against the squab.

"We need a plan for speaking with Mr. Akers at the Yellow Dog." She glanced over at Hadrian. "I've been wondering if we'll have better luck with money or threats."

"Since Dorris almost certainly paid him to be his messenger, I would think money would work quite well," Hadrian replied. "It's just a question of how much."

"I'm sure you're right," Tilda agreed. "How's your head after the vision in Fellows's office?"

"I've a mild ache, but I don't need lavender oil yet." He sent her a smile. "I plan to have a glass of ale at the Yellow Dog, so I can touch something Mr. Akers has handled."

"Well, I have the lavender oil for afterwards, should you need it," she said.

They arrived at the Yellow Dog a few minutes later. Leach opened the door of the coach, and they stepped down.

"I'll move the coach up to the end of the street and wait for you there," Leach said.

"Thank you," Hadrian said as he floated his hand against the small of Tilda's back, his fingers barely grazing the base of her spine.

Though the touch was brief and separated by her layers of clothing, she felt it intensely. Perhaps that was because his hand was still bare. A warm flush rose up her back, and she found herself wishing he would press his entire hand against her.

They entered the pub, with its narrow common room and low ceilings. A bar of about twelve feet stretched in front of the back wall. The barkeep stood wiping down the wood. He was not the same person they'd seen the other day. This man was around fifty with a shiny bald pate and a large, sturdy build. He looked as though he could pull a tree from the ground, roots and all. Tilda hoped this was the publican, Mr. Akers.

"Afternoon," Hadrian said. "A pint of ale, please."

The barkeep glanced toward Tilda.

"I'll have the same." She gave him a meek smile.

When the barkeep returned with the ale, Hadrian handed him payment. Tilda could see it was a bit too much, but that was likely on purpose.

"Are you Akers?" Hadrian asked.

The barkeep narrowed one blue eye. "I am. Who's asking?"

"Lord Ravenhurst, and this is my associate, Miss Wren. We'd like to ask you some questions about an arrangement you have. You traffic messages for a man called Dorris and the jeweler, Mr. Timms."

Akers grunted. "Timms was killed. I don't think I'll be delivering any more messages."

"Yes, he was," Hadrian said. "We're trying to locate some stolen items that may have come to him from Dorris." Hadrian dropped a few coins on the bar, and Akers swept them up instantly.

"I don't know anything about stolen goods," Akers said.

"Then what can you tell us about Mr. Dorris?" Hadrian asked.

Akers shrugged. "I don't know what I should say, especially after what happened to Timms." Akers glanced about, but Tilda didn't think he looked particularly nervous.

"We won't reveal how we learned whatever you tell us," Hadrian said evenly. "And we're certainly not going to disclose anything to Mr. Dorris."

"I don't want to end up like Timms," Akers said, his gaze uncertain.

Tilda gently nudged Hadrian's arm with her elbow. Hadrian set more money on the bar. Tilda hated paying Akers, but she was desperate for information. She just knew that Dorris's scheme—whatever it was—had to be connected to her father and the thefts he'd been investigating when he was killed. What she didn't know was if these thefts had anything to do with his death. But that was what she meant to find out.

"Do you at least admit that you work with Dorris, and you act as his go-between with Timms?" Hadrian asked.

Akers scooped up the additional coins. "I have done that."

"For how long?" Hadrian said.

"I can't remember. Years, I suppose."

"Five years? Ten years?" Hadrian prompted.

"At least ten," Akers replied.

"What can you tell us about Dorris? Where does he live, for instance?"

"No idea where he lives. Can't say much about him, except he's Quality. Wears expensive garments. Talks like you." Akers nodded at Hadrian.

"That's all you know, after ten or more years?" Hadrian asked, sounding incredulous and perhaps a bit irritated. Tilda hoped that didn't discourage Akers from saying anything else.

"It's not always Dorris that comes," Akers said. "There are others who come in his place sometimes."

Hadrian's gaze didn't waver. "Do they work for Dorris?"

Akers nodded once more. "There's two of 'em. The friendlier one is a short, squat fellow called Rymer. He's an ugly bloke with pockmarks all over his face and a wide gap between his front teeth."

Tilda tensed, and her pulse spiked. Was Rymer the same man with the pockmarked face whom Hadrian had seen in his vision? That man had been holding Mrs. Goodwin's missing silver salver.

"The other's called Bant," Akers went on. "He's frightening. Has deep-set eyes that look as though he'd just as soon cut your throat as speak to you and a thin, angry mouth. And he's got a wicked scar on his hand. Looks like he was bitten by a dog or some wild animal."

Hadrian glanced at Tilda. She gave him a slight nod. This was good information. These could very well be the two men who committed the robberies for Dorris. But who was Dorris?

"Have those men been around as long as Dorris?" Tilda asked.

"Seems so," Akers said. "They, including Dorris, don't come terribly often, especially the last few years."

"Would you say their visits have decreased over time?" Hadrian asked.

"I suppose so, but I can't say I've marked it much." Akers shrugged again. "Months go by now, and I don't see them."

"How does this process of communication work?" Hadrian asked. "Dorris or one of his minions comes to you with a message?"

"When Timms wanted to send a message to Dorris, he would bring it to me."

Hadrian eyed the barkeep steadily. "And how do you deliver the message to Dorris?"

"We have a signal." Akers glanced toward the front of the pub. "I put a candle in the window upstairs."

Tilda disguised her excitement at the prospect of drawing Dorris out. "Could you do that now to signal him to come?"

Akers looked at her as if she'd sprouted a second head. "Timms is dead. What message would I have for Dorris? I already told you, my business with Dorris is finished. That's all I can tell you."

Akers walked away from them to the other end of the bar.

Tilda exhaled, wishing they'd learned more but glad they'd discovered that much. She watched as Hadrian wrapped his bare hand around the glass of ale. His eyes glazed, and she knew he was seeing something. She could only hope it would be helpful.

After a few moments, he blinked, took a drink, and made a slight face.

"You don't care for the ale?" she whispered.

"Not particularly, but you should drink a little so we don't appear rude."

"I suppose, though we paid for it, so what would Akers care if we drank it or not?" Tilda took a sip and kept herself from making an even bigger face. It was terrible. She turned from the bar, and Hadrian escorted her out to the street.

When they reached the coach, Hadrian directed Leach to take

them to Inspector Lowther's house. Once they were seated together in the coach, Hadrian looked over at her. "I believe I saw Bant. He was in the pub on the other side of the bar from Akers. He looked as Akers described him—mean eyes and rather thin lips. The scar on his hand is quite nasty. He should be easy to identify."

Tilda frowned with disappointment. "Except we don't know where to look for him. It seems these two men, Rymer and Bant, are the thieves who stole from Mrs. Goodwin—and almost certainly others. Since Akers recalls seeing them over a number of years, it would seem they have long worked for Dorris."

"Do you find it astonishing that Dorris's scheme has gone on for so long?" Hadrian mused. "I wonder why the communication between him and Timms occurred so intermittently."

"Perhaps he just doesn't want to get caught," Tilda suggested. "Consequently, they don't commit these robberies very often."

"Dorris is going to have to find a new jeweler now," Hadrian remarked.

Tilda cocked her head. "Perhaps he's used another jeweler all along. It's possible their thefts *aren't* intermittent, and they use multiple places to fence the items."

"That's entirely possible," Hadrian said. "I think if I were going to traffic stolen items, I might use a variety of people to help fence them."

"I'm anxious to see what Teague can find in terms of police reports about thefts like Mrs. Goodwin's," Tilda said. "And I'm eager to speak with Clement about whatever newspaper articles he may have found."

Hadrian narrowed his eyes slightly. "I would love to know who Dorris is. Akers thought he was a man of quality."

"Could he be a gentleman?" Tilda wondered.

"It's possible. We know that social position and rank do not preclude someone from even the most heinous of crimes." He was referring to their first case in which the villain had been a viscount. His crimes had been horrendous, but he was, thankfully, dead.

Hadrian met her gaze. "You seem disappointed."

"A little, but I think it's because I'm more agitated about this case than usual."

"Of course, you are. It's personal."

"Yes, but I shouldn't allow it to be," Tilda said. "I'm not sure I'm doing my best work if I'm emotionally distracted."

She realized that statement could mean more than just the investigation. Kissing Hadrian was also an emotional distraction.

Hadrian's expression gentled. "I don't think you're capable of doing anything less than your best. Or at least trying."

"Thank you. This case has made me doubt myself and my skills." Perhaps it had pushed her so off-kilter that she wasn't able to examine what was happening between her and Hadrian. She knew he cared for her, and she absolutely cared for him, but now was not the time to determine what was to become of that.

Setting those too-consuming thoughts aside, she opened her reticule and found the small bottle of lavender oil. "Do you need this?"

"I should probably apply a little. I've only had two visions, but I do find that when I work to focus and exert great thought, the pain lasts longer. It's still a steady ache."

Last time he'd used it, Tilda had rubbed it into his forehead. She didn't want to touch him in that way again—not today. She would be overcome with emotion and may end up kissing him again.

That would not do.

She handed him the bottle. "I'll let you apply it. I'm rather distracted by our upcoming meeting with Lowther. I don't want to leave without obtaining the information we need."

"It's what you *deserve.*" Hadrian said as he opened the bottle. "We're going to find out what happened the night your father died and what he had to do with Dorris's theft scheme."

"Do you think his death was connected?" Tilda asked.

"I think someone killed your father and hid what truly happened. Right now, we can't discount any possibility." His dark blue eyes gleamed with an almost ruthless promise. "Tilda, I won't rest until we find the truth—no matter the cost."

CHAPTER 16

*H*adrian began Monday morning with his secretary, Elton. When they finished, he dashed upstairs to change his coat after noticing a loose thread.

Sharp met him and accepted the garment. "I'll fetch a fresh coat from the dressing chamber."

"Thank you. I'll need my hat and gloves as well," Hadrian said. "I need to leave shortly."

Tilda had sent him a note yesterday evening asking him to meet her and Clement at the coffee shop this morning. The reporter had information to share. She'd also invited Detective Inspector Teague in the hope that he'd reviewed past police reports and would also be able to share information.

Hadrian knew she was keen to learn something useful. Unfortunately, they hadn't been able to speak with Lowther on Saturday because he wasn't at home. Tilda had decided not to bother him on Sunday. She planned to speak with him today, no matter what.

Sharp came into the bedchamber with a coat and the requested accessories. He set the hat and gloves on a table where Mrs. Goodwin's tureen happened to be. Moving behind Hadrian, the valet helped him don the garment. "I've been meaning to ask you about that tureen. Shouldn't that be in the dining room?"

"It belongs to a client of Miss Wren's." Hadrian had spent a great deal of time trying to obtain additional memories from the item. He'd finally found some success last night, though his head had pained him terribly. He'd taken a bath liberally sprinkled with lavender oil.

"But you haven't returned it to her yet," Sharp replied.

"Not yet." Hadrian pulled the coat tight over his shoulders and turned to face his valet. "It may yet be of use to us in our investigation."

Sharp assessed Hadrian's appearance and flicked something off his shoulder. "You still haven't given her the mirror."

Hadrian didn't respond but narrowed his eyes slightly at Sharp.

"Is her birthday soon, perhaps?" Sharp asked.

"No."

Sharp's hazel eyes lit with an idea. "You can give it to her when you solve this case. A sort of celebration."

"Has anyone told you that you're intrusive?"

Cocking his head and stroking his chin in a shameless display of pretending to deeply contemplate Hadrian's question, Sharp blinked. "I'm sure someone has, but I can't think of who just now..."

Hadrian snorted.

"Do you plan to dance with Miss Wren at the Trumbull ball tomorrow night?" Sharp asked.

Though Hadrian wanted to, he wasn't sure she would. She'd indicated that she was not an accomplished dancer. Perhaps he could convince her. The waltz wasn't difficult, and he could guide her easily.

"Who can say?" Hadrian picked up his hat and gloves from the table. His gaze fell on the tureen briefly. He looked forward to sharing what he'd seen with Tilda.

"*You* can," Sharp called as Hadrian left the bedchamber.

When he arrived in Marylebone Lane, Tilda was waiting outside. He stepped out of the coach to greet her.

"I take it you're eager to leave?" he said as Leach held the door.

Tilda grimaced. "With the Trumbull ball tomorrow, my mother is in peak directorial form. If I have to engage in one more conversation about how to style my hair or what accessories I should wear, I shall scream."

"Well, we don't want that," Hadrian said with a chuckle. He helped her into the coach and followed behind, sitting beside her. Leach closed the door, and they were soon on their way.

"Thank you for coming this morning," Tilda said.

"I confess I was surprised that Vaughn had delivered a message from you."

She looked over at him. "He said he didn't see you."

"No, we did not meet," Hadrian replied. "But my butler told me Miss Wren's butler delivered the message. He couldn't have walked." Vaughn had a rather shuffling gait and was too old to be traveling so far on foot.

"He took a hack," Tilda explained. "He also had to deliver a note to Teague's house."

"That is an expense. Can you include it in Mrs. Goodwin's invoice?"

Tilda shook her head. "I don't think I'd feel right. Whilst this investigation into the stolen items that Dorris has been fencing will hopefully lead us to her missing salver, it's also heavily tied to the investigation into my father's death."

"I don't think she'd mind paying for the hack as part of your investigative expenses. You are indeed trying to find her salver. She indicated it was of special value to her."

"I suppose you're right. I'll consider it."

"Speaking of the salver, I've news to share," Hadrian said

eagerly. "I finally saw something useful from the tureen last night."

Tilda's brows shot up. "Did you?"

"I saw the tureen and the salver and the other items that were stolen from Mrs. Goodwin," Hadrian said. "I don't know whose memory it was, but the person separated the salver from the rest, which he put into a bag. I could tell the hands were masculine, but there was no scar—so he wasn't the thief called Bant."

"That's helpful," Tilda said. "Now we know the salver was separated from the other items. I wonder why."

"Did you change your mind and call on Lowther yesterday?" Hadrian wouldn't blame her if she had.

Tilda shook her head. "Though it was difficult." She smiled briefly. "You know me too well."

"I know how eager you are to speak with him, as am I."

"We'll talk to him later today." Tilda's eyes glinted with determination. "I don't plan to leave his house until he arrives at home."

Hadrian nodded. "I'll wait with you."

They arrived at the coffee house a few minutes later and made their way inside. Clement was already waiting for them at his regular table, but Teague was not.

A file folder sat on the table before Clement along with his cup of coffee. It occurred to Hadrian that he and Tilda never obtained coffee when they came here. Tilda and Hadrian sat opposite the reporter.

"I can hardly wait to hear what you've learned," Tilda said.

Clement glanced toward the door. "Is Teague usually punctual?"

"Yes," Tilda said. "We can wait a few more minutes, or you could just repeat yourself when he arrives."

"I'm fine doing that." Clement flashed a grin as he opened the folder. It appeared to be a stack of newspapers, but on top was a handwritten paper. Perhaps those were Clement's notes.

Clement regarded them from across the table, his eyes bright with excitement. "I found one article from 1857 and, as luck would have it, the reporter, Qualley, still works for the *Daily News*. I spoke with him, and he helped me locate other articles, many of which were written by him. Qualley remembers these cases clearly—there was a cluster of thefts, but not just silver and jewelry. There were paintings, vases, and other art pieces, even a few tapestries, and a *statue*." Clement laughed. "All the items were stolen from wealthy, prominent homes in the mid to late 1850s."

"That *is* lucky you found Qualley," Hadrian said.

Clement went on. "He dubbed the crimes the 'Stag Robberies' because so many items had stags. The thefts diminished, then dropped off entirely by 1860." Clement looked at Tilda. "The articles detailed the items stolen, so I compared them to the list you gave me. Well, I compared the silver and jewelry. Obviously, I couldn't do that with the other items."

"And the silver and jewelry match the list from Timms?" Tilda asked.

"Not entirely," Clement replied with a smile. "In each case, one or perhaps two, and in one instance, three items that were stolen were not on your list—meaning they weren't fenced, at least not with Timms."

Hadrian immediately thought of the salver they still hadn't found, the one he'd seen in his vision being separated from the other items. He exchanged a look with Tilda that told him she was thinking the same thing. They couldn't share that bit with Clement unless Hadrian wanted to explain his visions, which he did not. He wondered if he would ever share his ability with anyone besides Tilda and wasn't sure he would. He supposed he was still afraid that people would see him, at the very least, as mentally unstable, or, at most, outright insane.

"I wonder who fenced the non-silver and jewelry items," Tilda said. "How does one even fence a statue?"

"How does one *steal* a statue?" Hadrian asked drily. "That

seems difficult, both in accomplishing the feat and not getting caught whilst doing so."

"That would be challenging," Clement agreed. "It seems these thefts had to be completed by more than one person."

"Yes, there were two," Tilda said. She glanced at Hadrian. "We learned that from Timms, the jeweler."

Hadrian admired her improvisation. They knew there were two from Hadrian's visions and from Akers at the Yellow Dog, but attributing it to Timms, who was dead, ensured they didn't have to explain how they knew.

"Will you try to find who was fencing these other items?" Clement asked.

"Absolutely," Tilda replied. "Though I'm not sure where to begin."

"Perhaps Teague will have information that will help." Clement frowned. "He's quite late now."

Tilda looked toward the door. "Yes, and that's not like him. I wonder if something came up in the Detective Branch."

"Do you have any idea why some of the silver and jewelry would not have been fenced or fenced elsewhere?" Clement asked. "It seems odd there was at least one item missing from every single robbery."

Hadrian met Clement's gaze. "The item missing from Mrs. Goodwin's robbery is a salver with a coat of arms etched into the middle and delicate beading around the edge."

"Does the coat of arms have a stag?" Clement asked with a smirk.

Tilda laughed softly. "Indeed, it does."

Clement drummed his fingers on the table as his brow creased. "Perhaps it would be helpful to put notices in the newspaper about these missing items now," he suggested as his hand stilled. "I know it's been several years, but if someone recognized one of these items amongst their possessions, we may be able to trace where it came from."

"That's not a bad idea," Tilda said. "We'll have to consider it."

Clement narrowed his eyes at the door. "A constable just came in, and he's coming this way."

Tilda turned as did Hadrian.

The young man was from Scotland Yard. He stopped at their table and inclined his head. "Lord Ravenhurst, Miss Wren, I have a note for you from Detective Inspector Teague."

He handed a piece of paper to Tilda. She unfolded the parchment and almost immediately clapped her hand over her mouth. She thrust the paper at Hadrian. He read the words and his blood chilled.

Teague was, in fact, busy. He'd been called to an alley off the Strand because a body had been found.

It was Inspector Lowther.

CHAPTER 17

A rushing sound filled Tilda's ears, and she knew it was her blood pumping frantically. As upset as she'd been with Inspector Lowther, she'd never wished him ill.

She looked up at the constable and clasped her hands together to keep them from shaking. "Are you going there now?"

"I am," the constable replied.

Tilda stood, nearly knocking her chair over in her haste. "We'll come with you."

"Yes." Hadrian leapt up.

Clement closed his file folder and rose. "May I ride with you?"

Tilda wasn't sure what Teague would think of them bringing Clement along, but she didn't wish to exclude him. Clement was a helpful part of the investigation. The constable instructed them where to go, and they followed him from the coffee house.

"Are you walking?" Tilda asked the constable.

He paused and turned to face her, his expression faintly perplexed. "Yes."

"Ride with us," Hadrian said before giving the direction to Leach.

They all climbed into the coach. Tilda and Hadrian sat on the forward-facing seat, whilst Clement and the constable sat on the rear-facing seat. Tilda set her reticule on her lap and clutched it fiercely. Hadrian reached over and gently clasped her hand for a brief moment. His gaze met hers, and his concern was unmistakable.

"I'm sorry," he murmured.

She didn't trust herself to speak, so she only nodded. She couldn't help thinking of Mrs. Lowther and their children. Did they even know yet?

A few minutes later, they arrived in the alley off the Strand near the Waterloo Bridge. They quickly departed the coach and found Detective Inspector Teague. He stood with a sergeant from the Detective Branch, a tall, slender man around Hadrian's age, with light brown hair and small, sharp blue eyes, .

Teague looked over at Tilda as they approached, his expression grim.

Lowther's body lay on the ground, chest down, his head turned so she could see his profile. There was something odd about the way he was positioned.

"That doesn't look natural to me," Tilda observed. "What I mean is that Lowther doesn't appear as though he fell down."

Teague shook his head. "He looks as though he was put here."

Tilda crouched down to look at Lowther's face more closely. His lip was split, and his chin and eye were bruised. "Looks like he was in a fight."

"I sent the constables to ask around," Teague said. "This is Sergeant Wycombe. We estimate Lowther's been dead since late last night, perhaps around eleven."

"I would make the same assessment." Emotion welled in Tilda's throat, but she tamped it down. Now was not the time to be melancholy. She froze as she noticed Lowther's neck. It was hard to see since he was prone. But now that she was close, she could see his throat had been cut.

She turned her head to look up at Teague.

"You see it," Teague said flatly.

"Another member—or former member—of the Metropolitan Police with their throat slashed," Tilda noted with alarm. "And each time, there was an accompanying crime. The apothecary shop and Padgett's lodgings were both robbed, and now Lowther looks as though he was in a brawl. Are his watch and money missing?"

Teague nodded. "Of course."

"There doesn't seem to be enough blood here." The same as with her father. Gooseflesh formed on Tilda's neck.

"I agree," Teague said. "I lifted the body to check but set him back down the way I found him. I'm waiting for the coroner to come before moving him."

Tilda looked to Hadrian, who offered his hand. She clasped him firmly, and he helped her rise. Aside from the help, she appreciated the warmth and strength of his grip. It reminded her that she was not alone.

Had she felt alone? After her father had died, she'd certainly felt that way. Lowther's death reminded her, painfully, of that loss. Perhaps because she'd always associated Lowther with her father's death—first in good ways, but more recently in bad.

Tilda felt cold. She wrapped her arms around herself.

"All three murders appear to have involved theft, but Padgett's death stands out as different. He was choked." Teague took a breath, his features dark with consternation. "It seems there's something larger going on here. I must consider ensuring Jurgens and Fellows are protected until we find the killer."

"Unless one of them murdered all three men," Tilda said.

Teague's brow formed deep furrows. "I suppose that's possible. Damn, I hate thinking someone from the Met could be guilty of such crimes." He glanced at Sergeant Wycombe, whose expression turned dark.

Tilda pressed her fingertips into her arms. "And yet, you

know these men from the Met lied about what happened the night my father died. They're all guilty of deception at least."

"And Fellows isn't with the Met anymore," Hadrian interjected.

Clement had moved to stand near Lowther's head. "Where is his hat?"

"We didn't find it," Teague replied.

Tilda surveyed the body. Lowther's hands were at his sides, and the right arm was bent at the elbow. She leaned down and scrutinized his flesh. "There should be wounds on his hands if he was in a fight. He was right-handed, and his knuckles are undamaged."

Teague stepped around Lowther and bent down to look at his left hand. "There's a scratch on this one—on the back."

Hadrian crouched to investigate the right hand. He surreptitiously grazed his fingers against Lowther's flesh, lingering for a long moment. When he rose, he looked toward Tilda and gave his head the barest shake. She understood; he'd tried to see a memory and failed, or he'd seen something that wasn't helpful.

One of the constables returned. Teague, rising, asked what he'd found.

"Nothing, I'm afraid," the constable replied. "I spoke to several people in the area, and no one saw what happened. No one even knew Lowther was here, except the woman who found him."

"Who is the woman?" Tilda asked.

"She lives nearby and saw Lowther lying in the alley," Teague said. "She thought he was a drunk and told the barkeep at the tavern around the corner. He came out here to move the man along and discovered he was an inspector and that he was dead."

Clement wrote in his notebook, his pencil scratching furiously over the paper.

Teague narrowed his eyes at the man. "What are you doing?"

"Making notes," Clement replied as he barely glanced at Teague.

"If you're going to write about this, you must promise not to share these details," Teague said firmly. "We don't know why Lowther was killed."

Tilda agreed. She released her arms and let them drop to her sides as she fixed on Clement. "You can't say anything about the connection between these three deaths. We don't want to alert the killer."

Clement nodded. "I understand."

Teague sent a glower toward Tilda and Hadrian. "You probably shouldn't have brought him," he muttered.

"I promise I won't disclose anything you don't approve of," Clement vowed. "This doesn't appear to be a matter of public safety, so I don't feel compelled to make it known. This killer is targeting specific people. But why?"

"The conspiracy is cracking," Hadrian said.

She'd thought the same thing. "We met with Fellows on Saturday, and my impression was that he is either an excellent liar about what happened the night my father died, or he knew nothing. I don't see how the latter is possible."

"I don't either," Teague said. He looked to the inspector from the Detective Branch. "Wycombe, you and I will need to interview Fellows. And Jurgens. I'd planned to, but now we must prioritize those meetings."

Tilda wouldn't mind speaking to Jurgens again. She had time since she would not be going to Lowther's house later. Except she probably should visit Mrs. Lowther and the children. With Mrs. Acorn's biscuits, which she'd planned to bring anyway.

"Has Mrs. Lowther been notified?" Tilda asked softly. She would likely not be worried that her husband had been gone all night. That was not an odd occurrence in his line of work. Hadrian edged closer to Tilda, so that their arms nearly touched. She was grateful for his proximity.

"Not yet." Teague exhaled. "I'll be calling on her after the coroner arrives and we transport the body to Scotland Yard. Graythorpe should be here soon."

Tilda hadn't yet told Teague about her father's diary and the connection she'd made to her investigation regarding Mrs. Goodwin's stolen items. "I've been meaning to speak with you about my case."

"That will need to wait, I'm afraid," Teague said apologetically.

"It can't because it's tied to my father's death." Tilda watched Teague's surprise widen his eyes and flare his nostrils. "My mother found a diary from when he died. In it, he describes a case he's working on regarding stolen items. He mentioned a brooch that was among the items Timms sold."

"Timms is the jeweler who sold the items?" Teague asked.

"He *was*," Tilda replied. "He was murdered last Friday at his shop. More specifically, his throat was cut, and several items were stolen."

"*Blast.*" Teague put his hand over his mouth and chin for a moment. When he lowered it, his lips were pulled into a deep frown. "To be murdered in that way with an accompanying theft is too coincidental, especially after what you read in your father's diary. Remind me of all you know about this fencing situation at Timms's shop."

Tilda and Hadrian reviewed everything about Timms, the items he had record of selling, Dorris, and his scheme with the publican at the Yellow Dog. They concluded with telling him about the cart speeding toward them on the street.

"You didn't tell me you were nearly run down," Clement said, aghast.

"At the time, I thought it was more likely to do with me poking into my father's death," Tilda said. "However, now I know that the thefts are related to that. Or at least to my father."

Teague put a hand on his hip. "We must consider that the case Sergeant Wren was investigating played some role in his death."

"I think so too," Tilda said with some relief. "I'm glad you said so. My father was working on the investigation with an Inspector Knowles at the Detective Branch. Unfortunately, we can't speak with Knowles because he died earlier this decade."

Teague frowned. "That's unfortunate."

"Clement did some research into old newspaper articles about thefts of silver and jewelry. He found a series of them that were called the 'Stag Robberies,' and they included more than silver and jewelry." She looked at Clement. "Will you tell Teague everything, please?"

Clement nodded and proceeded to repeat everything he'd revealed at the coffee shop. When he was finished, Teague blew out a breath.

"The missing pieces from the stolen lots are puzzling. What happened to them?" Teague asked.

"We don't know. At least one of them has a stag," Tilda said. "It's part of a coat of arms etched into Mrs. Goodwin's missing silver salver, which we were not able to recover and Timms said he never received. Now that we know there are other items—paintings, vases, and the like—I want to find who was fencing those."

Teague crossed his arms over his chest. "How do you plan to do that?"

"To start, I want to look for police records with the non-silver and jewelry items in the articles Clement found."

"That will mean reviewing the occurrence books in the divisions in which the thefts occurred," the sergeant pointed out with a faint grimace.

"Yes, we have the dates of the thefts, and we'll know in which division to look." Tilda looked at Clement. "Can you provide me a list of the robberies detailing what was stolen as well as when and where it happened?"

Clement nodded. "I already made you a copy. We just hadn't got to that part before you received Detective Inspector Teague's note. It's in the folder, which I left in Ravenhurst's coach."

"Let's divide the work by division," Teague said. "Give one or two divisions to Wycombe. He can start on that this afternoon." He glanced at the sergeant, who inclined his head eagerly.

"I can take a division too," Clement offered.

Tilda smiled at the reporter. "That would be helpful, thank you."

"I'll fetch the file." Clement turned and hurried toward the coach.

Tilda pinned Teague with an expectant stare. "When do you plan to speak with Jurgens and Fellows?"

"Today, I hope."

"Then we should plan to meet this evening or in the morning," Tilda replied crisply, glad things would be happening quickly. "You can share what you learned from them, and the rest of us can report on what we find in the occurrence books."

Teague gave her a patient look. "I know you're eager to have answers, but I think it will take you longer to obtain what you need from the divisions. They may not be able to provide the occurrence books immediately. In some cases, these are from more than a decade ago."

"Are you saying we should meet tomorrow?" Hadrian asked.

"Perhaps, but more likely Wednesday morning," Teague replied. "Of course, if anything urgent happens, we must notify one another."

Clement returned with his folder. "Shall we divide the work?"

"I can tell the divisions by the locations if you have them listed," Wycombe said.

"Why don't you go into the tavern around the corner and divide the assignments?" Teague said.

Wycombe nodded. "I can do that quickly."

"I'll come with you." Clement joined the sergeant, and they disappeared around the corner.

Tilda's gaze slid to Lowther's body. "Do you want me to

accompany you to speak with Mrs. Lowther?" She looked to Teague and held her breath.

Teague's eyes lit with compassion. "That isn't necessary, unless you really want to. It might be better if you console her later, after she's had time to accept what's happened."

The memory of learning of her father's death rose in Tilda's mind. That had been the worst day of her life. The superintendent had come to the house and spoken to her mother. Tilda had listened from the entrance hall and walked into the parlor before he'd finished.

Tilda had asked the superintendent if he could be mistaken, that it wasn't her father who'd died, but someone else. He'd assured her that it was Sergeant Wren, and Tilda's entire world had shattered. It had taken her weeks, months even, to truly accept what happened. Sometimes, she wondered if she ever had. She felt awful for the Lowther children. The thought of suffering such a loss was unconscionable.

The coroner arrived, and Teague moved to speak with him. Tilda could have joined them but didn't see the point. Right now, she only wanted comfort. She turned toward Hadrian and considered resting her head on his chest.

Instead, she looked up at him. "Let's go to the tavern and then onto one of the divisions."

Hadrian lightly touched her arm and stroked her sleeve. "I'm so sorry, Tilda. For the loss of Lowther and also for what you must certainly be feeling about your own father right now."

His eyes glowed with concern and something Tilda couldn't name—a warmth that made her feel cared for. Perhaps even... cherished.

That was both wondrous and terrifying.

CHAPTER 18

*H*adrian looked over at Tilda as they drove toward Great Marlborough Street. She'd chosen to review the occurrence books at C Division in the hope that she could speak with Inspector Jurgens again. She looked tense and sad. Hadrian wished he could soothe her, but sometimes one had to simply live in the darkness of a particular moment.

"It's good to have Teague fully on board with this investigation," Hadrian said. "I'm glad he so readily accepted the connection between the stolen items case and your father's death."

Tilda glanced at him. "Yes, I was also pleased, but not terribly surprised. Teague has always been logical and rational."

"He accepts you are an excellent investigator and doesn't question your methods or conclusions." Hadrian was glad Teague recognized Tilda's brilliance. "And he's right to do so."

"Thank you." A faint blush briefly tinted her cheeks, which was a trifle odd. She typically didn't reveal such things, but perhaps her emotions were too close to the surface just now. "If we're right and my father's death is connected to these thefts, I'm trying to think of who would be behind it all. Is it Dorris? And how would he have obtained the support of the Met?" Tilda shook her head. "I shouldn't get ahead of myself and make assumptions," she added with a wry smile. "I always say not to do that."

Hadrian smiled in return, hoping to reassure her. He was definitely glimpsing a new side to her. Or perhaps she was simply allowing him to see deeper. "You do, but I think you need to give yourself some grace with this investigation. It's personal, and as much as you want to be clear-headed, I don't know if it will always be possible, and that's not wrong."

Tilda blew out a breath. "I know, but I don't have to like it."

They arrived at the station in Great Marlborough Street and went inside. Tilda asked the clerk at the desk if she could speak with Inspector Jurgens, but unfortunately, he was not present. Hadrian sensed her frustration, though she masked it well to others.

"As it happens, we have other business," she said. "We need to see the occurrence books from these three dates." She handed the clerk a piece of paper on which Wycombe had written the dates.

Clement was going to B Division, and Wycombe was taking care of D and E divisions. He was also going to review files in the Detective Branch for information about these thefts. They all hoped the Detective Branch might have investigated one or more of them.

The clerk scanned the paper Tilda handed him. "This will take some time. There's a bench where you can sit." He inclined his head, then disappeared through the arched doorway, presumably to wherever they kept past occurrence books.

"Shall we sit?" Hadrian suggested. He sensed Tilda's agitation.

"I suppose," she replied with a tone of resignation.

It was at least a quarter hour and probably closer to half before the clerk returned with two books. He handed them to Tilda. "The one on top has the first two dates and the other has the last one."

Tilda handed the lower book to Hadrian, then opened the

other on her lap. The scent of dust and old paper that hadn't been disturbed filled the air. She turned pages as she searched for the first date. "Here it is." She pulled the other paper Wycombe had given them from her reticule. It listed the items that were stolen and from whom.

"All these items match," Tilda said. "The constable who took the report was called Miller."

Hadrian looked over her shoulder at the entry, but from this angle, the scrawl was hard to read. "How did the thieves enter the house?"

"The lock was broken on the door to the lower ground floor facing the street. What I'd like to know is if any of the stolen items were recovered. However, we won't find that in the occurrence book, unfortunately." She looked over at him.

Hadrian met her gaze. "It's possible Sergeant Wycombe might find that information at the Detective Branch, isn't it?"

"I hope so." Tilda returned her attention to the book and flipped to the next entry they were searching for. Again, she matched up the stolen items. "The lock was also broken at this address, but on the front door to the house. The constable who took this report was Nicholson." She looked over at Hadrian.

Hadrian sat straighter. "That has to be the same Nicholson who took the report on Mrs. Goodwin's case."

"I'm sure it is," Tilda said. "I hope he's here so we can speak with him."

Hadrian opened the second book and found the third date. The report was also taken by Nicholson, and the items matched what they had from Wycombe. "Again, the lock was broken."

Tilda handed Hadrian her book. "I'm going to go ask for Nicholson."

"Wait just one moment," Hadrian said quickly. He removed his glove and set it on the bench beside him.

"Oh, of course." Tilda sent him a grateful smile.

Flexing his hand, Hadrian looked at the entry again and

focused his mind on Nicholson and the act of writing the report into the book. He pressed his fingers to the words then flattened his palm against the page.

A man with brown hair shot with gray and a round face, his expression angry, appeared before him. Looking down, Hadrian saw the occurrence book. His hand—that of the man whose memory he was experiencing—was writing the man's name and details of the theft. This had to be Nicholson's memory.

The vision faded, and Hadrian couldn't help frowning slightly. "That wasn't terribly helpful."

"What did you see?" Tilda asked.

"Nicholson's memory of taking the report. The man whose items were stolen appeared very angry."

"What were you hoping to see?"

Hadrian shrugged. "I don't know. I did focus on Nicholson recording the theft in the book, so I shouldn't be surprised to see that."

"No, in fact, you should feel rather accomplished," Tilda said. "You're becoming quite good at targeting what to experience."

"Sometimes," he said wryly. "Whilst that is helpful, I don't want to close my mind to seeing something that I haven't even imagined. Something that could be pivotal."

"That is a very good point." She touched his sleeve. "We're making progress. I'm going to ask for Nicholson."

He nodded, and she stood whilst he pulled his glove back on. As Tilda strode to the desk, Hadrian held onto the occurrence books, his blood thrumming with anticipation. He hoped Nicholson would be able to give them something useful. He didn't want Tilda to be disappointed.

Tilda returned to the bench, her eyes gleaming with excitement. "He's here. The clerk is fetching him."

A few minutes later, Inspector Nicholson approached.

Tilda rose from the bench, and Hadrian did the same.

"I take it you've come to talk about Mrs. Goodwin's stolen items?" Nicholson said with a faint smirk.

"Not exactly," Tilda replied. "I'm looking into some older thefts from 1856 and 57. You were the constable who recorded those thefts. Do you recall them?"

Nicholson's brows drew together as he let out a sharp, short laugh. "Not at all. I've recorded many thefts in my time here, and that was a very long time ago. Perhaps if you remind me what was stolen, I'll recall something."

Hadrian didn't care for the man's flippant attitude. "Some paintings and a stag statue."

The inspector's eyes lit with recognition. "I remember the statue. Who steals something like that and eludes capture or even notice?"

"I presume you never found the statue?" Hadrian asked.

Nicholson shook his head. "Though I think we recovered a stag painting from a gentleman who didn't realize it was stolen. I believe he said he purchased it from a shop in Clerkenwell."

Hadrian's pulse leapt, and he glanced over at Tilda, who appeared more animated than she had all day.

"Do you recall the name of the shop or the owner?" Tilda asked.

"It was on Clerkenwell Green. The name was March or something. Why are you looking into such old crimes?" Nicholson asked. He didn't appear so much suspicious as dumbfounded.

"I just am," Tilda replied.

Nicholson didn't react to her response, which added to his general air of befuddlement. "What about Mrs. Goodwin's things? Did you find anything?"

Tilda summoned a benign smile. "We're still working on it."

Hadrian was not surprised that she didn't share what she knew with Nicholson. They had enough people working on the case, and it seemed Nicholson wouldn't provide much help.

"We're finished with these." Hadrian handed the occurrence books to Nicholson.

"Thank you for your help, Inspector." Tilda glanced at Hadrian, then turned and walked to the door. Hadrian hastened to open it for her, and they left the station.

"We have a lead," Hadrian said.

"We do." Tilda frowned slightly, which was not the reaction Hadrian expected. "What's wrong?"

"As much as I'd like to go looking for this shop on Clerkenwell Green right now, I think I must go home to fetch Mrs. Acorn's spice biscuits and take them to the Lowthers."

"I understand," Hadrian said gently. "I'll drive you, and I'll wait in the coach whilst you're inside with Mrs. Lowther."

She turned toward him as they reached the coach. "Thank you for everything today. You've been wonderful." Her gaze held a warm glow that gave him a burst of joy.

Hadrian helped her into the coach and told Leach where they would be going next.

"Marylebone Lane, then Adelaide Street," Leach confirmed with a nod. "I do hope Miss Wren is all right," he added softly. "She seems a bit down."

"It's been a hard day," Hadrian said. "She's known Inspector Lowther a very long time."

Leach glanced toward the interior of the coach. "I see. Please convey my condolences."

"I will." Hadrian climbed inside and sat beside Tilda. Leach closed the door.

Hadrian turned his head toward Tilda. "Leach offers his condolences about Lowther."

"I heard," Tilda said.

"He was trying to be quiet," Hadrian replied with a faint grimace.

"I know," she said, a smile teasing her mouth. "It's sweet that he cares."

"He's grown quite fond of you." Hadrian wondered if he ought to say he felt the same. He wasn't sure he should, at least not now.

Soon he would need to reveal the depth of his feelings for her. He could only hope they would grow closer, but he honestly didn't know what to expect.

~

The late afternoon had turned chilly and gray as Tilda approached the door to the Lowther home on Adelaide Street. A black wreath already adorned the door, signifying the occupants were in mourning. Tilda carried a tin of spiced biscuits baked lovingly by Mrs. Acorn before she'd even known they would now be used to comfort the Lowther children after the death of their father.

Tilda couldn't shake the melancholy that had gripped her since that morning. Apparently, it was clear to everyone in the household that she should be left alone. There could be no other reason for her mother's lack of pestering about tomorrow's ball. It probably helped that Tilda had only been home for perhaps a quarter hour whilst Hadrian waited in the coach. They would have been there much longer if he'd come inside. In fact, her mother hadn't even mentioned the fact that Hadrian was in his coach. And she was certainly aware, since she'd been in the parlor when Tilda arrived. Perhaps she had more consideration than Tilda gave her credit for.

Taking a deep breath for courage, Tilda knocked on the Lowther door. It took a few minutes for someone to come, and it was Mrs. Lowther's sister-in-law who answered. She recognized Tilda, of course. Her eyes were red and puffy, as if she'd been crying. Emotion clogged Tilda's throat for a moment.

"I don't mean to intrude, Mrs. Halsey. I've brought biscuits for the children."

Mrs. Halsey and her husband, who was Mrs. Lowther's

brother, had two daughters of their own. One was grown and had her own household, whilst the other still lived at home.

"Come in." Mrs. Halsey gestured for Tilda to enter. "I'll take those, if you like."

Tilda handed her the tin of biscuits. "I believe the children are expecting them."

"How lovely." Mrs. Halsey smiled warmly. "Biscuits are always a welcome distraction."

"I'm glad. I'm so sorry for what's happened." Tilda pressed her lips together to keep her emotion at bay.

"I'll let Mrs. Lowther know you're here, if you'd care to wait in the parlor."

Tilda nodded and moved into the small room. The windows that faced the street had been covered with black crepe, and the mirror that hung over the mantel had been turned to face the wall.

Tilda desperately wished it hadn't come to this. She was more committed than ever to finding the person behind all these crimes. She was growing more and more certain there was one person behind everything—the thefts, the murders of the police, and the murder of Mr. Timms—and it was likely Dorris. If his name was really Dorris. They knew so little about the man. He could be anyone.

They needed to move quickly to prevent anyone else from being killed.

She wondered if Teague had been able to hide Jurgens and Fellows in order to protect them. Perhaps that was why Jurgens hadn't been at Great Marlborough Street earlier.

Or perhaps he'd arrested them and hadn't been able to notify Tilda and Hadrian yet.

"Tilda," Mrs. Lowther said softly from the doorway.

Tilda turned, and Mrs. Lowther began to cry again, for it was clear she'd been crying already. She walked farther into the room as Tilda met her, and they embraced for several minutes. When they finally drew apart, Tilda noticed that Mrs. Lowther had an envelope in her hand.

At first, Tilda thought it may already be the funeral invitation, but the envelope was not edged in black.

"Thank you for coming," Mrs. Lowther said after dabbing her eyes. "And for bringing the biscuits. The children are upset, of course, but this has brightened their spirits a bit, especially Michael."

"Mrs. Acorn is already making a second batch," Tilda assured her. "So, if Michael wants to eat the entire tin tonight, there'll be a replacement tomorrow."

Mrs. Lowther actually smiled, and Tilda's heart clenched.

"I know this is hard," Tilda said softly.

"Yes," Mrs. Lowther agreed. "I didn't think anything of it when he didn't come home last night. That happens from time to time. I know he's been very preoccupied with this investigation into Padgett's death. It troubled Edwin greatly."

"I'm sure it did," Tilda said, wondering how much Mrs. Lowther knew about her husband's association with Padgett, at least in the past. Tilda wasn't sure if she should say anything.

"This is for you." Mrs. Lowther handed Tilda the envelope. "Edwin told me to give this to you if anything bad happened to him. It's remarkable because he only gave this to me yesterday. It seems he may have expected—" Her voice broke, and she began to cry again.

Tilda put her arm around the woman and guided her to the settee. They sat down together. Tilda kept her arm around Mrs. Lowther whilst the widow wept softly.

After several minutes, she wiped her eyes with her handkerchief and took a deep, stuttering breath. "I'm afraid I can't stop crying."

"I'm sure it will be like that for some time." Tilda remembered the agonizing days and weeks of grief following her father's death. She'd felt as though she might never be happy again.

"Do you mind if I read this now?" Tilda asked.

"Not at all. If you feel comfortable sharing what he said, I'd like to know, if only because it's perhaps the last thing he wrote." Mrs. Lowther sniffed.

Tilda briefly clasped the woman's hand before opening the envelope. Tilda's pulse jumped. She held her breath as she read:

> *My dear Tilda,*
>
> *I hope you can forgive me for what I am about to share. I am horribly ashamed, but you must understand that I have my own family to protect.*

Tilda shifted her position so that she was angled toward Mrs. Lowther. She didn't want the woman to be able to read the letter.

> *There was more to your father's death, as you suspect. His body was moved to the apothecary shop, and it was made to look as though there was a robbery that your father had interrupted. However, he was killed behind a tavern on Clerkenwell Green called the Oak.*
>
> *I know all this because I helped move him from behind the Oak to the apothecary shop. I was not given a choice as to whether I wanted to be a part of the deception. I was told that if I didn't, I would lose my position, which I needed to take care of my family, especially Nancy. I took no part in his death, but my involvement in what happened after has long haunted me.*
>
> *With Padgett's murder, I worry I may be next. I don't know who killed him or why. I only know that some men from the Met, like me, have been used most horribly, and for that, I am deeply sorry.*
>
> *You must tell my wife whatever you think is necessary. I'm sure everything will come to light, especially with you on the case. I wish you a happy future, and I'm dreadfully sorry for the pain I have caused you.*
>
> *With affection,*

Edwin Lowther

ilda's hand was shaking by the time she finished. She quickly folded the parchment and returned it to the envelope.

"What did he say?" Mrs. Lowther asked.

It was easy for Tilda to decide not to share Edwin Lowther's misdeeds with his widow today. The truth would come out soon enough. For now, Mrs. Lowther needed to focus on her children and managing her grief.

"He was indeed concerned about something, though he didn't say what. I don't believe you have anything to worry about. Will you trust me when I say you're quite safe?"

Mrs. Lowther's eyes widened. She nodded slowly. "Yes," she whispered. "Thank you."

Tilda would speak to Teague about having a constable watch over Mrs. Lowther and her family. "Is there anything else I can do for you today?"

"Can you find who did this to Edwin?" Mrs. Lowther asked, her voice tremulous.

"I most certainly will," Tilda vowed. "You have my word."

Tilda departed a few minutes later. Hadrian stepped out of the coach and held the door for her as she climbed inside.

"Do you still wish to go home?" he asked.

She nodded. He confirmed their destination with Leach, climbed into the coach, and sat down beside her.

"I thought you'd be longer," he said.

"I couldn't stay, not after I read this." She handed him the letter.

He sucked in a breath partway through reading it. When he was finished, he refolded the paper and handed it back to her. "That's dated yesterday."

Tilda nodded. "He told Mrs. Lowther to give it to me if anything bad happened to him. She is worried that he suspected he would be killed. Well, she didn't say 'killed,' but she was very emotional, and I believe that's what she meant. I didn't tell her what the letter said, but I assured her that she and her children are safe."

"Are they?" Hadrian asked.

"I don't know for certain." Tilda clasped her hands together with worry. "Which is why I will ask Teague to have a constable watch over them. We probably should have stopped by Scotland Yard."

Hadrian shook his head. "You need to go home. Perhaps take a warm bath, drink some tea or sherry. I'll visit Scotland Yard after I drop you off."

"Thank you," she said, grateful for his help and presence. "You may as well take the letter with you and give it to Teague. He should see it." She handed it back to Hadrian.

His brows pulled together. "Are you sure you don't want to keep it for now?"

"No, I remember every word."

Hadrian tucked the envelope into his jacket.

"How am I to go to a ball tomorrow night?" Tilda asked in frustration.

"I don't know," Hadrian said. "Perhaps you shouldn't go."

"I'm afraid if I don't, my mother will never leave." It was worth it to Tilda to suffer through the evening if it meant her mother's departure.

"I suppose that's a good reason to go," Hadrian said wryly. "I'll be there. I promise to make it as painless as possible."

She sent him a grateful glance. "Thank you."

"I'm sorry things with your mother have not improved whilst she's been here."

"I doubt things will ever improve." Tilda exhaled. "We don't have a warm relationship, such as the kind you have with your mother. You are very fortunate."

"I know," Hadrian said softly. "I don't think I've always acknowledged that, but my mother is a strong and generous woman. She is truly the heart of our family." He sent her a cautious glance. "I've been considering telling her about my ability."

"You have been for some time, haven't you?" Tilda asked.

He nodded. "I've been afraid of her reaction. Then when I thought the power had gone, I felt a sense of relief that I hadn't told her. What if it disappears again and doesn't return? Then I would have told her for nothing."

"Don't play that game," Tilda advised. "Life is nothing but an endless series of unknowns. Look at the Lowther family. They never thought they'd go to bed tonight without their father and husband."

He pressed his lips together. "You're right. I'll find the right time to tell her. And soon, because I think I'll regret it if I don't."

"She'll understand. It's obvious she loves you very much. She'll support you no matter what." How she wished she could say the same about her own mother.

The coldness Tilda had felt on and off all day returned. She scooted closer to Hadrian and laid her head on his shoulder, but then quickly lifted it and looked over at him, her gaze meeting his. "Do you mind?"

"Not at all." He curled his arm around her as she put her head back down. Tilda closed her eyes and felt warmth seep back into her body.

The only other person who'd ever made her feel this safe and secure had been her father. She'd never loved anyone the way she'd loved him.

What, then, did she feel for Hadrian?

CHAPTER 19

It was clear—at least to Hadrian—that he and Tilda were growing closer. Yesterday, as she'd rested her head on his shoulder and he'd held her in the crook of his arm, he'd smiled with a bone-deep satisfaction. He didn't know if this intimacy would last, but he would appreciate every moment they shared.

He arrived at her grandmother's house and went to the door. Apparently, she wasn't going to meet him outside as she mostly did since her mother had come to stay. He wondered if Lady Pierce would be leaving after tonight's ball. Tilda almost certainly hoped so.

Vaughn opened the door and greeted Hadrian. "Miss Wren will be right down."

Hadrian stepped into the entrance hall. "Thank you, Vaughn."

Lady Pierce came from the parlor. She wore a blue plaid gown with an overskirt in the darkest blue from the pattern. Hadrian was always slightly jolted when he saw Tilda's mother wearing the most recent fashions, whilst Tilda and her grandmother did not. Though Tilda had acquired several new ensembles this year. However, they were simpler and less expensive than what her mother wore.

Hadrian supposed he was bothered by Lady Pierce—and more importantly, her husband—not providing an allowance for Tilda. But perhaps they'd offered, and Tilda had refused their money. He could see her doing that, actually. What was more, he could understand why she might. She was fiercely independent. Combine that with her fraught relationship with her mother, and it wasn't difficult to believe that Tilda wouldn't want to be dependent on Sir Bardolph.

"Good morning, Ravenhurst," Lady Pierce said with a bright smile. "Are you looking forward to the ball this evening?"

"I am. And you?"

"Oh, yes. Wait until you see Matilda's gown. I do hope you plan to dance with her."

"I would like to," Hadrian replied. "If she's amenable." He knew she didn't care for dancing.

Lady Pierce laughed, a light tinkling sound that rang a trifle hollow. "Of course she'll be amenable."

Tilda strode into the entrance hall wearing a blue gown and matching hat. She was just pulling on her gloves as she cast her mother a wary glance. "What am I amenable to?"

"Dancing," Lady Pierce said with great enthusiasm. "His lordship is expecting a dance at the ball."

Hadrian wished she hadn't phrased it that way. He never *expected* anything from Tilda. "Only if you are amenable," he said softly.

She gave him a wry look. "Shall we go?"

"Yes." Hadrian pivoted toward the door as Tilda moved past him.

"I hope you won't be gone long." Lady Pierce's tone held an edge of concern. "You must leave plenty of time to prepare for the ball."

Tilda sent her mother a flat smile. "We'll have ample time."

"Speaking of the ball, may I offer you the use of my coach?" Hadrian asked.

Lady Pierce fluttered her hand toward her chest. "My goodness, that is exceedingly kind. How will you find your way to the ball?"

"I have other vehicles," he said. "It's no trouble. In fact, I would be delighted if you would allow Leach to convey the three of you."

Tilda's mother's brows drew together in confusion. "Leach?"

"He is Ravenhurst's coachman, Mother." Tilda looked to Hadrian. "Thank you. We accept your offer of transportation." She turned and murmured her gratitude to Vaughn as he opened the door.

Hadrian inclined his head toward Lady Pierce, then followed Tilda outside. Before he could ask about her mother, Tilda looked toward him.

"Do you mind if we go to the Oak first? I'd like to see the alley where..." Her voice trailed off, but Hadrian knew what she wasn't saying.

"Not at all. I'll tell Leach."

They reached the coach, and Leach held the door whilst Tilda climbed inside. Though Tilda would hear him, Hadrian still lowered his voice to inform Leach of their next destination. The coachman nodded and closed the door after Hadrian climbed inside.

Sitting next to Tilda, it was difficult not to hope she might lean on him—physically as well as emotionally—again. "Is there anything you're hoping to discover?" he asked softly.

"I hope the publican might recall something," she replied. "Either about that December night in 1857 or anything else that may pertain."

"Do you think this pub may have a connection to the thefts, or more accurately, to Dorris, like the Yellow Dog does?"

She sent him a shrewd glance. "I had wondered, and I'm

pleased your thoughts turned in the same direction. It seems at least coincidental that another pub may be involved."

May was the primary word. The location of her father's death could mean nothing relative to the thefts. Even so, Hadrian didn't say anything.

"Although, my father was killed *behind* the pub." It was as if Tilda had pulled that from Hadrian's mind. "The Oak could have absolutely nothing to do with his death."

Hadrian inclined his head. "That's true. I do hope the publican can help."

"I just hope it's the same publican who was there ten and a half years ago," Tilda said. "Or that he can help us find this shop run by March or whatever his name is."

They had to learn something. Hadrian did not want Tilda to be disappointed. He felt as though they were very close to breaking through this case with her father. Thanks to Lowther. If only he'd spoken up much sooner. Tilda could have questioned him and perhaps uncovered more information—either details he was purposely hiding or didn't realize would be helpful.

The coach drove from Farringdon Road past the Sessions House. Hadrian noted that for something called a "green," it lacked lawn or much greenery at all.

"Do you see the Oak?" Tilda asked.

"Up ahead," Hadrian replied as the coach began to slow.

A few minutes later, he and Tilda walked arm in arm along the pavement in search of a way to reach the alley behind the pub. Past the Oak, they found an alley just wide enough for a single horse and narrow cart. Tilda glanced at Hadrian, and he could see her apprehension. He put his free hand over hers that clutched his sleeve and gave her a supportive nod.

They moved into the alley where there was a space between the buildings facing the green and those behind them. The area might have been made up of yards at some point, but now it was littered with crates, empty casks, and other detritus.

Tilda released Hadrian's arm and moved ahead of him to the area behind the Oak. A door with a sign above it that read, "Oak," clearly led to the pub.

Pausing, Tilda turned toward the door and stood silent for a long moment. Hadrian stopped a few feet away, giving her space.

"Lowther said my father died here." Her tone was surprisingly devoid of emotion. "I thought I would feel…something, but I don't." She pivoted to face Hadrian, her face pale. "What if Lowther lied?" Now, there was a break in her voice.

Hadrian took two large steps toward her. "Why would he do that?"

Tilda shrugged. "To continue to hide what really happened?"

"That doesn't make sense, not if he was concerned that something may happen to him," Hadrian argued. "He would not have written you a letter if he was trying to conceal the truth."

"I just don't understand why he lied to me all this time." Her voice rose, and now her emotion was stark and riddled with pain.

Hadrian ached to comfort her. "I know. I wish he hadn't."

Tilda looked around, her expression bleak and sad. "I hate that he died here. I hope he didn't suffer." She pressed her hand to her mouth.

Unable to stand another moment of not trying to absorb her anguish, Hadrian moved closer. He barely held up his arms before she turned and pressed herself against him. She wrapped her arms around his middle and buried her face in his chest.

She shook for a few minutes. He didn't think she was sobbing, but emotion was tearing through her. Hadrian held her close and stroked her back. He wished her hat wasn't in the way of him pressing a kiss, or at least his cheek, to her forehead.

After a few deep breaths, she settled. But she didn't release him, not for several minutes.

At last, she pulled back and quickly wiped at her face with the backs of her gloved hands. She looked up at him, and her eyes were bright.

Hadrian lifted his right hand and brushed her cheek with his thumb. How he wished he wasn't wearing gloves.

"I should stop leaning on you so much," she said shakily, a half-smile curling her lips.

"I hope you never stop," he whispered. He was overcome with his own emotions—all of them directed at her. He wanted to give her comfort, support, understanding, and most of all—the deep and abiding love he knew he would always have for her, no matter what happened between them.

He wanted to think that she reciprocated his feelings, at least partially. But she was a jumble of emotions at present, and rightly so. He would not burden her with his. Someday—soon—he would tell her how he felt. And he would suffer the consequences, whatever they were.

Tilda blinked several times as she withdrew her arms from him and stepped back. "Let's go into the pub."

Hadrian arched a brow and glanced at the door. "That way?" He used a wry tone hoping to lighten Tilda's mood.

She cracked a brief smile. "I suppose we should go through the front entrance."

They circled back around to the front of the pub, and Hadrian escorted her inside. "Do you want me to speak with the publican?" he asked in a low voice.

"This might be another instance in which the Earl of Ravenhurst is more than helpful," she replied with a nod.

The common room wasn't overly large, but it was nicely appointed with newer green curtains on the windows and well-kept furniture. An oak bar stretched along the left side, and Hadrian wondered if that was how the pub had earned its name.

There was no one behind the bar as they approached. "Where do you suppose the barkeep is?" Hadrian asked in a loud voice in the hope someone would hear.

A large man barely older than Hadrian popped up from

behind the bar. "Just maneuvering a new cask into place." He had thick, light brown brows and a wide forehead. "What'll you have?"

"Two pints of dark ale, if you have it," Hadrian said. "And mayhap a bit of information—also if you have it. I'm Ravenhurst."

The barkeep's brows rose sharply but then settled almost immediately as he went to fetch the two pints of ale. Whilst he was gone, Hadrian set down two coins that were more than the ale cost.

Returning with the ale, the barkeep set the pints on the bar in front of Hadrian and Tilda. He swept up the coins and deposited them into something beneath the bar. "What sort of information?"

"I don't suppose you're the publican, are you?" Hadrian asked.

"Aye. Oakley's the name."

Perhaps the pub wasn't named after the bar's material after all. "The pub is named for you then?"

Oakley nodded. "This was my father's tavern and his father's before that."

Hadrian heard the pride in the man's voice and hoped that would bode well for his character and desire to be helpful. "We're looking for a curiosity shop on Clerkenwell Green owned by someone called March or something like that."

The publican's features didn't register a reaction, and he quickly responded, "I don't know anyone by that name."

"It may not be March exactly," Tilda said. "But something similar."

Oakley looked at Tilda and shrugged. "Can't help you, sorry."

Hadrian wasn't sure he believed the man and sensed Tilda didn't either. He wanted to ask about the night Tilda's father died, but he wasn't sure Oakley would have been in charge then. Still, he was likely working here. "When did you take over the tavern from your father?" Hadrian asked.

"About five years ago. He's still around though." Oakley's green-blue gaze shifted upward briefly. "He lives upstairs."

"You must have worked here before that," Hadrian said. "I ask because we're interested in something that happened behind the pub in the alley. A man was killed in December 1857."

Oakley's eyes narrowed. "The hell that happened. I've been working here since I was fourteen—almost twenty years now. I would know if someone had been killed."

"Is there a chance you weren't here that night?" Tilda asked.

"Even if I wasn't, I would've heard that happened." Oakley was outraged, his voice rising and his brows pinching together as his eyes sparked with ire.

"No one is accusing you of having anything to do with the murder," Hadrian said calmly. "We know for a fact it happened, so if you can provide any information that would lead to the apprehension of those responsible, we would greatly appreciate it."

"The victim was a police sergeant," Tilda added, her lips curling ever so faintly, but Hadrian caught it.

Oakley exhaled, and he appeared to relax. "I honestly don't know anything. I can ask my father about it, but I doubt he knows anything either. I was twenty-one at that time—he would have told me that someone was murdered in the alley." There was a note of uncertainty in the publican's voice.

"May we speak with him?" Tilda asked. Her tone was polite, but Hadrian sensed the anxiety and tension simmering in her. Had she also caught Oakley's unease?

"No." The publican glanced at Hadrian. "I don't care who you are."

Tilda gave the man a stony glare. "What if a detective inspector from the Metropolitan Police comes asking?"

Oakley swallowed. "I'll talk to my father, but I'm telling you he won't know anything. Come back tomorrow."

Hadrian shook his head. "Now. We'll wait. Or we'll return

later today with the detective inspector." He shot a glance toward Tilda, who nearly smiled at him, admiration gleaming in her eyes.

"Wait here," Oakley said with irritation before disappearing through a doorway in the corner toward the back of the building.

"We need to ask him about Dorris," Tilda said quietly but with great urgency after Oakley was gone.

Hadrian turned slightly toward her. "How do we do that? 'Pardon us, but do you deliver messages for a thief to this March person you claim not to know?'"

Tilda let out a frustrated breath. "I'll come up with something."

"Then I shall do my part now. Perhaps it will help you determine what to say." Hadrian removed his glove and focused his mind. He wanted to know what Oakley wasn't saying. He thought of the December night in 1857 as well as any potential connection between this pub and Dorris.

Hadrian's vision blurred, then became clear once more. He was still in the pub, but it looked different. He was standing behind the bar and could see the common room. There was less furniture, and it was mismatched. The curtains on the windows were a dingy white. It was clearly another time.

A man stood on the opposite side of the bar, and he was speaking to whoever's memory Hadrian was seeing—likely Oakley's. The man had dark hair and angular brows. He looked vaguely familiar, but Hadrian couldn't place him.

The vision faded, and Hadrian worked to see something else. He saw flashes of the pub, but nothing specific or useful. He focused harder on the back alley, but he only saw a memory in which he carried a cask through the door and set it down.

"He's back," Tilda whispered.

Damn. Hadrian blinked several times as pain shot through his temple. He took a drink of the ale, which was quite good, to hopefully ease the sharp ache.

He looked over at Tilda and gave his head a slight shake. The disappointment in her eyes provoked an even greater frustration at his failure to see anything useful.

Oakley crossed his arms as he faced them over the bar. "It's as I said. He doesn't remember anything. You must be mistaken. Or we simply didn't hear about it."

Unfortunately, the latter could be true. The men involved with Thomas Wren's death had spent more than a decade hiding the truth. They could very well have kept the incident quiet from the moment it happened.

"Thank you for asking," Hadrian said.

Tilda sent Hadrian an expectant look and shot a glance toward his pocket. "I have one more question."

Understanding that she wanted him to offer more money, Hadrian withdrew two more coins and pushed them across the bar. "Your honesty is appreciated."

Oakley slowly picked up the coins but only held them in his hand. "I don't know if I can help you."

"Have you or your father ever delivered messages to someone?" Tilda asked.

"What do you mean?" Oakley's brows drew together.

Tilda leaned slightly forward. "Has anyone ever paid you to deliver handwritten notes to someone? The recipient may be called Dorris."

Again, the man's expression registered nothing. "No. I don't know anyone called Dorris."

"Perhaps you should ask your father again," Tilda suggested with barely veiled impatience.

"I already woke him. I'm not bothering him again." Oakley put the coins back on the bar and pushed them toward Hadrian. "You should go."

Hadrian plucked up the coins and tucked them in his pocket. "Thank you for your time and assistance." He turned and lightly touched Tilda's arm.

She hesitated but ultimately pivoted—rather sharply—and strode toward the door. Hadrian hastened to arrive before her so he could open it before she did.

Outside, she scowled. "He was hiding something."

"Perhaps."

Abruptly stopping, Tilda spun to face him. "What did you see when you touched the glass?"

"Not enough," he said with regret as he massaged his head. "But I did try."

Her features softened. "You need the lavender oil."

"And I will apply it when we are in the coach," he assured her. "I saw a memory of a man standing on the other side of the bar. The common room didn't look the same. The furniture didn't match and appeared worn and old. And the curtains were white, not green as they are now. I believe it was a memory from a different time, though I can't say how long ago it occurred."

"Did you recognize the man you saw?"

"No, but something about him was familiar, though I can't recall why. He had dark hair and angled brows—the kind that bend in the middle. I've never seen him before. I tried to see something from the night your father died, but all the visions were just flashes of people in the tavern." He frowned slightly. "I'm sorry, Tilda."

"Don't apologize. You tried, and I am grateful, especially knowing it causes you pain. I hate that." She looked at him with concern. "We should remove to the coach so you can apply the oil."

He appreciated her care, but he wasn't ready to go to the coach. "First, we should walk around the area and look for a curiosity shop, or someone named March or something similar."

Surprise flickered briefly in her eyes. "Of course we should. And thank you."

Tilda took his arm, and they strolled around Clerkenwell Green. However, they did not see a curiosity shop, nor any establishment with the name "March" or any name like that. They asked several people, including a few shop owners, about a curiosity shop or someone named March, and no one could help them.

This path of inquiry had led them nowhere.

Tilda tried to mask her frustration and disappointment, but Hadrian could see it as clearly as the man he didn't recognize from the vision in the Oak. He kept conjuring the face in his mind to see if he could recall why the man seemed familiar. The more he worked at it, the more he began to doubt that there was any familiarity at all.

When they were in the coach, Tilda handed him the lavender oil. He had his own supply beneath the rear-facing seat, but he took hers and applied it to his temples and forehead. The pain had begun to ease as they'd walked, and this helped even more.

"Was there any chance the man you saw was Dorris?" Tilda asked almost desperately.

"I thought of that, but I saw him in another vision, and this man didn't look at all the same. He didn't have spectacles or side whiskers. It was probably no one of import," he concluded with resignation. "Sometimes these visions aren't helpful."

Tilda crossed her arms over her chest. "What do we do now?"

"We'll make more inquiries. Or we'll take Teague to the Oak and have him speak to the elder Mr. Oakley."

"I suppose we could. In the meantime, I have to attend a ridiculous ball when I would much rather be working on this case." Her lip twitched with derision.

Hadrian took her hand and turned his upper body toward her. "I know you're upset. I am too. We will suffer through this ball together, and tomorrow we will make inquiries that will advance the investigation."

She gave him a faint smile. "How I adore your optimism and your efforts to cheer me." She squeezed his hand.

Adore. She adored him. Or at least some of his attributes. To some, that may seem a small thing.

To Hadrian, it was everything. But that didn't bring him as much joy as it should have, not when he saw Tilda's disappointment.

How he wished today hadn't been such an abysmal failure.

CHAPTER 20

*H*adrian arrived at the Trumbull ball in his father's old brougham, driven by one of his grooms. He was looking forward to seeing Tilda in her new finery and hoped she might dance with him. More than that, he wanted her to have a pleasant evening and not worry too much about their investigations. That was likely too much to expect.

Lady Trumbull stood at the doorway to the ballroom with her husband and a young man, whom Hadrian presumed was their son. When it was Hadrian's turn to address Lady Trumbull, she regarded him with a brilliant smile. Excitement lit her features.

"Lord Ravenhurst, it's an incredible honor to welcome you to our ball," she said with great enthusiasm. "I'm so pleased you could come. I was hoping your mother might be with you."

"I'm afraid she was not able to attend." In fact, Hadrian didn't know why.

"That's a shame," Lady Trumbull said with a touch of disappointment. She quickly recovered with another bright smile. "I'm delighted you're here. It is such an esteemed honor." She turned to look at her husband. "Trumbull, Lord Ravenhurst has arrived."

Lord Trumbull had a wide mustache with tapered ends that

curled into points. "I can see that. Welcome, Ravenhurst. I appreciate you coming."

"Looks to be quite a crush," Hadrian said.

"Does it?" Lady Trumbull batted her lashes. "I hope you'll tell all your friends."

Trumbull touched his wife's arm. "Leave him be, dear," he murmured.

Hadrian stifled a smile.

"Have you met my son, Ravenhurst?" Trumbull turned to the young man on his other side. "This is Monroe."

The lad looked to be approaching twenty years. He sent Hadrian a nervous glance and inclined his head. "Good evening."

"Evening." Hadrian glanced back at Lady Trumbull. She did not appear old enough to be the boy's mother. He vaguely recalled that she was Trumbull's second wife.

"Monroe just finished at Cambridge," Trumbull noted.

"What did you study?" Hadrian asked politely.

"The usual," the young man muttered.

When it did not appear he would say more, Hadrian returned his attention to Trumbull. "I'll look forward to speaking with you later." He nodded at Lady Trumbull, then made his way into the ballroom.

After the butler announced his arrival, Hadrian immediately scanned the room in search of Tilda. In fact, the ball *was* rather crowded, and he had difficulty finding his quarry. At last, he spotted her grandmother and Lady Pierce on the periphery. Where was Tilda? Could she be dancing? Hadrian hadn't even thought to look at the dance floor.

He turned his attention to where couples danced a quadrille. It took a moment, but he finally found her. His chest lightened. He felt as if he might float, buoyed by his delight in seeing her. It was silly, for he'd only left her presence that afternoon, and he felt as if he hadn't seen her in days.

She wore a dark coral gown with an ivory underskirt.

Flowers adorned her hair, and pearls dangled from her ears. She looked elegant and incomparably beautiful.

Hadrian was surprised she was dancing. Even from this distance, he could see she was moving rather stiffly. He didn't recognize her partner, a blond man around her age. The man grimaced faintly, and Hadrian saw Tilda react. It appeared she may have stepped on his toe. Selfishly, Hadrian was disappointed by the mishap, for it meant she may not want to dance with him.

"Ravenhurst?"

Hadrian turned at the sound of his name, recognizing the voice.

Captain Vale's hooded brown eyes lit as he smiled at Hadrian.

"What a surprise to see you here," Hadrian said. "I didn't realize you would be in town."

"I only arrived this afternoon," Vale replied. "I planned to send you a note tomorrow, but here you are."

"How do you know Trumbull?" Hadrian asked.

"I served with his younger brother, and we've remained friends."

"Is Thaddeus with you?"

"No, in fact he is preparing to leave for Paris soon. He plans to stay for the summer and perhaps into the autumn." Vale regarded Hadrian intently. "I was very glad to receive your letter that your ability has returned. I imagine that's a great relief."

"It is indeed."

Vale's brow pleated. "Have you any idea what triggered its return?"

"I did what you suggested," Hadrian said. "I meditated and focused my mind on regaining the power."

"What happened when it returned?" Vale asked.

"It was rather sudden, actually, and it followed a distressing event. A cart was speeding toward Miss Wren and myself. I rushed to sweep her out of the way. In the course of doing so, I dropped an item I was carrying. When I retrieved it, I saw a vision."

Captain Vale cocked his head. "That is rather dramatic. How did you feel whilst that was happening?"

"Terrified, to be honest." Hadrian thought back to those moments. He'd felt a stab of darkness and despair at the prospect of losing Tilda, but then also recalled how he'd felt that she was safe, along with the realization that he was in love with her.

"I don't suppose you had any revelations about Miss Wren?" Vale asked softly.

"I did, in fact," Hadrian replied, jolted with surprise. "You think my sentiments triggered the return of my power?"

Vale lifted a shoulder. "Who can say? But I think when we open our minds to thoughts and feelings, we open it to other things as well. It could be that the intense situation prompted your ability's return."

"Extraordinary," Hadrian breathed. He knew he would continue to ruminate on what Vale had said. "How long will you be in London?"

"A few days. Perhaps we'll meet at the club, or we can arrange another time. It would be nice to see Miss Wren," he added with a smile.

"I'm sure she would like that," Hadrian said.

The dance ended, and Hadrian was eager to make his way to Tilda. "You must excuse me, Captain."

"I imagine so," Vale said with a sly smile. "Do you have a dance to claim?"

Hadrian chuckled. "Not as of yet, but wish me luck."

Vale grinned. "You shall have it."

Hadrian made his way toward where Tilda was departing the dance floor with her partner. She left the young man, and Hadrian intercepted her. Her brows arched with surprise, then her expression relaxed with relief. "You're here."

"Of course," he said with a smile. "I see you were dancing."

"At my mother's behest," Tilda said with vague irritation. "I said I would dance with two gentlemen, and in return, she promised to consider leaving the day after tomorrow."

"And how many dances was that?" Hadrian asked, hopeful he hadn't missed his chance.

"Just one," she replied miserably.

"Never fear," Hadrian assured her. "I shall be your second dance, if you're willing."

She exhaled. "I suppose it can't be any worse than what I just endured."

"It wasn't that bad, was it?" he asked, trying not to take her lack of enthusiasm to heart.

"Were you watching?" Her gaze narrowed sardonically.

"I was, and I must say, your partner was not very accomplished," Hadrian said. "I will provide you with a much more favorable experience."

Tilda laughed softly. "That's shockingly arrogant of you."

Hadrian shrugged. "It's true."

"I'm not very familiar with this side of you," she said, still smiling. "I confess, it's somewhat alluring, which is also shocking."

It surprised Hadrian too, but he wasn't going to tell her that. He liked that she found him alluring and hoped she would continue to do so. "Shall we dance then and get it over with?"

"I suppose so," Tilda replied with resignation.

He took her hand and escorted her onto the dance floor. "It's a waltz, which is much simpler than the quadrille you just completed. I'll guide you. Try to relax, and perhaps even enjoy yourself."

Tilda sent him a wry glance. "That's easy for you to say. I imagine you've done this hundreds of times."

"I don't know about hundreds, but a great many." He swept her into the dance, and for a few moments, she focused greatly. Her brows pulled together as her forehead pleated.

"I said you should relax," Hadrian urged. He wanted her to enjoy this as much as he was. Having her in his arms was wonderful, and he particularly reveled in being with her in this public setting, away from their investigations, even for a few moments. "Try talking to me."

"I do need to speak with you, actually," Tilda said. "Teague called this afternoon. He spoke with Jurgens and placed him under protection with the Detective Branch until Padgett's and Lowther's murderer, assuming it's the same person, is captured. Jurgens was most upset to learn Lowther had been killed. He also confessed his involvement with my father's death. He knew the body was moved but said he did not participate in doing so."

"That's quite something." Of course they couldn't move away from investigating. That didn't bother him, for Tilda had relaxed in her movements.

"It is. However, Jurgens doesn't know why my father was killed, or why he was moved and his death made to look like an interrupted robbery." She fixed her gaze on Hadrian. "He was told to never speak of what truly happened."

"Told by whom?" Hadrian asked, thoroughly enjoying the dance, even if they were discussing their work.

"He said it was Padgett."

Hadrian felt the frustration he saw in the set of Tilda's mouth. "That's not terribly helpful since Padgett is dead."

Her eyes narrowed slightly. "No, and Teague said Fellows has not been seen at the Home Office since you and I met with him on Saturday."

"That doesn't sound good," Hadrian said.

"It does not," she agreed.

"Perhaps he's been killed like Padgett and Lowther."

"Yes, or he's the killer and has fled," Tilda noted ominously. "Teague has many men looking for him. This has been a most frustrating day, Hadrian."

"I know," he said sympathetically. "On the bright side, you're dancing beautifully."

"Am I?" Her foot grazed his. "You lie," she said flatly.

Hadrian laughed. "You *were* dancing beautifully before you started paying attention again. You're doing quite well, and the dance is almost over."

"That means I'll have to rejoin my mother." She didn't look too pleased about that.

"We'll take a stroll in the garden first," Hadrian said.

"That would be lovely," Tilda replied. "I'm a bit overwhelmed. I'm not used to all this finery."

"But you look so splendid in it," Hadrian said. "Indeed, when I spotted you on the dance floor, you quite took my breath away."

She snapped her gaze to his. "Thank you."

Hadrian couldn't contain his admiration. "Will you allow me to tell you that you're the most beautiful woman in the ballroom?"

"Now you're overdoing it," she said with faint sarcasm.

Hadrian grinned. "But it's true. At least in my opinion."

One of her blonde brows arched. "I suppose I shall have to accept that, because I do value and admire your opinion."

"Excellent." Hadrian wondered if she was aware they were flirting.

The music ended, and Hadrian escorted her from the dance floor. As he led her toward the doors leading to the garden, he saw Trumbull standing with another gentleman.

"Ah, Ravenhurst," Trumbull said. "Have you met Lord Strangfeld?"

"I have, but it's been some time since we've spoken." Hadrian inclined his head toward the viscount. Strangfeld was in his late forties. He had blond hair and shrewd, light-blue eyes. On the shorter side, he possessed an athletic build.

"Evening," Hadrian said.

"Evening, Ravenhurst," Strangfeld replied with a nod before looking toward Tilda.

"May I introduce Miss Wren?" Hadrian said. "She is Lady Pierce's daughter."

"I know Sir Bardolph," Strangfeld said, referring to Tilda's stepfather.

Tilda's attention locked on a pin on Strangfeld's lapel. "Is that a stag?"

Hadrian's pulse jumped. It was indeed a stag made of gold with what looked to be diamond eyes. How had he missed that? Tilda had, of course, seen it straightaway.

"It is," Strangfeld said.

Tilda smiled at the viscount. "It's stunning."

"Thank you." There was a note of pride in the man's voice.

"Pardon us," Hadrian said. "We're going to take some air."

"Lady Trumbull will be delighted that you strolled through the gardens," Trumbull said. "She's quite proud of them. Do tell her that you found them lovely."

Hadrian inclined his head as he guided Tilda from the ballroom. "You don't think his stag pin means anything?" he asked once they were outside.

"Probably not," Tilda said with a sigh. "I suppose it was just exciting to see it after the disappointment of today."

"That's understandable."

They walked along the path for a few moments. Tilda stopped short, tugging on Hadrian's arm. "Look at that." She sounded breathless.

Standing in the center of the garden was a large statue of another bloody stag.

CHAPTER 21

Tilda moved closer to the statue, pulling Hadrian along with her. She blinked, then turned her head toward Hadrian. "There was a stag statue in the list of stolen items in the occurrence book at Great Marlborough Street. How many statues of stags can there be?" That was an absurd question, as there were undoubtedly a great many. She exhaled. "It can't mean anything. We're just seeing stags everywhere."

Hadrian surveyed the statue. "Perhaps. But it is remarkable."

"It couldn't possibly be the same statue that was stolen, could it?"

"It's unlikely, but I think we can agree that, in our experience, stranger things have happened," he said drily. "It's also interesting that Strangfeld was wearing a stag pin. But you could be right—we're seeing stags everywhere now."

They continued their circuit of the garden. Tilda kept casting glances toward the stag.

"What are you thinking about?" Hadrian asked.

"The same thing that's been bothering me all day," Tilda replied. "How the stag robberies and my father's investigation are linked to his death, and what's happening now with the murders of Padgett and Lowther, and even Timms. I'm convinced it's all connected."

"That certainly makes sense," Hadrian said. "Perhaps Teague will find Fellows, and he'll provide the answers we're seeking. If he can."

At this point, Tilda doubted they would be so lucky. It was perhaps more likely that Fellows was either dead or, like Lowther and Jurgens, couldn't tell them anything useful, though Tilda still wasn't sure if that was true. Lowther and Jurgens could have both lied, though Hadrian's arguments that Lowther wouldn't have lied in a letter he'd written to Tilda expressing his regard for her made sense.

Hadrian had been such a wonderful support all day and every day. He'd even managed to coax her into dancing, and he'd kept her from making a complete fool of herself. Indeed, there were moments on the dance floor where she'd felt almost giddy. They'd engaged in a witty repartee that was most delightful. She didn't usually speak like that. Surprisingly, she'd enjoyed it and hoped it would continue.

Why was she thinking of such things when this investigation should be demanding all her attention?

She wanted to be annoyed by the intrusion of romantic thoughts, but instead they were a welcome brightness as she struggled to uncover the truth of her father's death. This would be so much harder if she was alone, but she wasn't. She had Hadrian.

Glancing over at him, she took in his handsome profile. She loved the little bump in his nose that kept him from looking too perfectly attractive. He was exceptionally handsome this evening in his fancy costume. His shirt and neckcloth were impossibly white against the ink black of his coat. Other men wore jewels on their costume, like Strangfeld with his stag pin, or rings on their fingers. But Hadrian bore no such adornment, nor did he need it.

They passed another couple on the path. The young man and

woman walked close together, their arms pressed tightly and their heads angled toward one another. They both smiled and giggled. To Tilda, they appeared to be in love.

Warmth bloomed in her chest as she thought of how wonderful that must be for them. She reminded herself that love was not something she looked for. Nevertheless, what if love found her anyway? She looked over at Hadrian again, focused on his mouth, and thought she would like to kiss him again.

They passed the stag statue once more as they approached the doors to the ballroom.

"I think I'd like to ask Lord Trumbull about that statue," Tilda said.

"Why not?" Hadrian guided her into the ballroom. As luck would have it, Trumbull was still standing near the doors, though Strangfeld was no longer with him. Their host finished speaking with a couple who moved away just as Hadrian and Tilda arrived.

"The gardens are spectacular," Tilda said. "I particularly liked your stag statue."

"Oh, that," Trumbull chuckled. "It's a favorite of mine, and it's Strangfeld's fault. He has a similar statue at his ancestral pile. I saw it there and had to have my own."

Strangfeld had a stag statue *and* was wearing a stag pin. Was that still a coincidence? "Did you obtain your statue from the same sculptor?" Tilda asked.

Trumbull shook his head. "I bought mine from a shop in Clerkenwell."

Tilda's heart shot into her throat. Clerkenwell could just be another coincidence, but for some reason, she didn't think so. She swallowed. "I don't suppose you obtained it from a shop owned by someone called March or something similar?"

"Marchant," Trumbull responded gleefully. "You've been there?" he asked. "Splendid place. I like to visit every few months, as he always seems to have something of interest."

Had Trumbull purchased the stolen stag statue listed in the

occurrence book? "When did you buy it?" Tilda asked, her mind fixed on the stag robberies.

"Perhaps five years ago?" Trumbull mused. "I'm not exactly certain, but Lady Trumbull would know." It couldn't be the same statue. Unless it had been in Marchant's possession since it was stolen more than a decade ago.

"Where is the shop located in Clerkenwell?" Hadrian asked. "I should like to pay a visit."

"St. John Street," Trumbull responded with enthusiasm. "You should definitely go, Ravenhurst. Marchant sells wonderful paintings, statues like this, oriental vases, all manner of things."

Tilda recalled what Inspector Nicholson had said about recovering a stag painting that the seller—who had to be Marchant—had said he didn't realize was stolen.

"That sounds like quite an array of goods," Hadrian said. "Where does Marchant acquire such things?"

Trumbull chuckled. "I've asked him that, for he has many items of great value. But he's very coy. He doesn't like to disclose anything. I've stopped asking because I don't wish to offend him. His prices are most reasonable."

Hadrian glanced at Tilda. Was he thinking what she was? That a shop with a wide range of goods at reasonable prices could very well mean Marchant was fencing stolen items, particularly given what Nicholson had told them about the recovered stag painting.

Tilda would inform Teague of this development and request they call on Marchant as soon as possible. At this point, she thought it best if Teague accompanied them and they made their inquiries together.

"Strangfeld must like stags," Hadrian noted.

Trumbull nodded. "His family crest bears a stag."

Tilda's pulse was still thrumming but gained even more speed. "I imagine that makes for an impressive coat of arms." She wanted to press for a description to see if it would match the salver that had been stolen from Mrs. Goodwin. However, a pair of gentlemen approached and clearly wanted to speak with their host.

"Pardon us," Hadrian said before guiding Tilda away from Lord Trumbull.

"I wanted to ask him about Strangfeld's coat of arms," Tilda said with disappointment.

"I know, but we needed to move on. He's the host and we can't monopolize his time."

Tilda blew out a frustrated breath. "Is there a book, such as Burke's or Debrett's, with illustrations of family crests?"

"I believe Burke's might include crests," Hadrian replied. "There are other books that have them. I'll look in my library later."

She shot him a grateful look. "If you find something, I hope you'll come and tell me."

Hadrian's brows rose. "Regardless of the hour? When I called rather late several days ago, your mother misinterpreted things."

"I don't care," Tilda said strongly. "This is vital to our investigation, and I won't let my mother be an obstacle. If Strangfeld's coat of arms matches the one on Mrs. Goodwin's missing salver, I think we must consider that he's involved, particularly when you think of the stag robberies. What if *his* statue is the one that was stolen?"

Hadrian nodded. "I won't keep you waiting until tomorrow if I find something, all right?"

"Thank you." She flashed him a relieved smile. "In the event you don't find anything in your library, will you fetch me before noon tomorrow to call on Teague at Scotland Yard before we go to find Marchant's shop?"

"Certainly." His blue eyes gleamed with anticipation. "I look forward to it."

Tilda did too. In fact, she wasn't sure how she would sleep tonight. She was anxious—more than she'd ever been before—to make progress with this investigation. "I suppose you should return me to my mother and grandmother now. Will you stay much longer?"

"For a while," Hadrian replied. "I wish I could remain in your company for the rest of the evening—and not just to keep you from dying of boredom. But it would be too conspicuous if we spent too much time together."

"We did that at Northumberland House," Tilda reminded him.

"We attended that together as business associates, and I made that clear from the outset," Hadrian explained. "This event is different, and for unmarried people such as ourselves, it is seen as an opportunity for cultivating marriage prospects."

Tilda made a slight face. "Well, I don't want to spark any rumors."

As they approached Tilda's mother and grandmother, her mother smiled widely. "Lord Ravenhurst," she said eagerly, "I saw you dancing with Matilda. Might I say you looked splendid together?"

"You did indeed," Tilda's grandmother agreed.

Whereas Tilda's mother looked absolutely thrilled, Tilda's grandmother appeared cautiously hopeful. Grandmama had always liked Hadrian. From the beginning, she had wondered if he and Tilda might form a romantic attachment. Tilda had assured her they would not.

Could she still make such assurances? She didn't know, nor did she want to think about it.

"Ravenhurst, since you're here, do you mind escorting me to the refreshment table?" Tilda's grandmother asked.

"It would be my pleasure," Hadrian said, offering her his arm.

He sent Tilda a rather dazzling smile, and she worked to ignore the urge to curl her toes with delight.

When they were gone, her mother edged closer to her. "You can't tell me that Ravenhurst isn't interested in pursuing a courtship with you. I can see his interest in you."

"Mother, we are professional associates. Please do not assign your hopes to his behavior. You're simply seeing what you want to." Except Tilda saw it too. She just wasn't going to admit it to her mother. "I've danced my two dances. May we leave?"

"Not yet," her mother said.

"But you said if I completed two dances, you would go home to Birmingham."

"I said I would consider it." She narrowed her eyes slightly at Tilda. "And I did not say we would leave after you danced twice. It's much too early to leave the ball. If you could find it within yourself to dance once or twice more, I will consider leaving. However, you may not be asked. Your first dance did not go well. But then you did dance with Ravenhurst, and that could encourage others to ask." She scanned the ballroom. "We shall see."

Once again, her mother used the word "consider," which Tilda now knew meant she was promising nothing. "If I dance with those who ask, will you please go home to Birmingham tomorrow or the day after?"

"That depends," her mother replied. "I find I would prefer to stay until you've settled this investigation into your father's death."

Tilda blinked. She was shocked her mother would care. "Why is that important to you?" she asked softly.

"I loved Thomas," she said plainly. "I know you think poorly of me because our marriage was not very happy near the end." She spoke softly so no one else could overhear them. "But I'd hoped we would find our way back to one another. I remain dreadfully sorry that he's gone."

"Thank you." Tilda hadn't known how much she'd wanted to hear her mother say something like that.

"So, the sooner you solve this case, the sooner I shall be on my way," her mother said brusquely. "Unless there's to be a courtship between you and Ravenhurst, of course." She arched her brows as her eyes sparkled with anticipation.

Tilda resisted the urge to roll her eyes. "Does this mean you approve of my profession now?"

"'Approve' is a strong word," her mother replied. "But I do understand your passion for investigation. I cannot deny your success, though I still hope you will wed and give it up."

That was not entirely what Tilda hoped to hear from her mother, but it was progress. "What if I wed and continue to investigate?"

One man had already offered exactly that, and Tilda had refused him. Inspector Maxwell, whom she'd worked with on her last investigation, had proposed marriage and a partnership where they would work together investigating for the City of London Police. Tilda had declined because she hadn't felt romantically toward him.

Her gaze locked on Hadrian as he made his way back to them with her grandmother. She had romantic feelings for him, much as she didn't want to, and he would almost certainly support her continuing to conduct investigations.

Could a countess even do that? How would it reflect on him to have a wife with a profession? How would it reflect on her profession to be married to an earl and, very possibly, be infamous?

The familiar fear she felt when she pondered a future with Hadrian gnawed at her once more. Was it because she was afraid that she couldn't be an investigator any longer?

No. Hadrian wouldn't want her to give that up. What was she afraid of?

CHAPTER 22

The following morning, Hadrian decided to call on his mother before fetching Tilda. He'd been thinking more and more about telling his mother of his ability, and seeing Captain Vale last night had convinced him to reveal the truth. That and watching Tilda and her mother together. Their relationship was fraught, whilst Hadrian was fortunate to be close with his mother. He didn't like keeping such an important aspect of his life secret from her, especially since it was likely permanent.

Unless it decided to disappear again. But Hadrian didn't think his power had ever really gone. It had just been dysfunctional for a while—until his mind had cleared and he'd acknowledged his love for Tilda.

His mother's butler, Peverell, greeted him with surprise. "Good morning, my lord. We weren't expecting you."

"I know. It wasn't planned," Hadrian said as he stepped into the entrance hall. "I won't take too much of my mother's time, but I would like to speak with her."

Peverell closed the door. "She is in her private sitting room."

Hadrian made his way upstairs to his mother's suite. The door was ajar, but he knocked anyway.

"Come in," his mother called.

"It's me, Mama," Hadrian said before he stepped inside.

Seated at her small round table, she held a newspaper that she'd clearly been reading. "Hadrian, did I forget you were coming?"

He shook his head. "My apologies for arriving unannounced."

"Is everything all right?" she asked with a bit of alarm.

"Yes, why?"

She set the newspaper down on the table and motioned for him to sit opposite her in the other chair. She was drinking tea and had likely finished breakfast a short while ago. "You don't usually arrive unannounced and never at this hour."

"I'm sorry for coming so early," Hadrian said a bit sheepishly.

"Didn't you go to the Trumbull ball last night?" she asked.

"I did. In fact, I was wondering why you didn't."

She waved her hand. "Too much new money. Trumbull married his second wife to improve his coffers. Her family are merchants."

Hadrian let out a faux gasp. "How awful."

His mother pursed her lips. "Those of you in the younger generation don't understand. Now, why have you come?"

"I have something important to tell you," Hadrian said. "You will find it rather shocking."

She clasped her hands together as her eyes rounded. "Are you engaged? I take back everything I said about the Trumbulls' ball if you have come away with a betrothed."

He'd walked right into that. "No, Mama, that is not what I want to say."

"Well, that is disappointing," she said with a sigh. "What could possibly be of more import than that?"

Hadrian stifled a smile and resisted the urge to leave now

before he told her anything. "It is important. I hope you will not look at me differently after I tell you."

The lines in her forehead deepened. "Now you have me worried, dear. What is going on?"

"You recall when I was stabbed back in January?"

"How could I forget that?" she asked, her hand fluttering to her chest. "I was afraid I was going to lose my other son. You aren't ill, are you?"

"No," he assured her. "When I was stabbed, I fell and hit my head. I had a concussion, if you remember."

"I do," she said. "You were quite ill for several days."

"Yes, and part of that was to do with what I want to tell you. The blow to my head prompted an odd…skill that I didn't have before." Hadrian took a deep breath. He'd rehearsed what to say in his mind, but everything he planned evaporated as he looked at his mother's concerned face. "I have developed the ability to see the memories of other people when I touch something or when I touch a person."

She stared at him. "I don't understand."

"Let me give you an example," Hadrian said. "If I'm at my club and I touch a glass with my bare hand, I sometimes see flashes of memories of other people who also touched that glass."

"What do you mean, you see them?" Her eyes were round but devoid of any wariness, which Hadrian found encouraging.

"I see the memories in my mind," Hadrian explained. "I suppose it's as if they're my memories, but they aren't."

"How terrifying," she said, appearing mildly horrified. "That's been happening since January?"

"Yes."

Her brow knitted with concern. "How do you manage?"

"It can be challenging." He was grateful, albeit surprised, that she wasn't responding with disbelief. "Thankfully, I don't see the memories of those who are close to me. That includes the people in my household and you, as well as the people in your household."

"This is most astonishing," she said, staring at him as if he'd grown a second head, but also…accepting that head.

"You believe me?" he asked.

"Of course, why wouldn't I?"

"Because it's preposterous."

She waved her hand again. "No more preposterous than speaking with the departed, which I believed was possible."

"Except we proved it was not," Hadrian noted.

"At least not by the mediums in the London Spiritualism Society," his mother replied. "But this power of yours gives me hope that speaking to the dead is actually possible. If one, why not the other?"

Hadrian wanted to tell her that the man who had run the Spiritualism Society—Lysander Mallory, also known as Thaddeus Vale—possessed the same ability and had used it to make it seem as though he could speak with the dead. However, he'd made a pact with Vale that they would not disclose their abilities to anyone else.

Instead, Hadrian moved on to the next part of his revelation. "As it happens, Mama, this ability is passed through families."

"I don't have any such ability," she said earnestly. "Who in our family has that?"

"I don't know for certain," Hadrian replied. "I suspect my great uncle, the original Earl of Ravenhurst, had it. I recently learned from Grandmama that he didn't die when they said he did. He was sent to an asylum."

His mother gasped. "Are you going to lose your mind?"

"I don't think so." Hadrian had been afraid of just that when he'd first been stricken with the ability. "It could be that my great uncle's ability was more complicated than mine and caused him great distress. I don't know what happened, but he died in the asylum eventually."

"I had no idea." She gave her head a shake. "I don't think your father had any such ability. I would have known."

Hadrian didn't doubt that. His father was unable to hide things from her, including his mistresses. "I don't think he had it either."

"Do you think Gabriel had it?" his mother asked.

"I don't know," Hadrian replied. "It seems to be prompted by a head injury. If Gabriel never sustained one, he may never have developed the ability. Perhaps that's why Father didn't have it either."

"How do you know all this?" For the first time, she sounded a bit wary.

"I've been fortunate to meet a few other people with the same ability. Please don't ask me who, because I'm not allowed to say. As you can imagine, this is not something I would want shared, nor do they."

His mother nodded. "Of course. I don't think I'd want anyone to know either." She stared at him a moment. "*Does* anyone else know?"

"Yes, Miss Wren is aware. In fact, it has been rather helpful in our investigations."

"Oh." His mother's eyes rounded once more. "I can see how that would be useful. No wonder you've worked together so closely. This makes so much more sense now."

"Why is that?" Hadrian asked.

His mother shrugged. "I didn't understand why you would want to work with someone like her, and you've never shown interest in investigating or solving crimes. I still don't understand why you do."

"I like helping people and ensuring justice is served." Hadrian didn't care for her choice of words regarding Tilda and wouldn't let them go unchallenged. "What do you mean by someone like Tilda?"

She frowned faintly. "There you go, referring to her so familiarly again. I hope you don't do that in front of anyone else."

"I do not," he said cautiously. "I thought you liked her."

"I *do* like her, but she is not from our station, and you can't deny that your association with her is becoming quite well known in our circle."

Hadrian wasn't sure he and his mother shared the same "circle," but he knew what she meant. "I can't help what people say. We are very careful to behave appropriately, and our relationship is entirely professional."

Almost entirely. He certainly wasn't going to reveal his feelings about Tilda to his mother, nor any of the intimacies they'd shared.

"I don't know how much longer you can continue to work with her without people making assumptions that aren't true. As much as you enjoy conducting investigations with her, it may be time to at least take a respite from your association."

Hadrian had been so relieved by his mother's reaction to his secret. But now the conversation had turned somewhat sour, at least for him.

"I'll keep that in mind," he said coolly. "I do hope I can trust you not to share my secret with anyone."

"Certainly! What about your sisters?" she asked, her eyes rounding again. "You should tell them, in case they have the same ability."

Hadrian hadn't considered that. He supposed he'd assumed that only men could have the power, since Vale was only aware of men possessing it. "I'll think about that. But I would ask you not to say anything to them. This is not gossip to be bandied about, even in our own family."

"I understand. I'm glad you shared it with me," she said. "I imagine it was frightening for you at first, until you became used to it."

"It was," he admitted. "I had no idea what was happening to

me in the beginning. I feared I was losing my mind, but Miss Wren"—he was careful not to call her Tilda again—"assured me I was of sound mind."

He would have gone on to say that Tilda had continued to be a great support to him as he learned to manage the ability, but he didn't want to encourage more discussion of his relationship with her. He loved his mother dearly, but she could be a prig, as indicated by her comments regarding the Trumbulls.

"It wasn't just new money at the ball last night," Hadrian said. "Lord Strangfeld was there."

His mother didn't appear impressed. "Strangfeld's viscountcy may be old enough, but his grandfather made poor investments, and his father gambled away the fortune. Strangfeld had to marry a woman from a lower class with money to refill his coffers."

Hadrian frowned. "I don't see why that is a reason to denigrate him."

"I'm not denigrating him," his mother insisted. "My generation just doesn't care to mingle with those ladies. We don't share the same sensibilities. You must understand that, and if you don't, well, it doesn't matter."

"No, I don't suppose it does." Hadrian stood.

"I'm glad you came to call," his mother said with a smile. "Thank you for trusting me with your secret."

"Thank you for believing me." He returned her smile, then turned to go.

"Don't forget what I said about Miss Wren," she called after him. "A break in your association would be welcome, I think."

Hadrian didn't respond before leaving. He had no desire to break from Tilda in any way. If anything, he hoped their association would deepen.

ilda left the house as soon as she observed Hadrian's coach driving up the street. Leach was just opening the door of the coach as Tilda strode toward them.

"Good morning, Miss Wren," he said.

Hadrian appeared in the doorway. "You are clearly in a hurry."

"You're a few minutes late," she replied, perhaps testily. "I'm eager to speak with Detective Inspector Teague." She turned her head to look at Leach. "You know to go to Scotland Yard next?"

He nodded. "I do."

"Thank you," she said before climbing into the coach.

Hadrian moved over on the seat, and she sat down beside him. It was strange, for their positions were reversed, since she usually climbed into the coach first.

Tilda set her reticule in her lap. "My apologies if I sound terse."

"That is perfectly understandable. I am sorry to be late." He sounded so caring, and Tilda regretted her tone even more. "Do you know if Teague will be at Scotland Yard?"

"I don't," Tilda said. "If he's not, we'll just have to continue to St. John Street ourselves." She met Hadrian's gaze. "I take it you didn't find a book in your library with any family crests?"

He shook his head. "I have Burke's, but it didn't have an illustration of Strangfeld's crest, only a very minimal description saying it bore a sword and a stag. Still, I think it's entirely possible the crest on Mrs. Goodwin's salver could be his. What do you think that means?"

"I don't know yet." Tilda had been pondering Strangfeld's potential connection to their investigation and hadn't yet come up with anything.

After a few moments, Hadrian asked if her mother was leaving today.

Tilda thought of the conversation she'd had with her mother last night at the ball. She had not seen her yet this morning, and since they'd arrived home rather late last night, Tilda didn't expect she'd come downstairs before noon. "No, she wants to stay until we've solved this case regarding my father."

"Really?" Hadrian looked and sounded as surprised as Tilda had felt when her mother had told her that.

"It seems she cared for my father more than I thought. She also acknowledged that I'm a good investigator." Tilda still couldn't believe her mother had said so.

Hadrian smiled. "That's wonderful. I'm pleased she recognizes your talent and supports you."

Tilda grimaced. "I wouldn't say she *supports* me. She did say she would prefer that I marry, whilst also noting that marriage would likely prevent me from continuing my profession. I didn't bother telling her that I have no plans to give up my work. Marriage or not."

"Does that mean you would consider marriage?" Hadrian asked.

"I don't know," she replied honestly. "Maxwell did ask. I could have been his wife and continued to be an investigator."

"That's true," Hadrian said quietly. "Do you regret refusing his proposal?"

Tilda glanced over at him and noted the tense set of his jaw. "Not at all. Whilst my mother sees benefits to marriage that are financial, a complete or fulfilled life must include sharing it with the right person. And Maxwell was not that person for me."

"That's a lovely sentiment. If you do choose to wed, your husband will be a lucky man indeed."

Tilda shifted uncomfortably. The only man she could even slightly envision in that position was sitting beside her.

"Speaking of mothers, I was visiting mine, which is why I was running late," Hadrian said.

"Is everything all right?" Tilda looked over at him with concern.

"Quite." He sent her a wry glance. His tone indicated there was more to the story.

"What happened?"

"I told her about my ability to see others' memories."

Tilda angled toward him. "You did?" She blinked, then stared at him a moment longer. "Finally. What prompted you to do so now?"

"You pointed out that she would not be upset nor judge me, that she loves me and would be supportive. I decided to see if you were right." He chuckled. "You were."

Tilda smiled as a warm satisfaction poured through her. "I imagine she was surprised. Or did she already know about people in your family with this ability?"

"She did not," Hadrian said. "She *was* surprised, but she didn't for a moment doubt what I was telling her, nor did she think I was losing my mind. I think what surprised her most was that I had only shared the secret with you."

"You told her that?" Tilda asked, wondering what his mother had thought about him confiding in someone he'd only known a handful of months.

"I explained to her why it was important for me to share it with you, because this skill has been an important tool in many of our investigations. That made sense to her. She did point out that it shouldn't surprise me that she believed me, since she also believed she'd be able to speak to her deceased son."

"That's a valid point," Tilda said. "Did you tell her the role your ability played in the London Spiritualism Society?"

Hadrian shook his head. "I made a pact with Thaddeus Vale that I would not share his secret, nor would he share mine."

Tilda knew Hadrian to be a man of honor, so this was not surprising. "It is good of you to uphold that bargain. I imagine you wanted to tell your mother the truth so that she would understand how she was truly being swindled."

He grinned. "You know me too well."

"I do," Tilda said, thinking she had never met a more honorable man, not since her father had died.

They arrived at Scotland Yard a few minutes later, and Leach helped Tilda from the coach. She waited on the pavement for Hadrian to join her, and they entered the station together.

The clerk, a young constable they'd met several times, greeted them immediately. "Good morning, Lord Ravenhurst, Miss Wren. How can I be of assistance today?"

"We're here to speak with Detective Inspector Teague," Tilda said. "I do hope he's here."

"I am, in fact," Teague replied as he walked into the entrance hall. "Though I was just on my way out."

Tilda relaxed with relief that he was here. "Excellent. We've made an important discovery. I would like your presence as we make our next inquiry. Can you delay your task to accompany us?"

"Certainly. I was just going to the Home Office to see if Fellows is in today, but that can wait."

"We'll take my coach," Hadrian said.

Teague nodded, and they left the building. Once they were situated with Tilda and Hadrian on the forward-facing seat in their usual places and Teague opposite them, Tilda told him about their inquiries at the Oak the previous day, as well as walking around Clerkenwell Green.

"We were not able to find the shop that Inspector Nicholson told us about," Tilda said. "But that's because we were looking in the wrong place."

"How do you know?" Teague asked, his brows drawing together.

"We made a rather remarkable discovery last night at the Trumbull ball," Tilda replied.

"At a ball?" Teague asked dubiously.

"Our host had a stag statue in his garden, and we asked him about it. He bought it from a shop in Clerkenwell perhaps five years ago." Tilda noted Teague's features animating at this revelation. "The shop is on St. John Street, owned by a man called Marchant. He has to be the same man who sold the recovered stag painting Nicholson told us about."

Teague leaned back against the squab. "Well done. Do you think the stag statue is the same one that was stolen? That was much longer than five years ago."

"It's possible Marchant had the statue in his possession all that time," Tilda said. "I should note that Lord Trumbull obtained the statue after seeing a similar one at Lord Strangfeld's estate. Strangfeld was also wearing a stag pin. His family's crest contains a stag."

"You think Strangfeld is involved somehow?" Teague asked with a frown. "I do dislike when peers behave poorly, as with Ardleigh. It complicates matters." His lip curled as he mentioned the villain in the first case they'd worked on together. The Viscount Ardleigh had committed a number of crimes, and Teague had been forced to shoot him to protect Tilda.

"It shouldn't matter who is committing crimes," Tilda said. "Though I do understand what you mean." She recalled her father discussing how some people were able to elude justice because of who they were or who they knew.

"We're going to Marchant's shop now, of course?"

"Yes," Tilda replied. "Lord Trumbull made a few comments about Marchant's shop that called its legitimacy into question—in addition to the fact that he sold a stolen painting."

Teague crossed his arms over his chest. "What did Trumbull say?"

"He encouraged me to visit the shop," Hadrian said. "He indicated Marchant's goods were varied, valuable, and obtainable at reasonable prices."

"Ah." Teague inclined his head. "It sounds as though Marchant is a fence."

Tilda nodded. "Precisely. Which is why I thought it imperative that you join us on this inquiry."

"I'm glad," Teague said. "I'm most eager to speak to Mr. Marchant."

They arrived at Marchant's shop on St. John Street. It wasn't a shabby area, but neither was it somewhere gentlemen such as Trumbull or Hadrian would typically shop.

"Why would someone like you come here to buy a painting or a statue?" Tilda asked Hadrian.

"I don't think I would," Hadrian replied. "Unless I was looking for something of lesser value. Or something that was stolen."

Leach opened the door, and Hadrian stepped out. He helped Tilda to the pavement, then Teague joined them.

"I'd like to be the one to speak with Marchant at first, if you don't mind," Teague said.

"Not at all." Tilda presumed he would want to do that. He was, after all, a detective inspector.

They walked into the shop, and Tilda was immediately struck by the quantity of items. Marchant had tried to display everything in an appealing manner, but it was quite cluttered. There were paintings, vases, statues and other *objets d'art* of varying size and materials. They stepped farther inside, and Tilda noticed a man standing next to an open doorway to the back of the shop.

Hadrian and Teague seemed to register him at the same time, and the man saw them as well. He locked gazes with them, his eyes rounding, then turned his head to look through the doorway.

"Bant!" he called. "We need to go."

Hadrian started toward the man, whilst Teague pulled a pistol from his pocket. As they drew closer, Tilda could see the man's face was covered with pockmarks as well as a fine sheen of sweat. She gasped. Could he be one of the thieves Hadrian had seen in his visions?

The man pulled something from his pocket—another pistol. He lifted the weapon and aimed it toward them.

"Get down!" Teague shouted.

They weren't fast enough. The man fired, and Tilda felt a nick in her shoulder. A stinging sensation shot up her neck and down her arm.

Teague fired his pistol, but Tilda couldn't see what happened. She only knew she didn't want the villains to escape. Despite the pain in her shoulder, she dashed toward the back of the shop. Teague was wrestling with Rymer on the floor.

Moving past them, she stepped into what appeared to be a storage room. A man with dark hair that had gone gray at the temples and a rather fashionable mustache stood with his hand pressed to the side of his neck. Blood seeped through his fingers. He lifted his other hand and gestured toward another doorway.

"He ran that way," the man, presumably Marchant, managed to say before slumping into a chair behind him.

Tilda raced to the door that led outside to an alley. There was no sign of Bant. Turning, she realized she hadn't seen Hadrian. Her blood iced as she made her way back into the storage room.

Hadrian was just walking in from the shop. Blood streamed from the top of his ear down his neck and stained the collar of his shirt.

Her heart stopped. "My God, Hadrian, you've been shot."

Hadrian gaped at her shoulder. "*You've* been shot."

CHAPTER 23

*H*adrian barely registered what she said as he rushed toward her. Her gown was stained red, but not excessively so. Her wound was minor, but his fear had been anything but. "Let me see."

"It's a scratch. But how could we both have been shot?" She focused on his ear, her brows drawn tightly together.

"We can't have been. There was only one bullet. I wasn't shot. The bullet hit a vase, I think, and a piece of the pottery grazed my ear. I imagine you were also hit with a piece." At first, Hadrian *had* thought she'd been shot. He'd never known a greater terror. If he'd had any doubt about his feelings for her, it had been completely banished.

He loved her. Fiercely.

Tilda glanced at her shoulder and winced. "That makes sense. I do think it might still be in there."

Hadrian didn't like that one bit. "Damn. We'll need to take you to a surgeon. Or fetch one to your house."

She looked at his ear. "Your wound does, in fact, look like a scratch, as if the shard of pottery sliced the flesh at the top of your ear. However, it's bleeding a great deal."

"Those kinds of wounds do," he said wryly.

Tilda turned and gestured toward the man slumped in a wooden chair. "His wound looks much worse."

He was pale, and blood seeped from his neck through his fingers. It was not, however, a gush of blood, indicating it wasn't a deep wound. Hadrian moved toward him, as did Tilda.

"Are you Marchant?" Hadrian asked.

The man nodded, then winced.

Hadrian whipped off his coat. "Move your hand, and I'll press this to your neck to staunch the bleeding."

Marchant lowered his blood-stained hand to his lap and closed his eyes as Hadrian applied his garment to his wound. The coat was thick and rather unwieldy, but it was better than nothing. Hadrian made sure to hold it against the man's neck in a way that allowed his bare hand to touch Marchant's flesh.

He was suddenly in a large space with dozens of crates. It was perhaps a warehouse, and a gas lamp provided the only light. He expected to see Rymer and Bant, but instead he saw the man he'd glimpsed when he'd touched the glass at the Oak yesterday. The man he hadn't been able to place.

Only, he looked slightly different. He had longer side whiskers. And if he wore spectacles, Hadrian would recognize him as Dorris.

Blast! The man Hadrian had seen in his vision at the Oak was a younger version of this man and the Dorris he'd seen the first time in a vision. Which meant Oakley had lied about not knowing Dorris.

Dorris gestured to his right to a stag painting standing against a crate. But Hadrian didn't see what happened next because Teague came into the storage room, and the vision faded.

Teague dragged Rymer—at least that was who Hadrian presumed he was, due to the man's pockmarked face—who was also wounded. The villain was bent over, his hand clutching his side. Hadrian could see that his coat as well as the shirt beneath it were bloodied.

"Is there another chair?" Teague asked.

"Here." Hadrian hastened to move one that stood in the corner. He pulled it near to Marchant, who'd opened his eyes.

"I don't want that brigand next to me!" Marchant cried.

"I'll seat him wherever I like," Teague barked. "I'm Detective Inspector Teague from Scotland Yard." He settled the man who'd shot at them in the chair.

Hadrian glowered at the man who'd wounded Tilda. "Are you Rymer?"

The man lifted his pockmarked face toward Hadrian. His blue eyes were round with fear. "How'd you know?"

"We know a great deal," Tilda said. "What were you and Bant doing here today?"

"Just doing business with Marchant." Rymer glanced at Marchant warily.

"What business is that?" Teague asked, crossing his arms over his chest as his brow furrowed. "Don't bother lying. As Miss Wren said, we already know much about your activities."

Hadrian appreciated Teague's tactic to convince Rymer to speak honestly. He wanted to touch the man as he'd done with Marchant to see what more he could learn. "Make sure you tell us all about Dorris."

Rymer swore softly and grimaced. He pressed his lips together. He was either in pain or didn't want to tell them anything. Perhaps it was both.

"Or *you* can tell us about Dorris," Hadrian said as he transferred his gaze to Marchant.

"He works for Dorris," Marchant said, sending an angry glare toward Rymer. "I've been doing business with them for years. Over a decade."

"What sort of business?" Teague asked again. "Fencing stolen goods?"

Marchant had the audacity to look affronted. "I don't know if they're stolen. Are they?" His outrage was almost convincing.

"Of course they are," Tilda said plainly. "Don't bother prevaricating. You can't have been oblivious to their provenance."

"I never asked." Marchant sniffed.

Hadrian pressed harder on the coat against Marchant's wound. "Explain everything about your business with Dorris and these two thieves."

Marchant gasped at Hadrian's pressure, then took over holding the coat. Hadrian was happy to remove his hand.

"Dorris approached me over a decade ago—must have been 1855, I think—with goods to sell," Marchant said. "He offered me an excellent price."

"You bought them outright?" Tilda asked. "You didn't sell them on a consignment arrangement or something similar?" That was the arrangement Timms had seemed to have. He sold the items, then provided the proceeds to Dorris.

"Sometimes I did, when the item was very valuable," Marchant replied. "Also, when I did not, ah, have quite enough funds to buy something."

"You shouldn't be telling them any of this," Rymer said darkly. "You'll pay for it."

"Don't threaten him," Teague snapped. "You're in enough trouble as it is."

"I need a surgeon," Rymer whined. He'd paled and looked almost gray. He was still perspiring heavily. In fact, his forehead was nearly dripping.

"You'll have one when I'm finished questioning you," Teague replied. "The quality of your answers will determine the quality of the surgeon, by the way."

A drop of sweat fell from Rymer's chin.

Tilda continued to interrogate Marchant. "Did the items you purchased from Dorris include stag paintings and statues or any other stag items?"

"Yes," Marchant replied. "Dorris has brought me a great number of stags, just the one statue though."

Tilda narrowed her eyes at Marchant. "Only one? You're certain?"

"Absolutely. I am meticulous in my memory as well as my recordkeeping."

Teague uncrossed his arms. "You kept records of what you bought from Dorris?" At Marchant's nod, he asked where.

"In the desk there." Marchant motioned with his free hand toward the corner where an oak desk stood. It was cluttered with papers and two of the drawers were partially open. Overall, Hadrian had the sense that Marchant was disorganized and could only hope his records were as orderly as he claimed.

Teague stepped closer to Rymer. "What were you and your partner, Bant, doing here today?"

"Collecting money," Marchant said before Rymer could answer. "Or so I thought. In truth, they'd come to kill me. As I went to the desk to fetch the funds, Bant came at me from behind with a knife. He sliced my throat, but I'd seen his movement in the mirror there." He pointed to a small, oval mirror hanging above the desk. "I was able to jerk to the side so that his strike did not cut deep."

Hadrian looked at Tilda and noted her grim expression. She had to be thinking the same thing he was—that Bant had intended to cut Marchant's throat as he'd done to Timms and to Lowther. What about Padgett, who'd died in a different manner? Or Tilda's father? Had Bant killed Thomas Wren all those years ago? A tremor of unease and sorrow swept through Hadrian.

"Why did Bant want to kill you?" Teague asked.

"I don't bloody know," Marchant replied angrily. He cut his hand through the air toward Rymer. "Ask him."

"I do think I need a surgeon," Rymer said weakly. "Already had another wound," he murmured as his eyelids fluttered, then closed.

Teague advanced on him and shook him by the shoulders. "Do not lose consciousness! Why did Bant want to kill Marchant?"

Rymer managed to open his eyes, but his lids drooped. "Told to. Always do what we're told."

"By whom?" Tilda asked, her voice tight with fury.

"Dorris," Rymer muttered as his eyes closed once more.

"*Who is Dorris?*" Tilda shouted, her voice thunderous, startling even Hadrian.

Rymer jerked. The hand he used to clutch his side fell slack. Hadrian worried he was losing consciousness, despite Teague's command. It wasn't as if the thief could help it. But damn it, Tilda needed to know the truth.

Teague shook Rymer again, but his head only lolled to the side as he fainted. At least, Hadrian hoped he only fainted.

"Is he breathing?" Hadrian asked.

Teague nodded. "But we do need him to see a surgeon as soon as possible. I don't want to lose him in this manner. He can pay for his crimes the proper way."

"Tilda also needs a surgeon," Hadrian said. "There's a piece of pottery lodged in her shoulder."

"Damn." Teague turned his head toward Tilda. "I didn't know."

"I'm all right," Tilda said, sounding completely unconcerned. "Discovering the truth of this scheme is more important." She turned a fiery stare on Marchant. "You must know who Dorris is after nearly fifteen years working together."

"He's a man of business," Marchant said.

It was clear to Hadrian that Marchant only offered the bare minimum of information unless he was pressed.

"You damn well know who he works for," Teague growled. "Tell us, or I'll make sure your surgeon is worse than Rymer's."

Fear flickered over Marchant's features. "Lord Strangfeld."

Hadrian watched Tilda's reaction. The tension in her jaw eased, but the light in her eyes only intensified. Now she had a target. And Strangfeld made sense. They'd suspected he was involved.

"Who obtained the stag statue you purchased from Dorris?" Tilda asked in a deceptively quiet tone. "Was it Strangfeld?"

Marchant shook his head. "I've never sold anything to Strangfeld. Why would I when the items came from his secretary? Presumably, his lordship would have got them straight from Dorris."

"And Dorris had Bant and Rymer stealing these items," Hadrian said. "Why?"

"As a profit scheme." Marchant rolled his eyes. "You must be a new detective inspector." He glanced at Tilda. "And who's the skirt, your wife?"

Hadrian didn't conceal his ire. "She is a private investigator, and *I* am the Earl of Ravenhurst."

Marchant's eyes rounded in surprise, and he blinked. "Apologies, my lord," he murmured.

Teague looked at Tilda. "We need to fetch a surgeon."

"I'm fine for now," Tilda said. She looked to Hadrian. "We can call on Dr. Giles over on Gresham Street when we're finished."

"I need to take these two to Scotland Yard," Teague said. "A surgeon can tend to them there. But I need transportation. Why don't you take your coach to the station on King's Cross Road and ask for assistance? That's the G Division headquarters, and they have a van that can take us to Whitehall."

Hadrian glanced at the two wounded men, one of whom was unconscious. Teague would be able to manage them. He stepped toward Tilda to offer her his arm.

She held up a hand, her features stoic. "One moment." She fixed a dark stare on Marchant. "What else can you tell us about Dorris or Strangfeld? Or about the stag robberies?" Recognition flashed in his gaze, and a satisfied smile curved her lips. "You knew these items were stolen. You received stag items, and you were aware of the so-called stag robberies."

Marchant blinked and looked away from her. "I might have guessed, but I didn't realize the items were stolen at the time."

"Yet you continued to fence items for Dorris until the present," Teague said with disgust. "I'd advise you to stop hiding the truth. We will discover it, and you will pay accordingly."

Hadrian fixed on Marchant. "Did you work with the publican at the Oak on Clerkenwell Green to communicate with Dorris? Did Oakley serve as a messenger?"

Surprise sparked in Marchant's expression. "Yes, when I sold items and had money to give Dorris, I sent word through Oakley." Marchant's eyes narrowed. "Did Oakley tell you that?"

Tilda did not give Hadrian a chance to respond, not that he'd planned to. "What do you know of Bant?" she asked Marchant. "Are you aware he may have killed others, including a man who owned a silver shop and also fenced items for Dorris?"

Marchant paled. "I had no idea."

For the first time, Hadrian believed the man.

"I do hope you catch him." Marchant sounded desperate now. "Find Dorris. He should be able to help you! Go to Lord Strangfeld's house!"

"Come, Tilda," Hadrian murmured. "We need to see about your shoulder."

She left with him, but he sensed her reluctance.

"I know you want to go to Strangfeld's straightaway, but we need to tend to your wound first." He frowned at her shoulder. "Not to mention, we may not wish to call on Strangfeld looking as we do."

"I suppose you make a good point. Your wound also requires attention." She looked toward his ear as they made their way through the cluttered shop. "At least it's stopped bleeding."

"It's hardly anything. I can't even say it hurts much. How is your shoulder?" He gave her a mildly stern stare. "Please tell me the truth."

She grimaced. "I confess it aches a bit—now, anyway. Before, when I was angrier, I hardly noticed it."

"That makes sense, given your state of agitation. We are closer to solving this, which I hope makes you feel better." He opened the door to the shop so she could step outside.

"I won't feel better until we've found Dorris and discovered the link to my father's death," she said as he came abreast of her.

"I nearly forgot to tell you about my vision when I touched Marchant." Hadrian shook his head with irritation directed at himself. "I saw Dorris, and I realized the man I saw when I handled the glass at the Oak yesterday was also Dorris, but when he was younger. Oakley lied when he said he didn't know Dorris."

"That's why you asked about Oakley serving as messenger." She was most impressed. "Excellent work, Hadrian."

"I'm just glad my ability is proving useful after being absent."

Tilda was fixated on how this scheme related to her father's death—and it must. "Do you suppose my father discovered the link between Oakley, Dorris, and Marchant? That appears possible, given where my father was murdered in the alley behind the Oak. We know Bant is at least an attempted murderer. It seems clear that he killed Timms and Lowther, and, more than likely, my father too."

Her gaze was blistering. Hadrian could feel her anguish, and he wanted nothing more than to soothe it. "I'm sorry he escaped. But we'll find him."

"We will, and he'll pay for all he's done," she vowed. "Everyone involved will."

~

"Must you go back out again?" Tilda's grandmother asked with deep concern as Tilda pulled on her gloves in the entrance hall. "I think you should stay home and rest." She flicked a glance toward Tilda's shoulder.

It had been impossible to hide the injury, for when she'd arrived home, her bloodied gown drew immediate attention. Tilda had hoped to change before encountering her grandmother, but Grandmama had been in the parlor and came into the entrance hall to greet her.

"The doctor said I am fine," Tilda said for the fourth or fifth time.

After fetching the police van to transport Teague and his prisoners to Scotland Yard, Tilda had surrendered to Hadrian's insistence that they visit Dr. Giles in Gresham Street. They'd met Dr. Giles, who was both a physician and a surgeon, during their last investigation. He'd been pleased to take care of Tilda.

"But surely you should rest!" Grandmama pleaded.

Tilda summoned her patience. She was eager to find Dorris and determine the connection between these thefts and her father's death. Nothing was going to prevent her from forging ahead—certainly not two tiny stitches or the dull ache in her shoulder. "I am truly fine, Grandmama. We are close to solving this case, and I must continue."

"Because this involves your father," her grandmother said quietly. "You may think I'm not aware of your agitation, of how much this investigation is affecting you, but I am. Painfully so. As is your mother."

"I doubt she is *pained*," Tilda noted sardonically. But she didn't like that her grandmother was upset. She exhaled. "I don't want you to worry. I am close to discovering the truth. When justice is found, I will be quite satisfied."

"I want you to be happy," her grandmother said. "Sometimes I think losing your father has made it difficult for you to seek or accept joy. After your grandfather died, I used to think I needed to cling to my grief in order to keep his memory strong. But it is through happiness and contentment that I feel him with me, because I know he would want me to live my life fully." She looked into Tilda's eyes with warmth and love. "You won't forget your father if you are happy or if you find love. I hope you'll allow these things. You certainly deserve them."

Tilda worked to swallow past the sudden lump that had formed in her throat. She nodded.

"Lord Ravenhurst is here," Vaughn said. He opened the door for Tilda.

"Thank you, Vaughn." Tilda took her grandmother's hand and gave it a squeeze. "And thank you."

Her mother sailed into the entrance hall, her brows pitched into a V. "Is that Ravenhurst's coach? Isn't he coming inside?"

"No," Tilda replied. "We've an important inquiry to make."

"But I heard you were hurt," her mother said. "You can't leave."

Tilda looked to her grandmother. "Would you mind explaining?" She flashed her a grateful smile, then turned and left the house, glad that Vaughn closed the door behind her with alacrity.

Hadrian stood outside the coach and helped her inside. She settled herself on the seat as he sat down beside her.

"How is your shoulder?" he asked.

Tilda had never needed stitches before and was grateful for the ether spray Dr. Giles had used to minimize her discomfort. He'd told her to rest and return in a week so he could remove the sutures. He'd also offered to come to her to provide the service.

"It's fine. I have the money to reimburse you for Dr. Giles's fee." She reached into her reticule and removed a banknote.

Hadrian held up a hand. "I refuse to accept your money."

"You can't pay for such things," she argued. "It's…unseemly. Or at least inappropriate."

"I had to pay for my care, and it was easier to just pay for yours too. No one knows," he said with a shrug.

"Dr. Giles knows."

Hadrian gave her a wry stare.

"*I* know," Tilda grumbled. "I prefer to pay for my own expenses."

"I realize that, but in this case, I would ask that you allow me the pleasure of taking care of this." His gaze met hers with a deep concern, along with other emotions Tilda didn't want to investigate. "I feel terrible that you were wounded."

"It wasn't your fault." Tilda looked down and put the banknote back into her reticule. She would find a way to give him the money, even if she had to sneak into his house and leave it in his study. She could not allow him to pay for her expenses, regardless of how she felt about him.

And now she feared she knew exactly what she felt. When she'd thought he'd been shot, she'd been struck with a horrible dread. She'd felt similarly when he'd been struck in the head at the end of their previous investigation, and when he'd been shot in the arm during one of their prior cases.

However, in this instance, her fear had intensified. The idea of losing him had caused a visceral reaction, and she now suspected it was because she was more than fond of him. He was a vital part of her life, both professional and personal, and she simply couldn't imagine not having him beside her.

That had to be love, didn't it?

But love should fill her with joy. Instead, she felt weak and nervous. Utterly vulnerable. She didn't particularly like it.

Perhaps that was because he didn't know how she felt. The joy might come from telling him. Except she couldn't. Not now, with the case moving quickly.

Her grandmother's words flitted through her mind. Was Tilda holding herself back from happiness—from love—in order to hold onto the grief of losing her father? Ten years he'd been gone, and in a few years, she would have lived half her life without him. Her memories of him would fade. Some already had.

Emotion welled within her. She blinked and swallowed and

took a deep breath, cleansing her thoughts so she could focus on the case and finding Dorris.

"How is your ear?" she asked. Dr. Giles had cleaned Hadrian's wound and declared it would heal nicely—and quickly. Indeed, no one would ever know he was struck.

"It doesn't even hurt," he replied.

"I'm glad. And your head doesn't ache from Marchant's memory you saw earlier?"

Hadrian had explained what he'd seen when he'd tended to Marchant.

Hadrian shook his head. "I'm ready for more visions," he said eagerly and with a brief smile.

They were on their way to Strangfeld's house on Gilbert Street in Mayfair. Teague would meet them there.

"I do hope Lord Strangfeld will lead us to Dorris at last," Tilda said. She didn't think she would be able to sleep tonight if they didn't find him. "We're so close to discovering the link between his robbery scheme and my father's death."

"Do you have any theories?" Hadrian asked.

"I do not, which is most frustrating." Tilda could not think of how Dorris, a viscount's secretary, could influence the police to lie about her father's murder.

Hadrian hesitated before speaking, his expression sympathetic. "Have you considered that the two may not be connected after all?"

Tilda did not think that was likely. "My father was investigating the same robberies we are, and he was killed in the same manner as Timms and Lowther—and nearly Marchant."

"But not Padgett," Hadrian noted. "And he was, according to Jurgens, the one behind moving your father to the apothecary shop. Bear with me, but what if your father was killed for an unrelated reason? What if Padgett and perhaps Fellows were behind his murder, and they forced Jurgens and Lowther to help them?"

Tilda hated that his logic made sense. "I suppose that is possible," she muttered.

"I know you don't care to make assumptions," he added.

"You needn't go on." He'd made his point—and very well. "I will take care to find proof that my father's death is tied to these robberies and those responsible."

"I know you will," Hadrian said with confidence.

The coach arrived at Strangfeld's house, an elegant terrace with white stone and red brick. Sergeant Wycombe stood outside.

Tilda and Hadrian departed the coach and approached Wycombe. "Is Detective Inspector Teague already inside?" Tilda asked.

"No, he's been detained at Scotland Yard. He's hoping to speak with Rymer. The man awakened briefly, then lost consciousness again." Wycombe's brow furrowed. "It seems he had another injury beyond the wound that Teague inflicted when he shot him."

"He'd mentioned something about already being wounded," Hadrian said. "What sort of injury?"

"A cut on his forearm, which has festered and caused blood poisoning," Wycombe explained. "The surgeon thinks he sustained the wound a couple days ago. Teague and I wonder if he was involved with Lowther's death. That was two days ago. Perhaps Lowther injured him—he appeared to have fought with his attacker or attackers. Whatever happened, Rymer is now quite ill."

That didn't sound good. "I'm glad Teague is staying close to him." Hopefully Rymer would recover. Or at least regain consciousness long enough for Teague to obtain more information about Dorris and the robbery scheme. Tilda didn't wish the man ill health and not just because it would mean he couldn't help them.

Hadrian inclined his head toward Wycombe. "What of Marchant?"

"He's been patched up and is in a cell. He claims Dorris is behind everything and says he's told us all he knows." Wycombe's expression was dubious.

"You doubt his honesty?" Tilda asked.

"Teague does."

"Smart," Hadrian remarked. "Marchant was loath to reveal much unless he was forced."

Tilda was anxious to see if Dorris was here or if they could learn his address. She looked to Wycombe. "Are you coming in with us?"

"Yes, though I'll just be taking notes for Teague." He pulled a small notebook from his coat pocket along with a pencil.

They made their way to the door, where Hadrian knocked. A rather short and thin butler answered the door. He was also somewhat ancient. In fact, he made Vaughn look positively spry.

Behind his thick spectacles, the butler's blue eyes appeared rheumy. He surveyed the three of them, his gaze widening slightly as he registered Sergeant Wycombe.

"Good afternoon," Hadrian said pleasantly. "We're looking for Mr. Dorris. We understand he is secretary to Lord Strangfeld. I am Ravenhurst. This is Miss Wren and Sergeant Wycombe."

"Mr. Dorris isn't in." The butler's voice was high and feeble.

Tilda tried not to be terribly disappointed. So long as they obtained his address, she would be satisfied. "We need to speak with him about an urgent matter." She glanced toward Wycombe to underscore the importance of their call. "Where can we find him?"

"You'll need to speak with his lordship. I will see if he's receiving." The butler looked expectantly at Hadrian.

Removing a card from his pocket, Hadrian handed it to the butler with a benign smile. "We'll wait inside whilst you determine Lord Strangfeld's availability."

The butler clutched Hadrian's card and opened the door wider for them to enter. Tilda moved into the center of the towering entrance hall. Once Hadrian and Sergeant Wycombe had joined her, the butler closed the door and ambled past them through an archway toward a grand staircase.

Hadrian looked around whilst they waited, and Tilda did the same. The space was impressive, the ceiling soaring through the first floor to provide an auspicious entry. Paintings adorned the walls along with a pair of swords crossed over the family crest.

The crest!

Tilda tried not to gasp. It was exactly the same as what was etched into Mrs. Goodwin's missing salver. "Hadrian, look." She pointed up to the wall that faced the front door.

He followed her finger, and his lips parted. "A stag, a sword, the chevron in the middle, and three martlets on the bottom."

"What does that mean?" Wycombe asked.

"It means Mrs. Goodwin's salver was etched with the Strangfeld crest," Tilda said. "She said she received it as a gift from her son last year. It was crafted by Hester Bateman, so it was made in the last century. I imagine it once belonged to this family."

"We know Rymer and Bant stole the salver," Hadrian said. "And that they work for Dorris."

Tilda worked to control her excitement. They were moving closer to the truth. "It is not a coincidence that Dorris works for Strangfeld and has employed thieves to steal items with the Strangfeld crest as well as stags. But why was he doing that?" Most importantly, at least to Tilda, what did Dorris—or Strangfeld—have to do with her father's death?

A few minutes later, the butler returned. "Lord Strangfeld will see you." He led them—again, slowly—upstairs to the drawing room.

Lord Strangfeld was already present. He stood in the middle

of a large seating area and greeted them with a smile. "What a surprise to see you again so soon," he said.

"Thank you for receiving us," Hadrian replied. "You recall Miss Wren, I'm sure. This is Sergeant Wycombe from the Metropolitan Police Detective Branch."

Strangfeld's blond brows rose. "The Detective Branch? I understand you wish to speak with my secretary, Arnold Dorris. I'm afraid I don't expect him until tomorrow afternoon."

"Can you tell us where to find him?" Hadrian asked.

Strangfeld studied Hadrian. "Forgive my curiosity, but why are you involved with the Detective Branch?"

Hadrian offered a brief, tight smile. "Miss Wren is a private investigator and was hired to find some stolen items. On occasion, I assist with her inquiries. Her investigation has led us to Mr. Dorris."

"You think Dorris is a thief?" Strangfeld's features creased. "He would never do anything illegal. He's worked for me for over twenty years and is absolutely above reproach." He sounded slightly affronted.

"We don't wish to cause offense," Hadrian said benignly. "We merely need to speak with Mr. Dorris. May we have his address?" He glanced toward Wycombe. "Scotland Yard would greatly appreciate your cooperation."

Tilda wanted to hug Hadrian. He was handling this superbly.

"Of course." Strangfeld turned and went to a desk that stood on the far wall. He bent at the waist slightly and the sound of a pen scratching over parchment carried to them.

The viscount returned and handed a small piece of folded paper to Hadrian. "He lodges in Frith Street near Soho Square."

"Have you seen him today?" Tilda asked.

"No," Strangfeld replied. "He can't be in any trouble. I simply won't believe it. I hope you are merely making an inquiry."

Tilda gave Strangfeld an engaging smile. "I couldn't help noticing your family crest in the entrance hall. At least, I presume it's the Strangfeld crest?" Tilda wanted to be sure. She supposed it could be his wife's, if he was married. Or perhaps it was another family's entirely, and he merely liked it. But that would be odd to display someone else's crest in one's entrance hall. Furthermore, he'd been wearing a stag pin last night and had a stag statue at his country estate. It made sense that his crest contained a stag.

"Oh, yes, that is the Strangfeld crest," he replied with a smile. "I had that made last year."

"It matches one of the stolen items I am seeking," Tilda said, her pulse racing.

Strangfeld blinked in surprise. "Does it? What is the item? If I may ask."

"A silver salver designed by Hester Bateman," Tilda replied. "I have to think it belonged to your family at some point since it is the Strangfeld crest."

"I have a Bateman salver with the Strangfeld crest," Strangfeld said with a befuddled look. "That can't be the same one."

"May I see it?" Tilda asked.

Strangfeld nodded. He passed by them and went to the door, where he pulled a cord to summon someone. The ancient butler appeared, and Strangfeld asked him to fetch the salver.

Joining them once more, Strangfeld's mouth pulled into a slight frown. "I only just recovered the salver recently."

"When?" Tilda asked. She noted that Wycombe furiously took notes whilst she questioned the viscount. Hadrian was watching closely, and she knew he'd interject if he wanted to.

"Perhaps a month ago?" Strangfeld mused.

Mrs. Goodwin's salver had been stolen on the thirtieth of April, just over one month ago. The timing certainly matched. Tilda didn't say anything. She wanted to see the salver to confirm it was the same piece.

The butler returned carrying a silver salver. He presented it to Strangfeld, who indicated it should go to Tilda.

"Thank you," she murmured, then sent a meaningful glance

toward Hadrian. He removed his gloves in response, conveying his understanding that she wanted him to touch the salver.

Tilda surveyed it first and knew right away that it was Mrs. Goodwin's. In addition to the etching in the center that clearly displayed the Strangfeld crest, which was the same design Mrs. Goodwin had described, the edge of the salver was decorated with delicate beading, a hallmark of Hester Bateman's work.

"This looks to be Mrs. Goodwin's salver," Tilda said as she handed it to Hadrian. "Do you agree?"

He took the silver piece and held it up in front of his face. Tilda immediately understood he was doing that to block Strangfeld from seeing the blank expression in his gaze that seeing a memory would cause. She marveled at Hadrian's cleverness.

After a long moment, Hadrian lowered the salver. "It is her salver," he said, returning it to Tilda. Then he turned his attention to Strangfeld. "Why is it now in your possession?"

CHAPTER 24

"*B*ecause it belongs to *my* family," Strangfeld said with distress. "My great-grandfather commissioned it with Hester Bateman."

"But you only recently recovered it," Tilda pointed out. "Surely you realized it was missing."

Strangfeld blew out a breath and moved to sit in a chair. He slumped down, bracing his elbows on the wooden arms. "My grandfather sold a great many of our family's heirlooms nearly forty years ago after losing much of our fortune." His lip curled. "You may have heard of his financial and social downfall. He was soundly ridiculed for his foolishness with investments."

"I was not aware," Tilda said, but she stored the information away. She looked at Hadrian, wondering if he'd known of the Strangfeld family's troubles.

"I suppose I had heard something about that," Hadrian said. "Now that you mention it."

Tilda was eager to hear all of what Hadrian knew and would ask as soon as they departed. She held the salver in front of her chest, almost like a shield, not that she needed one. "Your grandfather sold this salver, along with other items, to settle his debts?"

"That's correct," Strangfeld replied. "My secretary, Dorris, has miraculously acquired much of what was sold during the past decade or more. This salver was his most recent acquisition. He was quite thrilled to present it to me." The viscount rubbed his hand over his brow, then looked toward Sergeant Wycombe. "You suspect Dorris stole this salver?"

"We can't discuss the case with you," Wycombe said. "We just need to speak with him."

"This is most upsetting." Strangfeld stood abruptly and moved behind the chair to pace. "He's recovered many of my family's treasures. I never imagined he would have done so illegally." He shook his head. "I can't believe it's true."

Tilda pressed her lips together. It seemed as though Strangfeld had no notion whatsoever that his secretary had been stealing his family heirlooms. Or was he merely feigning ignorance? It occurred to Tilda that a man in Strangfeld's position would likely have the appropriate influence to persuade members of the Metropolitan Police to lie. Was Strangfeld somehow involved? He didn't appear to be.

"Did you ask Mr. Dorris to obtain your family's treasures?" she asked.

Strangfeld's eyes rounded briefly. "I said I wanted to regain as many of them as I could, but I didn't think it would be possible. He's surprised me over the years by recovering several." His face creased with anguish. "If Dorris is guilty of theft… This is my fault. He was only trying to please me."

"Did you ask him to obtain the items through any means necessary?" Tilda asked. Strangfeld shook his head. "Then you are not to blame. You'll need to provide a list of the items Dorris has recovered for you to Sergeant Wycombe. When can you prepare this?"

"Right away," Strangfeld said. "I won't be able to rest until I know what's happened. Do you want to wait whilst I compile the list? It may take me a few hours. I confess I can't quite recall everything exactly. I'll need to consult with my retainers and with Lady Strangfeld. I do not expect her return until this evening." He locked his gaze on Wycombe. "I could bring the list to Scotland Yard if that's convenient?"

Wycombe inclined his head. "That would be most helpful. Thank you, my lord."

Tilda wasn't sure they ought to entrust Strangfeld to create the list. If these were items that had once belonged to his family, he may not want to part with them.

Strangfeld looked sadly at the salver Tilda held. "I suppose you'll be taking that."

And with that, he confirmed that Tilda was right to be skeptical. "Yes. It is evidence in a crime as well as belonging to someone else. I'm sorry to take it from you. Perhaps it would be easier if Wycombe assisted you with cataloging the items that Dorris has procured." She gave the viscount a sympathetic smile. "I imagine it will be difficult to return these items to their rightful owners."

"I confess it will," Strangfeld said. "I would welcome Sergeant Wycombe's assistance." He looked toward the sergeant, who nodded.

"I could help you with that tomorrow," Wycombe said. "Today, I am at Detective Inspector Teague's behest, focused on making certain inquiries. Are you acquainted with a pair of men called Bant and Rymer?"

"Certainly. They are grooms in my stable," Strangfeld said. "Why?"

Tilda was torn as to what they ought to reveal. Strangfeld gave the impression he was innocent of any illegal activity, but what if he simply excelled at deception?

"Is Bant here?" Hadrian asked.

"I'm sure he's at the mews, as is Rymer." Strangfeld grimaced. "Are they also part of your inquiry? Like Dorris, they've worked for me for a great many years."

Wycombe poised his pencil above his notebook. "Where are your stables?"

"Davies Mews," Strangfeld replied.

"Thank you." Wycombe wrote in the notebook, then looked over at Tilda and Hadrian. "Do you have anything else to ask?"

"Not at the moment," Hadrian said.

Tilda narrowed her eyes slightly at Strangfeld. "How did Dorris know which of your family heirlooms to look for?"

Strangfeld's brows pinched together. He was silent several moments as he seemed to ponder her question. "There was an auction, and my father kept the list of items. He vowed to buy them all back some day, but he was no better with financial matters than his father. I can only think that Dorris must have found that list."

"Thank you, my lord," Tilda said. "We appreciate your assistance today."

"I'll return in the morning to record the items that Dorris recovered for you," Wycombe said. "If you could gather them all together in one place, that would be most helpful." He closed his notebook and gave the viscount a nod.

"I'll do my best," Strangfeld said. "This is all so troubling."

"We do understand." Hadrian sent the man a sympathetic look.

Tilda squared her shoulders. "If you see Mr. Dorris, it would be best if you didn't tell him the police wish to question him. We don't want him to flee."

"Certainly not. I will make sure he cooperates with your investigation. Forgive me for thinking he will have some sort of explanation for everything." Strangfeld grimaced as sadness shadowed his expression. "Perhaps I am being naïve."

They took their leave but gathered outside on the pavement. Wycombe glanced toward the house. "His lordship seemed quite distraught about his secretary's thievery."

"He did," Tilda agreed. "I confess I'm skeptical that he could be completely unaware of what Dorris has been up to for over a decade, but I suppose some people only see what they choose to, especially those in places of privilege." She sent Hadrian an apologetic look—she didn't mean him.

"I propose we separate to pursue both Bant and Dorris," Wycombe said. "Since Bant seems the more dangerous of the two, I will dash over to the Great Marlborough Street station to fetch some constables to accompany me to the Davies Mews. I will also send someone to meet you at Dorris's lodging."

Hadrian handed Wycombe the paper Strangfeld had given him. "Here's the address. I've committed it to memory."

Wycombe accepted the paper with a nod. "Whilst I'm at the station, I'll send an urgent message to Detective Inspector Teague at Scotland Yard, informing him of our progress. I could also have the salver delivered to him." He inclined his head to the piece Tilda still carried.

"I'm happy to keep it with me," Hadrian offered. "My coachman can keep hold of it and ensure it's safe. It's an important piece of evidence."

Tilda knew what he wanted to do—he planned to touch it again and see what else he might learn, as he'd done with the other items that they'd obtained from Timms. "That's an excellent idea." Tilda gave Hadrian a subtle nod.

"That may be best, as I'd like to move quickly," Wycombe said. "In fact, I'd best be on my way. Let us meet up again at Scotland Yard after completing our errands—hopefully with suspects in custody."

"Indeed," Hadrian said.

Wycombe departed on foot, moving rapidly as he'd intended. Tilda pivoted with Hadrian, and his hand grazed her back. She had to resist the urge to press back against his touch or even to lean toward him. It seemed she craved his physical support as much as anything.

The realization she'd made earlier came flooding back. Could she be in love with him?

The notion filled her with a combination of apprehension and anticipation, and perhaps, just a smidgen of joy. She pushed that away. Now was not the time to contemplate such emotions, nor should she be feeling joy as she worked to find her father's killer and the reason for his murder.

Hadrian instructed Leach where to take them next, then helped Tilda into the coach. He sat down and turned his head toward her. "You understood why I wanted to keep the salver?"

"I did. Did you not see anything when you touched it in Strangfeld's drawing room?"

"Only murky images. I didn't have enough time to latch onto anything solid. Even so, I sensed something important. I'll try again after we hopefully find Dorris. I don't want to do it now lest I suffer a terrible headache. I'd rather approach Dorris with a clear head."

"That's smart," Tilda said. "How is your head now?"

"Mild pain, but nothing bothersome." He gave her a brief and incredibly warm, intimate smile. "I shall never tire of your concern."

Tilda felt a blush rising in her cheeks. She quickly turned her head toward the window. "I hope it doesn't start raining, though it looks as if it might." *What a silly thing to comment on just now.* But she'd needed to distract herself—and Hadrian—from…whatever was between them.

She needed to focus on this case!

Taking a deep breath, she pressed her shoulders against the squab and glanced back toward Hadrian. "My father was also investigating these thefts. I wonder if he was murdered because he was close to solving the case—or had solved it. But who killed him? Who directed his murder be covered up? It had to be someone with influence in the Metropolitan Police. I wish Teague had been able to find Fellows."

"Perhaps he'll do so today." Hadrian's gaze darkened as he frowned slightly. "Or perhaps I should meet with the Home Secretary again."

"That might be necessary," Tilda said.

They arrived at Dorris's lodging house in Frith Street. It was a respectable-looking terrace of dark red brick. Hadrian stepped from the carriage and helped Tilda to the pavement.

"You take the lead with your title," she said. "We don't have time to persuade the landlord or landlady to talk to us."

Hadrian nodded. "Understood." He escorted Tilda to the door and knocked.

A few moments later, a woman garbed in a plain brown gown that was more than a few years out of fashion answered. She wore a cap over her sleek, dark-gray hair. She perused Hadrian with interest and merely glanced at Tilda. "Yes?"

"I am Lord Ravenhurst," Hadrian said with warmth, but he didn't smile. "We need to speak with one of your tenants—Mr. Arnold Dorris."

"I'm afraid he's not here," she replied, her expression turning reverential as she regarded Hadrian.

"Do you know when he left?" Tilda asked.

The landlady turned her attention to Tilda. "I do not monitor my lodgers, Lady Ravenhurst."

Tilda would normally have corrected her, but she didn't have the patience at the moment. "Is there a time of day he generally returns?" She schooled her tone to be as pleasant as possible.

"I can't say. Sometimes I see him when he returns from dinner down the street or wherever he goes."

"What is down the street?" Hadrian prodded. "Is there a place where you know he dines?"

Shrugging, the landlady lifted her hand to her chest briefly. "Some of my lodgers dine at the chop house down the way—Bickley and Son."

Hadrian inclined his head. "That's very helpful, thank you." He turned toward Tilda.

She exhaled, then thanked the landlady. They returned to the coach, where Hadrian directed Leach to drive to Bickley and Son.

Dorris wasn't there either, but the proprietor said he dined in the chop house a couple of times each week. As they returned to the coach, Hadrian suggested they ask Teague to assign a constable or two to watch the place in case Dorris showed up.

"That's a good idea." Tilda glanced at the salver sitting on the opposite seat, wrapped in a cloth that Leach had procured from under his seat. "I am disappointed in our progress, but I have hope you will see something with the salver. Do you think you're up to trying now?" She hoped she didn't sound too eager. "Only if you're feeling up to it."

His features gentled as he regarded her. "Of course." He leaned forward and picked up the salver, his hand only touching the cloth.

He unwrapped the piece but didn't yet put his bare flesh to the surface. "Give me a few moments. I want to direct my entire focus, and it may take time for me to see anything."

"I understand." Tilda held her breath as he pulled the salver from the cloth and gripped the edges with both hands. She watched as his face went blank and his eyes stared toward the front of the coach.

Finally, she remembered to exhale and draw another breath. Her fingertips dug into her lap as she waited for something—anything—to happen. But his silence and lack of expression likely meant he was in the throes of someone's memory, which was precisely what they wanted.

Suddenly, he gasped. Tilda started. She grabbed his arm and turned her body toward him, her eyes wide.

"What did you see?"

CHAPTER 25

*H*adrian's heart pounded. His entire body thrummed in reaction to what he'd just seen. At Strangfeld's house, he'd glimpsed a shadowy scene. He'd thought it was the alley behind the Oak—where Tilda's father had been killed.

Now, with this vision, he knew that was the place. He saw Bant, along with two other men he couldn't identify due to the darkness. A small shaft of light streamed into the alley from the back door of the pub, which was ajar. It was enough for Hadrian to look down at Bant's hands and see a bloody knife.

He was also able to make out the form of a man lying on the ground. He wore a police uniform. Whilst he couldn't confirm it was Thomas Wren, Hadrian was certain the body was his.

Looking over at Tilda's eager expression, he wasn't sure he wanted to tell her what he'd seen. Her lips were parted and her eyes wide, as she waited for him to speak.

Hadrian set the salver in his lap and covered it with the cloth once more.

"Why did you gasp?" she asked finally.

"From the pain," he lied, lifting his hand to rub his temple. "I was trying very hard to see something, but I was only glimpsing shadows." Hadrian felt bad not telling her the truth, but he didn't want to say anything until he was sure that was her father's body on the ground. She was already so frustrated and upset. He would keep trying with the salver and hope he could tell her something more definitive, including the identities of the other two men in the alley.

Tilda opened her reticule and rummaged inside. She pulled out the vial of lavender oil and sprinkled some onto her fingertips. "May I?" she asked as she lifted her hand toward his forehead.

"Please." Hadrian lowered his hand and surrendered—happily —to her ministrations. She massaged the oil into his forehead and temples. The lavender helped, but he wondered if her touch was the true balm. "That feels better already."

"Good." She finished, then withdrew her hand. "As much as I would love for you to try again with the salver, please don't. I don't want you to suffer any more than you already are."

He thrilled at her concern. That his well-being was more important to her than discovering the truth filled him with joy. "But we'll need to give the salver to Teague. Wycombe will ensure we do."

She nodded. "I know."

They arrived at Scotland Yard and went inside. Hadrian carried the cloth-wrapped salver. The clerk was busy, and whilst they waited, Wycombe entered.

The sergeant frowned upon seeing them. "It doesn't seem you found Dorris, and nor did I locate Bant."

"You are correct," Tilda said with a bitter edge. She explained their visiting Dorris's lodgings and then looking for him at the chop house. "We think it would be smart to assign a constable to Bickley and Son, to watch for Dorris in case he shows up."

"I can arrange for that," Wycombe said. "We'll also put constables at Dorris's lodging, the Davies mews, and at Strangfeld's, as we discussed. We'll nab Dorris and Bant," he said with a confidence Hadrian wasn't sure he shared.

"I wish I was as certain," Tilda said, echoing Hadrian's thoughts. "I fear Dorris has fled—perhaps with Bant."

Wycombe's brows drew together. "That is possible, but I hope not. Let's go to Detective Inspector Teague's office."

As the sergeant led them upstairs, Hadrian realized he may have one last chance to see something with the salver. He also recalled that seeing memories whilst he was walking could result in imbalance, and it was possible he may stumble. Alas, he didn't see any other option.

Hadrian exposed an edge of the salver and clasped it with his bare hand. He skimmed his other hand along the railing as they ascended the stairs. Though he moved very slowly in order to focus on seeing everything in the alley, it was difficult to walk. Compounding matters was the incessant and deepening pain in his head. His efforts to see more sharpened the ache.

There! He saw the alley again. He worked hard to see the other two men cloaked in the shadows. At last, the first visage came into view—it was Padgett. And the other was Fellows.

He remembered to look down at the hands of the person whose memory he was seeing. They were dry and calloused, with broken nails.

Hadrian blinked and pain sliced through his temples. He gripped the railing and briefly closed his eyes. His breath had snagged in his lungs, and he forced it out as he opened his eyes. He'd stopped near the top of the stairs.

"Hadrian?" Tilda asked from above him.

He lifted his gaze and fixed on her. "I'm coming."

Now, he would tell her what he'd seen—when he could. Even though he hadn't identified her father's body, he didn't think it could be anyone else, particularly since both Padgett and Fellows had looked a decade younger.

Taking care to wrap the salver securely once more, he

followed Tilda and Wycombe to Teague's office. The detective inspector was not there when they arrived.

"I hope he's here at Scotland Yard," Wycombe said with a frown. "I didn't think to ask."

Tilda was eyeing Hadrian with curiosity, her brow slightly furrowed. He subtly gestured with the salver and gave her a small nod, hoping she would understand that he had something to share.

Sergeant Wycombe started toward the door. "Let me go find him." He departed, and Hadrian moved to the seating area.

"Did you see something more?" Tilda followed him, and they sat in the pair of chairs situated by the hearth. "Is that why you were loitering on the stairs?"

Hadrian rubbed at his head, not that he would ease the terrible ache that had rooted. "Yes. I saw the alley behind the Oak."

Her brows shot up. "Where my father was killed?"

"Yes, and more importantly, I believe it was *when* he was murdered. It was dark, but I managed to see Padgett and Fellows. They were not as they look today but appeared younger. I also saw a man lying on the ground. He wore a police uniform. Though I could not see his face, I am certain it was your father." He hesitated and gave her a grim look. "Bant was there too. He held a bloody knife."

Tilda swallowed. The tension in her neck and jaw was evident. "Have you any idea whose memory you were seeing?"

"Not entirely, but my guess is Rymer, since he would have touched the salver. And he was almost certainly there, since he and Bant seemed to have been working with Dorris all this time."

"Couldn't it have been Dorris?" Tilda said darkly. "You didn't mention him."

"I didn't see him there," Hadrian replied. "I don't think it was his memory. The hands were rough, more suited to a groom than a secretary."

Tilda blew out a breath, but then her features instantly creased as she met his gaze. "How are you?"

"I'm all right." Before he could elaborate, they were interrupted by the arrival of Teague and Wycombe. Both men looked disappointed, their expressions tight.

"What's happened?" Tilda asked.

"Unfortunately, Rymer has died," Teague replied as he moved to sit behind his desk. "From the infection due to his earlier wound."

Wycombe took the chair positioned on the opposite side of the desk and moved it in order to see Teague as well as Tilda and Hadrian. He sat with a deep frown. "He did not regain consciousness, so we weren't able to learn anything more from him."

Hadrian watched Tilda's reaction. She didn't reveal much, just a hint of frustration in the purse of her lips and set of her jaw.

"That is unfortunate," Tilda said. "We've had no luck finding Dorris or Bant."

"That's what Wycombe told me." Teague glanced at the sergeant before fixing on Tilda. "I promise we're going to find who killed your father and why."

"I want to know how they were able to conceal what happened," Tilda said fiercely. "Who made sure no one revealed the truth? Who was behind the deception of moving my father to the apothecary shop?"

"Those are excellent questions." Teague's eyes were dark with anger. "I want to know the answers as much as you do. Whomever is behind this scheme has tarnished the Metropolitan Police, and that must not be ignored."

"I think it's likely Bant who killed Thomas Wren," Hadrian said, glancing at Tilda. "He tried to cut Marchant's throat, and that's how Timms, Lowther, and Wren died."

Teague nodded. "I'm inclined to agree with you, but we don't have Bant or evidence beyond the method of murder. It will be especially hard to link to him to Sergeant Wren's death over a decade ago."

Hadrian briefly met Tilda's gaze. "I do think Fellows has an important role in this. Did he report to the Home Office today?"

"He did not," Teague responded. "And I've sent constables to his lodgings, at which he has not been seen since Sunday. In fact, I have them watching at all hours now and will do the same for Dorris and Bant. Wycombe has spoken to me about where to station our men."

Tilda looked to the detective inspector. "What do you think happened to Fellows?"

"I'm not sure anything happened *to* him. I'm concerned he was involved in this entire scheme and has fled, along with Dorris and Bant." Teague smacked his palm against the top of his desk. He muttered an apology as he scowled into the distance.

"I should like to know who killed Padgett," Tilda said. "He was murdered in a different manner than the others, so it's possible his killer is not the same person who killed the others. Are you no closer to solving that crime?" She looked at Teague expectantly.

"No," Teague lamented. "I've searched Padgett's lodgings thoroughly—twice."

"Would you mind if Ravenhurst and I conducted a search?" Tilda asked.

Teague exhaled. "It couldn't hurt and would likely help. Tomorrow?"

Hadrian looked over at Tilda in question. She nodded. "We'll do that," Hadrian said.

"We just need to find one of these men," Wycombe said. "And we will."

Hadrian appreciated the sergeant's optimism, just as he understood both Tilda's and Teague's frustration. "I agree," he said, preferring to hope for the best.

"Is that the salver you recovered from Strangfeld?" Teague asked.

"It is." Hadrian stood and took the silver piece to Teague's desk, where he set it down.

"I'd like to inform Mrs. Goodwin that I've found her salver," Tilda said. "Do you take any issue with my doing so? When I have time, that is."

"Not at all," Teague replied. "After Wycombe assists Strangfeld with the inventory of the stolen items in his possession, we'll be notifying many people that we've recovered their long-missing items."

"I imagine Strangfeld will be sad to part with his family's heirlooms." Hadrian would hate if his grandfather had been forced to sell a great many treasures and understood Strangfeld wanting to regain them. Losing them again, through no fault of his own, would be distressing.

"If he's desperate to keep them, he can always offer to buy them from the owners," Tilda suggested.

Hadrian tried to imagine having to purchase items that had once belonged to his family. Whilst that was the only thing Strangfeld could do if he wanted to try to keep those heirlooms, Hadrian understood how it would grate. If he were Strangfeld, he'd be livid with Dorris.

Tilda rose, her attention fixed on Teague. "When will you have the constables in place in their various assignments?"

"I have already dispatched them," Teague replied. "If they encounter any of our quarries, they will bring them here immediately."

"Will you please send word?" Tilda asked. "I should like to return to hear what they have to say, even if you won't include me in the interrogation."

Teague nodded. "I will. I know how important this is to you."

"Thank you." Tilda gave the detective inspector a brief smile that did not quite reach her eyes.

Hadrian could see she was agitated and perhaps tired. This had to be wearing on her.

He escorted Tilda from Teague's office and out to his coach. "Marylebone Lane," he said to Leach, who inclined his head as he opened the door for Tilda.

"I hate that I'm going home with so many questions unanswered." Tilda climbed into the coach.

Hadrian noted the sullen set of her jaw as she dropped her reticule in her lap and turned her head toward the window. He sat down beside her, and Leach closed the door.

"Today was not completely unsuccessful," he said quietly. "We did capture Rymer and Marchant, and we learned that Dorris works for Strangfeld. We made many useful connections."

Tilda exhaled and slumped back against the squab. "We did. It just feels as though we've been chasing Dorris for a long time, and we're hardly any closer to finding him."

"We know where he works and where he lives." Hadrian didn't want her to lose hope. "It's only a matter of time until we have him—and the entire truth."

"What about Fellows? Or Bant? They were present when my father was killed and can tell us why he was moved, as well as who was behind concealing the truth."

"I've been thinking about that," Hadrian said. "If Bant is truly the one who killed your father, I am concerned he may come after you. Your father was potentially murdered because of his investigation into these robberies—that's the only thing that makes sense."

Tilda turned toward Hadrian. "Yes, because Bant was involved with those robberies, and he almost certainly murdered my father."

"Exactly." Hadrian heard the anger and sorrow in her tone. He would ensure Bant and the others paid for their crimes against her father especially. First, however, he needed to keep her safe. "Bant knows we're close to solving this case. It's likely why he's in hiding now. I think we must prepare for him coming after you in the way he did your father."

Hadrian's pulse pounded as he considered that. He wanted to snatch Tilda close and hold her tightly until everyone to do with these robberies and murders was in custody. But he could not, so he would do the next best thing. "I would like to assign a few of my footmen to watch over you at home, on a rotating schedule, until Bant and the others are caught. Will you allow me to do that?"

Tilda nodded. "Certainly."

"Thank you." Hadrian felt slightly better. Still, he wished *he* could be the one to watch over her. Perhaps someday.

It was early evening when the coach stopped in front of Tilda's grandmother's house, and Hadrian walked her to the door. It had been an exceptionally long day.

Vaughn greeted them, opening the door wide. "Miss Wren, you've a caller."

Ezra Clement stood in the entrance hall, his red and gray plaid trousers drawing Hadrian's eye. The reporter looked rather excited, his brown eyes gleaming. "I'm so glad you're here. I've news to share."

"As do we," Tilda said. "Let us sit." She removed her gloves, then her hat, setting them on a table in the entrance hall before moving into the parlor.

Hadrian followed her, and Clement trailed him. Tilda perched on a chair whilst Hadrian took another. That left the settee for Clement.

The reporter removed his hat to reveal his thinning, light brown hair and set it on the cushion beside him. "I interviewed some of the people from whom the items were stolen. Two of them reported purchasing their items at auction—they belonged to the Strangfeld family. Apparently, the grandfather of the current viscount was forced to sell many of their treasures to settle his debts nearly forty years ago."

"We also learned that today," Tilda said somewhat dejectedly. "We spoke with Strangfeld. His secretary, Dorris, was fencing the stolen items with Timms, along with a man called Marchant, who has a shop in Clerkenwell."

"Well, that is fascinating," Clement said. "I have more. Shall I continue?"

Tilda's eyes lit with interest. "Please."

"One of the people I interviewed, Mr. Horace Derwin, purchased two things from the Strangfeld auction: a painting of a stag in a forest on a moonlit night and a silver snuffbox bearing the letter S entwined around a sword. He bought the snuffbox as a gift for his brother, and the painting was for himself. The painting was stolen more than a decade ago."

"And the snuffbox?" Tilda asked eagerly, giving voice to Hadrian's rising curiosity.

"Derwin's brother died last year, and he left it to Derwin's son." Clement paused, and Hadrian surmised it was for dramatic effect. "It was stolen about a fortnight ago."

Tilda sucked in a breath. "Was anything else stolen?"

"Yes, some items from the younger Derwin's study, where the snuffbox was kept. However, the thief did not steal any of the several illustrated medieval manuscripts that Derwin owns. They are on display in the study, and the elder Derwin was shocked that they weren't stolen."

"What if the thieves didn't know their worth?" Hadrian mused.

"I think we can deduce that Rymer and Bant were the thieves," Tilda said.

"Who are they?" Clement asked, his forehead furrowed.

Tilda explained, culminating with what happened at Marchant's shop earlier.

Clement had listened raptly. "I'm sorry to hear Bant escaped, but glad Rymer is in custody."

"Unfortunately, Rymer has died at Scotland Yard," Hadrian said.

"That *is* unfortunate," Clement replied with a frown.

Tilda cocked her head. "Knowing they are the thieves, it seems Dorris instructed them to steal the items that had been sold at the Strangfeld auction. I would theorize they were also told to take other pieces, so that the thefts would not only be items from the auction. Doing so would distract from the true purpose of the thefts."

Hadrian looked at her with admiration. "That's brilliant— your deduction, I mean. The scheme would make the motive behind the thefts much more difficult to detect. Indeed, it's taken someone—you—well over a decade to do so."

Clement's expression turned rather smug. He smirked at Tilda. "Hold out your hand."

The space between Tilda's brows pleated as she did what Clement asked. The reporter withdrew something small from his pocket. Hadrian sucked in his breath as Clement placed a silver snuffbox in Tilda's palm.

"This is that very snuffbox," Clement announced proudly.

Tilda stared at the item in her hand. "Where did you find this?"

"It found me, actually," Clement said. "A pawnbroker brought it to me at the newspaper offices. He was given the snuffbox to keep safe."

"By whom?" Hadrian hung on Clement's every word and suspected Tilda was doing the same.

"Dorris," Tilda guessed.

Clement shook his head, and a smile much like that worn by a cat who'd just caught his dinner lifted his mouth. "Padgett."

Tilda gasped. "Why did the pawnbroker give it to you?"

"He said Padgett brought it to him the day he was killed. He instructed the pawnbroker to only redeem the ticket for the snuffbox if it was presented by a man called Strangfeld or Padgett himself. If anyone else tried to claim it, Padgett paid him to deliver it to me."

"That means someone else tried to claim it." Tilda turned the snuffbox over in her hand. "Did the pawnbroker know who?"

"He said he assumed the man was a secretary or clerk of some sort—he had that air about him. He described him as having gray at his temples and long side whiskers, and he wore spectacles."

Tilda looked at Hadrian. "That has to be Dorris."

"When you mentioned Strangfeld's secretary a few minutes ago, I presumed it could be the same man," Clement said. "May I assume he matches the pawnbroker's description?"

"Yes," Tilda replied. "We haven't met him in person, but he's been described to us."

Furthermore, Hadrian had seen the man in a vision, and he just knew it was the same person who'd tried to redeem the pawn ticket for the snuffbox. "What took the pawnbroker so long to bring the snuffbox to you?"

Clement gave him a wry look. "I asked him the same thing. The man said he considered selling it, but then he recalled that Padgett was a retired inspector and decided he didn't want to be embroiled in this matter. So, he brought it to me today."

"That is astonishing." Hadrian returned his gaze to Tilda. "How do you think Padgett came to have this snuffbox in his possession?"

Tilda stood and walked to the window, where she turned and came back toward them, her expression creased. She clutched the snuffbox in her right hand.

"We know Padgett was corrupt." Tilda narrowed her eyes as if she was scrutinizing something before her, but Hadrian knew she was examining the various threads of their investigation in her mind. "And we also know he was present when my father was killed."

Now it was Clement's turn to react with shock. "How do you know that?"

Hadrian's heart pounded as he snapped his attention to Tilda. What had possessed her to reveal that? The only reason they knew was because he'd seen it in someone's—likely Bant's—memory. They could not explain that to Clement.

"Lowther told me in a letter that his wife gave me," Tilda replied smoothly. "He was there too. We know that he and Padgett, along with Fellows and Jurgens, were involved with my father's death and the subsequent concealment of what happened. What I don't yet know is why they moved my father's body to the apothecary shop. Lowther did not know the reason or so he said, and unfortunately, I can't ask him. I suspect the purpose was to hide where my father was really murdered—and why."

"You've discovered the answer to that." Hadrian didn't ask if she had. He could see it in her eyes.

"I don't think it took over a decade for someone to detect the motive behind these thefts," Tilda said quietly. "I believe my father determined the scheme that Dorris was executing—to recover Strangfeld's heirlooms—and he was killed."

Clement frowned. "But how would Dorris convince four members of the Metropolitan Police to assist him with murder and make it look like something else?"

"That is the remaining question," Tilda said. "We know Bant and Rymer took orders from Dorris, whilst Jurgens and Lowther were directed by Padgett. What was Fellows's role?"

"Perhaps he was the one who ensured the other men helped with hiding what really happened," Hadrian suggested.

"That would make sense. But we're still missing something to do with Padgett." Tilda put her hand on her hip and thought for a moment, her brows drawn tightly together. "He died differently than the others—he was strangled whilst their throats were cut. Furthermore, he was planning to give you"—she looked to Clement—"a piece of paper with my father's name and the date he was killed to prompt you to look into what happened. And now we learn that he, not Dorris or one of the thieves, was in possession of one of Strangfeld's items. Someone killed him for it."

"I agree," Clement said. "I would say Dorris is the likely suspect. He could be behind all these murders, including your father."

"It does seem likely." Hadrian looked at Tilda. "I wonder if he wears a ring." He would try to see a memory with Dorris in it and determine if he did. He moved his focus to her hand where she held the snuffbox. Perhaps he could use that to see someone's memory of Dorris.

"Why?" Clement asked.

"Padgett's killer wore a ring." Tilda inclined her head toward Hadrian. "Ravenhurst noticed that when he surveyed Padgett's body at the inquest. The marks on his neck indicated the killer was wearing a ring on his little finger."

"Well done," Clement said with a nod toward Hadrian.

"We'll need to give this snuffbox to Teague," Tilda said.

"I can take it to him." Clement held out his hand.

"Actually, I can, if you don't mind," Tilda offered, glancing at Hadrian, and he knew she wanted him to try to see a memory from the snuffbox. "I'd like to discuss the case with him."

"This will be quite a story," Clement said with an anticipatory smile. "To solve the stag robberies after all this time will be of great interest, as will the connection to someone of Lord Strangfeld's stature."

Hadrian frowned briefly. "I'm not sure Strangfeld will appreciate having this publicized."

Clement stared at him. "I must tell this story, my lord."

"Of course," Hadrian assured him. "I didn't mean to imply you shouldn't."

"Thank you for your help," Tilda said to Clement. "I can't thank you enough for telling us of this snuffbox straightaway."

"What is your next move?" Clement asked.

"We must find Dorris, Fellows, and Bant," Tilda replied sternly. "Teague has several men searching and watching for them. Jurgens has already been questioned and is being protected in case he is the next target. We are concerned the three missing men have either fled or been murdered."

Clement's brows arched briefly. "It would make sense for Dorris to have killed them if he wants to ensure his crimes remain hidden." He fixed an earnest stare on Tilda. "What can I do to help with the search?"

"I don't know that you can, but I'll share where they live, in case you find yourself in those areas and want to be on guard." Tilda provided the addresses of their lodgings and pointed out the chop house Dorris frequented.

"I know where I'm dining this evening," Clement said with a smile. "I'll let you know if I see any of these men. We'll find them." He sounded as confident as Hadrian had tried to be.

After Clement left a few minutes later, Tilda sat and motioned for Hadrian to join her on the settee. When he was seated beside her, she held the snuffbox out to him. "Ready? I hope this won't overtax you after all the work you did with the salver."

"I'll be fine." His head still ached, but he was not going to delay touching the snuffbox.

Tilda placed the silver piece in his palm. Hadrian closed his hand around it and focused on seeing something to do with this case.

A dark room came into view. It was night. The person whose memory he was seeing lit a small lantern sitting on a mantel. The room illuminated, and Hadrian saw a mirror above the mantel. He glimpsed the face of the man whose memory this was: Padgett.

He turned from the mirror and went to a desk. Starting with the top drawer on the right, Padgett searched the contents. Not finding what he wanted, he moved on to the center drawer. Right away, his gaze locked on the silver snuffbox. Padgett picked it up with an immense feeling of satisfaction.

Pocketing the box, his mind turned to covering his tracks. Hadrian could sense his thoughts, that he needed to pilfer a few other things so the snuffbox was not the only item missing. He also knew this snuffbox was the last item that needed to be stolen.

"Oh, Lord Ravenhurst, I didn't realize you were here." Tilda's mother's voice broke into the vision, and it immediately vanished.

Hadrian swallowed a curse. Fighting the arc of pain slicing through his head, he managed to stand and offer a smile. "Good evening, Lady Pierce." He slipped the snuffbox into his coat pocket.

"Perhaps you should stay for dinner," she said eagerly.

"Mother, we're in the midst of working on our investigation," Tilda said with mild exasperation. "You must excuse us, then Ravenhurst needs to be on his way."

He did, for he needed to fetch his footman to watch over Tilda and her household.

Lady Pierce pouted briefly. "That is unfortunate. Perhaps you could plan to come for dinner tomorrow."

"We'll discuss it." Tilda appeared to try to mask her impatience, but Hadrian saw it. He knew she wanted to hear what he'd just seen, and they couldn't talk about that in front of her mother.

"Good." Lady Pierce smiled at Hadrian. "I hope to see you tomorrow!" She sent a slightly perturbed glance toward Tilda before turning and leaving the parlor.

Tilda fixed her attention on Hadrian as he sat back down next to her. "What did you see?"

He shared every detail. "You were right about them stealing things other than what was purchased from the Strangfeld auction in order to conceal the motive behind the thefts."

"I'm a bit surprised you saw Padgett's memory since he is dead," she noted.

"I think it's because he handled the snuffbox whilst he was still living."

Tilda nodded. "That does make sense. I wonder why Padgett, instead of Bant and Rymer, stole the snuffbox."

"Padgett has been involved at least since your father died," Hadrian said. "Perhaps he's been helping to locate these items. As you said, we know he's corrupt."

"What if he was working with Fellows to find the Strangfeld heirlooms and ensure no one from the Met discovered what was happening?" Tilda suggested. "When my father did, he was murdered."

"That sounds quite possible," Hadrian said darkly. "I haven't said, but I'm very sorry your father's colleagues were instrumental in his death."

"I just wish they would face justice." Tilda pressed her lips together, and Hadrian had the sense she was fighting her emotions. "I fear they will all be dead without having done so."

"I remain hopeful that we will find Fellows," Hadrian said. "And at least Teague has Jurgens."

Tilda nodded but did not look appeased. She grimaced faintly and touched her wounded shoulder.

Hadrian looked at her with concern. "Are you in pain? You should rest."

"It pulls a bit is all," she said. "What about your head? You need lavender."

"I shall have it as soon as I'm in my coach," he assured her with a smile. "I should go and fetch Brian. I'll feel better with him watching over you." He touched the snuffbox through the fabric of his coat. "Would you mind taking the box out of my pocket? I fear I'd rather not touch it again."

"Of course," Tilda said quickly. She moved closer and slid her hand into his pocket.

The action was rather intimate, and Hadrian caught her familiar floral scent. Finally, he could recognize the specific flower. It was jasmine, and he wondered if she wore a perfume or if it was just her soap. He had a sudden image of her stepping into a bath, which was perhaps the most sensual thing that had entered his mind whilst in her presence.

He met her gaze and recognized the same heat in her eyes that he felt, well, everywhere at the moment. "I should go," he repeated, except he didn't move.

She finally blinked, and the spell between them broke. Withdrawing the snuffbox, she clutched it in her hand as she stood. "Go ahead and bring Brian to the house. I'll tell everyone that you thought we needed a footman whilst my mother is here." She cracked a smile as she slid the silver box into the pocket of her gown.

Hadrian chuckled. "An excellent and highly believable reason for his presence." Sobering, he regarded her intently. "I'll see you soon. Please rest that shoulder."

"Please take care of your head," she replied.

As Hadrian departed the house, he was not as agitated as he expected to be. He was still very concerned for Tilda's safety, but his love for her was pushing all other emotions aside just now.

He couldn't wait to tell her how he felt.

~

After Hadrian left, Tilda went to the sitting room where she and her grandmother typically spent their evenings after dinner and poured a small glass of sherry. They'd fallen out of the habit somewhat since Tilda's mother had arrived.

Her grandmother walked in. "I heard Lord Ravenhurst was here along with a journalist. I didn't want to intrude whilst you were working."

"I appreciate that, Grandmama. Mother had no such hesitation." Tilda sipped the sherry.

"You've had a very trying day," Grandmama observed, glancing toward the glass in Tilda's hand. "I'm glad you're home now and can finally rest."

"I am too." Tilda gave her grandmother a reassuring smile. "Can I pour you a sherry?"

"I suppose so. I don't want you to tipple alone," Grandmama said with a wink.

Tilda set her glass down on the cabinet where the sherry decanter and glasses stood and poured the wine. As she delivered the sherry to her grandmother, Vaughn entered.

"I'm sorry to disturb, Miss Wren, but there's a constable at the door with an urgent message for you."

Excitement rushed through Tilda, making her pulse speed. "Thank you, Vaughn." She looked to her grandmother. "Please excuse me."

Tilda moved past the slow-moving butler on her way to the entrance hall. She opened the door to see the constable waiting outside. Dusk had fallen, but it wasn't yet dark.

"Miss Wren?" the constable asked tentatively. He was young, perhaps not even as old as Tilda, and had faint freckles across his cheeks.

"Yes?"

"I'm Constable Roth. Sergeant Wycombe sent me to tell you that they've found Mr. Dorris."

Tilda's excitement surged. "Where?"

"At his lodging. I'm to take you there at once," Roth said with enthusiasm.

As desperate as Tilda was to finally speak with Dorris, she considered waiting for Hadrian. He would be here any moment, surely. That was also an excellent argument for why she could go now.

She turned to Vaughn. "Lord Ravenhurst will be arriving

soon. Please inform him I have gone with Constable Roth to Dorris's lodgings. He knows where that is."

Vaughn nodded. "Certainly."

"Thank you, Vaughn." Tilda turned and followed the constable toward the street, walking briskly to keep pace with him. "Are you from the Detective Branch?" she asked as they arrived at the…hansom cab? Why hadn't he come in a police van?

"Yes," Roth replied as he gestured for her to precede him into the cab.

Tilda hesitated. She turned to the constable and looked at his insignia. It wasn't for the Detective Branch at all. It was for K Division in the east, which made no sense. A terrible sensation swept through her. In her haste and excitement, she worried she'd been extremely foolish.

"Are you driving?" she asked. If so, she reasoned that she could likely get away. If only she had her pistol or even her reticule to use as a weapon!

"No, I am." The deep voice came from behind Roth. The man stepped around the constable, and though Tilda had never met Bant, she saw his widow's peak and immediately suspected it was him. Looking toward his right hand, she wanted to confirm that he had a scar. Unfortunately, he was wearing gloves. He was also holding a cloth.

Fear ripped through Tilda. She pivoted slightly and tried to push past Roth's other side. But Bant—if this was Bant—grabbed her right arm, and Roth seized her left.

Bant slapped the cloth over her mouth, and the unmistakable, cloying scent of chloroform filled her nostrils. Tilda tried to wrest herself away and was able to pull her arm from Roth's grip. She clutched at Bant's wrist, her fingers gripping the sleeve of his coat, and tried to pull his hand away, but her limbs began to feel like they were no longer connected to her body. She felt something come loose from his coat before the edges of her vision dimmed.

Suddenly she was flying. Then everything went black.

CHAPTER 26

The moment Vaughn opened the door, Hadrian knew something was wrong.

The butler's gray brows were pitched with worry, his eyes dark with fear. "Thank goodness you're here, my lord."

"What's happened?" Hadrian managed to keep his tone even.

"Is that Ravenhurst?" Lady Pierce strode into the entrance hall as Hadrian stepped inside.

The footman, Brian, followed right after him. Tilda's grandmother walked in behind her daughter-in-law—her face was ghostly white.

Hadrian knew a moment of stark terror. "What has happened?" he asked again, but now his voice was low and a bit unsteady.

"A constable came to the door," Vaughn said, his features twisting into an apprehensive grimace. "His name was Roth, and he told Miss Wren that Mr. Dorris had been found. He said she was to accompany him to Mr. Dorris's lodgings. I was to inform you of this when you arrived."

So far, none of that sounded bad, but Hadrian presumed there must be more to the story. "Then what happened?"

Lady Pierce stepped toward him. "I arrived in the entrance hall after she left, and I was disappointed to have missed her. I went into the parlor to watch her leave. I saw her standing next to a hansom cab."

"A hansom cab?" Hadrian repeated.

"The constable arrived in a hired vehicle, apparently." Vaughn gave Hadrian an apologetic look. "I'm afraid I didn't notice."

"Well, I did," Lady Pierce said. "It was a hansom cab, and the driver climbed down. Both he and the constable were speaking with Matilda. Something happened, and she tried to get away from them. The driver put something over her face, and Matilda began to fall. He scooped her up and thrust her in the cab. And the constable climbed in with her. Then the driver returned to the back of the cab and drove away." Deep furrows creased her brow. "What has happened to my daughter?"

Hadrian's stomach fell to the floor, and his chest squeezed until he feared he couldn't draw breath. Indeed, for a moment he could not. His pulse sped and sweat broke out on the back of his neck. "How long ago did this happen?" he asked.

"Not even a quarter hour," Lady Pierce replied.

"Less than," Vaughn put in. "Perhaps ten minutes."

Hadrian wanted nothing more than to bolt out the door after Tilda, but he needed to take a moment to think. He looked to Vaughn. "The constable said they were going to Dorris's lodgings?" Vaughn nodded. "And what did this constable look like?"

"He was young and eager." The description didn't sound like any of the men they were looking for, Hadrian thought—neither Bant, Fellows, nor Dorris were young.

Vaughn wiped a hand over his brow, and Hadrian noticed the man was perspiring. "I'm afraid that's all I recall. Forgive me, my lord." He sounded most upset.

"It's all right," Hadrian assured him. "We'll find Tilda." He wouldn't consider any other outcome.

"What has happened to her?" Lady Pierce raised her voice.

"Has she been kidnapped? I've told her that her work is dangerous. She should have listened to me!" Her tone turned strident, and Hadrian snapped his gaze to her.

"Please do not say such things. Now is not the time for admonishment. Yes, your daughter has been kidnapped. But I *will* find her." Hadrian heard Mrs. Wren gasp, and he spared a moment to move toward her. He took Tilda's grandmother's hand and looked into her frightened blue eyes. "I promise you I will bring Tilda home safely."

"Thank you," Mrs. Wren whispered. "I'm so glad you are here."

Hadrian squeezed her hand, then released her before turning back to the door where his footman stood.

"With your permission, my lord, I'll go outside and look around," Brian said.

"Please." Hadrian noted it was nearly dark. "Can you fetch him a lantern, Vaughn?"

"Right away, my lord." The butler moved into the parlor faster than Hadrian had ever seen him move.

Brian had already gone outside when Vaughn returned with two lanterns. Hadrian took them both and went outside. Lady Pierce followed them.

Hadrian looked back at her. "Where was the cab?"

She pointed to the street somewhat between their house and the one next door. "Just there."

Brian was already looking in that area. Hadrian hurried to give him one of the lanterns as Leach rushed over from the coach.

"What's amiss?" the coachman asked.

Hadrian held the lantern aloft as he looked about. "Tilda has been kidnapped by someone likely posing as a constable, and a second man. They took her away in a hansom cab about a quarter hour or so ago."

"What are we looking for?" Leach's tone was dark and clipped. He was not a man that displayed great emotion, but

Hadrian knew he cared for Tilda and was likely upset by her kidnapping.

"I found something," Brian called out as he bent to the pavement.

Hadrian stalked toward the footman as he straightened. Brian handed him a brass button. The cool metal warmed quickly in Hadrian's bare palm, for he hadn't bothered to don his gloves since leaving Tilda earlier.

He closed his hand into a fist around the button and turned slightly away from Brian and Leach. Marylebone Lane faded from his sight, and he was transported to a different place.

He was in a well-appointed house. And he wasn't alone. Standing opposite him was Lord Strangfeld.

Whose vision was Hadrian seeing?

He prayed for a mirror so he could identify the memory holder. But there wasn't one. Instead, Hadrian hoped the memory would allow him to see the man's hands... There! He glimpsed the man's right hand and saw a scar. Hadrian had to be seeing Bant's memory.

But where had the men taken Tilda? Hadrian clung to the vision. The two men were having a conversation, but he couldn't hear what they were saying. Never had he been more frustrated that he couldn't hear what was happening in the memories he saw. Sometimes, however, he could detect the person's thoughts.

Hadrian focused on what Bant was thinking at this moment whilst speaking with Strangfeld. Something about Cow Cross Street—

"My lord?" Brian's concerned query splintered the memory, and Hadrian was back on the pavement in front of Tilda's house.

He muttered a curse. Then he blinked several times and put his palm to his forehead. A terrible ache, like he'd never before experienced, threatened to crush his skull.

"Are you all right?" Brian asked.

"I'm fine," Hadrian replied through his gritted teeth.

Lady Pierce had seen two men—the young constable and the driver. Perhaps Bant had been the driver, and it was his button Hadrian clutched. He slipped it into his pocket.

Hadrian felt certain he needed to hurry to Cow Cross Street. But he also thought he should check Dorris's lodgings as well.

"Brian, I want you to fetch a cab and go to Dorris's lodgings in Frith Street." Hadrian handed him coins for the fare and provided the exact address. "If you don't find Tilda—or anyone—there, come and find me in Cow Cross Street."

Brian nodded.

"Go now," Hadrian urged, and the footman hastened on his way.

"Where is he going?" Lady Pierce called.

Hadrian pivoted toward them. Tilda's grandmother stood in the doorway, and Vaughn was behind her. Everyone watched him with an air of agitation.

"We're going to find Tilda," Hadrian vowed. He was torn between catching a cab himself to Cow Cross Street and sending Leach to Scotland Yard to fetch Teague, or whoever he could, but he reasoned that Leach would deliver him to Cow Cross Street faster than anyone else.

Hadrian moved closer to them. "We're going to Cow Cross Street. If Detective Inspector Teague or Sergeant Wycombe or someone sent by them calls, tell them where I've gone. But only after you've verified their identity."

"Constable Roth said he was sent by Wycombe," Vaughn said.

"Damn it," Hadrian swore quietly. "Then we can't trust anyone. Don't answer the door for the rest of the evening, until I return or Detective Inspector Teague arrives. You know him, don't you, Mrs. Wren?" He fixed his gaze on Tilda's grandmother.

She nodded. "I do."

"Good. Now go inside. I need to be on my way." Hadrian spun about and raced to the coach.

Leach was there. "I heard." He was already climbing into the driver's seat. "Cow Cross Street. As fast as possible."

Hadrian climbed into the coach and prayed they would find Tilda before it was too late.

~

When Tilda awoke, a wave of nausea swept over her. She swallowed and realized there was a gag in her mouth. Her head throbbed, and she vaguely wondered if this was how Hadrian felt after he had a vision.

Hadrian.

He would have gone to look for her at Dorris's lodgings, but Tilda feared she wasn't there. Opening her eyes, she knew immediately, despite her weakened state, that she was not. Had Hadrian determined that she'd been kidnapped? Of course, he had. Which meant he was searching for her.

Tilda's hands and feet were bound, and the cloth gag drew what little moisture she possessed in her mouth. She tried to blink away the cobwebs in her eyes and in her head. It took a few minutes for her to study her surroundings.

She was in a warehouse with crates and items draped with cloth. A statue of Dionysus stood uncovered, and beneath the hem of a sheet, she could make out the gilded frame and lower edge of a painting.

Her ability to see came from a faint flicker of light behind a stack of crates. She heard male voices and wondered if it was "Constable Roth" and Bant. She still couldn't confirm the driver had been Bant, but she would wager he was.

The sound of boots on the wood floor made her try to straighten, but it was impossible to move from her slumped position on the floor against a crate. The light grew brighter, and a man carrying a lantern came into focus. Tilda recognized the aristocratic, attractive features of Lord Strangfeld.

"Miss Wren," he said in a ridiculously polite tone.

Tilda could not speak, of course, nor did she try. She was most perturbed with herself for not recognizing that Roth, whomever he was, had not been a constable at all, and for falling for their scheme to kidnap her.

However, she was even more upset that she hadn't deduced that Strangfeld was behind everything. He'd fooled her well that afternoon. She'd been too focused on Dorris, Bant, and Fellows—the men she knew to be involved in her father's death. Her emotions had claimed her good sense.

She glared up at Strangfeld.

The viscount chuckled. "I can see that you're angry. I would be too if I were trussed up as you are. I am sorry it has come to this, but you are far too close to the heart of things. In fact, you have already ruined everything, for I cannot keep any of my family's things without paying for them." He pursed his lips at her.

"You should have to," Tilda tried to say, but her words were garbled and likely unintelligible.

Strangfeld frowned. "I think you're trying to say that I should pay for them, which is ridiculous. I shouldn't have to purchase things that are rightfully mine."

Tilda tried again to speak. "They were legally sold."

"Your participation in this conversation is not required," Lord Strangfeld said sharply. "Do be quiet, or I will have Bant cut out your tongue, though that seems unnecessary, as you will soon be dead."

Tilda swallowed as her blood chilled. She wanted to hope that someone, *anyone*—especially Hadrian—would find her. But how would he find her here, wherever *here* was?

As she pulled at the rope binding her wrists together, she was rewarded with a sharp pain in her shoulder and barely managed to keep herself from making a sound. Instead, she bit down on the gag.

"Since your time is short, I will keep this brief." Strangfeld's tone had become genial once more. "You will die because you have ruined my plans, just as your father tried to do over a decade ago. Thankfully, we were able to stop him before things went too far and anyone else discovered our scheme. I hated to do it, to be honest, just as I don't particularly care to kill you either. Of course, I won't be doing that myself. I don't do such things." He made a tsking sound. "Dorris thought that having Bant nearly run you down would frighten you off, but you're a persistent chit, aren't you?"

Tilda glared at the viscount. If she could speak, she would have told him that nothing could have stopped her from investigating her father's death.

Strangfeld set the lantern on a crate, and for a moment, his right hand was illuminated. Tilda saw—which she had failed to notice when she'd seen him that afternoon and at the ball last night—he wore a ring on his little finger.

How Tilda wished she could speak. She didn't believe for a moment that Strangfeld hadn't killed anyone. He may not have killed Timms or Lowther, or her father, but she was certain he'd killed Padgett. And why? How was Strangfeld linked to Padgett, Fellows, and the others in the Met?

The hell with it. She was going to die anyway. Probably. "You killed Padgett, didn't you?" She spoke as clearly as she could around the offensive cloth in her mouth and despite the persistent throb in her head.

"I still can't make out your nonsense. Did you just say Padgett?" Strangfeld scoffed. "He was a loyal servant for a very long time, until he wasn't."

"I have your snuffbox," she said, realizing she may have a card to play in this losing hand. She tried to motion with her head toward her pocket, then tried to use her shoulder, but again, a sharp pain bit her. This time she moaned softly, breathless.

Strangfeld gave her a look of pity. "I'm sorry you're in pain, but it's not for much longer now."

"No, you don't understand," Tilda tried to say around the gag. "I have your snuffbox in my pocket."

It seemed she'd done well enough for Strangfeld's brows to furrow. "My snuffbox? You have it here with you?"

Tilda gave him a mutinous stare, daring him to let her speak.

"Take the gag down," he said.

A man moved out of the shadows. It was the driver. He came toward her, and as he drew close, Tilda finally saw his bare right hand. There was a scar, which meant this was indeed Bant, the man who'd almost certainly killed her father.

A deep, sweltering rage clouded her sight. She began to shake.

Bant pulled the gag down but flashed a knife in front of her face. "Don't cry out, or I'll do to you what I did to your father."

Tilda looked at the man with a hate she had never felt before. It was terrifying—both his presence and the horrible emotion inside her.

"Where is my snuffbox?" Strangfeld demanded.

"It's in my pocket," Tilda said tersely. "Padgett stole it for you, but I thought he"—she glanced at Bant—"and Rymer stole everything for you. Why did Padgett steal this particular item?"

Strangfeld sneered. "Padgett's role was to find the items sold by my grandfather at auction decades ago, and he was paid handsomely. Once he located an item, he notified me, and I informed Dorris, who managed this fellow." He gestured to Bant. "And the other groom." Did he not recall their names, or were they too beneath him to deserve recognition?

"However, Padgett didn't tell me he'd found the final treasure —my grandfather's snuffbox. Instead, he stole it himself and threatened to reveal the entire scheme if I didn't pay him an enormous sum in exchange for the item."

"You killed him because he was greedy." It wasn't a question. Tilda was nearly certain it was true.

"I prefer not to dirty my hands with such things," he said coldly.

She didn't believe him. A man like him could not be trusted. "Bant didn't do it." She glanced at the murderer, whose knife was still poised at her throat. "He uses his knife, and Padgett was choked to death by a man who wears a ring on his right little finger." She inclined her head toward Strangfeld's hand. "Like you do."

Strangfeld's features hardened, but he said nothing.

Tilda supposed Dorris still could have murdered Padgett, *if* he wore a ring, but she knew it was the viscount. "Where is your other loyal servant, Mr. Dorris?"

"Nowhere anyone will find him," Strangfeld said with a chilling satisfaction.

Tilda wasn't sure what that meant exactly. "Is Dorris dead?" She hoped not, for she dearly wanted the man to pay for his crimes under the law.

Strangfeld's eyes burned with anger. "I could not risk him exposing the scheme. He'd become nervous of late—when *you* began to circle too closely." He curled his lip at her before tossing a glance toward Bant. "Remove the snuffbox from her pocket."

Bant thrust his free hand into the left pocket of Tilda's dress, but it wasn't there. She squirmed against the intimate invasion of his hand, then steeled herself when he plunged his hand into the right pocket. He withdrew the snuffbox with a smile that revealed his graying teeth. "Found it."

Tilda twitched with revulsion.

"Throw it to me," Strangfeld said.

Bant complied, tossing the silver box to the viscount, who caught it easily. Strangfeld held it in front of the lantern, and a slow victorious smile spread across his lips.

"At least I can keep this," he said with glee. "No one will know I have it in my possession. It was the most important thing anyway. The box belonged to my grandfather, and he always promised me that one day it would be mine. When it was among the items he sold, I felt betrayed. He fell down the stairs a month later. It was such a tragedy." He stared at the snuffbox a moment, his eyes wide and a touch wild.

Had he just admitted to killing his grandfather? Tilda wasn't sure, and she wasn't going to ask. She began to realize that Lord Strangfeld was not entirely sane.

"Do you mind if I pose a few clarifying questions before you have Bant kill me?" Tilda asked. "I simply want to close my investigation before I meet my maker."

Strangfeld smiled at her. There was no warmth in the expression, just a horrible emptiness that chilled Tilda to the bone. "I imagine your father will be delighted to see you. You have been a formidable investigator. He ought to be proud. I suppose I could answer a question or two."

"This scheme to recover your family's heirlooms was yours from the beginning, wasn't it? Dorris was merely your agent in reacquiring everything. He oversaw Bant and Rymer, who stole the items that Padgett found. Was it your idea to have them steal more than just your family's heirlooms in order to conceal the purpose behind the thefts?"

He looked at her with frank admiration. "Well done, Miss Wren. I didn't want to draw notice, but your father put it together as you have. I had to make sure that Fellows covered our tracks better after that."

"How did he accomplish that?" Tilda asked, glad to finally learn Fellows's role. "And why Fellows? How did you become associated with him—and with Padgett, Lowther, and Jurgens, for that matter?"

"Padgett was easy," Strangfeld replied with a chuckle. "I spent some evenings at the Standing Bear nearly fifteen years ago now. I observed members of the Met and deduced he could be bought. I was, of course, correct, and I hired him to seek out my family's heirlooms. He brought on Fellows to assist, who worked his way into the Home Office—with my recommendation, which still mattered for something, despite my family's misfortune—where he ultimately became the criminal clerk. He ensured that reports were misplaced, among other things. You'd have to ask Fellows exactly what he did, but I'm afraid you can't do that either," he added with a nonchalant shrug, as if he hadn't just implied the man was dead.

"Has Fellows also been killed?" Tilda held her breath. She wanted these men—Lowther, Padgett, Fellows, Rymer—to find justice, and now they would not.

"Indeed." Lord Strangfeld's reply held no remorse. "He also asked for a sum of money, though not quite as large as Padgett, so that he could run to America. I found that extremely rude."

Strangfeld continued. "Bant is most efficient, except for dispatching Marchant, the failure of which, I believe, was your fault when you interrupted him earlier today."

A movement in the shadows well behind Strangfeld drew her notice. She didn't think it was the young man known as Constable Roth or anyone else that might be working for Strangfeld, because the figure didn't come forward.

She didn't know who it was, but she decided to try to buy herself more time and distract Strangfeld, and hopefully Bant too. If she had a chance to avoid ending up like Marchant or, worse, her poor father, she would take it.

"The Metropolitan Police and the Earl of Ravenhurst will discover you are behind everything. What will you do then?" she asked in a mildly taunting voice. "Will you kill more members of the Met? Will you kill an earl?"

Strangfeld's lip curled, his expression seething with anger. "If I must."

Tilda laughed. "You must know you won't get away with all that." Except she didn't think he did. His mind was too far gone with satisfying his own grievances.

"It will actually give me great pleasure to kill someone like

Ravenhurst," Strangfeld said. "Perhaps I will choke him myself, as I did Padgett. Men like him befriended my father and grandfather and led them astray, robbed them blind, first with investments and then the gaming tables."

Glad that she'd lured him to confess to killing Padgett, Tilda continued to press onward. He was distracted now, and whomever lurked in the shadows could make their move. "You don't think it's more likely that your father and grandfather made their own mistakes?"

Strangfeld let out an inhuman cry as he kicked the crate beside him. The lantern fell over as the viscount bared his teeth. "Gag her again and kill her!"

"No!" Tilda managed to cry before Bant replaced the gag in her mouth.

Then he leered at her as his lips spread into an anticipatory smile. Tilda knew in that moment that Bant took pleasure in killing his victims. She felt sick.

What was the person in the shadows waiting for?

This was not how it was all supposed to end. She'd been such a fool. Her father had no reason to be proud of her. She would never see Hadrian again and never be able to tell him that she loved him. Despite the fact that her emotions had spun horribly inside her tonight, she could no longer deny them. Not for the seconds she had left.

Was this what her father had thought about in the moments when he'd seen death coming? Or had he been completely surprised, the life snuffed from him as a flame was extinguished?

Tilda felt his loss keenly. No, it was sharper, fresher. How was that possible after all this time?

Because the pain wasn't coming from losing him. It was from leaving Hadrian. She now knew her fear—that death would steal him from her as it had done with the other person she loved most in the world.

Hadrian's face rose in her mind, and her heart swelled with

love. She was glad that her last moments would be thinking of him, despite the bittersweet agony of knowing she wouldn't see him again.

Bant's knife glinted in the light that she suddenly realized had grown. The crate on which the lantern had tipped over had caught fire.

Just as the blade touched her throat, she saw the face of the man she loved moving toward Strangfeld. But Hadrian wasn't in her mind. He was real.

Then she heard the shot of a pistol.

CHAPTER 27

*H*adrian was glad he'd decided Leach should have the single pistol that was stowed in his coach. The coachman's shot at Bant hadn't missed. He'd saved Tilda's life.

But Hadrian couldn't rush to her side, not whilst Strangfeld was free. Hadrian leapt at the man and tackled him to the floor. He heard something clatter but paid no mind as he focused on the viscount beneath him.

Strangfeld had gone down face first and now tried to squirm to his side. Snarling, Hadrian grabbed the back of the man's head and slammed it onto the wood floor. Strangfeld let out a cry of pain.

"You're not escaping this," Hadrian growled. "You will hang. Is Tilda safe?" he called out. He feared his heart might exhaust itself.

"Yes," she replied. "Leach shot Bant in the neck. You're an excellent shot, Leach. I had no idea."

Hadrian exhaled with a loud vocalization of relief. She was safe.

"I'm just glad you're all right, Miss Wren," Leach said, echoing Hadrian's thoughts.

"The fire," Strangfeld ground out.

Hadrian was suddenly aware of a heat behind them. He looked over his shoulder and saw the flames had spread from the crate. Sliding off Strangfeld, he dragged the man away from the fire.

But Strangfeld tried to escape. He pulled away from Hadrian, just as Tilda appeared and crawled along the floor.

"Bring the rope so we can tie up Lord Strangfeld!" she shouted.

Hadrian lunged after Strangfeld and grabbed his ankle. The viscount exclaimed in pain as he twisted to his back in an effort to shake himself free of Hadrian's grip.

Leach appeared then. He carried rope and the pistol from the coach.

Hadrian held out his other hand as Strangfeld tried to pull his leg away. "Give me the pistol."

The coachman handed him the weapon. "I haven't reloaded it."

"I know." Hadrian leaned down and used the weapon to knock Strangfeld unconscious. "Help me carry him. We'll bind him outside."

Tilda took the pistol from him and the rope from Leach. Hadrian clasped Strangfeld's arm and hauled him up. Leach hastened to help, taking Strangfeld's other arm. Smoke filled the air, and Hadrian, already short of breath from his exertions and his fear for Tilda, fought to breathe.

They made their way to the door, which Tilda rushed to open. At last, they emerged onto Cow Cross Street. The night air filled their lungs, and Hadrian breathed deeply to clear the smoke away.

They set Strangfeld down and bound him the way he had Tilda—his hands behind his back and his feet together.

"Why don't you reload the pistol, just in case?" Hadrian said to Leach.

With a nod, the coachman hurried back to the coach, which

was parked across and up the street away from the warehouse. As soon as he'd seen the name "Marchant" on the outside of the building they'd just departed, Hadrian had known where Tilda would be. He'd pounded on the roof of the coach for Leach to stop and hadn't waited for it to completely stop before launching himself to the street.

At last, he turned to Tilda. "Are you all right?"

Her pale face was illuminated by a gas lamp as well as the fire that was on its way to consuming the warehouse.

"Fire!" someone called.

"We need to move away from the building," Hadrian said. He took Tilda's hand and started to cross the street.

"Don't leave me!" Strangfeld shouted. He must have regained consciousness.

"I'll come back." Hadrian wouldn't leave the man to die in the fire, no matter his crimes.

"How did you find me?" Tilda asked as she gripped Hadrian's hand.

"Your mother saw you being tossed into the cab, and Brian found a button on the pavement outside your house."

Her eyes rounded as they reached the other side of the street. "*My mother?*"

He nodded. "She was quite worried for your safety, as was everyone."

"My poor grandmother." Tilda shook her head. "I was incredibly foolish and put myself in terrible danger. I was so eager to find Dorris that I believed the young man who came to the door was actually a constable. What happened to him?"

"I don't know." Hadrian cupped her face and looked into her eyes. "You mustn't blame yourself. You were driven to find your father's killer. You're safe now."

Her gaze softened as she stared up at him. "Because of you."

Hadrian wanted nothing more than to take her in his arms and kiss her. He was desperate to tell her he loved her and that his whole world had been threatened when he'd learned she was gone. But people were rushing along the street now. Reluctantly, he lowered his hands to his sides.

"I still don't know how you found me here," Tilda said.

"It was the button." Hadrian smiled. "I'm so grateful I regained my power because the moment I held it, I experienced Bant's memory, and I was able to hear his thoughts. He was speaking to Strangfeld and thinking of Cow Cross Street. When I saw the name 'Marchant' on the warehouse, I knew where you were."

"You heard his thoughts?" Tilda shook her head. "I suppose that's happened before, but it's astonishing, nonetheless. And incredibly helpful. You knew Strangfeld was behind everything before you arrived."

He nodded. "I gathered that from Bant's memory."

"The fire brigade is on their way!" someone called.

"Here comes a police van!" someone else shouted.

The van stopped beside them, and Teague leapt down from the seat, whilst several constables came from the back. The detective inspector looked at them with relief. "Thank God you're all right," he said to no one in particular.

Wycombe had also been on the driver's seat with Teague and the driver. He climbed down and stood next to Teague.

"You need to fetch Strangfeld," Hadrian said, pointing toward the viscount laying on the opposite pavement.

Tilda held up her hand and focused on Wycombe. "Wait. The young man who impersonated a constable and drew me from my home earlier said Wycombe had sent him. Are you involved in this conspiracy?" She narrowed her eyes at the sergeant.

Wycombe's eyes rounded. "Absolutely not! I didn't send anyone to your house. Who is this young man?"

"I don't know," Tilda said with a scowl. "I'm sure he was employed by Strangfeld to play the part, however."

"Strangfeld?" Teague asked in surprise.

Tilda nodded. "He's behind everything—the robberies, the

cart nearly running us down, and the deaths of Lowther, Timms, Fellows, and Dorris. And my father. Actually, Bant killed all those people, and he was driving the cart that nearly struck us." She glanced toward Hadrian. "At Strangfeld's command. He took pleasure in doing so."

Hadrian felt her shiver and wished he had the chance to kill Bant a second time. "My coachman shot Bant. He was about to kill Tilda in the same manner he murdered the others."

Teague nodded toward Wycombe. "Go. Take the others with you." He turned his attention to Tilda, his eyes dark. "I'm glad Ravenhurst and his man arrived in time."

"No gladder than I," Hadrian said, shaking with how close he'd come to losing Tilda.

"But Strangfeld killed Padgett himself," Tilda told Teague. "Padgett tried to blackmail him for a large sum in exchange for the final item from the Strangfeld family auction that he had yet to reclaim."

"What was that?" Teague asked.

"A silver snuffbox," Tilda replied. "Did Wycombe tell you about that?"

Teague nodded, and Hadrian realized that was what he'd heard hit the floor when he'd tackled Strangfeld. "It's inside the warehouse. I know where it is. I can run in and fetch it."

"No," Teague said firmly. "The fire is moving too quickly. Nobody's going in there." He looked to Tilda. "You heard Strangfeld's confession?"

"Yes."

"I did too," Hadrian said. "So did my coachman. We have plenty of witnesses to ensure Strangfeld hangs."

"Good," Teague replied.

Wycombe and one of the constables had hauled Strangfeld up from the ground and were guiding him across the street.

"Put him in the van and take him to Scotland Yard," Teague said, casting a glower toward Strangfeld.

"What about Bant?" Hadrian asked.

"As I said, we can't go into the warehouse, not with this fire raging." Teague blew out a frustrated breath.

The red steam fire engine arrived, and several firemen jumped down, their brass helmets shining in the light of the gas lamps and the growing fire. They set to work as Teague focused on Tilda and Hadrian. "Are you coming to Scotland Yard now? I'll understand if you want to wait until morning."

"I think it's best if we come tomorrow." Hadrian glanced at Tilda with concern. "Tilda has been through enough today."

"Agreed." Teague gave her a heartfelt smile. "Thank you once again, Miss Wren. You've provided an invaluable service to the Metropolitan Police, just as your father did."

"The truth of his death must be made known," she said. "Mr. Clement will write about it in the *Daily News*."

"I understand." Teague pressed his lips into a grim line. "This is an embarrassing series of events for the Met, but we will make it right. I don't suppose you learned what Fellows's role was?"

Tilda nodded. "Fellows was working with Dorris and Strangfeld all along. He also tried to squeeze more money from Strangfeld in order to flee to America. Strangfeld said he was killed, but that we wouldn't find him. He said the same about Dorris—that we wouldn't find him—though he didn't actually confirm the man is dead."

"Can we assume he is?" Hadrian asked. If not, he would hunt him down.

"I think so, which is unfortunate." Tilda sounded disappointed. Hadrian knew she wanted justice to be served.

"I confess, I'm disappointed we only have Strangfeld to bring in front of the magistrate, but I suppose that will have to suffice." Teague, of course, shared Tilda's view on ensuring justice. "I'll see you both tomorrow."

Hadrian nodded, then escorted Tilda to his coach, where

Leach was standing. As they walked, Hadrian held her close to his side. She pressed into him, her head leaning against him.

"I have never known a fear like the one I felt when I found you were missing," Hadrian said softly.

"I thought I was going to die," she whispered.

"You were afraid." Hadrian hated that he wasn't there with her.

"I think I was more angry," Tilda said. "At myself for being so stupid. At Bant for killing my father." She paused and looked up at Hadrian. "If my hands hadn't been tied, I think I might have killed him myself in much the same way Strangfeld murdered Padgett—with my bare hands. Or I would have tried to anyway."

"I'm so sorry, Tilda." Hadrian brushed his knuckles against her cheek as he looked into her eyes. "If you would let me, I would protect you for the rest of our lives. I love you, and I want nothing more than for us to be together, not as business associates or as friends, but as husband and wife." He paused as he allowed a small, perhaps sad, smile to lift his mouth. "I understand if that isn't possible for you, and if you aren't able to reciprocate my feelings. I just needed to tell you. I couldn't go another moment without doing so."

"I—" She abruptly pressed her lips together.

Hadrian's joy wilted. But then she clasped his hand and drew him toward the coach.

She smiled at Leach. "Thank you for your assistance this evening, especially for saving me."

"It was my honor," Leach said proudly. "I am beyond glad that we arrived in time."

Tilda released Hadrian's hand and hugged him. The coachman's cheeks flamed as he helped her into the coach.

Hadrian clapped Leach on the shoulder and followed Tilda inside. When he was seated, he turned to see that she was already angled toward him.

"I didn't want to have this conversation out there." Her eyes were dark and full of emotion—but he couldn't tell what kind. "I'm glad you told me how you feel. I want to do the same." She took a deep breath. "Hadrian, I'm afraid."

~

Tilda's pulse galloped as the coach lurched forward. Hadrian's features gentled from tense to sympathetic.

"This has been a harrowing experience," Hadrian said. "I should not have said all that tonight."

"No." She saw the flicker of unease in his gaze. "That is, you should have. I'm glad you did. Didn't I already say that?" She laughed then pressed her hand to her mouth.

Now, he looked confused.

"This *has* been a terrible evening, but it has been wonderful too." That probably didn't help his consternation. "I also said I want to tell you how I feel."

His expression became wary. "You said you're afraid."

"I was. I still am. I didn't realize that was what I was feeling, why I kept finding ways to keep myself from recognizing that I love you too."

"You do?" Joy lit his features.

She nodded as she felt suddenly shy. She'd never experienced such strong emotion, nor had she had it directed at her. "I've been hesitant…for all the reasons you already know. I value my independence and my job."

"I don't want you to give up either of those," he said fiercely. "I promise you, if we are wed, we will continue to solve cases together, just as we are now."

As much as Tilda wanted that to be true—and she did—she hoped he wasn't being naïve. "I very much doubt the circle you move in will approve of such behavior. Even if I stopped investigating, they still wouldn't approve of my background. Your mother has said as much."

Hadrian scowled. "Forget my mother. Her sensibilities are outdated."

"That may be true, but I don't think she is alone in having them. It will be uncomfortable at best and extremely challenging at worst. I just don't know if I want that, Hadrian—for me or for you. And that has nothing to do with my love for you."

He exhaled. "I understand. Truly, I do. I have tried to consider the matter from your perspective, but I think perhaps I need to ponder it even more." He took her hand. "Tilda, I would do anything for you to be my wife. Could we perhaps try a courtship to start? If things don't progress well, you can cry off."

Tilda drew in a sharp breath, and her cheeks hollowed briefly. "I can't do that to you, not after Beryl broke your engagement. I won't subject you to that again, not the spectacle of it, and especially not the emotion of it."

He smiled at her. "I did not think I could love you more, but I think I shall find that I love you more and more every day, perhaps every moment. And it is because I love you that it doesn't really matter what happens next. My love will remain, and I will have to find a way to live without you if that's what you decide."

"*No.*" The fear she now recognized cut through her. "That is what I'm afraid of, Hadrian, that one of us will have to live without the other. You've come close to death—at least, I thought you did—during the course of our investigations. I couldn't bear to lose you, not like I lost my father. I'm not...close to many people."

"My love." His mouth curved into a slight smile as he stared into her eyes. "I have also been afraid I would lose you—this very evening in fact. Still, I would take whatever days we have than none at all. We can't know the future, but I know I want to be with you now and forever, however long that may be. Not too long ago, a very wise person told me that 'life is nothing but an endless series of unknowns.' She encouraged me to set aside my fear, and I did."

Tilda couldn't help smiling. "That was me. I told you that."

He nodded. "Yes, you did. Can you set aside your fear? I understand if you need time. If you recall, it took me awhile to overcome mine and speak to my mother about my skill."

"I *would* like some time to acclimate myself to this new emotion," she squeezed his hand with gratitude—and boundless affection. "Or perhaps to recover from this evening."

"God, yes," Hadrian said with a laugh. "Please, take as long as you need."

"Does that mean I shouldn't ask you to kiss me?" she asked hesitantly.

Hadrian grinned. "On the contrary, I've wanted to do that from the moment I saw you in the warehouse and that you were all right. I mean, except for the fact that you were tied up and gagged." His grin faded, but Tilda laughed.

"Yes, except for that. I was so happy to see you. I prayed you would find me, and you did." Tilda's pulse thrummed with anticipation as a delicious heat spread through her. She scarcely understood how she could feel this way after all that had happened. But perhaps it was *because* of the day's events that she was ready, even eager, to step into the unknown with Hadrian.

He cupped her face once more and lowered his mouth to hers. Tilda basked in the warmth and comfort of his embrace. She kissed him back, tentatively, and slipped her hands beneath his coat. The loss of just that one garment between her hand and him gave her an entirely different perspective. She began to comprehend why one might *choose* to wed.

The coach stopped, and Tilda quickly drew back before they were interrupted by Leach opening the door.

"Did that upset you?" Hadrian asked with concern.

"Not at all. I just don't want to shock Leach."

Hadrian laughed as the door opened. He leaned forward and whispered, "I shall warn him not to open the door without knocking in future."

Tilda felt her cheeks warm. "Won't he…guess why? That can't be appropriate."

"Leach will never tell." Hadrian waggled his brows at her, and Tilda smiled. She liked when he flirted with her.

Hadrian climbed out of the coach and helped Tilda down. "Do you want me to just walk you to the door, or would you like me to stay for a while?"

"Perhaps stay for bit. I'm exhausted, and I know there will be questions. You can help me answer them." She looked over at him as they made their way to the door. "If you don't mind."

"My dearest, Tilda, I am your humble servant in all things. Forevermore, if you allow me." His eyes glimmered with hope and with love.

What was Tilda going to do if his proposed courtship didn't end well? She was terribly uncertain and perhaps a little scared about how this could possibly work. But perhaps she was more afraid of not pursuing her feelings at all.

Her lips lifted as she held his gaze. "I am certainly going to try."

CHAPTER 28

*L*ast night, after escorting Tilda inside, Hadrian had stayed for nearly an hour, answering everyone's questions about the investigation and pouring her two glasses of sherry. The wine had helped her relax and ultimately sleep.

First, however, she'd bathed. She'd needed to wash away not just the physical grime of the day, but also the lingering revulsion of coming face to face with her father's murderer.

Hadrian was due in a short while, and they would go to Scotland Yard to provide testimony about what had happened. She was relieved they hadn't gone last night. It truly would have been too much.

"How is your shoulder?" Clara asked as she finished arranging Tilda's hair. The maid had dressed the wound last night after the bath.

"Much better today, thank you." Tilda turned and stood to face Clara. "I want to thank you for all the extra work you've been doing since my mother came to stay. I have been too distracted and should have said so sooner."

"That's quite all right," Clara assured her. "I know how important this investigation is. Whilst I have been spending more time with your mother, I hope you know that I'm loyal to *you*."

Tilda chuckled. "That is heartening." She patted Clara's arm before picking up her hat and gloves and departing the chamber.

As she walked downstairs, her stomach kept fluttering. She was nervous to see Hadrian. Though she'd thought extensively about a courtship with him, she hadn't come to a decision. Her heart wanted to take the risk, but her mind was too aware of all that could go wrong.

Vaughn greeted her as she stepped into the entrance hall. "Let me take those." He reached for her accessories, and she surrendered them with a smile. Everyone had taken wonderful care of her since she'd returned last night, not that they didn't always.

"Thank you, Vaughn."

"Your mother and grandmother are in the parlor," he said. "They were hoping to see you before you leave with his lordship."

Tilda was surprised that her mother was downstairs this early. Turning, she went into the parlor. Grandmama was in her favorite chair near the window, and her mother was perched on the settee. The tension between the two of them that had been evident when her mother had arrived had eased. Tilda wondered if something had happened to prompt that but didn't ask. That wasn't a topic she wanted to broach at the moment.

"You look well rested," her mother said with an approving nod.

Her grandmother regarded her with love and concern. "How is your shoulder, dear? I trust you slept well."

"My shoulder feels much improved. And I slept quite soundly, thank you." Tilda sat in a chair across from the settee and clasped her hands in her lap. "Vaughn said you wanted to see me. Was there something you wished to discuss?"

"Not me," her grandmother said pertly. She turned her attention to Tilda's mother.

"*I* wanted to speak with you." Her mother smoothed her hand over her skirt, brushing something away that Tilda couldn't see. "I was shocked to hear the truth of your father's death last night. I am deeply sorry you had to face his...*killer*." She whispered the last word. "Solving this case is an astonishing achievement. I'm very proud of you."

Her words made Tilda slightly uncomfortable, whilst also filling her with a bright happiness. Could nothing between them be simple?

"Thank you," Tilda murmured. "Though I didn't entirely solve it." She was still bitter that she hadn't deduced Strangfeld's role and probably would be for some time.

"Ravenhurst said you connected all the threads," her grandmother said. "I trust his judgment. Just accept the accolades, my dear. Anyway, you've solved many cases, and you're becoming much in demand as an investigator. I'm sure your mother is also proud of that." She sent an expectant look toward her daughter-in-law.

Tilda's mother hesitated. "I am. It's just... As I've told you, I don't know that a husband will want an investigator for a wife."

"Someone will," Tilda replied confidently. "I already received one proposal of marriage from a gentleman who not only supported my investigative endeavors, he looked forward to our partnership in conducting inquiries together."

"Who was that?" her mother demanded in shock. "Why did I not know this?"

"He's an inspector with the City of London Police. I don't think you would approve," Tilda said wryly.

"Why not?" Her mother sounded indignant. "*I* married a constable."

Tilda did not point out that she'd also grown to resent that. "Well, I declined his offer."

Her mother's features fell, her eyes darkening with abject disappointment. "Does this mean you truly will never marry?"

"No, it does not." Tilda weighed whether to tell them

about a potential courtship with Hadrian. Part of her wanted their advice—especially from her grandmother. However, she also feared her mother's reaction. A courtship with Hadrian was precisely what she'd been hoping for. If things went poorly and they broke things off, her mother would be devastated. And Tilda would probably never hear the end of it.

Tilda's grandmother stared at her in surprise. "You're considering marriage? I thought you'd definitively decided against it." Her eyes lit with joy. "I confess this makes me very happy." She had long wanted Tilda to find a mate, because she worried Tilda would be lonely after she was gone.

"Dare we hope there is someone specific you're thinking of?" Tilda's mother asked with an expectant smile.

Whilst Tilda wanted to believe they both desired her happiness above all else, she wasn't sure that was her mother's goal. She'd made it clear that marriage, at its best, was about security and status. Tilda decided that for her, marriage must be about love. Without that, there was absolutely no reason to surrender her independence.

"No one specific." Tilda couldn't bring herself to tell them about a possible courtship with Hadrian. Not until she'd made her decision.

Her mother looked slightly disappointed. "If there was someone, I would only say that you will make an excellent countess. I mean, an excellent wife."

Tilda couldn't help but laugh, and her grandmother did the same. Composing herself, Tilda focused on her mother. "When will you return to Birmingham?"

"Tomorrow, but Bardolph and I may return to London sooner than later," her mother said with a light shrug. "Perhaps our presence will be required." She gave Tilda a sly smile with a thinly-veiled sheen of anticipation.

A movement outside the window caught Tilda's attention.

Hadrian was just stepping out of his coach. She felt a pulse of joy seeing him and had to suppress a smile.

Standing, she looked to her grandmother and then her mother. "I must go. Ravenhurst is here."

"Can't he come in?" her mother asked in a cajoling tone. "I'm leaving tomorrow, and I won't see him until my next visit."

Tilda might once have said that she oughtn't assume she would see him at all, but for the first time in many years, she felt somewhat at peace with her mother. She preferred it and hoped the sentiment would last.

"Yes, do invite him in," her grandmother added with an eager smile. "I want to thank him again for keeping you safe last night."

"All right." Tilda knew he wouldn't mind delaying their departure for a few minutes. "But we do have an appointment at Scotland Yard, so we must be on our way *soon*."

Hearing the door open, Tilda hurried into the entrance hall to intercept Hadrian. "You must come in."

"Your presence has been doubly requested," Vaughn said to Hadrian with a chuckle.

"I see," Hadrian murmured as he handed Vaughn his hat. He looked to Tilda and slightly arched a brow in question.

Tilda gathered what he was wondering—did her mother and grandmother know anything about a potential courtship. "My mother wanted to be sure and see you before she leaves tomorrow." She appreciated the hint of a smile he displayed at that news. "And Grandmama wishes to thank you again for saving me. Truly, we should invite Leach inside so she can thank him."

"Indeed, we should. I've already increased his wages." Hadrian lifted a shoulder. "It seemed the right thing to do, given all he does to support our investigations."

Our investigations. Tilda liked the sound of that.

She'd thought a great deal about what Hadrian had said regarding the continuation of their work together if they pursued a romantic attachment. She wanted to believe they could continue to conduct investigations, but she just wasn't sure an earl and his countess who were also private investigators would be accepted in Society. And surely that was a primary requirement for Hadrian's countess—she had to be accepted. Tilda had no desire to be a pariah, or to make Hadrian one.

Tilda turned toward the parlor, and Hadrian joined her. In the few steps they made to the doorway, she leaned her head toward him.

"I did not tell them anything about our discussion in the coach last night," she whispered. "I haven't made any decisions yet."

"There's no hurry." Hadrian sent her a smile that made her feel rather giddy, then directed it at her mother and grandmother. The two of them glowed in response, and in that moment, Tilda could not think of a good reason to deny a courtship.

What would her father have thought of Hadrian? She looked at the photograph of her father on the mantel and had the sense he was watching—and that he would approve of the man who cared deeply for his daughter. He was also the partner who'd helped her solve this most important of cases, and shortly they would go to Scotland Yard to provide testimony. Together, they would bring justice to the man who'd killed Thomas Wren, as well as the man who'd directed his murder.

She felt a sense of satisfaction, of being...whole. Whilst she didn't think this had been her best investigative work, she couldn't be disappointed in the result. Though she did wish that Fellows and Dorris—even Lowther—could have answered for their crimes in front of the magistrate.

There were many lessons here, mostly to do with her own emotions—how they'd affected her investigation and the surprising discovery that love wasn't only something she was capable of, it was something she desired. She was not, as she'd feared, like her mother, but then she'd also learned her mother did feel love, even if she didn't demonstrate it. Tilda decided she would purposely seek to be more like her father. His sentimentality and capacity for love were qualities she wanted to emulate.

She shifted her attention to Hadrian, where he stood greeting her grandmother and mother. The question of their potential courtship weighed heavy on her mind.

Would the love she felt for him be strong enough to withstand the difficulties that surely lay before them?

~

Two days later, Hadrian called on Tilda with a bouquet of pink and white roses and peonies. The scent reminded him of her—fresh, floral, and stunningly beautiful. He'd also requested a few sprigs of lavender, in a nod for the care she always showed him with his headaches when he saw a memory.

He'd considered gifting the silver mirror to her but had decided he didn't want to give it to her after all. The mirror had been owned by a man who'd played a role in the crime her father had been investigating. Hadrian had to think the mirror would ultimately remind her of her father's death.

Instead, he'd sent it to a girl whose care he'd assumed at the end of their last investigation. Her brother had been murdered, and he was her only family. Hadrian now paid for her to attend a school for girls. He hoped she would like the mirror.

Vaughn answered Hadrian's knock, and his brows rose as his gaze fell on the flowers. "Good afternoon, my lord. What a lovely posy." He opened the door wide, wordlessly inviting Hadrian into the entrance hall.

"Shall I take your hat?" Vaughn offered.

Hadrian handed him the accessory. "Thank you."

Vaughn set the hat on the small table against the wall opposite the doorway to the parlor. "I'll fetch Miss Wren."

Hadrian moved into the parlor to await Tilda. He'd become quite comfortable here, which made sense since he'd spent a great deal of time in Mrs. Wren's home. His mind wandered to what might happen if Tilda agreed to a courtship and that progressed to marriage. Tilda managed this household. Would she hire someone to do that in her stead?

No, she would want to oversee her grandmother's care herself. Hadrian would make it clear that Mrs. Wren was welcome at Ravenhurst House—and at Ravenswood, his country home. And what of the rest of their household? Hadrian didn't need a housekeeper or cook or a butler.

"Hadrian, I wasn't expecting you." Tilda's arrival interrupted his thoughts, and as soon as he turned to look at her, he couldn't have recalled what he was even thinking about.

She was incomparably lovely in her dark green gown, one of the newer garments she'd acquired since they'd met. He imagined her in the latest styles, with a wardrobe full of smart ensembles that represented her expertise and accomplishment as a private investigator. She would argue that her appearance shouldn't matter, but the truth was that if she looked successful, people would naturally assume she was.

Tilda surveyed the flowers he held. "Those are beautiful."

"They are for you." He handed them to her, and she smiled. Her features softened, and when she looked at him, he saw something he'd never seen before. Was it love? He wasn't sure, but there was a warmth and sparkle, and it filled him with a ridiculous glee.

Hadrian hadn't ever felt this way before. Definitely not when he'd been betrothed to Beryl. He'd been fond of her and thought he might love her or that the possibility was at least there. But this was different. This was emotional and physical—it was visceral. What he felt for Tilda was primal and necessary, and whatever happened, he knew he would never be the same.

"Doesn't it signify something for you to bring me flowers?" she asked, perhaps a touch warily.

"I've brought you flowers before."

She nodded. "You have. Though these are quite splendid."

"It's much easier to buy flowers in June than when I brought them last time in, I believe, March?"

She chuckled. "True. Fortunately, my mother is gone, else these would have sparked a great deal of assumption." She gave him a slightly admonishing gaze, but there was a twinkle of mirth in her eye.

He laughed. "I am adept at managing your mother's insinuations. At least, I think I have been."

"You have indeed. Let me give these to Vaughn, and he can see that they are displayed in a vase." Tilda pivoted and went into the entrance hall, then returned a moment later without the flowers.

"Are you on your way somewhere, or would you like to stay for a bit?" she asked.

"I would stay for a bit, if you are amenable," he replied, glad that she'd invited him.

"Certainly." Tilda moved to sit, taking a chair. Hadrian had been hoping she would choose the settee so he could sit beside her.

Hadrian took the chair near hers. "I arranged for Michael Lowther—and his sisters, as it happens—to visit my horses tomorrow afternoon."

Tilda's eyes brightened, then her features softened. "That is so very kind of you."

"When I stopped by earlier, it was clear all the Lowther children wanted to meet the horses and perhaps even learn to ride."

"You would teach them?" she asked, agog.

"Not me, but my grooms. I have no quarrel with it, if that's what they would like." Hadrian was just glad he could offer the poor children something. Mrs. Lowther had been tearfully grateful.

She shook her head as her lips curled into a brief smile. "You are the kindest man."

"I don't know about the kindest," he said with a self-deprecating tone. "I had extremely unkind thoughts about Strangfeld and Bant."

"That is not only acceptable, it's encouraged," she replied pertly.

Hadrian chuckled. "I wondered if you had a new case yet."

"I do have a few potential inquiries regarding stolen items," she replied. "And I expect more will be forthcoming, since Clement's story was published today."

"I read it." Clement had detailed the corruption surrounding the stag robberies, which included more than just "stag" items, as well as the person behind the robberies and the murders associated with them—the Viscount Strangfeld. Tilda had once again been named as a vital part of the investigative team that had solved the case. Because of that, she was right in thinking that she would likely receive more inquiries for her services.

Clement's article also teased a follow-up story regarding the tragic death of a beloved police sergeant, which would appear in the paper soon. "Are you pleased your father's story will be told separately?"

"I am," she said with the hint of another smile. "Clement called yesterday after I returned from speaking with Mrs. Goodwin and told me of his plan. I am touched that he wanted to honor my father especially."

"How was your visit with Mrs. Goodwin?" Hadrian asked. "Was she disappointed not to receive her items back just yet?" When they'd gone to Scotland Yard the day before yesterday, Teague had said they were still identifying stolen items and matching them to their owners using division occurrence books, police reports, as well as Timms's and Marchant's records. However, even the items that had already been identified, such as Mrs. Goodwin's, would not be returned right away.

"No, she understood why it was important for Scotland Yard to keep them until Strangfeld is tried in the House of Lords." Tilda paused and studied him a moment. "Have you been to Westminster since he was arrested? I expect everyone is talking about it."

"I was there yesterday, in fact. But the majority of discussion is happening at the clubs, of course." Hadrian shook his head. "It's a scandal, to be sure. I understand his wife is so distraught that she is under the care of a physician." He felt bad for the poor woman and indeed the entire household. It turned out that "Constable Roth" was one of their footmen and had been pressed into playing the role. He'd tearfully confessed and expressed his regret.

"The trial will likely be a spectacle." Tilda looked down at her lap. "It's good that hangings are no longer public, else that would be one too."

Hadrian agreed with her assessments.

She lifted her gaze to his. "Do you think there's any chance he'll be acquitted?"

"None whatsoever," he replied with firm confidence. "The evidence is too strong. You did your job well," he added with a smile.

"As did you. Your skill—you called it that instead of a power at one point and I like that—was most helpful. It *is* a skill, and you've honed it quite well." She cocked her head. "Do you know how you were able to regain the skill, or was that simply a fluke?"

"I cannot be sure of, course, but Captain Vale believes it was to do with the realization of my feelings for you. Apparently, love opens one's mind, and that was what made it possible for my power to return. Or wake up, for I don't think it went away. It was simply knocked into a period of dormancy when Draper hit me in the head." As he'd spoken, Tilda's eyes had rounded slightly, and her lips parted.

"That is…astonishing."

Voices from the entrance hall carried into the parlor, and a moment later, Vaughn shuffled in to speak with them. "Miss Wren, a Mr. and Mrs. Chadwick are here. They would like to speak with you about engaging your investigative services. Their need is most urgent. May I show them in?" He sent an apologetic glance toward Hadrian.

"Of course. Thank you, Vaughn." Tilda looked at Hadrian. "It's convenient you're here." She stood, and Hadrian rose with her.

A man and woman entered. With gray hair and drooping eyelids, Mr. Chadwick appeared to be in his fifties. He had a rather bushy mustache that was a shade darker than the hair on his head. Mrs. Chadwick looked several years younger—her blonde hair didn't have a strand of gray, and her eyes were a lustrous blue. She was very attractive, but lines marred her features with worry.

Tilda smiled in greeting. "Good afternoon, Mr. and Mrs. Chadwick. I am Miss Wren." She gestured to Hadrian. "This is my investigative partner, Lord Ravenhurst."

Chadwick's brow rose as he regarded Hadrian. "I didn't realize you had a partner, Miss Wren, let alone one so illustrious. Indeed, I can scarcely fathom why you would be working as an investigator." He stared at Hadrian in bewilderment.

"Ravenhurst is a valuable ally in my investigative work, Mr. Chadwick. Please sit and tell us why you've come today. I believe you said your business is urgent?" Tilda sat back down, and Hadrian waited for the Chadwicks to perch together on the settee before he followed suit.

Mrs. Chadwick took her husband's hand and looked at him expectantly.

Chadwick cleared his throat. "Miss Wren, it seems you have a gift for finding things that are stolen."

"She does indeed," Hadrian said, casting a proud look at Tilda.

With an affirmative nod toward Hadrian, Chadwick fixed his

attention on Tilda as he went on. "We would like to hire you to find our daughter. She has been kidnapped."

"How awful," Tilda said with alarm. "When was she taken?"

"Two days ago," Mrs. Chadwick replied in a soft, rather broken voice. "Her maid went to wake her, and she wasn't there."

"Had her bed been slept in?" Tilda asked.

"It seems so," Mrs. Chadwick said. "Honestly, it's difficult to say, as Delia has always been a tidy sleeper. Her bed never looks disheveled." She blinked rapidly as if she were trying not to cry.

Tilda looked at the woman with sympathy. "When was the last time someone saw her?"

"The night before Delia went missing." Mrs. Chadwick sniffed. "Her maid, Bannet, is always the last person in Delia's chamber." She sent Tilda a pleading stare. "You must find her. She's only nineteen. I'm certain she's terrified."

So far, Hadrian wasn't convinced there had been any malfeasance. Delia Chadwick could have stolen away from her bedchamber. Perhaps she'd eloped. "How do you know she was kidnapped?"

"There was a note on her pillow," Chadwick responded gruffly. He reached into his coat and removed a folded piece of parchment. Releasing his wife's hand, he came off the settee enough to extend his arm and deliver the paper to Tilda.

"Thank you." Tilda opened the parchment and quickly scanned the note. Pursing her lips, she handed it to Hadrian with an expectant look. She was, of course, waiting to see if he experienced anything when he touched the paper.

Hadrian focused his mind, but nothing came to him immediately. He didn't want to take too much time and draw attention, so he tipped his head to pretend to read the missive.

He tried for another moment to summon a vision. A glimpse of something flashed in his mind, but it wasn't so much what he saw, for it was almost complete darkness. It was, instead, what he felt—a deep and chilling fear. What an odd thing for the kidnapper to feel. Unless...had Delia Chadwick come into contact with the letter? Was Hadrian experiencing her fright?

An exceedingly sharp pain sliced through his scalp. It was as if the intensity of the emotion he'd felt was echoed in his head, worsening the typical ache. Blinking, he read the note.

We have your daughter. You will exchange twenty thousand pounds for her safe return. Another note with instructions will be delivered soon. Do not contact the police for assistance. If you do, Delia will die.

Yours,

Spring-heeled Jack

Succinct. Direct. And absolutely terrifying. Hadrian couldn't imagine reading those words about his own child—*we have your daughter*—and he was not even a parent. Yet. Hopefully, someday he would be. His gaze shot toward Tilda for the barest moment. Her brow was creased as she looked upon the Chadwicks, whose expressions were ravaged by worry and fear.

"Have you any idea who Spring-heeled Jack may be?" Tilda asked.

"Of course we do!" Chadwick responded angrily. "Haven't you heard of him? He hasn't been seen much of late, but everyone knows he's still out there, lying in wait to terrorize us all again."

Spring-heeled Jack was a frightening story told to children to keep them from misbehaving. There was no real "Spring-heeled Jack," for no one had red eyes and could spit blue and silver flame.

As he thought those things, Hadrian couldn't ignore his own unbelievable and inexplicable power to see others' memories. Still, what he was able to do did not compare with something as fantastical as spitting flames or jumping from the ground onto the top of a coach, which was how Jack had earned the descriptor of "spring-heeled."

"Spring-heeled Jack has not been proven to be real," Tilda said calmly—and gently. Her expression conveyed understanding and, again, sympathy.

Hadrian wondered what she was really thinking.

"You weren't alive when those girls were attacked thirty years ago," Chadwick said. "I recall the events distinctly. They never caught Spring-heeled Jack. He's still out there and has taken our daughter."

"I don't believe he ever kidnapped anyone," Tilda noted. "However, rest assured that I will make a thorough investigation to discover the truth."

Chadwick exhaled, and Mrs. Chadwick pressed her hand to her chest as she closed her eyes. "I'm so relieved you will take our case," Chadwick said. "What is your fee?"

Before Tilda could answer, Chadwick waved his hand. "A thousand pounds. And another thousand when Delia is safely returned."

That was more money than Tilda had probably ever possessed. Hadrian watched her reaction and was impressed she did not betray even the slightest hint of elation—or anything else.

"That is…more than I typically charge," she said slowly.

Chadwick leaned forward, his brown eyes intensely dark. "I want you to drop everything and find Delia. I will spare no expense to rescue my daughter from this foul heathen!"

Mrs. Chadwick opened her eyes and dashed away the tears that threatened to spill over. "Thank you, Miss Wren. You can't imagine how this feels—to lose your only daughter." A sob escaped her mouth, and she pressed her hand to her lips.

"I can imagine, though my experience is not the same," Tilda said quietly. "I lost my father at a young age, and it was devastating. I will do everything in my power to bring Delia back to you as soon as possible."

"I know you will," Mrs. Chadwick said tearfully. She removed a handkerchief from her reticule and dabbed at her eyes and cheeks.

"I would like to come to your house to see Delia's bedchamber," Tilda said. "When would that be convenient?"

"Right now, if you can." Chadwick started to rise.

Tilda waved him back down. "Not just yet." She gave him a kind smile. "I have a few more questions before we go to your house. Have you reported your daughter's disappearance to the Metropolitan Police?"

Chadwick's cheeks flushed. "Heavens, no! You read that devil's letter. He will kill our dear Delia. You mustn't consult with them either."

Mrs. Chadwick's eyes widened with fear. "Promise us you won't!"

"I will not." Tilda continued to use a soothing tone.

Chadwick pinned Hadrian with a desperate glare. "You mustn't either. Nor can you tell any of your powerful friends."

Hadrian inclined his head. "Where is your house?"

"Number Seven Belgrave Square," Chadwick replied.

"Will you come right away?" Mrs. Chadwick looked at Tilda with hopeful, even pleading, eyes.

"Yes," Tilda said. "Lord Ravenhurst and I will depart shortly." She stood, and Hadrian did the same. "I will collect a great deal of information from you when we arrive, such as a full description of Delia, including what she was wearing. I will also want to speak with her maid as well as other members of your household. Do you have other children?"

Chadwick nodded as he stood and helped Mrs. Chadwick to her feet. "Two boys, but they are not currently in London. One is in the navy, and the other is currently traveling."

Hadrian held up the note from "Spring-heeled Jack."

"May we keep this?" he asked, glancing toward Tilda, who gave him a slight nod to indicate she wanted it.

"Certainly," Chadwick replied. "You may have whatever you require. I shall pay you when you arrive."

"We shall discuss those terms later," Tilda said. "We'll see you shortly."

The Chadwicks left a few moments later, and Tilda turned to face Hadrian. "That was not how I expected today to progress. Did you see anything from the letter?"

"Not really. There was a flash of darkness, but I don't know if I was seeing that so much as feeling it."

Tilda cocked her head, her eyes bright with curiosity. "What do you mean?"

"I felt a terrible fear, which I found odd for a kidnapper. I wonder if Miss Chadwick touched the letter and I was feeling her emotions." He grimaced faintly and touched his head. "Left me with a rather acute headache."

"You need lavender," she said with concern.

"I'll use it as soon as I get to the coach."

She nodded. "I will let you know what I learn at the Chadwicks'."

"I assumed we would go together," Hadrian said. "Don't we always?"

"Yes." She smiled. "You don't have other plans today?"

"None that didn't revolve around you." He enjoyed the faint blush that rose in her cheeks. "I thought we might take a stroll."

She gave him a wry look. "Instead, we will embark on a rather serious case."

"With a very serious fee," Hadrian noted. "I'm curious why you seemed to hesitate in accepting what Chadwick offered."

Tilda rounded her eyes briefly as she looked toward Hadrian. "It's an enormous sum. Far greater than I would feel comfortable taking."

"You are worth every shilling. I'm sure Chadwick would agree, particularly when you find Delia and deliver her home."

"*If* we find Delia," Tilda said darkly. "We cannot be sure we'll find her. I find the invocation of Spring-heeled Jack to be interesting. Whoever took her—if someone actually kidnapped her—seems to want to stoke terror."

"You don't think she was kidnapped?" Hadrian asked. "I confess, my first thought was that she may have eloped. But perhaps my mind was simply too full of thoughts of romance." He winked at her, and she let out a brief laugh.

"If we are to be courting, I must insist you not flirt whilst we are working. Can you agree to that?"

Hadrian's breath snagged. "Does that mean… Have you decided we should court?" He hoped he didn't sound overly enthusiastic. It was difficult when he felt like grinning and sweeping her into his arms.

"It's not entirely up to me," she said.

"No, but I do believe I've made my intentions clear." He was still holding his breath.

"I think—" She glanced away. "That is, I would like to…try." Her gaze met his once more. "But I meant what I said about no flirting. We mustn't let whatever happens between us…romantically interfere with our investigations."

"Agreed." Hadrian finally exhaled and allowed a smile, when what he really wanted to do was inform everyone in her household that they were now courting. He wanted to tell his own household too. And his mother. As well as all of London—no, England.

"Hadrian?"

He blinked, realizing he'd been woolgathering. "My apologies, I was just thinking of what our first event together might be. My mother will know the right way for you to be presented in Society."

Tilda held up a hand. "Please don't put the cart before the horse. We have a very important and urgent case on which to focus. Our courtship and anything to do with it must wait."

A chill of disappointment snaked through him. But she was

right. They needed to help the Chadwicks. Hadrian would hope they would solve the matter quickly. It was highly likely that Miss Chadwick *had* eloped, perhaps with someone her parents would not deem appropriate.

"One other thing," Tilda said, drawing Hadrian's attention once more.

"Yes?"

"I realize I am not well-versed in courtship, let alone one conducted at your level of Society. However, I do not wish to be presented to anyone, nor do I want to be displayed like a prime piece of horseflesh."

Hadrian frowned. "I would never do that to you."

Her features gentled. "I know. But you cannot control how others act or what they will expect, including your own mother. Is it possible for our courtship to be…quiet and private?"

He understood her concern—at least, he wanted to. "Not in my position," he said apologetically. And she was right about his mother. She would have expectations for their courtship and Tilda may not agree to meet them. The same could be said for when they wed. *If* they wed.

Already, this was becoming complicated. Hadrian desperately didn't want it to be.

However, how could the courtship between an earl and the daughter of a police sergeant who worked as a private investigator possibly be *un*complicated? Add in his mother's almost certain disapproval and her mother's certain unadulterated glee, and this courtship had the potential to be a complete fiasco.

But Hadrian was going to make sure it was a happy ever after.

AUTHOR'S NOTE

When I was researching silversmiths for the stolen items in this story, I was delighted to find Hester Bateman. Born in London in 1708 or 1709, she did what was expected—she married and had six children. Her husband was a gold chain maker. When he died in 1760, he willed his tools to his wife and she took over the family business. She registered her first sponsor's mark, HB, in 1761 at the Goldsmith's Hall. She was not alone in her practice, as there were other women working in this trade at the same time, such as Elizabeth Godfrey. Two of her sons joined her in business and they specialized in household silverware such as salt cellars, teapots, and sugar bowls. Hester Bateman's designs are particularly known for their elegant beading. When she retired in 1790, her sons took over the business. Her daughter, Letitia Clarke, ran her own business as a goldsmith and jeweler. When one of the two sons died in 1790, his widow, Ann, assumed his place in the business.

I encourage you to search for Bateman's work online, if you can. It's exquisite.

ALSO BY DARCY BURKE

Historical Mystery

Raven & Wren

A Whisper of Death

A Whisper at Midnight

A Whisper and a Curse

A Whisper in the Shadows

A Whisper of Secrecy

A Whisper in Darkness

Historical Romance

If the Duke Dares

Because the Baron Broods

When the Viscount Seduces

As the Earl Likes

Until the Rake Surrenders

Since the Marquess Demands

What the Scoundrel Desires

How the Devil Sins

The Phoenix Club

Improper

Impassioned

Intolerable

Indecent

Impossible

Irresistible

Impeccable

Insatiable

The Matchmaking Chronicles

Yule Be My Duke

The Rigid Duke

The Bachelor Earl (also prequel to *The Untouchables*)

The Runaway Viscount

The Make-Believe Widow

Marrywell Brides

Beguiling the Duke

Romancing the Heiress

Matching the Marquess

The Untouchables

The Bachelor Earl (prequel)

The Forbidden Duke

The Duke of Daring

The Duke of Deception

The Duke of Desire

The Duke of Defiance

The Duke of Danger

The Duke of Ice

The Duke of Ruin

The Duke of Lies

The Duke of Seduction

The Duke of Kisses

The Duke of Distraction

The Untouchables: The Spitfire Society

Never Have I Ever with a Duke

A Duke is Never Enough

A Duke Will Never Do

The Untouchables: The Pretenders

A Secret Surrender

A Scandalous Bargain

A Rogue to Ruin

Love is All Around

(A Regency Holiday Trilogy)

The Red Hot Earl

The Gift of the Marquess

Joy to the Duke

Wicked Dukes Club

One Night for Seduction by Erica Ridley

One Night of Surrender by Darcy Burke

One Night of Passion by Erica Ridley

One Night of Scandal by Darcy Burke

One Night to Remember by Erica Ridley

One Night of Temptation by Darcy Burke

Secrets and Scandals

Her Wicked Ways

His Wicked Heart

To Seduce a Scoundrel

To Love a Thief (a novella)

Never Love a Scoundrel

Scoundrel Ever After

Legendary Rogues

Lady of Desire

Romancing the Earl

Lord of Fortune

Captivating the Scoundrel

Contemporary Romance

Ribbon Ridge

Let Go (a prequel novella)

Get Lucky

Sparks Fly

Fall Hard

Can't Stop

Break Free

Hold Me

Turn On

So Right

This Love

Prefer to read in German, French, or Italian? Check out my website for foreign language editions!

ABOUT THE AUTHOR

Darcy Burke is the USA Today Bestselling Author of historical romance and mystery and contemporary romance. Darcy wrote her first book at age 11, a happily ever after about a swan addicted to magic and the female swan who loved him, with exceedingly poor illustrations. Join her Reader Club newsletter for the latest updates from Darcy.

A native Oregonian, Darcy lives on the edge of wine country with her guitar-strumming husband, incredibly talented artist daughter, and imaginative, Japanese-speaking son who will almost certainly out-write her one day (that may be tomorrow). They're a crazy cat family with two Bengal cats, a small, fame-seeking torbie named after a fruit, an older rescue Maine Coon with attitude to spare, an adorable former stray who wandered onto their deck and into their hearts, and two bonded boys (a Russian Blue and a Turkish Van) who used to belong to (separate) neighbors but chose them instead. You can find Darcy in her comfy writing chair balancing her laptop and a cat or three, attempting yoga, folding laundry (which she loves), or wildlife spotting and playing games with her family. She loves traveling to the UK and visiting her cousins in Denmark. Visit Darcy online at www.darcyburke.com and follow her on social media.

facebook.com/DarcyBurkeFans

instagram.com/darcyburkeauthor

pinterest.com/darcyburkewrites

goodreads.com/darcyburke

bookbub.com/authors/darcy-burke

amazon.com/author/darcyburke

tiktok.com/@darcyburkeauthor

bsky.app/profile/darcyburkeauthor.bsky.social

A small press bound by the belief that every voice matters.

Sign up for our newsletter to learn about new releases and more.
https://oliver-heberbooks.com/subscribe/

Follow us on social media:

facebook.com/oliverheberbooks
instagram.com/oliverheberbooks
amazon.com/oliverheberbooks
youtube.com/@OliverHeberBooksPublisher

9 798900 430539